TRIPPING ARCADIA

TRIPPING ARCADIA

A NOVEL

Kit Mayquist

DUTTON

DUTTON

An imprint of Penguin Random House LLC
penguinrandomhouse.com

Copyright © 2022 by Kit Mayquist

DUTTON and the D colophon are registered trademarks of
Penguin Random House LLC.

LIBRARY OF CONGRESS CATALOGING-IN-PUBLICATION DATA
has been applied for.

ISBN 9780593185209 (hardcover)
ISBN 9780593185216 (ebook)

Printed in the United States of America
1st Printing

BOOK DESIGN BY ALISON CNOCKAERT
Interior art: floral background by Ola-la/Shutterstock

To those who have sought beauty in the world and have the scars to prove it.

May you never be afraid to bite back.

TRIPPING
ARCADIA

1

THE SCENT OF DEATH IS SWEET. A cologne of something chilling and saccharine—like spoiled figs, and honey, and mud. I know this because all my memories of Arrow's Edge will be forever tainted with it. A miasma left to drift into the psyche late at night, when I'm driving, or walking, or given more than a second alone. When the frost begins to gather on windows and the sign of a New Year creeps in with all its flashing glory, that scent with its unique and terrible power consumes every part of me, until the very thought of each gilded room and once-polished floor is stained with it as much as the wallpaper still sits forever stained with their blood.

Months of my life can now be boiled down into these simple impressions: Wineglasses in hands and heels on marble. Herbs and the rise of steam from beakers. Perfume and grinning lips. A clink. A cut. A whisper. Each of them accurate but each of them simple, dreamlike things far prettier and far more poetic than the full reality. If that's not what the mind is good for—to repaint and repossess every small horror of our lives—then perhaps it's the heart's doing. After all, it was my heart, as much as my hand, that led to their deaths.

It happened quickly, hitting the newsstands like whiplash: the fateful downfall of the Verdeau family and their empire. None of the tabloids ever managed to come close to the truth. Even if they tried—and some did try—they never stood a chance. Yet as I sit here now, almost a decade since I first came into their lives, there is not an ounce of marrow remaining in my bones absent of the details. While an indulgent game transpired between private rooms in Boston and the now-cobwebbed walls of Arrow's Edge, a series of poisons took their toll, and of the hands that crafted them, one is the very same that attempts to write this now.

I guess some might call this a confession.

THERE WAS NOTHING SWEET IN THE AIR as I stepped off the train and walked down the tree-lined street in Boston's historic neighborhood of Back Bay. Not then anyway. Not that day. Autumn was still weeks away, yet the air was crisp and clean. Verdant, from the grass along the Charles River being freshly cut. But if there is to be any starting point for all this, then it was there, my heels covered in pollen, a gentle breeze in the curls of my hair, and the New England sun beating down on my face in a way that felt familiar and yet oddly foreign.

I had recently returned from living with my aunt in Italy and after two long years away had just set my suitcases down in the living room of my childhood home when my father handed me the want-ads page of the newspaper. Unemployment checks, he had explained to me over the phone the week before my flight, weren't enough to cover the family anymore. The tired look in his bloodshot eyes the day of my arrival convinced me that he hadn't been exaggerating. Something in him had changed in my absence, and the piles of pain meds and constant phone calls from the debtors told me I had no choice. In my parents' eyes, my vacation was over. Responsibility was calling, and anyone in the family who was old enough to work was expected to do their share.

Six months prior my father had been cut from the payroll at his job. No notice given and, to my knowledge, no clue that it was coming either. If there had been, his pride wouldn't have let him say. His pride, as it were, had also prevented him from sending an e-mail to let me know. At least until the meager savings we had as a family ran out.

The situation had made him and my mother more sour and resentful of my time abroad in the first place, a fact that made my homecoming less enjoyable by the second and made me yearn for the chance to return to my aunt's side and back to a semblance of peace.

My aunt, Clare Ricchetti, was well known in the academic world so long as you studied botany or medieval history. Which, admittedly, not many people do. She was the most successful in her field out of any of us—another thing, I think, my parents resented. My mother especially, considering that Clare was her sister.

By the age of thirty-five, Aunt Clare had a fully established research garden outside a small village near Montefalco in Umbria, specializing in the reconstruction of medieval apothecary blends and once-lost strains of herbs. It was a tremendously useful garden niche as it was, and as a result of this specialty she frequently sold remedies to homeopathic companies and pharmacies alongside hosting Ph.D. candidates from illustrious places like Cambridge and Yale. She was always busy, tending to plants and doing interviews for documentaries in front of the lush greenery and fervent hum of bumblebees. She lived there, away from everything, in her beige dresses and lab coat, looking part scientist, part witch, and I loved her immensely for it. I also, I think, saw myself in her, and she in me.

I was a twenty-two-year-old mess of a med-school dropout when she offered me an internship. A girl doing her best to claw herself up from feelings of failure as I arrived on her doorstep, my ego bruised and fingers nervously clutching my suitcase. Saying I was a dropout isn't entirely true, though. I only considered myself one. That's what happens when you elect to defer your second year of med school due to burnout and a declining GPA. When you stare at the quickly accumulating debt and can't convince yourself you'll ever pay it off, so why bother getting more?

Europe in those days was far enough away from the disappointment of my life to seem like the best option. It was romantic, pastoral, and still close enough to family to be viable, thanks to Aunt Clare. Italy was a place my heart had always yearned to travel to after teenage years filled with falling asleep to documentaries on the Borgias or dreaming of scenic tours through Tuscany, but finances had never allowed me the chance to visit. Family vacations never happened beyond the continental United States, if beyond the Massachusetts border at all, and so I couldn't say no when she offered. Plus, while it wasn't much, it paid, saving me from suffering in a customer-service job while I tried to get my act together.

The sunrise every morning was misty and picturesque, filled with a pink-and-orange glow that I will never forget. At night the stars were brighter than I had ever seen and more numerous than my years growing up in Boston had led me to believe was even possible. It had been a slice of heaven and a time where my passion for medicine had only just begun to grow again. A sapling of a thing, bruised yet lovingly tended to in her care.

But family had beckoned me home. So I sat there, jet-lagged, over a dinner of chicken and boxed mashed potatoes as my father explained to me once more the details about the cutbacks at Ellerhart, a culling that followed the company's purchase by some massive conglomerate eager to downsize. That, combined with a back injury from a fall he had neglected to mention to me before, made it difficult for him to find employment, and a series of medical bills without insurance to cover them meant that there was only one choice: I had to get a job as soon as possible, in the worst economy in decades.

And so it came to be that not a month later I found myself hovering at the door of an ornate brownstone in Back Bay. My coffee had been chugged, and I had paced the street for a good ten minutes while popping gum stick after gum stick into my mouth in hopes of not smelling like cookie dough, or coconut, or whatever obnoxiously sweet syrup I had chosen to load it up with in a fit of nerves the hour prior.

My nerves were not any better.

Caffeine had a poor track record with that.

I stood there surrounded by brick and greenery and glistening sports cars, with three minutes until my first official interview after weeks of applications. Then I took a breath, spit my gum into the bushes, and knocked.

Ten seconds passed, maybe twenty, before the door opened with a slow and dramatic creak.

"Yes?" a voice asked. The disdain was unimaginably thick.

My back straightened as I tried to hand over my résumé.

"I have an appointment. Lena. Helena," I corrected. "Gereghty? It's for two-thirty."

The old man looked at the paper for a second and then sighed.

"Mr. Verdeau is not well. All appointments have been canceled for the day."

My outstretched hand dipped a little in disappointment. "Not feeling well? What's wrong?"

Again I received a look of annoyance.

"I'm not at liberty to discuss."

"Well, where's his physician?"

"Tending to him. Look, Miss Gor—"

"Gereghty," I said. "Like clarity."

"Miss *Gereghty*, I'm sure you came a long way." His sagging face tilted down as he peered at my outfit. As if somehow a man in his sixth or seventh decade could detect my zip code from the thread count of my shirt. "But perhaps we should reschedule."

The butler's eyes looked away from the transit card sticking out of my pocket and back to the freshly printed résumé in my hand.

"If your phone number is on that, then I can have Mr. Verdeau call you for rescheduling when his health has improved."

No.

It was the only thought running through my head at the time. Rent was due in a week and a half. It was this or nothing.

"But why? If he's ill, and his physician is there, wouldn't that make for an ideal interview?"

"Are you implying that the suffering of my employer is a prime time for him to make a business decision?"

"What? No, I—"

"Because if so, then perhaps I should hand this back to you."

"No! No, but . . . if there was any time for the physician to need assistance, now would be it, wouldn't it? To . . . test my skill."

He raised a gray eyebrow.

"Could you ask him?" I insisted. "Please."

The door creaked again as the man glanced behind him into the vast interior of the home.

"Perhaps."

"I'll wait. I'm happy to wait."

At last he nodded and motioned with a finger for me to stay put. I ignored how it was the same motion I used on our old dog and instead bade him a quick thank-you before he shut the door and shuffled off into the unknown, leaving me to wait outside.

I stared down at my feet, at how the ragged soles of my mother's borrowed heels appeared in sharp contrast to their surroundings. Never before in my life had I stood on a porch like that. A classic brick, so polished and clean it was hard to imagine that a weed could even consider sprouting up. Two streets over were brownstones whose small yards were filled with weeds, but not this one. It was as if the decay of history had never touched it. The bricks sat in charming little patterns, a far cry from the peeling, grayish paint and wood rot back home.

My feet tapped, an anxious habit, as I tried to go over anything that could be said to still give me a chance at the job.

It had been two years since I'd officially done anything in the medical field, but on paper my job at Aunt Clare's counted. I even had a few instances of informally administering a shot of antivenin during the summer, which was exciting, especially since I wasn't entirely sure if it was legal.

I glanced around the well-trimmed shrubbery and tried to imagine the likelihood of a surprise snakebite.

It seemed low.

After another moment the door opened and the butler motioned with a perfectly bent arm and straight fingers past the marbled entryway and toward what looked like a living room. It was then I realized that despite the building's looking like a standard set of three or four town houses on the outside, it was in fact one. Just one, and it was immense.

"Can I get you anything? Water, perhaps?" he asked.

"Sure . . . water would be great, thank you."

The little clicks of my shoes echoed in the chamberlike space until my feet came upon a pale Oriental rug. The room was larger than the entire first floor of my parents' apartment. The walls a warm cream, illuminated by the lingering summertime sun as it filtered in beyond the ornate glass windows. It wasn't clear to me whether the forbidding feeling of the furniture was a genuine one or simply a mistaken impression from my never having been in such a grand space in all my life. The small couch, with its carved wooden frame and tapestry cushions, probably cost more than a month's rent. The rug, I didn't even want to know.

I glanced back for the stern figure who was apparently the Verdeau butler, only to find him pacing across the entry with a tray neatly balanced on his palm. He set it down on a golden coffee table and began to pour a glass of water from a pitcher.

Little lemon slices caught my eye as they danced just atop the ice.

"If you need anything else, my name is George. Please, have a seat. It will be a moment before Mr. Verdeau is available."

I reached forward to take the glass and did as asked.

Moments passed in absolute silence, other than the occasional car driving past and the muffled sound of a conversation from somewhere within the house. After some time and enough fidgeting, I picked up my résumé from where George had placed it on the table and began reading over my qualifications, some fabricated and some truthful but exaggerated. Just when I began to silently pray that I was not in deeply over my head, the sharp scent of licorice filled the air. I turned to George just in time to see the flash of something popped into his mouth and a familiar Amarelli candy tin slipped into his breast pocket.

From the back of the home, a door opened, followed by the sound of hurried footsteps growing closer.

"George! There you are," said a man who was short in stature and balding, with a booming voice. He stopped and looked to me. "Who's this?"

Before he could answer, I stood and extended my hand.

"Helena Gereghty. I'm here for the physician's assistant position. We had an appointment."

He looked at my hand and then to George before finally giving it a shake. His palm slicked in sweat as he held on to me, as if he were trying to crush my bones underneath as he squeezed.

"Martin Verdeau," he said, letting go. "Thank you for coming by. As I'm sure George here has told you, we're all a bit under the weather today. I'm going to need you to reschedule."

I looked at this man, eager to see what the problem was, but merely found him slightly pallid and avoidant of the light streaming in from the windows. An annoyed squint to his eyes.

A hangover, I realized.

He was going to send me away because of a hangover.

"I see," I said, "but if you're under the weather, it might be a good time to test my skills. A trial run. So long as your physician is here."

Martin looked at me, quiet, but I kept my back straight and my voice firm. A minor miracle.

"My physician has stepped out at the moment," said Martin. "So I'm sorry, Miss Grat—"

"Gereghty."

"Miss Gereghty, but your timing is off today."

"I see," I said again.

Satisfied with himself, and apparently *dis*satisfied with me, Martin motioned with his hand toward the door. I refused to move.

"Perhaps you can tell me more about the position," I suggested. "You seem like someone who otherwise would be in fantastic health, so why the need for an assistant?"

Martin stared, silenced.

"Because it's not for him," came a soft but earnest voice from just behind a pillar in the entryway. "It's for Jonathan."

I turned to the sound and was instantly greeted by a blond girl in a cream satin slip. A dressing gown not meant for outside eyes, but the delicate golden chains of her necklace told a different story—as did her tights and heels. She was cherubic, sharp-eyed, and soft-cheeked. Beautiful, actually.

"Audrey!" Mr. Verdeau shouted. "I told you to wait upstairs."

"I wanted coffee," she said with a shrug. "Besides, Georgie wasn't anywhere to be found, so I figured I'd wander on down myself. Who's this?"

Her voice was as poignant as her gaze, and at the sound of it my mouth went dry.

"My apologies, Miss Audrey," George said quickly. "This is Miss Gereghty. We were interviewing her to help Dr. Prosenko."

"I figured it was business," Audrey said with a swift glance to Martin, sounding bored. "I just didn't know her name."

She looked at me again, her cropped hair twirling about her jaw, and raised an eyebrow in expectation.

"Lena," I said, my nerves at last catching up to me. "Well, Helena really, but my friends call me Lena."

"And what am I to call you, then?"

"I'm sorry?"

"I'd hate to think you were a friend and embarrass myself by calling you incorrectly," she said, a corner of her mouth curling up into a smile. "Or even worse, offend."

A flush rose to my face. She had the kind of friendly voice I once wished popular girls would use with me back in high school but never did. No doubt a skill obtained from growing up in the upper echelons of society. Her use of it then was especially powerful.

"Um, Lena . . . is fine."

"Brilliant," said Audrey, seemingly pleased. "Well, *Lena*, good luck."

She popped her teeth along with a mint that was in her mouth before turning her attention to her phone and striding back across the entryway and toward what I assumed was the kitchen. The living room, at the loss of her, almost grew dimmer.

Mr. Verdeau sighed and pressed his fingers to the sides of his nose. "You'll have to excuse my daughter."

I looked to him, confused. "Why? She seems . . . charming."

The man let out a great puff of air. "That's a word for it. Charmed her way into having me pay for three years of law school."

"Three? Did she drop out?"

I cursed my lack of a filter.

Mr. Verdeau humphed, not seeming to mind. "Worse," he told me. "Graduated summa cum laude."

Damn.

I tried to return to the task at hand.

"Mr. Verdeau, what did your daughter mean by 'it's not for you'? The job description didn't give many details. I just assumed."

He made a face as if some great lie had been revealed.

"Yes, so you caught that. Well, at least you've got good ears. No, Audrey is right. In some ways. Dr. Prosenko tends less to myself and more to my son. But your duties—"

I bettered my posture.

"Should you be hired," he cautioned, "would be to assist with—oh, how should I put this?— smaller jobs. As they arise."

"You mean I would be on call?"

"In some ways."

"This is part-time? It didn't say that in the advertisement."

"No," Mr. Verdeau confirmed with a hearty chuckle. "I should hope not. Wording like that tends to deter the more qualified candidates."

I didn't enjoy the implication but did my best to hide it. "How many hours, then?"

"Twenty-five to start," he explained, at last seeming to realize he had been conned into continuing the interview despite his earlier efforts. "One to six on weekdays with the occasional weekends. But I want to be clear that the weekly wage is set at eight hundred dollars. That is the salary. The only additional wages you might receive would be a bonus for being called in or working events."

It was a decent sum, despite his tone. More than decent. Astounding, considering it wasn't full-time. A single week's wages would help significantly with the rent for the month and was more than I was rightfully qualified for. It would go a long way in helping my parents out, maybe even with a bit to put aside for student loan repayment. Something I was champing at the bit to do.

Still, a few details in his speech were concerning, and so I asked him what he meant by "events."

"I mean fund-raisers, parties, dinner clubs," Martin answered. "I have a profile to maintain, Miss Gereghty. My family receives a great deal of attention. Are you good around people?"

The truth was, I was abysmal. Not in any sort of way that would be embarrassing, but more in the awkward sense of avoiding prom my senior year because of an overwhelming anxiety about mingling in a sea of nylons and being judged. I had grown taller and, for the most part, evened out into a form I was okay with, but the old wounds still stung. The thick curls and dark hair, like my aunt's, and the freckles from my father's side that spread across my nose and cheeks made sense now but hadn't when I was younger. All that, combined with the fact that the wealth brackets between my family and his were stratospheres apart, made the old insecurities of childhood arise once more.

I swallowed them. "I like to think so."

"Hmph," said the man across from me.

Over the course of the last few minutes, his already pale and clammy complexion had grown ghostly. There was no question. I had seen a hundred similar hangovers my freshman year of college.

"Well, thank you for coming by, but I think we should wait until Dr. Prosenko is back to do any sort of real interview."

Martin extended his hand, and I shook it with the tightest, surest grip I could manage. With a few more thanks, I was ushered out by George and left to watch as the door shut briskly behind me.

That was meant to be the end of it, I thought, and with the way I'd pushed him, it should have been. I had been far too desperate, and standing there, I couldn't help but run over every moment of the interview when I'd placed my foot in my mouth. Every sentence where I should have just shut up but hadn't.

For reasons I still do not understand, grace afforded me a second chance. Not five minutes later, as I began my walk back to the T stop, I reached into my pocket to find my CharlieCard gone.

I could have just gotten another one. Wasted another three bucks that I didn't have for a one-way ticket I'd already paid for. Only something urged me to return, despite my humiliation and growing anger at my own mistakes, and thankfully I listened.

I rushed back down the tree-lined streets and past brownstone after brownstone, and I came to stand on that stoop again. As I knocked ferociously, my knuckles making a quick rhythmic tap on the wood, the door swung open and my words flew out as fast as they could manage with both politeness and brevity.

"Hi again. Look, I'm sorry, but I think I left my card here, and I—"

"Lena?"

I looked up, expecting a dark three-piece and wrinkles.

Instead I came face-to-face with Audrey Verdeau.

"It is Lena, right?"

"Oh. Yes. Hi."

She smiled. "You said that already. Did you leave something?"

"Yeah, my . . . uh, my train card. I can't find it, and I think it might have . . . uh, well, fallen on the couch."

The entire situation only seemed to grow more embarrassing by being spoken out loud, but Audrey, to her credit, didn't seem to mind. Instead she opened the door wider and waved me in.

"Well, you're welcome to check for it."

"Thank you."

Walking back into the brownstone felt strange. Slower, even as my feet hastened to cross the shining marble entryway and return to my former seat. Audrey stood at the threshold, watching me with her shoulder elegantly pressed to the trim, a mug of coffee in one hand and her phone in the other. As I stuck my fingers between the cushions, she eyed me like a hawk, the steam rising from her cup and curling under the delicate curve of her jaw, until some minuscule sound had her turning back toward the staircase.

A grumble echoed, and then a heavy clunk sounded against one of the steps.

A man laughed.

"Audrey!" he shouted. "Audrey! Where's Dad?"

I pretended to stare between the crease of another cushion as she shouted back.

"What are you doing out of bed?"

"What's it to you? Where's Dad?"

She hurried off toward the steps with a face ready for battle, her blush at once becoming war paint. The tone to her voice changing.

"He's gone to the office! Get back upstairs!"

From my spot in the side room, there was another echo of a thud from the steps. The sound of unsteady feet, heavy and languorous. Then the loudest sound, that of a body slipping. Crashing hard as it fell.

"Jonathan! Shit."

With Audrey's shout I immediately abandoned my search to run out to the entryway. As soon as I crossed that threshold, I saw a man, not much older than myself, face white and hair dark, unconscious halfway down the steps in what looked to be an incomplete set of pajamas.

"What happened?!" I shouted, rushing over to Audrey's side.

Her mug of coffee had been left on a small table, and she hovered, one hand clinging tightly to her phone and frozen as to what to do.

"He just—he fell. He's fine."

"Did he trip?"

As I reached him, I saw just how pale the man was. Eyes rimmed in bruised circles and cheekbones sharp enough to rival the edge of the step that his head currently lay on. He looked ill. Drastically ill, and yet his lips were noticeably purple with the stain of merlot, the same color as the silk of his robe.

I moved past Audrey and reached to tap his cheek, gaining no response.

"Help me sit him up!" I called back to her, but she didn't move. I waited two beats and then shouted, "Come on!"

Lifting his head slowly, I checked for blood, my fingers thankfully coming back dry, and as Audrey at last walked those few steps, I hoisted him up and motioned for her to sit.

"Here, cradle his head. Like this," I told her, positioning him. "You said he's your brother, right?"

She nodded, just watching me and cautiously accepting her new position.

"What's his name, again?" I asked, and checked his eyes.

"Jonathan."

"Jonathan!" I shouted. "Hey! Jonathan, can you hear me?"

Still there was no response.

"Does this happen often?" I asked.

She looked at me still. Hesitant of something. "Yes. Sometimes."

"Has he eaten? Is it low blood sugar? Heart issues? Kidneys?"

She paused and then gave an odd, stunted laugh, rolling her eyes up to the ceiling. "Everything."

My hands finally stopped. "What?"

"He hasn't eaten," said Audrey. "He never does, and he used to be on dialysis."

"Is he diabetic?"

"What? No."

I scanned the room, still worried that he hadn't responded to anything yet. Then I spotted the coffee and ran to grab it.

"His pulse is low. See if you can get him to wake up. If he does, have him drink this. As much as he can. Where's your kitchen?"

"Our kitchen? What do you . . . ?"

"Where?"

"Just down that hall, but—"

I ran, my heels skidding on the floorboards before I at last came to a large kitchen on the opposite side of the home. It was absent of any cooks, but I found the sink and threw open the cabinet doors to look under it.

Bleach . . . detergent . . . *shit.*

"Audrey!" I shouted as loud as I could. "Cleaning supplies! Where's the rest of your cleaning supplies?"

"How would I know? Sascha takes care of all that!"

Cursing, I hoisted myself up and turned to rummage in all the cabinets until at last I found a closet near the back that contained a series of large plastic bottles. I grabbed the ammonia and snatched a dish towel on my way back through the kitchen.

"Is he up?" I asked, returning to kneel by them both on the stairs.

"No, he— Wait, what's that?"

Hastily I poured a splash of the ammonia onto the towel, the scent quickly rising to burn the inside of my nose and fill the room with its noxious fumes.

"Ugh! It smells awful!" Audrey said.

"Cover your nose."

I waved the bundled towel under his chin, mimicking the motions I once used in childhood after rescuing my friends from fistfights. It was crude, and it hardly would have been recommended in med school, but it always worked, and I prayed it'd work this time, too. The smell was acrid and burned my eyes, but it took only a few seconds before Jonathan suddenly lurched up from his sister's lap, eyes wide.

Then, before I could register what was happening, I was yanked away with force, my body left stumbling off the stairs and out the front door, pulled by a man's firm hand, a blur of gray and the golden glint of a watch. Voices shouting something too quickly to catch.

I hadn't heard the front door open.

I had missed seeing Audrey look up in surprise.

All that I saw was Jonathan, and life rushing back into his dark hazel eyes. Then that wooden door, slamming shut in my face before my nostrils had the chance to stop burning.

In the shock of finding myself alone again, I took a deep breath, the quiet of the street catching up to me, and shouted, "Fuck!"

2

I AWOKE TO THE SOUND of my phone ringing ceaselessly and to the blaring red digits of my alarm clock displaying a sharp and cruel 7:40 A.M. At some point I had fallen asleep without realizing it, leaving my mouth stale and teeth feeling fuzzy. Even after I'd blinked my eyes into focus, the phone continued to ring from its spot on the floor, nestled in the back pocket of my discarded jeans.

For a moment I forgot that I still had job applications out, my head foggy from drowning my embarrassment over the interview during a night out with friends and one too many beers. Cheap beers, as my dwindling funds would necessitate. The thought caught up, though, flooding my veins with adrenaline as I sat up and fetched my phone.

Ignoring the room's spinning, I answered the unknown number before my oncoming yawn had the chance.

"Hello?" I murmured.

"Ah. Yes, is this Helena Gereghty?"

"Oh, uh, yeah, I mean yes. Yes, this is her. Sorry, who is this?"

"This is Dr. Prosenko from Arrow's Edge calling. As I understand, you came to the town house yesterday for an interview? Is that correct?"

Had I not been awake before, I was at those simple words. I sat down on the edge of my bed and prayed it wasn't a formal rejection. Then again, that was all I reckoned it could be.

"Yes," I said cautiously, ". . . I did."

"Excellent. I wanted to apologize for how shortly we ended it. Martin and I, that is. If you have the time, could you come in again today so we might properly meet?"

"Oh . . . oh! Sure. Yeah! It's no problem. What time?"

There was a pause.

"Nine o'clock? If you can make it."

I looked at the clock again—7:45 A.M. It might be close.

"Of course," I told him anyway. "I'll be there as soon as I can."

"Good! Good. We'll see you then."

Shakily I hung up the phone and then stood to stumble into the nearest clean pair of pants I could find.

"Ma?" I shouted. "Ma! Can I borrow the car?"

"What for?" her voice called from in front of the TV. The TV that lately had begun at 5:00 A.M. sharp as my father got ready for the opening shift at his new temporary job in the neighborhood hardware store.

"Work!" I shouted louder. "It's for work!"

For a moment the house fell into silence, except for the echoes of a cereal commercial's jingle. Then she shouted back, both loud and excited. "Keys are by the door!"

I RACED ACROSS TOWN AS SOON AS I could shower and twist my hair into a messy braid. Even with the chaos of Boston's traffic, my parents' hatchback managed to make it from Roslindale to Back Bay with seven minutes left to find parking. Although upon seeing the immaculate street again, I circled back to park a few blocks over. Somehow I didn't think the car's rust stains and boxy frame would be appreciated, parked among all the newest Buicks and Lincolns.

Still, it was less embarrassing than going back for a lost three-dollar transit pass, I supposed.

But not by that much.

Knocking for the third time felt stranger than the second. As my knuckles rapped against the polished wood once again, a part of me hoped Audrey would be there to answer, a cup of fresh coffee in her hand and some new cream-colored dress to make my own outfit feel woefully insignificant. I also hoped she was okay, after everything that had happened.

That Jonathan was okay, too.

Although really, if he hadn't been, I doubted they would have called me back.

The door opened, and true to both my previous experiences with the Verdeau family's front door, someone new answered. This time it was a taller man. Taller than Martin at any rate. He had receding gray hair, once dark and likely curly but now short and kept tidy with pomade, and a square jaw hidden by a trimmed salt-and-pepper beard. He looked older, once handsome and now just incredibly tired. He turned to me with striking gray eyes.

"You must be Helena Gereghty."

I nodded.

"Good!" he said loudly, and looked to the golden Rolex on his wrist. "Right on time. Excellent. Come on in. We spoke on the phone. I'm Dr. Prosenko. I work for Martin and the family."

He extended his hand, and immediately I recognized it as the same one that had grabbed me during my quick exit the day before.

"You'll forgive me for not getting the chance to meet you yesterday," he continued. "I had stepped out to take care of some errands, you understand."

I was speechless, and he paused awkwardly before ushering us half-way into that same sitting room I was getting to know quite well.

"Miss Gereghty?"

"Yeah. Sorry. I just—" I couldn't help it. I glanced at the stairs. "With the way things ended, I didn't expect to be back."

Dr. Prosenko looked at me, and again I felt the urge to curse myself for saying such unnecessary things, but then he nodded.

"No," he reasoned. "I suppose not. Please, sit."

I did as asked, pulling down the back of my blouse before it could ride up.

"Is he all right?"

"Who? Jonathan? Yes, yes. I assure you that happens with him from time to time," Dr. Prosenko explained. "You'll learn. You'll also, hope-fully, learn not to use *ammonia*."

My eyes, which had until that point been nervously staring at the table, looked up, mildly bewildered. "Sir?"

Dr. Prosenko gave another smile. "Would you like a tour of the house?"

Before I could decide on an answer, the doctor was already walking away, leaving me to see only the back of his suit jacket and listen to the shuffle of his shoes as he headed toward the entryway. Then he motioned for me to follow.

"You know this part already, I presume," he said as we neared the kitchen. His tone told me they had no doubt found the mess I'd left the kitchen in.

"A bit," I confessed.

"I can't say we've ever had someone rummage through our cook's quarters during an interview."

"It wasn't during the—" I cut myself off as Prosenko looked back to me with a raised eyebrow.

"No?"

"I just mean he passed out after I returned. To get my card."

"Second interview, then," he said, motioning to the kitchen proper. "This area is mostly off-limits between seven A.M. and eight A.M., as our cook, Daniella, gets breakfast set up. Coffee is always on the pot there in the corner if you find you need it or if someone asks you for it. Audrey only drinks her fair-trade coffee in the burlap bag, but I wouldn't worry, since she goes out for lattes mostly. Jonathan will drink whatever you give him, though I'm going to have to ask you to not give him anything, precisely for that reason. Even if he asks."

"Because I gave him ammonia?"

"Because I monitor his state *closely* and I can't do that if he has you sneaking him eight cups of coffee and who knows what else before he so much as attempts a proper breakfast."

"Oh . . . right."

Prosenko eyed me closely, making sure I understood the severity of his rule. When he was satisfied, he moved on to the dining room.

"Breakfast, lunch, and dinner are each served here. Breakfast is at eight, lunch at twelve-thirty, and dinner at six. I can't say Jonathan nor Audrey can often be found at meals, but Daniella prepares them anyway. Staff are always welcome to leftovers if there's anything good and it happens during a shift. No one here is vegetarian—well, Audrey is, depending on who's asking and whatever it is she's read that week—but if you have any allergies, let Daniella know. I've found that she's quite accommodating with enough convincing. Now, moving on, cleaning supplies and spare medical equipment like alcohol swabs and the second defibrillator are in that pantry there, and the bathroom is around the back. Any questions?"

I had many.

The more Prosenko spoke about the rooms and the daily schedules, the more my head spun with the memories of the day before and with the implication that somehow I had been hired for the position without realizing it. Instead I shook my head, not wanting to give him any more reason to take my new, seemingly fragile sense of employment away, and thus he carried on.

"Ordinarily George is here, but he must be out. He takes care of the estate and the household finances as well as the family's schedules. If you have a question about the houses or events, he's the person you'll want to find. Otherwise there's Daniella and Sascha in the kitchen and then Martin, Jonathan, Audrey, and of course myself."

It was a smaller household than I expected, but one detail stood out.

"No lady of the house?"

Prosenko's lips thinned. "No, and you'd be wise to not mention it. Let's move on."

After the kitchen we looped back past the bathroom and turned down the western hallway, otherwise accessible only through the living room. There, in a side room, an old hunting tapestry caught my eye as it hung on a sharp white wall beneath the intricate molding. Its colors were rich and dark, in contrast to everything else in the home. Full of ambers and forest greens, with deer and huntsmen and dogs along the borders.

"Arrow's Edge," I said, remembering the name from the phone call that morning. "That's what you called this place on the phone, right? Kind of seems like a strange name for a town house."

Prosenko stopped just before the other room.

"That's because this *isn't* Arrow's Edge."

"It's not?"

"No, Miss Gereghty," said Prosenko, almost amused. "This is just where the Verdeaus like to stay during workweeks. One of many properties. I thought I mentioned that before."

"Then what is it? Arrow's Edge?"

He hesitated, thinking. "The main house, you could say. If you choose to accept, then you'll see it soon enough."

"Accept?"

Dr. Prosenko paused as realization dawned. "Yes. The position, Miss Gereghty. That's why I called you here, after all. Why else would I give you the tour?"

"You mean you're actually . . . you're really offering me the job?"

"You sound like you don't think you deserve it."

"No! I mean yes. I just thought maybe there'd be another interview or other candidates or—"

"Or something else. I understand. Truth be told, Martin wanted to interview a few more. However, after some consideration of the way you handled Jonathan's collapse *and* the fact it miraculously did not reach this morning's round of papers . . . well, it gave me all I needed to know to make the call. Miss Gereghty, the job is yours if you'd like it."

"Yes!" I blurted before thinking, grace and etiquette abandoned. "Yes, of course!"

"Great," he said, a small smile pulling his lips. "Well then, with that settled, let's finish the tour, shall we? Then I can take you to Martin for the paperwork." Prosenko checked his Rolex. "If we can waste another ten minutes or so, he should have a moment."

I couldn't believe it.

Standing in that hallway, I really couldn't.

I had botched the interview. It had been so apparent that it took three hours at the pub with my friends taking turns buying pints to get over the embarrassment of just how badly I'd fucked up, but here it was, not even a full twenty hours later, and I was being offered the job. It seemed as surreal as it did miraculous, and foolishly I followed behind Prosenko, past more paintings hung on the walls and expensive art pieces and clearly modernized bathrooms, still in a state of disbelief.

Most of the rooms were small and cramped, as with most of Boston's brick units, but nonetheless the house itself was expansive. Every turn revealed a new, smaller room to memorize, including storage archives and rooms filled with medical equipment. I can't say that the reality of his offer truly struck until we moved back to the staircase. Those same fateful steps where I so clearly recalled Audrey cradling her brother's head like a modern pietà. Only now I was being led up them and not ripped away.

As we at last approached Martin's office, shouting echoed through the walls, and I hesitated to go any further. Prosenko merely sighed and continued. There was nothing kind about the shouts, just muffled orders in two male voices. One paused to let out a series of coughs, which quickly seemed to turn the hall to silence.

We barely had time to consider a retreat before the office door swung open to reveal Jonathan, upright and now clearly rivaling Prosenko in height. His dark brown hair hung in messy, greasy-looking waves over his eyes, framing hollow cheeks. The deep maroon of his bathrobe did nothing to conceal the protruding collarbones nor the sick pallor of his skin where it poked out from a thin white undershirt and a pair of striped boxer shorts.

"What are you looking at, old man?" said Jonathan sharply, eyeing his doctor with a purple-rimmed gaze.

Prosenko said nothing, and I waited, quiet as I could manage, before Jonathan turned to me. All I could do was look at him, partially stunned by finding myself face-to-face with the source of the shouting and equally so by his still wretched state.

He scoffed and quickly brushed past me with a slam of our shoulders before rounding the corner and disappearing to the other side, back to his domain.

Prosenko let out a sigh and gave me a not entirely sympathetic look.

"Don't take it personally," he said, and then rapped three times on the wooden door, waiting for Martin to signal us inside.

The moment came all too soon.

Let me just say that if it's not considered good for one's safety to step into the middle of a fight, then it's only marginally less risky to go talk to a man two seconds after that fight has finished. There was no blood in the office, no sign of broken furniture or black eyes, but there at his desk Martin Verdeau was red-faced and sullen, and I could sense that it was not the best time to be signing a new letter of employment, despite Prosenko's intentions.

"So," said Martin, "you're back."

"I gave her a tour, and Miss Gereghty here has accepted. All she needs to do now is sign the offer."

I waited, trying to be polite even as Martin stared me down while the anger in his face slowly drained.

"Hmph," he said at last, turning back to Prosenko. "And you think she can handle it?"

"I think she proved that yesterday, don't you?"

"Sure proved something," he grumbled, opening a desk drawer to pull out a small file folder and set it on the desk in front of me. Clearing his throat, he opened it to reveal a basic offer of employment printed on a business letterhead I was too distracted to read.

"Well, go on and read over it and let me know if you have any questions," he said, and then reached for a pen, twisted it open, and set it beside my hand. "But make it quick. I've got a call to Zurich in five."

"Already?" Prosenko asked, seeming slightly surprised at Martin's words.

Martin only gave the doctor a displeased look, refusing to indulge Prosenko's inquiry any further.

As I read the paper, I could see that it seemed like a basic offer. Nothing in the few brief paragraphs gave me any cause for alarm. It cited almost exactly what Martin had mentioned the day before. I would be an assistant for Dr. Prosenko and work part-time, salaried, with the option for bonuses at special events. I would help the family and file papers and run errands and respect their privacy. Everything seemed in order and nothing beyond my capabilities. Though even if there were things I didn't think I could do, I wasn't going to admit it then. I needed a job, and I wasn't about to return to my father empty-handed when his pain meds were due for a refill.

In one easy motion, I nodded and picked up the pen. It was heavy. One of those pens that come in marble and gold, packaged in boxes with expensive ink. Leagues above the standard Bic.

I held it, before catching the second hand of Prosenko's watch from the corner of my eye. It was 10:45 A.M. Ten minutes until my parking meter ran out, a five-minute walk away.

Maybe that's why I didn't ask any questions, why too easily I signed my name so Martin could get to his call and I could go run to the hatchback. Just as quickly, Martin filed it away, reached out, and shook my hand with an unnecessarily firm grip and a practiced, "Welcome aboard. George'll send you everything else."

They excused me as soon as the contract was signed, and hastily I took my leave. Brushing past the doors of that hallway and back downstairs, I could hear the loud echo of a television in the sitting room, which should have been my warning. Not two seconds later, Jonathan Verdeau stepped out, waltzing his way back from the kitchen with a corkscrew and a glass in hand.

At the sight of me, he stopped, his somber frown disappearing as a small smirk overtook his lips. Hazel eyes twinkled with something dark and lost as Jonathan waved the glass in front of my face and disappeared into the room, just below the portrait of a blond woman.

My mouth opened, but my brain hadn't thought of any words to say. It was too late. He was gone, and the seconds ticked by as I ran down the hall and out the door, letting it slam behind me. By the time I reached the car, the red expiration warning was flashing, but my windshield was empty and clear.

3

Desperately in need of grease and carbs before I could consider going home, I met up with my friends again for lunch at the neighborhood pancake house. It wasn't much from the outside. A faded and run-down seventies-style brick building with a plastic sign and an interior covered in close to five decades of grime to make it seem all the more authentic, but it was home. Slick Rick's Pig and Pancake was one of the top-ten things I'd missed during my time with Aunt Clare. The idiots sitting in the metallic blue booth with me were numbers one and two.

Beside me Anna let out a loud laugh, half choking on her soda and inelegantly catching the sugary liquid with the sleeve of her hoodie before it could drip. We were all a basket of onion rings and a round of sodas into what was a solid and time-tested tradition.

Slick Rick's had seen us through the worst of it. It had seen Rumi five hours after he'd broken his arm junior year when a winter joyride took a wrong turn, serving up a platter of hash browns and a steak knife to cut off the ER band. It had seen Anna too many nights with tears on her face and a backpack of clothes after her stepdad had kicked her out yet again,

and it had held her as she wrote out her scholarship essays for Harvard—
and rewrote them and rewrote them—and even as she snuck in birthday
candles and a small statue of St. Jude for an impromptu prayer session
before finally sending them off. Then of course it had seen me. Crying
through breakups and bad test scores and all the joys of new adulthood.
Slick Rick's had been there when I first got into med school and consoled
me in that dark hour after I decided to leave.

In a sense Slick Rick's owned a bit of our souls, and in return we gave
it ample patronage in the form of too much soda and pitchers of iced tea
and bountiful hordes of anything fried that came from their kitchen.
French fries, onion rings, hash browns, and even the occasional corn dog.

That day was no exception.

"I just can't believe they called you again," Anna continued after she
was no longer in danger of choking on Dr Pepper. She brushed a lock of
dyed-green hair out of her face.

I snagged an onion ring from the communal basket and took a bite.

"I know, but it's like I said: He called me back this morning, and by the
end of the meeting he was taking me up to the big guy to sign the papers."

Anna whistled. "I need to call Aunt Clare and thank her for whatever
miracle she pulled. Never thought I'd see the day you got back into medicine again."

I looked across the booth to her and glared. Though she was right.

"No, no, no!" Rumi chimed in. "This is great. Really. You could've
wound up making lattes or something, but now you're the— Wait, what
are you, again?"

"I'm the . . . physician's assistant."

Anna's eyes widened. "Lena, you didn't graduate. You're not qualified to—"

"I know that! I'm just . . . assisting."

"The physician."

"Right."

Anna looked skeptical, knowing all too well my lack of a genuine certification and the ten short months of schooling I got under my belt before bailing. I just chose to ignore that at the time.

"And who exactly is trusting you with this, again?" Rumi asked. "You never said."

"Yeah, Lena, who actually managed to hire you?"

I shrugged. "Some big shot in Back Bay. Big business family. The doctor is named Prosenko. Main guy was Martin."

Anna slammed her small hands on the table. "Verdeau? You don't mean Martin *Verdeau* hired you, right?"

I looked to her, confused. "Yeah, that's the name. You know him?"

This time Rumi looked to Anna and then pulled the basket of onion rings away before I could snag another one.

"Why would Martin Verdeau hire *you*?"

"Yeah, what for? Is his health that bad?" Anna continued.

Stealing the basket back, I frowned.

"Guys, you know I'm not allowed to tell you that. HIPAA."

Anna gave me a look, then slung her hypothesis to Rumi.

"I bet something's wrong. It's probably Jonathan. Or no, maybe Audrey. You know, I was reading this blog yesterday, and it said she wasn't at her usual Sunday-brunch place last weekend. Plus, she's been in the papers a lot less over the past year."

"Yeah, but if that's the case, they would have found someone better than *Lena*."

"Okay, how do *you* know them?" I finally asked.

Rumi paused. "You mean you really don't?"

"Am I supposed to?"

If I had to admit it, my friends' interest made me feel better about my new employment. Prouder, if a bit too much like a con was quickly getting away from me. It also proved I knew nothing about the family that had just hired me. Luckily, Anna was all too happy to explain.

"I don't know much about the company. It's like a big tech producer or something, but lately it's been in the news because it keeps buying up these smaller businesses and people aren't sure what to make of it. But it doesn't matter. The company is the boring bit."

"What's the name of it?"

"Hm? Oh. Uh . . ." She turned to Rumi. "Avaxla? Avelux?"

Rumi shrugged.

I pulled out my phone to remind myself to do a quick search of the name later. "So what have you guys heard about the family?"

Rumi stifled a laugh and then said dully, "Martin's scum, Jonathan's a drunk, and Audrey's a bitch."

Anna looked appalled. "She's not a bitch!"

"Only 'cause you have a crush on her."

She blushed. "Shut up."

Rumi took a sip of his soda and turned back to me. "The family's a mess. If that's what you want to know."

"Yeah. I gathered that much."

"So you really met them?" he asked. "Audrey and her brother?"

"'Met' is . . . an understatement."

"What?"

Anna grabbed my shoulder. "Lena, what did you do?"

"HIPAA, guys. HIPAA! Patient privacy laws. I can't tell you."

"But you've met her," Anna insisted. "Audrey Verdeau? Five-four, blond, and usually carries a small beige Birkin bag."

"Well, I don't know about the Birkin, but yeah, that sounds like her. She seemed . . . nice."

Nice. Sure, it wasn't as if I'd seen her for more than a few moments, and yet her face now seemed to appear every time I blinked.

"Huh," mocked Rumi, noting how Anna had grown silent. "Look at that, you've stunned the poor girl."

Anna frowned and gave a sharp stab to his toes with the heel of her boot beneath the table, which earned a yelp.

"You're telling us Audrey Verdeau is nice," she said, still in disbelief.

"I mean, she was polite enough, I guess," I told them, growing increasingly confused as to why they cared and wishing they would stop before too much of a blush could rise to my cheeks. "She offered to help me find my CharlieCard after I left it on their couch."

Anna sighed. "Jesus Christ, Lena, you left it on their couch?"

"Oh, shut up and order some more onion rings," I told Rumi.

"Hey! We're only trying to help you!" he said with a laugh before crawling out of the booth.

The teasing tone and laughter died down as Anna leaned over to me, careful not to catch Rumi's ear.

"Audrey's not that bad," she said. "The blogs just pick on her a lot. I really don't know that much about Jonathan. Just that . . . well, Rumi wasn't wrong," Anna warned me further. "He's kind of a drunk."

The image of Jonathan's collapse and the grin as he waved the glass and corkscrew in front of my face came back with Technicolor force. "That makes sense."

"You meet the guy yet?"

"Briefly."

Anna raised an eyebrow.

"He was probably drunk," I confessed.

Anna shot me a knowing look just before a steaming plastic tray of onion rings was dropped onto the table and Rumi climbed back to his spot.

"Who's drunk?"

"Jonathan," said Anna, catching him up.

"Oh. Duh."

"He can't always be drunk, though," I tried. "Right?"

"Of course," said Rumi cruelly. "I'm sure he can be hungover, too."

I couldn't help that a small part of me grew defensive of Jonathan despite what my friends were saying. They hadn't seen him collapsed onto the stairs or so terribly, deathly pale. In the part of my conscience that had formed through too many anatomy and physiology courses, I knew even then that Jonathan Verdeau seemed sick beyond what could be attributed to alcohol, but professionalism, among other things, kept me quiet. Fear of further taunting from my friends, as well as a contract that specifically mentioned respecting the family's privacy on top of the standard ethical expectations of health care, meant that I couldn't offer any explanation to them or do anything to dissuade their opinions. Instead in my silence grew a sort of frustration at his family for letting him drink the way he did and at the doctor who was now my boss and didn't seem to care.

With reluctance on my part to keep it going, the conversation soon died down, and when the new basket of onion rings was still half full, I took my leave of Slick Rick's with the false excuse that I had to run errands before work the next day. After a series of quick and well-rehearsed hugs that had become second nature, I told Anna and Rumi good-bye and drove the thankfully brief six minutes to my parents' house.

Back inside the old living room that I had snuck into so many times as a teen, my father lounged in his recliner, the TV echoing as he snored. I tried not to pay attention to the orange pill bottles beside him, emptier than I remembered them that morning. Or how there was a time not too long ago when he'd refuse even an Advil. He never spoke about what caused the back injury, and in my weeks at home my mother changed the subject anytime I asked. Still, I found it hard not to miss the man my father had been before. Now it seemed he was either unconscious, in a haze, or angry, and I wasn't sure which I preferred.

As quietly as I could, I shut the front door, slipped off my shoes, and headed upstairs to my room. It would have been a quiet trip, too, had my newly vulnerable toe not run straight into the corner of a large wooden crate waiting for me at the foot of my bed.

With a yelp, I hissed, bouncing my way to the mattress to sit down and rub the sting away.

My door creaked open, and my mother poked her head through.

"Oh, good. You're finally home," she said. "That arrived for you earlier from your aunt. Had to sign for customs. From the looks of it, the thing's been stuck at the border since that plane of yours landed."

The searing pain from stubbing my toe finally began to fade, so I leaned over and ripped off the notice taped to the top.

"Aunt Clare didn't say she was sending anything."

My mother frowned. "She spoils you, if you ask me. Haven't so much as gotten a Christmas card in five years, but oh, no, she'll waste hundreds to mail you some useless shrubs. Where's the car keys?"

I ignored her, reading the return address with a fondness, and letting my thumb linger over the words.

"Helena."

"Fine. Here," I said, and tossed the keys toward the door.

She fumbled to catch them. "Brat."

I looked up then. "Wait, why do you need them?"

She sighed and walked into my room to steal a glance at her hair in the mirror on the back side of my door.

"Anthony stayed late at school, and I've got to pick him up."

Anthony, or rather Tony, was my younger brother, scarcely fourteen and bitter about it. I missed two of his birthdays when I was in Italy, and since I had come back, he'd hardly spoken a word to me, instead spending all his time at school or who knows where.

"He could've called me," I said. "The school was on my way home. I could've taken him to Rick's."

She stopped fussing with her hair. "Tch, he doesn't need to be eating that crap before dinner. Besides, picking him up was never a problem before we had you stealing the car."

"You're the one who said I could borrow it."

"This morning! Now it's past five and I haven't even been able to get groceries for dinner, so the store's gonna be a mess and your father's gonna have to stay up late to eat."

"Well, you could have told me."

She sighed, dramatically frustrated. "I shouldn't have to. Your aunt may have let you do whatever you wanted, but we have schedules in this house. It's not all wine and sunbathing."

My mother did her best to avoid eye contact with me and instead rummaged through her purse until she found her lipstick and refreshed it.

"But you should e-mail her," she said. "Thank her for the trouble."

"Yeah, Anna already told me to."

"For the package?"

"For the help."

"Hmph, well. I can't see how that help of hers has made much of a difference the last few weeks. That woman's credentials can't possibly be—"

"I got the job, Ma," I finally told her. "That's why I had the car so long."

She stopped fussing at last. "Doing what?"

I shrugged. "Just helping some rich family. Taking notes for a doctor."

"Hm. Well. Good. At least it's somewhat related to that schooling of yours you started." She headed back out the door. "You don't need the car again tomorrow, though, right? You can bus there? I can't do this every day, Lena. We don't have room in the budget for all the gas you've been using, and I've got an interview later this week."

"No, it's fine. I'll take the train."

"Good. I'll be back later, then. If your father wakes up, don't let him snack and don't ask him about his day."

"How *was* his day?"

"How d'you think?"

I didn't answer, and my mother simply gave me a look as if her point had been well made and then shut the door.

Alone in the darkness of my room, I stared down at the wooden crate, willing it to take me back to Umbria and the safety of my aunt's garden, where there wasn't sunbathing but there *was* a glass of wine at the end of a long day. Where Aunt Clare never pestered me about the car because we always walked to the stores and where, on nights when we needed more groceries than we could carry, we'd all pile into one of the vans—a mess of Ph.D. students, awkward limbs, laughter, and beginner-level Italian.

It hurt, the kind of nostalgia that was still so fresh it seemed as though I could just turn around and fly back to get a hug that smelled like lavender lotion and warmed soil and love. But those days were over, no matter how much I longed to return. There was no place like that garden and no one who understood me like she did.

Aunt Clare was not just any botanist. She went far beyond it in my eyes. She was practically magic, funded in part by various pharmaceutical companies to create antidotes and graft together new strains of plants once thought lost to time. A sort of archaeobotany. She grew herbs whose leaves were crushed and boiled to make ink and flowers that if pollinated correctly could influence the appearance of other plants. She grew poisons like belladonna and hemlock and monitored their effects on other plants in the garden.

I'd arrived at the garden clouded by months of memorized chemical compounds and knew nothing about herbs or poisons, but by the time I returned to Boston, I'd come to know every herb that could be used to treat a burn, reduce swelling, or cure gout. I knew the fifty ingredients of mythological cures for the plague, a half dozen theriacs meant to relieve any ailment, and the herbs one could burn for prophetic dreams. I knew the works of the medical greats like Galen and Pliny and Celsus. I could identify the properties of almost every plant she owned and each one's protein chains, which, when broken down, might ease symptoms of a given illness. Or potentially cause one. I knew that echinacea could build your immune system and that rose hips, horsetail, and calendula were good for the skin.

It seemed archaic in contrast to the bleached white walls of med school and far too outdated to be relevant. More like good-luck charms and empty promises that my old professors would have scoffed at, but it had saved me. It made medicine feel real to me again, and alive, and that was a greater gift than I could have hoped for. So on the hour I bade Aunt Clare good-bye, in my hand was a thermos of herbal tea to soothe my flight anxiety and in my bag was a book of three dozen recipes of my own concocting and records of all our trials. Pages stained with the oils and dyes we had wrung from berries, noting every failure and every success.

I peeled my eyes away from the return label and tied my hair back before crawling over my mattress to the bedside table. Opening the drawer, I fetched my Leatherman tool and ran downstairs to rummage through our toolbox for a small hammer.

The crate wasn't that difficult to open. I had packed similar ones only a few months earlier when a student wanted a gene-spliced mustard plant shipped back to his home in Dorset for further study. I just never expected to be on the receiving end of one.

Carefully I popped the seal and slid the top to the side enough to let me peer at the lush green contents. There were six plants that I could count. Some smaller and some in larger pots, like the fragrant strain of rosemary I had used so often to make bread with her on Sundays. The inside of the crate smelled like home and flooded my senses, making it hard for me to fight the swell of yearning, a feeling and a love my mother never understood but that Aunt Clare always had.

Each potted plant bore a small label she had printed, indicating the row in the nursery it was from, its genus, and the date I'd planted it, as well as the date she'd transplanted it to send to me. Each leaf, now all much in need of water and sunlight, was proof I'd been there in that garden in a way that I desperately needed the longer I was in Boston.

One by one I took them out and placed them on the spare shelves of my room, taking care to put the right ones by the window or in the shade depending on their needs. There was rosemary, comfrey, and angelica, herbs used for treating the hair, the skin, and even bruises. There was absurdly fragrant basil and a small assortment of wildflowers that were less from the garden itself and more from the village. Then there was another plant, kept to the side and separated by plastic so as not to touch the others. Its leaves were thick and wide, similar in their appearance to sage but with little dark purple and green spots. A likely member of the Lamiaceae family.

I knew it by *Nebula sanctorum*—the medieval Latin moniker. Saint's Fog.

It had been the one plant we struggled with, its having been described in an old leechbook from the 1400s as some kind of medicinal grown by Franciscan monks and finally sourced in the Occitania and brought back to us. Except it never worked how it should have, according to records. There were no visions induced or easing of any heart pains or headache. It did nothing. No matter how many tests we performed or how many hours I spent with its leaves under the microscope, my eyes parsing the toxicology reports in the hope of something, anything to show that it could do the sort of things attested to.

It couldn't even be used for cooking: When we'd tried, it smelled like a sour mix of anise and spoiled fruit.

Aunt Clare assumed it was a plant that just needed a bit more maturity, or that the mentioned properties in the text referred to a berry that it grew in the right climate. I, on the other hand, had merely viewed it as an enormous failure after six months of built-up hopes and cautious care and testing, with soil under my nails and dreams of having my name printed alongside hers in one of the pharmaceutical journals. The Saint's Fog had been my project. My main task in the months just before I was beckoned home. I had hunted it down to a likely source and been in the car with the heat of summer burning my cheeks as I smiled wide, seeing the hill in the distance, crested with its leaves.

But no matter how much of my hope I poured into it, the Saint's Fog never amounted to anything. It was a failure, and one that quite frankly I didn't want to be reminded of and wasn't entirely sure why I was being forced to look at now.

I placed the plant by the others on my windowsill and ran to the bathroom to grab a cup of water to refresh them after their long journey. Then I pulled out my laptop to e-mail my aunt and update her on what she had missed.

Aunt Clare,

I just received your gifts! I cannot believe you sent them. Each little (mildly withered and underwatered) leaf is a reminder of my time there and how much I miss you. I hope the new batch of students are as fun as the last, although maybe less troublesome than Patrick and Delphine (is she still there, or did they yank her back to the archives yet?).

Speaking of troubles, I admit I've had a few of them since my return. The stress in this house is so thick you can cut it with a knife. I still don't know why they kept it from me for so long. It's worse than whatever Ma's been telling you, I can at least assure you of that. But we'll get through it. The good news is, I've managed to find a new job. A miracle if there ever was one. It's for some rich family out here that needs an assistant for their doctor. I've got to say I've never seen a family so well-off. I mean,

not personally. I'm nervous but . . . It should be all right. The
daughter is nice at least. It's a bit of an odd setup. The son, Jonathan—

Jonathan.

I typed the name and then deleted it, remembering the code of privacy that I'd signed myself to. Still, it hung in my head, and I recalled
what Anna and Rumi had been so keen to say.

Before I could finish, I minimized the e-mail window and did a quick
Internet search for Jonathan Verdeau. Naïvely, I suspected I'd get some
blog articles and a LinkedIn page. A few people with similar names,
perhaps. Only when the results loaded, all I saw was his face, staring back
at me, and looking much more lively than when I had seen him in
person.

Like it was the first time I was really seeing him.

Tall and thin in build, Jonathan Verdeau was a statue come to life,
with dark hair, overgrown enough to show the hint of a curl and a Roman
profile that was nothing like his sister's. His lips curved, bold and obscene,
when he grinned—which, judging from the photos, was not often—and
his eyes looked seldom sober. Over and over again, page after page of
news articles and blog entries and links to Instagram accounts filled my
screen. I saw him in T-shirts and blazers with the same messy dark hair
and dark circles under his eyes from five, six years before. The same
hauntingly frail frame that earned him hashtags comparing him to run-
way models. There were articles about Jonathan going back to his teens,
photos of him outside police cars and only a few in business suits. All of
the pictures damning in their own way. Each of them precisely what my
friends had warned me about.

Audrey, when I searched, fared only minimally better.

Her results held considerably fewer police lights in the background
than her brother's, and her images stuck to a classic beige, gold, and black
palette, with the exception of more formal, sharp outfits worn at Fashion

Weeks and dinners. Only a few articles hinted at scandal, and most at first glance had to do with businesses and fashion faux pas, as opposed to Jonathan's mess of ambulances and accidents. I browsed her social media to find it filled with photos of her at brunch in Beacon Hill drinking mimosas and flaunting manicures, and then after a few more clicks, there were the paparazzi photos. The zoomed-in snapshots of her arms around models and lipstick kisses on her cheeks that caused my heart to flutter.

Apart, the siblings appeared to be entertaining, enigmatic creatures, but in photos together they defied all rationale. As if a baroque painting had somehow birthed two figures straight from myth and placed them among the brick and grit of Boston.

An hour passed without my realizing it. The minutes flew by as I remained engrossed in the kind of morbid curiosity that could only come with seeking out the sordid reputation of someone else my age, someone with a lifestyle so far above my own that it seemed fictitious. The kind with diamond necklaces and designer handbags and fresh-pressed juices every day. Marble countertops and private jets. Altogether it hinted that what I'd seen in my brief visits to their brownstone was only the tip of the iceberg.

The Verdeau children were French in name and thoroughly American in class, apparently raised with the lingering morals of 1980s Wall Street. Were it not for the lavish Old World charm of their home, it might have been difficult to view them as being born of genuine wealth and not simply spoiled, conceited twenty-somethings based on all the paparazzi photos. It would have been hard to recognize them as siblings at all.

Audrey did her part to look nothing like her brother, and she succeeded. Whereas his hair was dark brown and nearly the color of night, hers was bleached a ghostly pale and always trimmed into some form of bob, hovering just low enough to kiss her jawline. Her style appeared effortless and for most would have been unachievable. She lived in smooth textures and clean-cut lines that would have made a Dior muse weep with envy. Nothing was excessive, everything was sharp and crystalline and carried with it a mature poise that failed to meet its true potential due only to her family's crude reputation.

Jonathan, in contrast, lacked any sort of poise or maturity at all. In the most recent photos I could find, he was always in a button-up, but it was either crooked or had a collar askew. His jackets were either black or gray or plum, and his clothes hung on him in such a way that made him look consumptive, with legs that would have given a heron a twinge of jealousy. He could have looked classical if he tried. Instead he looked the very opposite of his sister—disheveled, weak, and sad.

Martin's search, by the time I got around to it, was considerably less interesting and bore nothing but the faces of aging, bloated white men, handshakes, hotels, business deals, head shots, and a few paparazzi photos of him rushing out of a courthouse probably fifteen years earlier.

Still, bit by bit the reality of my new employment felt greater than I could handle and far more than I could have imagined.

Over my time with the Verdeau family, that feeling never faded.

4

AN HOUR INTO MY FIRST SHIFT, Prosenko made it clear that he had no intention of viewing me as anything more than a low-level medical assistant. It would have been more accurate to describe the position as a personal assistant for a doctor and some reluctant family members on the side, rather than anything that required a proper medical background. Which was probably for the best and, at least initially, put me in a position of considerably less legal trouble.

Still, Prosenko strove to drill into me the rules I was expected to follow and the routines of the household, including everything from asking Daniella to show me where the deliveries were placed to how to take notes and what shorthand he preferred. Every detail of Jonathan's own schedule was explained, as it would apparently be my task to track him down daily and report anything suspicious. Seeing him carrying a half-full bottle of malbec while the sun was prime in the sky, I learned, was no cause for concern. Yet my so much as handing him water was forbidden, without Prosenko's approval first.

When Prosenko said I was to give Jonathan Verdeau nothing, he meant it in the most extreme way. If Jonathan asked for ibuprofen, I was to alert Prosenko. If he wanted toast, or orange juice, or ice for his scotch, I was to alert Prosenko and him alone. If his sister gave him something and I happened to catch it? It was expected that Prosenko would be informed posthaste.

I came to realize that Audrey Verdeau had not been wrong in what she'd said the hour of that first interview. Prosenko's main task was Jonathan. Everyone else came second, including Audrey herself.

No matter how much I willed myself to see her poking her head out from behind a wall or strolling down the stairs with a to-go cup of coffee, she remained elusive. The only remotely familiar sight I had those first few days was of the butler George, eyeing me with a scrutiny even greater than Prosenko's own. Then there was Sascha.

Sascha Oswick was the Verdeau family do-it-all. She was short, with brilliantly red hair and a round face that looked barely beyond high-school age. The cleaning lady by technicality, she also worked as Daniella's assistant during meal hours and as George's assistant for whatever George decided he needed. That and watering the gardens. Out of anyone in the house, Sascha was probably the person who best understood my own position, which was vague at best.

It was close to three o'clock that first day before I was given a pause long enough for me to realize that I was starving. The timing of my shifts, starting at one o'clock, meant that Daniella's freshly prepared lunch was always just barely missed. As a result my employment during the weeks was perpetually haunted by the fading smell of a recently cooked feast. However, that day, too nervous to eat beforehand and finding myself hopeful for scraps, I wandered back to the kitchen, and that was where I first met Sascha.

She had been doing the dishes as I passed through for a cup of coffee and caught me rummaging through the cupboards in a hurry to find any sort of snack before Prosenko yanked me back to sorting a stack of lab reports in his office. At some point without my seeing, she ducked away and returned with a cloth napkin full of croissants, presliced and filled—one with jam, the other with cheese.

"They're in a basket in the lounge," she offered. "Not sure if he showed you."

Hastily I took it, thanking her. "I'm still learning the place."

Sascha giggled. "This place is nothing. Just wait until next weekend."

"What?"

But before she could answer, Prosenko ducked his head into the kitchen.

"Gereghty!" he shouted. "I've been looking everywhere for you. You're not to disappear, understand?"

"Yes, sir," I said quickly, and reluctantly handed the cloth back to Sascha.

"Has she taken her break yet?" Sascha asked boldly, leaning over to face Prosenko eye to eye. "We're allowed breaks, you know."

Prosenko went quiet and then gave a grumbling sigh. "Fine. Find me in five minutes."

"She gets ten, Doc."

"And she's wasted five already," he said, and then looked back to me. "Five minutes, Lena. Then find me so we can go over how I want you to file the toxicology reports. There's seven years of backlog."

"Yes, sir."

The moment he was gone, Sascha gave another small laugh and shook her head. "Don't let him get to you."

"He's not so bad," I told her, unwrapping the croissants again to take a large bite of Muenster and sweet, flaky bread. "But anyway, thanks. I should be getting back, though."

"Well, maybe I'll see you around?"

"We can hope!"

I dashed out of the kitchen, my mouth full of half a croissant, a cup of coffee in hand. The few minutes that were left of my unintended break felt small and not worth using, and given Prosenko's sour mood that day, I didn't want to risk being in any more trouble. Following the cramped hallways, I circled through the back of the town house, beyond the lounge, the coatroom, and the bathroom once again before looping past the back side of the stairs and to his office.

Only when I arrived, Prosenko wasn't there. Just before I ventured down the hall to search for him, the front door to the house slammed open, followed by the loud laughter of men and a rush of footsteps in my direction. Instinctively I darted back to the underside of the staircase, where, safely out of view, I listened as the echoes of their voices drew closer and closer still.

They all stopped just short of Prosenko's office, Jonathan's voice rising above them with the audible confirmation of handshakes and backslaps. Then they disappeared into the study.

In the shadows of that staircase, I took a breath and pulled the remainder of the croissant from my pocket. Eavesdropping, I heard the familiar metallic scrape of a liquor cap being unscrewed and the glug of what was probably raspberry Stoli or whatever else rich boys drank at 3:00 P.M. on a Wednesday.

That unsettling brew of concern and irritation rose in me again. It was my first official day, but my third seeing Jonathan Verdeau, and not once had I seen him sober nor void of some form of suffering. The afternoon had been spent peering over his medical charts and Sharpied-out reports that I presumed Prosenko simply didn't trust me with yet, and I now knew in oddly intimate detail the fragility of Jonathan's condition. A weak pulse, weak liver, weak lungs . . . All the while I had yet to see him stray too far from alcohol or his pale lips untinged with the maroon of a French red. In that moment every boom of laughter from his friends and boyish slurred joy that echoed out of that study was like adding coals to a fire of quickly growing resentment. A frustration fueled by his own obvious disregard for his state and the disregard of those he kept around him and apparently considered friends.

I didn't see Jonathan for the rest of the day. After Prosenko found me, there was only an hour left to my shift, which was spent taking inventory of a new shipment of syringes and alcohol pads, among other office supplies. As far as first days go, it had not been the worst. I had survived it well enough, and my time with Prosenko and the family was less than five hours each day. Even the inventory checks and note-taking weren't that far of a stretch from my work with Aunt Clare, despite the drastic shift in surroundings. All in all, it was well worth the eight hundred dollars a week to me, despite any ethical and medical concerns about Jonathan's treatment.

In spite of my burnout, med school had actually treated me well, and the overall field of medicine and I once had a positive relationship. I had aced every anatomy course I ever took. Every physiology and chemistry course. My fingers had been stained more than enough times by the ink rubbed off flash cards in the midnight hours, and I had confidently led countless study groups toward success. By the time I took my MCAT, I knew chemical compositions and contraindicated medication lists so well that I could sing them to myself like lullabies.

But none of that means a thing when you look at a larger-than-average class size and an underfunded grant program and wonder day after day if it's really worth it. If you can keep on like that. If you have it in you.

Still, I knew enough about medicine to see that Jonathan Verdeau was genuinely sick beyond what could be blamed on alcohol. So when Prosenko asked me the next day to track Jonathan down for his daily medication, I did so willingly, despite still being unable to shake my annoyance at his habits.

After I'd wandered the town house for ages, Jonathan was still nowhere to be found. Not in his usual study nor on the second floor, and I dared not go to the private quarters of the third. It wasn't until I heard the flush of the bathroom toilet downstairs that I jogged down the steps in time to see him walking out the door and wiping at his mouth with the edge of his robe's sleeve.

He paused and glanced to me, then shuffled back to the study.

"Prosenko's looking for you," I called out, but he didn't stop.

"Then he can get me himself," Jonathan grumbled.

"He says it's time for your meds."

"Tch," he said before plopping down on the antique sofa.

I waited there in the doorway for what was probably too long, unsure of what to do, and watched as he picked up a wineglass and sipped from it, eyeing me from over the rim.

"Well?" he said.

I frowned, finding my tongue uncharacteristically caught, and promptly took my leave.

Embarrassed, I did the only thing I could do at that moment and went to get Prosenko. I watched from the hall as he came in with a black leather bag and a tray with a glass of water and a little paper cup. Inside it were two small black pills, which Jonathan quickly swallowed before opening his mouth wide for Prosenko to confirm they didn't linger.

Prosenko then turned and motioned with his hand for me to stop loitering and enter the study properly.

"Record the time and anything I say. Got it?"

"Yes, sir." I stood there with a pen and clipboard, monitoring as Prosenko went on to check Jonathan's chest with a stethoscope, then his lymph nodes.

"Bowels?" he asked routinely, and Jonathan looked up at me awkwardly and then back to Prosenko.

"Yeah, they're workin'," he said.

Prosenko sighed and turned back to me. "Just write 'loose.'"

Prosenko finished giving Jonathan the once-over and told him to finish his water, which Jonathan chugged with spite worthy of a teenager.

He then brushed past us and down the hall.

"He's a full-time job, Miss Gereghty," said Prosenko. "I hope by now you've realized that. He also values his privacy."

"I won't say a word."

"No, I believe that much."

"What's wrong with him? You never said."

Prosenko stayed quiet a moment, leaving us to listen to the echoes of the toilet flushing and the running of water.

"He drinks too much," he said. "And if the press happens to ask, you tell them exactly that."

I wanted to ask about the pills, and looking back, I wish it were the first thing I'd done, but Prosenko made it clear I wasn't trusted with that information, same as with the censored toxicology reports and the blood-work results, and at the time I could hardly blame him. I was still an outsider, and I remained such for the entirety of my first two weeks.

I would show up for a few hours, take notes or type old ones from before my hiring. I cleaned equipment and counted out bulk containers of everything from ibuprofen to Percocet to Valium. I watched silently, studiously, as Jonathan disappeared from view one day, sullen and quiet as he sulked about the various rooms, and was loud and boisterous with his friends the next. I spied him, painfully thin and stealing croissants from the lounge well after breakfast, and too often found half-empty bottles of wine in various rooms throughout the town house. No business meetings, no job as far as I could tell. He was like a listless teenager, trapped within the walls of his home. Yet still he never said a word to me. Even as we passed in the halls or as I stood there taking notes during Prosenko's daily exams. To him I might as well have been a ghost, and I began to think that despite any wishing on my part, to Audrey I was even less.

Most days Audrey was gone before I arrived, leaving only the straggling trail of photographers hoping to catch a glimpse of her, and she seldom returned until the evening. Where she went, I never learned, although often she came back with shopping bags, and if I did see her, she would only smile briefly and continue on her way. The more my hours were filled with Prosenko and chasing Jonathan down, the more I yearned to see her instead, or have a chance to say hello again. However, in the span of ten days' time, I never saw more than a glimpse of Audrey Verdeau, and half of those glimpses came just prior to the chaotic shouts and slamming of doors from her brother's domain up the stairs.

This was how my employment went that late summer, relatively simple and with little improvement as the days wore on, and I expected it to remain as such. I came to anticipate my hour commute on transit each way for a brief afternoon shift and dread the horror of a typical return at rush hour. I quickly established the best opportunities to see Sascha and snag a croissant and determine what sort of notes Prosenko expected. I learned to grab coffee before arriving and to expect nothing more beyond those basic offerings during my hours at the town house.

However, on a fateful Thursday toward the end of September, I was walking from the Roslindale Village station to Slick Rick's when my cell phone rang and I found Prosenko's deep voice on the other end.

"Miss Gereghty," he said, "I was just calling because George informed me you have not been driving to work and was concerned as to how you expected to get to the estate tomorrow?"

"The estate?"

"Yes, the party. It was added to your schedule today."

At the word "party," my stomach sank.

"When?"

"A few minutes ago."

"Um . . ."

"So how will you be arriving? You will be driving, yes?"

"I don't know. Is it just at the town house?"

Prosenko sighed. "No, Miss Gereghty, it's at the estate. Arrow's Edge. Do you not have the address?"

Arrow's Edge. There it was, I thought, that name again. "No."

On the other end, Prosenko grumbled. "All right. I'll have George send it over. Let him know how you expect to get there."

"Wait! What time tomorrow?"

"Seven P.M. Sharp. I'll need you to help me set up the parlor."

"Until?"

"Talk to George," he said, and then promptly hung up.

5

I don't like parties.

I will henceforth strive to emphasize this point, but I do not think any words I choose can drive the fact forward enough that I have never met a party I genuinely enjoyed. Not even birthdays. Perhaps this was my most fatal flaw. The error in my soul's construction. Perhaps, I thought, this was the thing that was going to get me fired.

Ordinarily I was not someone who so readily feared such a thing. I had never been fired from a job in my life, and no mistake I ever made was the reason for my leaving nor any cause for punishment beyond a few high jinks in high school. So this fear that came with the Verdeau party was a strange one, even for me, and it to this day retains some gnawing sensation—one I believe to be sourced from the feeling that I was never meant to be there at all.

I had been waiting for the shoe to drop after that first interview and every second since. The fact that I was expected to work a party at some distant and unknown location with all of Martin's elite surely, I thought, spelled out my end.

The good news was that Arrow's Edge was an easier drive from my home in Roslindale than from Back Bay, as far as traffic was concerned. It was considerably longer, however, by about two hours, and I wished that when George finally called with the address, it had not come with a Berkshires zip code clear across the state. I also wished he'd given me an estimated end time, but even in a household of billionaires, George was probably the least giving person in the room.

Of all the mistakes that have now come to define that weekend, my first was borrowing the hatchback to get there. "Borrowing" is also a loose term. I stole it without so much as a word to my mother, then promptly decided to leave my phone on silent for the remainder of the night to avoid the potential for conflict.

My second mistake was arriving twenty minutes late due to the peculiar and unmarked nature of the address.

Most roads in the Berkshires region of Massachusetts are tree-lined. It is a picturesque playground of New England charm in the far western part of the state, with winding driveways that turn the most fluorescent shades of orange and red come autumn. Despite living in Boston, my family and I had driven out only once when I was a child, but the trip left me with memories of picking apples and sipping cider and my mother almost crashing our car into a family of deer.

That evening, as the darkness just barely began to creep its way across the horizon, I drove the hatchback up a long and well-secluded road past mansion after mansion with acres between them until finally I came upon the correct turn, missed twice already. There, up a twisting driveway, a vine-covered manor home slowly came into view, framed by an old brick-and-metal gate bearing a plaque that read proudly, ARROW'S EDGE (1887).

Arrow's Edge could have been called anything. It could have been Meadow's Edge and sounded like another cookie-cutter suburban community of pristine driveways and neutral-colored sidings. Innocent.

Simple. Instead it held a fearful name that from its first utterance by Prosenko summoned the image of a time when the estate had served as a summer hunting ground for the sort of people who I imagined would have been thrilled at the thought of owning more than one place where they could kill.

I parked the hatchback and peered up to where the house stood, an imposing graystone presence atop a small green hill, the light fading into an unfitting halo, and came to understand it all too well. Arrow's Edge was not a home. It likely was never meant to be. In place of anything remotely comforting, or even livable, stood a ruthless and dangerously virile relic, cold yet cluttered. Uniquely American in its opulent, turn-of-the-century enthusiasm.

Although it was historic and from all appearances a certain result of the Gilded Age splendor that dotted the region, I had never heard of it before, even growing up in New England. In those youthful days when television and movies had encouraged me to imagine a life of riches and wealth, it was more the mansions in Los Angeles or the high-rises in New York that dominated my daydreams. Back then I admired everything new, and glimmering, and clean. Arrow's Edge was too imposing for that. As if with one wrong move I would find myself trapped forever. Lost to some curse or mystery of hallway planning.

There was no one outside waiting for me when I arrived, and with the growing knowledge that each minute I failed to report to Prosenko put me closer to unemployment, I found the largest, heaviest door I could and opened it with hopes that it would be the right one.

Crimson wallpaper greeted me, a smothering, dark shade of damask print, inlaid with gold. Across from the entryway was a hall featuring stone urns filled with peacock feathers and portraits set amid pastoral scenes. Each of these elements accosted me, bold and lavish and unlike anything I had seen before. Farther inside I heard the clamor of lights being set up and watched as tables were adorned with silver trays of food, telling me that I must be in the right place.

As I paced the manor, rooms intersected each other with clashing wallpaper and furniture, only their opulence left to bind them together as belonging to the same home. Walking in search of my employer, I found myself lost in a sea of antiques—be they furniture, statues, or Ming vases. In Arrow's Edge everything seemed to be filled with detail, indulging my eyes and willing me to stare longer.

Still, the gallery was what stood apart.

The length of it was awash with light, a shocking contrast to anything else in the home. A series of tall, expansive windows stretched the length of the room, and everything inside was marble and gold, with mirrors, palms, and art hanging along the walls. Smaller rooms extended outward from it in hallway-like branches, their shadows all the darker in contrast.

"Gereghty! There you are!"

Prosenko's voice bounced along the walls, and following its sound I caught sight of his sour, exhausted reflection in one of the mercury-glass mirrors. I turned to face him.

"Sorry, I got lost and—"

"Never mind, never mind." He waved his hand in dismissal. "You're late, which means I've already started the preparations on my own. Is that what you're wearing?" His gray eyes lingered for an unsettlingly long time on the top button of my shirt.

I turned away. "You didn't tell me there was a dress code."

"Hmph! Didn't think I'd need to. Look where you are! But I guess that's what I get. . . . All right, there's no helping it now. Follow me."

Prosenko led me farther down the series of halls with a speed gained from years of experience. My eyes struggled to keep track of his white coat in the cluttered chaos of each room we passed. In my naïveté I had not imagined what sort of party it was that awaited me, but as Prosenko shoved Narcan into one pocket and handed me a series of condoms from his other, I began to understand.

The entirety of the entry level had been decked out with low lighting, no brighter than candles. On tables sat towering chocolate fountains, and lavish food displays with gold flakes encrusting everything from doughnuts to poultry, and enough caviar to impress a Russian oligarch. There was everything from intricate ice sculptures to a rainbow of ecstasy pills laid out in crystal bowls for the taking, and more couches and velvet-cushioned beds than a single room had any right to bear. Yet all of it fit with the lines of the old manor. A mishmash of golden cherubs, grotesques, and the glimmering delights of the Roaring Twenties. The only thing that stood out to me was the lack of anything modern. There were no LCD screens or showy tech beyond the speakers for the music. Compared to how I imagined it would be, Arrow's Edge remained shockingly manual. Archaic.

The parties, I was to learn that night, seemed to come in two parts. Darkened, historic rooms for depravity and affairs and larger ballrooms and dining halls for exhibitionism. You could snort your coke on the rim of an antique globe while men sipped scotch and played cards, and then you could find yourself wandering down the halls, following the sconces like will-o'-the-wisps into a den of chaotic reverie.

None of this had begun during my arrival at half past seven o'clock. That night, as I moved through the space, the only inhabitants were hired staff I had never seen before, and the only sign of what was to come was what I had been hastily told by Prosenko as he yanked me from my bewilderment into a side room.

"You are to keep out of the way," he told me after chewing me out again for arriving late. In one hand he had a plate of chocolate-covered strawberries and in the other a package of syringes. "If someone scrapes their knee, give them a Band-Aid. If they need a condom, hand it out, but if there is anything worse, you are to notify me directly. Understood?"

I nodded.

"Good. Now, I don't care where you go. In a half hour, the guests will start arriving, and I don't have time for a tour, so if you get lost, find George and he'll direct you. Otherwise just keep to the walls and carry a rag."

"What do I need a rag for?"

"Do you want the list?"

I did not.

"So that's it?" I asked him after following his errands from one adorned room to another. "Just stay out of the way?"

"And help when it's needed."

"Oh, well, that seems easy enough."

"Hopefully. But, Lena," he said gravely, drawing his gray eyes to my own. "Remember, you are here with one simple rule."

I arched an eyebrow in curiosity.

"If the police get called, you don't get paid."

The words had seemed unnecessarily ominous. Illegal, yes, but even beyond that they were enough to send a shiver down my spine. This was a party, I thought. One with liquor flowing as steady as water but also one run by a man who looked sixty.

Stepping onto the estate earlier, I had imagined little more could be in store that night than the drunken ramblings of CEOs and perhaps an ill stomach or two. Now, surrounded by the open displays of drugs and with Prosenko's warning ringing in my ear, it was clear that I'd been woefully wrong. Mere hours later the scene of Martin's glamorous party began to grow into something beyond recognition and something deserving of far greater warning.

Limousines and luxury cars made their way up the winding roads with ease, all gathering at the circle just beyond the view of the gallery windows. There was no flash of paparazzi bulbs or gathering of reporters as I had half expected. Instead it was just the partygoers themselves, each draped in jewels so bright they caught every light Arrow's Edge had to offer as they crossed the threshold, their white teeth grinning with a performative ease.

The gallery and its central arm, the grand ballroom, were the center of the parties. It was here where Martin reigned over his kingdom proudly, welcoming each guest as they arrived. Grinning face and aging hands outstretched perpetually. One with a glass and the other shaking and grasping whatever bit of flesh he could.

I had never seen the man look so open, nor as happy as he did on nights like this. Nights when he was the center of a luxurious world where each patron in some way was indebted to him. As if every hour in a boardroom condensed and compressed the worst of his impulses, until the hour came where he could release them here in his home, with a smiling face and unrestrained joviality.

Increasingly disgusted and ill at ease, I paced the halls, willing my being to blend into the oiled woodwork as I watched all levels of the elite throw their heads back in laughter. I saw Chinese businessmen in matching suits clasp their hands onto the hips of secretaries slurring in Swedish. I heard the booming laughter from the punch lines of Arabic jokes and saw the way men whose wallets had been thinning since the last recession shifted their posture so as to stand taller as they downed a sixth martini.

The ballroom was Martin's kingdom, complete with an actual red velvet throne, and it was there I opted to remain that first hour before at last venturing deeper into the building.

Parties in a place like Arrow's Edge allowed for the utmost intimacy. The corners had corners, and in the moments when the music lulled or the rattling of the floor ceased, you could always hear shouts amid the clamor. A ghostly slam of bodies in an embarrassing rhythm on the other side of the wall. Moans. Slaps. Punches. Falls. The estate hid each of these like a protective spirit. And what could not be hidden did not need to be.

With but one exception.

People as a whole are terrible at temperance, but they are also vain. While Martin had a slew of maids at his beck and call that night to clean up the spilled liquor and vomit, he had only one doctor, and overdose was not a mess he could be rid of easily.

Almost as soon as I had realized my purpose, it became too much. The sickening reality that called forth Prosenko's earlier warning. I wasn't there to tend to the needy. I was there to tend to their reputations.

Over and over I watched as men of all ages drank themselves stupid from crystal glasses. Judging silently as they knelt over onto the backs of women years my junior or kissed away a pill that had them dazed until dawn. Each vision stacked on top of the other in my mind, piling into a tower of hatred with Jonathan's own disregard for his health at the foundation, which had been steadily built in my short time tending to him as my charge. I knew he had to be somewhere in the mess. I knew that Audrey, despite what I might have wanted to believe, was likely among the crowd as well.

From the ballroom a side door slipped open into a back hallway that led to an old library. Exhausted, and with the shaking bass having taken its toll on my patience, I elected to explore it.

The library of Arrow's Edge, I discovered to my dismay, was where Jonathan and his friends wasted the night. They were not entirely secluded from the growing hysteria but sectioned off so as to be onlookers. It kept Jonathan safely at arm's length from anyone he didn't like and perpetuated the idea of a lazy prince instead of an ill one.

Surrounding him on an antique green couch were the same three men I'd seen before and would come to know the names of slowly over the next few months. They were an odd, annoying group that Jonathan always had in tow for occasions where company was needed or was at the very least better than the alternative.

Dylan was the first I spotted as I entered the room, showing the usual gusto that made Jonathan seem meek. In his hand was a glass of clear liquid filled nearly to the rim, with a smell coming off it that told me it wasn't water. Beside him stood Brodie, his own glass half empty and his eyes focused on the screen of his phone. It was his Instagram account I had used to find photos of the siblings during my night of research. I think that's the only reason he stuck around. Verdeau parties made for good social-media posts, even if he could only get away with blurred images and shadow-filled snapshots.

Lounging in the leather chair closest to Jonathan sat Elliot Hayworthe, the ginger son of an antiques importer and heir to a string of international auction houses. Out of everyone in the group, he seemed to get along with Jonathan best. When Dylan had drunkenly hurled himself into a sixteenth-century painting, Elliot was the only one who seemed to care and was the one who walked over to inspect the damage while Jonathan threw his glass in anger at the disrespect, missing Dylan's skull by a millimeter.

It wasn't long before I was spotted, and within seconds the group were shouting jeers and waving their arms to motion me over.

"Settle down, boys," said Jonathan, his voice dripping with boredom and something I couldn't place but that nonetheless made my skin prickle. "She's with Prosenko."

Dylan looked at me with a twinkle in his eye. "Well, good on him. Doc got a little sugar baby."

"I'm his assistant," I clarified sharply.

"And my uncle married his secretary. Don't mean shit to us, sweetie," said Dylan before taking a swig from his glass, which I now recognized by the smell on his breath to be the same raspberry Stoli suspected from his visit to the town house before.

"You didn't tell us Prosenko got an assistant," said Elliot over the music.

"Yeah," Jonathan said, eyeing me coldly. "Didn't seem important."

Someone among them snickered, and my face grew hot with anger. Same as all the other times I'd encountered Jonathan, I turned around to take my leave, only this time with the added sting of knowing the eyes of his crew lingered on my back by the belittling whistle I heard as I left.

Fighting the embarrassment, I continued to wander with growing exhaustion and at every turn came to see faces I felt I should have known. Businessmen and tycoons from around the world. People whose grins were toothy and straight, which made me feel progressively smaller, as if my thrift-shop thread count could be detected even through their blood-shot eyes.

But I was invisible. I wasn't a guest, only a fly on the wall. For anyone who managed to catch me as Prosenko's assistant, I was just some girl there to hand out condoms. I was as much of an outsider as someone could be, and it was then, in this low hour, that I saw her. A familiar face shuffling about and tripping in heels, with the sticky residue of champagne spilled on her wrists.

She looked nothing like how I'd known her, and had traded in her mom jeans and paisley blouses for a black-and-green dress from the clearance rack, but there was no question in my mind that it was her. Natalie Gainsborough.

Our families had been friends since I was a toddler. Her husband, Tom, had been a colleague of my father's back at Ellerhart. I'd lost track of the number of dinners we'd had over the years. I'd babysat her kids at one point, when I was in high school and needed the cash, but the woman in the crowd did not look like the tired mom of three I'd come to know and who had once slipped me a twenty-dollar tip after a two-hour gig because she hated stealing my Friday nights like that.

No. I didn't recognize the heavy eye shadow on her aging eyes. Or the heavy Swarovski earrings that stretched her earlobes. All the same, even from twenty feet away, I knew it was her.

I couldn't place why she of all people would be there, dolled up and on Tom's arm. Even he had traded his seafoam-green polo shirt and khakis for a tailored navy suit. Helpless to resist my curiosity at the sight of a familiar face, I stood there for a moment, surrounded by mirrors and sofas and the surprisingly exposed breasts of women just like her.

The music blared loud, and I lingered, silent in the shadows as the lights danced about her and her flushed cheeks, the crowd moving in waves of clinging limbs and shaking hips. No matter how long I watched, the woman across the room was not the one I'd known, and I struggled to understand why she was even there at all.

Tom had disappeared at some point, and in his place stood another man, grinning with pearly white teeth in a horror of crooked shapes. From my hidden place, I watched as he leaned in to whisper something that made her smile falter and then awkwardly grow as she shrugged and turned away from him, only to be pulled back by his hand. At the motion I took a step forward, my mouth half opening to defend her as I would have any one of my friends, but then I stopped, once again forced to remember my place among the crowd.

I watched as she was urged to take a sip from his drink and as he forced the rest of it down her throat with a laugh, the liquid dribbling onto her chin. And still I waited, thinking surely Tom would be back or she would snap out of it and shove the guy away for good. Only she didn't, and Tom was nowhere to be seen. Instead, transfixed, I watched her cheeks flush deeper and her eyes glaze over as she laughed at jokes I failed to hear through the music. I watched as she danced and mingled and tried to join conversations she was promptly shoved out of, over and over again for what seemed like an hour. Then, amid the smiles and the ceaseless thrum of moving bodies, I watched her stumble as her feet tripped over each other. Her own smile falling as her body gave way and she hit the floor with a slap.

Instantly I rushed over, forgetting my place as I shoved myself through the crowd that separated us. I reached my hand to her wrist to take her pulse, adrenaline flooding through me faster than any drug. As my mind tried to count the passing seconds and each beat of her heart, the sound of laughter increased overhead, louder and closer.

"What happened?" I shouted, the gathered anger and fear seeping through my teeth, but no one paid any mind.

A small circle had formed around us, but the man, whoever he was, had already disappeared. I held her, my heart racing with a feeling I hadn't known since my first day on the steps of the brownstone with Jonathan, and begged for help to no reply.

I realized then, after too long a pause and too long without anyone in that smaller ballroom seeming to give a damn, that the laughter echoing in my ear wasn't because of any conversation I had missed. It wasn't the laughter of a group in the corner, unaware of the scene before me. It was from the mouths of those around us.

As Natalie lay unconscious and messy on the expanse of the Turkish rug, Tom appeared from somewhere in the crowd and lingered frozen as he glanced to me, his eyes filled with shameful recognition. His fingers twitching as he fought between concern for his wife and the businessman who had newly turned his back to him.

That was when I understood it at last. That there, cradled by the walls of Arrow's Edge, its patrons wouldn't be considered fools for ignoring her. Even Tom wouldn't be. Only I would, for trying to help.

In the world of the Verdeaus, someone could collapse with a nose rimmed in white and still have their dignity in the morning. Maybe not that night, but in the boardroom or the limo later they would get their chance. That's what their money bought them. The problem was that Natalie Gainsborough didn't have any. She couldn't buy her reputation back with a wink like everyone else in the room. She couldn't afford for people to care.

In her I saw the face of my mother, of my father, innocent and out of place in a hedonistic den such as this. She didn't belong here any more than they would have, and the crowd around us knew that. I knew that. Because I didn't belong either.

This, I realized with redness flooding my vision on that rug, was at the heart of it. This was the thing that separated me from people like the Verdeaus. Not my skill or my clothing but my own impulsive efforts to save them from their self-perceived immortality.

Then I felt it. The slosh of Dom Pérignon as it fell into my hair like holy water of the most corrupt kind. The liquid that spilled onto my pants was worth more than what I'd be earning that night, and at the sight my fingers on Mrs. Gainsborough's arm tightened, and the cacophony of the room blurred into a sharp and unwelcome ringing.

Humiliation flowed through my veins like a venom. The blinding rage of being forced to feel small, all because of the number in my bank account. The world vibrated all around, the bass of the music pulsing the air as people jumped and laughed, and somehow I absorbed every action as if it were a dart aimed straight for my nerves.

Then a hand reached forward through the ever-shifting bodies and grasped my arm.

"Lena," Audrey said as the room spun. "Get up."

My eyes refused to focus. "But she . . ."

"I know," her firm, kind voice said. "Get up."

I looked back to Mrs. Gainsborough as her husband hoisted her up, slinging her arm over his shoulder while the flash of smartphone cameras went off around us.

"Will she be okay?" Audrey asked, and for a moment her perfume overshadowed the scent of champagne. A breath of something merciful, like coming up for air.

"What?"

"Can you fix this?"

"I . . ."

"There's two others like her in the parlor," she said.

"Where's Prosenko?"

"The parlor."

"Then what do you—"

The realization hit me, and like that I was being pulled through the crowded hallways. With Audrey's hand clasped around my own, I did my best to keep track of where we were going and guide Mr. Gainsborough and his wife through the unacknowledged revelry of the new, shadowed wing.

I never would have found the parlor again had Audrey not led me there with the surety of years of experience. She slipped through the crowd expertly, a crystal coupe glass still in her hand, and never once let it spill. In her beige stiletto Louboutins, she dodged men two seconds before they collapsed as if it were a dance, never losing her poise, and together we darted from room to room, from corners to hidden hallways. In the safety of her grip, I caught sight not of the bodies threatening to crash into us but the portraits that hung ignored on the walls behind them. On the vases that still stood, miraculously unscathed. With each turn I held on to her desperately, her small hand warm and grounding me through the shifting scenes and the blur of the music. Then at last we stopped, and the spinning world around me stilled into focus.

The parlor was a decent-size room with white curtains hung up like those in an army hospital. Chaise lounges had become beds filled with dazed figures, IV drips in their arms. Leather couches became beds for men to wait on, their fingers clutching plastic bags and their faces green and pallid. Antique coatracks lined the walls to preserve the most expensive suit jackets and silk ties, and a small bin held empty boxes for adrenaline shots.

"Prosenko!" Audrey shouted, earning shudders and winces from everyone in the vicinity. A few voices, shielded from view, laughed.

"Is this . . . is this legal?" I asked, only to be ignored, and so I just watched as Tom dropped his wife into the nearest available chair, her body still unresponsive.

"Prosenko! Now!" Audrey shouted again, irritated at being made to wait.

"All right!" came a low and distant reply. "All right already, just let me—"

Somebody, hidden, yelped.

"There we go!"

To say that I was woefully unprepared for this part of my job was an understatement of the highest order. Standing there in the parlor, with hatred and disbelief still coursing through my body, I watched as men and women reduced themselves to drunken toddlers and dazed-out lunatics. The smell alone made me cover my mouth to keep from gagging, and by the time Prosenko appeared from the maze of makeshift hospital beds, I was ready to run.

"Who's this?" he asked, pointing to Mrs. Gainsborough, and Audrey quickly explained what had happened.

"Can you take care of it?" she asked. "I need to get back."

"Of course. Of course," said Prosenko, rubbing his gloved hands on a nearby sanitary rag. "Go on now."

"Good," said Audrey, and then she turned to me, placing her palm, no doubt laced with my own sweat, onto my shoulder. "A word of advice, Lena, love . . . Try not to cry. It . . . well, it only makes them laugh."

Her fingers dragged along the cloth of my shirt and rose to gently brush at my cheek as her eyes looked sympathetically into my own, and then, before I could open my mouth or will her to stay with me, she turned and drifted back into the crowd.

It was terrible advice. I knew that, no matter how sweetly she had told me. It was the very last thing I wanted to hear, and already my eyes were wet and burning with anger, my sense of uselessness only growing along-side my fury. Still, I knew she was right.

"Gereghty!" Prosenko shouted, taking his stethoscope off his neck. "Nice of you to show up! Where the fuck were you?"

"You told me to wander!"

He shook his head and took Natalie's pulse at her wrist. "Doesn't matter. Jesus Christ, can't people hold their benzos anymore?" He sighed and, dropping her arm, waved a finger toward the back of the room. "Grab a mask, check on Reynolds and Al-Hazan in the back there. Send 'em out if they can manage to stand up."

The order was simple and militaristic in its apathy, and this, I learned, was Prosenko's greatest strength, if he had any. The net worth of the men and women in his care meant nothing when time was on the line. Not to save them. Not to do anything for their health. Just to keep control.

So it went.

I saw no more of Martin Verdeau, nor Jonathan or even Audrey. From midnight until dawn, I ran about that small, overcrowded room, checking pulses and administering diltiazem and changing out IV bags. I was a battlefield nurse, without any sort of proper training, but I couldn't be asked to care. By the second hour, I had taught myself to successfully focus on the blaring music as opposed to the gags and crash of bile into plastic bags. By the third I had found a rhythm and a pragmatic apathy all my own.

Dozens left that room, and as the night wore on, dozens more came in. Most just needed a place to ride out the worst, some liquids to ensure that their hangover wouldn't cost them come Monday. Others would trip in, clinging to the molding, with red cheeks and maddening grins as they reached for a fistful of condoms and then disappeared back into the darkness.

Despite what occurred outside, that small room housed the worst of Martin's party, and through that single door I watched as the celebration carried on without us. We remained there as exhaustion took hold, stuck in a purgatorial place for people to fall when they lost their charm and glamour, people who were all too eager to leave once their bodies ceased their momentary betrayals.

I worked until Mrs. Gainsborough was safe from the worst of what wound up being a toxic dose of alcohol, ecstasy, and a date-rape drug that was apparently so "popular" that Prosenko had a routine treatment for it—one that had already been administered four times that night and, sadly, was to be administered a half dozen more.

For each hour I spent in Arrow's Edge, my soul felt increasingly burdened and weary, and it wasn't long before my body succumbed as well. By then the worst was over, and that parlor room and its makeshift beds were empty when the music dulled and my body finally gave out.

6

Slowly I peeled my cheek from the sticky surface of a leather sofa, and for a moment the events of the night before felt like a horrid dream. Around me sat the same series of chairs and sofas, only there were no curtains between them, no roller carts of equipment and cords. The rancid smell that had plagued me so persistently had faded, disappearing through open windows and newly replaced by the scent of fresh soap.

The parlor room was unrecognizable.

It was quiet.

Just then an envelope appeared, blocking my view.

"Good. You're awake. I have a headache," Audrey said from behind a pair of Prada sunglasses. Her lithe fingers were raised to her temple. "Can you do something about it?"

I winced at the sunlight and accepted the envelope, tossing it onto the sofa. "Take an aspirin?"

Audrey frowned, watching me as I stretched. "Well, yes, I know that. Do you happen to know where they are?"

I shrugged. Everything in the room had been moved. In front of me,

Audrey sighed. "Right, you haven't been here before. It's fine, I'll find them somewhere. Brunch is almost ready, by the way," she said.

I realized that I was starving, having not eaten dinner the night before and having rejected all the ornate food on silver platters that had passed me by: I hadn't been entirely sure what the items offered had consisted of and what they might have been tainted with. Only now I very much wished I'd grabbed a lobster roll when Prosenko stole the tray off a passing waiter.

A hint of bemusement edged Audrey's pink lips. "Hungry after all that work? Well, it'll have to wait a bit longer. I only mentioned it because Jonathan should try to eat a few hours before taking his pills or he'll just retch it all back up. Have you seen Prosenko? I'm hoping it's not too late. I feel like I've been calling for him for the last hour, but you're the first sign of life in this place that I've seen." She stared at me through the dark lenses, her mouth still turned up into a near-flirtatious smile. "Not that I mind."

Feeling my own cheeks warm at what I thought I surely was imagining, I instead glanced around the room and then shook my head. "No . . . I . . . I haven't seen him. What time is it?"

"Half past ten," said Audrey, following my movements as I stood quickly, shoving my mess of hair back into a sloppy but more manageable bun.

"Shit, I don't even remember falling asleep."

"Enjoy the champagne after all?"

I turned to her, my eyes likely rimmed in a shade of dark circles that only sleep deprivation and dehydration could give. Not entirely unlike the ones her brother possessed. "No. Of course not. I was working."

She shrugged, not seeming to mind the thought that I might have. "Well, you'll find your car parked down the road. Georgie had it moved last night to make room for all the limos and such."

I looked at Audrey, confused. "But how? I have the keys. How did he—"

"He has his ways. . . . And any aesthetic insult to Arrow's Edge like that beat-up thing is one of the greatest motivators for the old man you can find. Oh, no offense."

"Noted."

"Grand, and send Prosenko over if you happen to find him on your way out, okay?"

"Sure," I told her, and then called out a quick, "Wait!" just before the soft pink of her skirt had a chance to disappear. "What's this?"

She turned back and eyed the envelope in my hand. "You mean your pay?"

"Oh."

"There's a bonus in there, too! See you Monday."

Abandoned to the silence of the room and with an ever-growing emotional hangover, I reached back to fetch my phone from my pocket. I found it not only silent but dead. Even as a powerless plastic brick, it expelled an aura of unmistakable disappointment. I was reluctant to think of how many calls I'd missed or how many angry voice messages awaited me.

I stood and peered at my face in one of the gilded mirrors, trying to tidy any drugstore eyeliner that remained. I could feel the sweat on my forehead and the grease in my hair in a way that was leagues beyond what even my last international flight had summoned, but I was too tired, too beaten to care.

After wandering the empty halls and gallery spaces, awash with morning light and without a speck of glitter to be seen, I found the front exit and made my way out without seeing Prosenko, nor George, nor anyone other than a single lingering maid with a high-powered vacuum.

The hatchback was not where I'd left it, true to Audrey's word. It wasn't in the circular drive or anywhere that I could see on the property. Fearing the worst, I began to walk down the long, winding driveway to the main road, shooting up a small prayer that when George had it taken care of, that hadn't meant a tow truck.

Thankfully, being stranded in the Berkshires was not in the cards that day. Instead I found the old car, half covered in fallen green leaves, on a small side trail meant more for golf carts than parking. My heart leaped with relief, and I opened the door, let the heat escape, and climbed in.

For a moment I sat with my hands on the wheel, staring out the windshield as Arrow's Edge stood tall, perfectly framed by the leaves. In the morning light, the brick looked almost charming and picturesque. The wide windows that I had passed in the gallery now appeared welcoming, and the steps that led up to the door were clean and framed with potted plants, an entrance clear as day and thoroughly innocent. At first glance it was nice. Ultimately it taunted me.

Everything about Arrow's Edge felt like a lie, and I suddenly understood why Martin favored it so much for the parties, as well as why he favored it for his main home.

It was his castle.

My fingers slowly gripped the wheel tighter as the night caught up with me, and my body began to tremble with a tired rage that simmered every sinew in hatred and shame. Sitting there staring up at that pathetic excuse of a mansion, I struggled with the realization that I had wasted my night in an unwanted fever dream for a family that didn't give a damn. The residual champagne in my hair confirmed my place in their hierarchy, and even with the peace of the morning and a few hours of sleep under my belt, I hated myself for it. I hated how easily I could recall Dylan's voice and leering gaze. I hated Jonathan for the way he had dismissed every attempt I'd made to help him for the last few weeks. Then there was Mrs. Gainsborough. The memory of her so strong I could still feel the clamminess of her skin beneath my fingers and the stench of bile coming off her lips. I hated that she had been hurt, recovered or not. She never should have been there, and neither should I.

With no one to hear, a small, weakened whine of a scream tore through my throat as my hands squeezed the sun-warmed steering wheel tight enough to burn. If this was the job I'd been hired for, it wasn't one I could continue with. That in and of itself came with a particularly familiar sting.

I was a med-school dropout, and this was my proof of the matter. My wretched proof of unworthiness and shame that everyone had tried telling me would come, roundhouse-kicking me with a bonus punch of classism.

I chose the worst route home. The one without toll roads that took almost two hours longer, but it gave me more time to think, more time for the burning in my veins to settle down before no doubt being ignited again by my mother. The ancient radio of the hatchback blasted Top 40 for a hundred miles, and I willed it to drown out any new memory or guilt that could bubble up. That little envelope of Audrey's sat abandoned on my passenger seat, ignored.

Sixty miles from Boston, I pulled over for gas and some much-needed iced coffee and gas-station fare. It was a Saturday, and the roads at noon were packed with convertibles and SUVs making their way to some weekend escape before the foliage died and the lingering warmth of summer faded. I had had enough of escapes, even though I would happily have wasted another year before going home to face whatever punishment no doubt resided in wait at the hatchback's return. With the condensation from my coffee dripping over my hand, I opened the door again and tossed a bag of chips and a prepackaged muffin onto the seat, knocking the envelope to the floor.

Across the street I saw a sign for one of my bank's branches, and practicality told me I had just spent forty bucks I didn't have on gas, so I resolved to reach down and pick up the envelope to see whatever measly sum I had earned. I reckoned that as soon as I'd taken their money, I would go home with my tail between my legs and begin the search anew for a job—one that wasn't as absurd and one that didn't come with the Verdeau name or anyone like them attached. No George. No Jonathan. No Audrey. No parties.

I tore the envelope open.

Inside was a simple check, written in Martin's own hand, and a letter written on the same familiar Avelux letterhead as my contract. The check was for six thousand dollars.

$6,508.63 to be exact.

Hastily I unfolded the letter and began to read.

Miss Gereghty,

Your pay is included in the attached check as well as your bonus as discussed. One thousand per instance where emergency services were rendered unnecessary due to your direct action. I have, of course, removed the fee for relocating your vehicle.

Dr. Prosenko will notify you of your next shift.

Sincerely,
Martin Verdeau

"Fuck." The word escaped over my breath.

In my hand was a sum of money I had never seen. A check that on any other morning, I'm ashamed to say, could have bought anything of me I was unwilling to give. It was the kind of money that had been pinned to inspiration boards back in school to complement daydreams of my future as a physician.

This was the kind of money I presumed Prosenko made, but certainly not me.

Six thousand dollars was not a lot of money in the long run. It was not a lottery win, but it was precisely enough to give me a logistical whiplash and make my decision to seek other employment seem foolish. Ethics aside, this was the kind of money that would pay my parents' rent. It would pay our bills and, eventually, my crushing student debt. If there was anything in that hour that could have convinced me not to quit, it was that. I should have known it was something Martin Verdeau was willing to part with.

After snapping a commemorative photo of it with my phone, I drove to the bank and deposited the check, holding my breath as it cleared without issue. There it was, I thought. Almost seven thousand dollars in my bank account.

The drive after was something of a daze. The chips sat abandoned on the seat, and the ice in my coffee melted while I waited in traffic all the way back to Roslindale. The anxiety of any fight to come had failed to manifest. Instead my thoughts were occupied with a newly written future. How was Prosenko dealing with Jonathan that morning? Did Jonathan manage to take his pills? Would he have picked another fight with Audrey?

Hell, I was even concerned to know if Audrey had gotten her aspirin after all.

When I finally arrived at the run-down triple-decker rental that was home, I was tired beyond words and in such an exhausted state that I naïvely unlocked the front door and stepped inside.

"Where the *hell* were you last night?" my mother shouted before the lock on the door could catch. She stormed out from the kitchen, foil-wrapped frozen burrito in hand and slippers slapping the carpet.

"Work," I told her.

She watched me silently as I removed my shoes. Her graying hair had been straightened as always and was now in a messy, thinning long bob to her shoulders. Disheveled from her running around the house.

"You could have told us you'd have the car until morning, you know. Your poor brother had to take the bus home. Put him nearly an hour late for dinner!"

"I'm sorry."

"You're sorry? Hah! Sorry doesn't cover it, Lena. You need to get your act together, you know that? Ever since you've been back—"

"What, Mom! What? Ever since I've been back, what has been so bad?"

She frowned. "I didn't raise you to be such a spoiled brat, Helena."

"Ugh!"

"You're twenty-four years old, for Christ's sake! When do you plan to start acting like it?"

"I don't need this right now," I said, and gripped the banister to go upstairs to my room.

Hastily she grabbed my wrist. "No. You don't get to run from this! You come home, no phone call, no notice, stealing our car, and for what? To lie to me, saying it was for work when you smell head to toe like the bars? You don't get to do that, Helena. Maybe at your aunt's, but not in my household."

"I wasn't at the bars!" I shouted, still furious. Ashamed, even though I knew I had no reason to be. "I told you, I was at work! Taking care of— Never mind."

A need for justice urged me to tell her everything. That people had thrown champagne in my hair and that my feet ached from the worst twelve-hour shift of my life. I wanted so badly to just scream at her the sorts of details that only came from a sleep-deprived lack of filter, but I just couldn't. There was no explaining Arrow's Edge, and I knew it.

I couldn't even tell her about Mrs. Gainsborough.

Despite everything, I knew there was no way to get her to understand, even with $6K in my pocket to show for it. I knew my mother well enough to know she would have assumed that something else had given me that money. Something she would have considered distasteful. To her, anything would have seemed more likely than the job I'd been hired for with my shitty qualifications.

Finally she let go of me. "Then why were you out so long, hm?"

"I had to drive there. To work."

"Lena, you take the T. You've told us they're just some rich family in Back Bay!"

"No," I insisted. "I mean, I do. Just not for this."

"It still shouldn't have taken you that long!"

"It was a work party!" I managed. "It ran late!"

"Tch! A work party? Oh, come on. So you had to go to the Hilton downtown, that don't explain it."

"It wasn't downtown!"

"Then where was it, huh?" my mother huffed. "Rich folks don't have parties just anywhere, Lena. It's not like you were out there at some flashy thing in the Berkshires!"

The words rang out, and seeing my face, she stilled.

As flippant as my mother's statement seemed, something in it caught us both the moment she said it. We held each other's eyes with growing hesitation. Natalie Gainsborough's name hovered on my lips, and something unknowable hovered on hers. Something that told me maybe, just maybe, she would understand more than I thought she would.

"Actually," I said, softer, "yeah, that's . . . where the party was. The Berkshires." I looked to her again, closer this time, trying to read something in her expression. "Did you—"

The foil of the frozen burrito crinkled in her grip.

She gave a laugh. The kind of stunted laugh that mothers often use when they need to dismiss something more serious than they're comfortable with. She was a professional at that laugh and could easily turn a conversation on a dime with it.

"So it was a work party, you said?"

"Yeah."

"I remember those. Boring, aren't they? Just seem to go on forever."

She turned away from me and shuffled back to the kitchen, tossing the burrito onto the counter with a thunk.

Unsure if I really wanted the answer, I couldn't help but try to ask again. "When'd you ever go to a work party, Ma?"

She fiddled quietly with the foil, peeling it back. "Oh, I don't know, it was a bit ago. Back before the merger."

"Merger? You mean with Dad?"

"That's the one."

I paused, then stepped into the kitchen. "You never told me that."

"Well, you were gone. Didn't seem important. Anyway, it was just a couple of work parties, Lena. An effort to save his job that didn't pay off when Avelux came in and overhauled the place."

Avelux.

"Avelux," I repeated. "*That's* who bought Ellerhart? *That's* who fired Dad?"

She ripped the foil off and crumpled it up, slamming the burrito onto a plate to pop into the microwave.

"It doesn't matter. Your father's back will heal, and he'll get something else. You know the hardware store is just a temp that Benny offered him to get the unemployment audit off our backs. Until he doesn't need the pain meds anymore."

"Yeah . . . I know that. Wait, how did he hurt—"

"He'll stop the meds when the doctor clears him," she insisted. "It's just a setback. Then the bills will be better again. . . . Just a setback," she repeated, and then cleared her throat. "You have the keys, right? To the hatch? I'm going to need to run some errands. Maybe pick up something for dinner. Giorgio's sound okay? They have that cacciatore you like. It's my treat."

"Sure . . . sounds great," I said in a daze, and handed over the keys.

In the back of my mind, the name Avelux repeated over and over again. The image of my father in one of those rooms at Arrow's Edge. Injured and helpless on the floor just like Mrs. Gainsborough.

My mother was gone before the microwave dinged, leaving me with the smell of sizzling cheese and beans and a ravenous stomach that growled as pieces slowly came together in my mind. I grabbed the burrito, ran upstairs to get my laptop, and promptly set up station at the dining table.

News that my parents had tried to mingle with businessmen like Martin to save my father's job wasn't what was surprising to me. Before I'd left for Italy, my father had been through his fair share of job-hopping, and as a man who struggled against those twenty years younger with business degrees and internships, he found it harder and harder to meet expectations. All he could offer was experience and loyalty, and as a start-up, Ellerhart had accepted that when I was in high school. We had seen it grow, the business moving from a small office no bigger than a basement to three floors of a suburban office park, and my father was damn proud of it, just being part of it as a regional manager. It had been the typical climb, starting from sales, but he'd done it.

Even when I left for Italy, he told me everything was great. Our dinner conversations were filled with talk of new acquisitions, of business partners in Oklahoma, and of the Chinese market. It never seemed like a thing that could end. The thought of him, with my mother on his arm, wearing her best pearls and some new dress that was grossly unsuited to the lascivious nature of Martin's parties, flew through me. They didn't belong in a world like that any more than I did. My father was rough but hardworking, a man who everyone assumed was blue-collar but had worked his way up with nothing to go on other than his determination to support his two kids.

Avelux stole that from him without so much as a severance package.

Avelux left him a husk of a man. Injured without insurance. Without a job.

I had heard them shouting the details ever since I got back—the new prescriptions, the unpaid medical bills, the constant calls to insurance companies—though somehow I never put it together. His growing addiction or just how bad things had gotten. Even though my return home occurred months after he was laid off, the bickering by that point was never-ending. Late at night the walls echoed every complaint and threat of embarrassment, and rage, and I had listened, swearing I would do anything to make it stop if I were just given a chance. Hoping that if I could bring in more money, the stress would lessen and maybe, just maybe, the pain my father was feeling would shrink into something manageable without the pills.

I never imagined I'd be face-to-face with the devil himself, much less tending to his children.

With this revelation, any humanity I'd been able to muster with regard to the Verdeau family disappeared. The same anger that had been dulled by the influx of funds to my bank account returned with a vengeance. I dug into the burrito and began an afternoon of research.

Over the next hour, my fingers typed as fast as they could, following link after link, only this time with the focus on Martin and not photos of Audrey and fashion hashtags. Each click only brought me further beyond the edge of disgust.

My father, as it turned out, was one of hundreds whose jobs had been destroyed following an Avelux acquisition.

Avelux was a shadowy backbone to the technology industry, a manufacturer rather than a brand, with fingers that reached internationally, the

Verdeau name at the center of it. Which is to say, Martin and his people were the idea people, and his power came from a more primary source than most. Namely plastic, and more recently software development.

In the 1970s, Martin's father died, leaving him as the owner of a moderately sized rubber and petroleum manufacturer, and roughly $3.5 million in stocks. He doubled them, and through a surge in the 1980s had managed to make his first billion, officially starting Avelux.

Avelux owned the patents and production rights to the plastic that old CD players were made of. It owned the rights to a highly specific metal compound that some MP3 players used between 2004 and 2006, and to the glue that sealed smartphone motherboards. It had a hundred failed inventions under its belt, but none of that mattered because at least half of them would still make him money, from a manufacturing standpoint. His practice over the past decade had been to buy out small software and programming companies and force them to develop tech that would use his materials. A penny here, a nickel there, and most consumers never noticed the difference or that a monopoly was forming behind the scenes. The employees like my father, though, men and women whose job it was to secure materials from abroad and strike up deals with manufacturers, got dumped in the process.

My father never stood a chance at that party.

I wondered then how many others last night were there for reasons like his. How many had arrived wearing old suits and shoes they'd shined themselves, just to be let go the following Monday via a phone call? Was Mrs. Gainsborough one of them? Was her husband? He had worked side by side with my father, so surely if he was at Arrow's Edge, then he'd survived the cut somehow.

How many innocent men like my father had I treated last night, crudely in the shadows of an overcrowded room instead of a hospital, all for Martin's reputation? Worse still, how many parties like that one had

Jonathan and Audrey reveled at, knowing full well the status of the crowd and their father's games?

The six grand that clung to my name was hush money, and now I knew it.

At half past five, my mother had yet to return from errands, and the burrito sat unfinished by my side. My eyes were blurring from exhaustion, but I couldn't stop reading until a knock at the front door ripped me from the screen.

"Hey," said Rumi, an iced coffee in his hand. "Shit. You look like—"

"Shit," I echoed. "Yeah, I'm sure."

I cracked the door open enough for him to walk in, and Rumi plopped down on the sofa, handing me the coffee.

"What happened to you? We kept trying to call, but it went straight to voice mail. Thought you were dead in a ditch somewhere."

I took a sip from the cup, desperate for the caffeine, before rubbing a hand over my eye. "Yeah, sorry, it wasn't me that died. Just the phone."

"Long night?"

"The longest."

He laughed. "You actually may look worse now than after that week-long study bender you did before the SATs."

"Tch, I feel it."

"Work?"

I collapsed onto my father's recliner, careful not to knock over the tray of empty beer cans I still wasn't used to finding. "They made me drive across the state."

"North or south?"

"West," I told him. "The Berkshires."

"Damn! What the hell did they want with you out there?"

"A party," I said, venom dripping.

"You? At a party?" Rumi said, and then, noting my disdain, let out a long, dramatic whistle. "They *have* met you, right?"

"It was horrible. I'm not even sure *you* would've liked it, Ru."

He propped his feet on the coffee table. "Depends on what went down."

Even though Rumi, given our long, chaotic history together, was probably the best person around to understand the story, I also felt obligated not to share. In all my research, there hadn't been a single reference to parties. Not one. Any Instagram photos of Jonathan and his crew had been posted without details, and it was only now, after the party, that I knew what they were. That I could recognize the ornate moldings and paintings in the shadow-filled background of countless photos from Arrow's Edge on Brodie's account. No, the house itself remained a closely guarded secret, and increasingly I found myself worried about what might happen were I to be the one to expose it, no matter how much I wanted to.

"You guys were right," I said instead. "About them. I should have listened."

The grin on Rumi's face slowly disappeared, replaced by concern. "What do you mean?"

"It's just—" I began, but the words quickly failed me. "They think they can get away with anything. All they do is take drugs and drink and destroy people and make fun of them and treat it all like some game. Like we're not even people, and if I so much as expect to be treated as one? Then I'm a joke."

"Lena . . . what happened?"

"Nothing," I said, even though the warmth of exhaustion-fueled tears came to my eyes. "Nothing. I just hate this."

"This?" he asked. "Your job?"

"No . . . I don't know." Finally the tears fell. Not many, but enough so that I couldn't hide it easily with a brush of my hand. "Everything just feels *wrong*. . . . I keep trying and trying, but I can't seem to do anything right. . . . I want to miss school, but I *can't* because I have to work and I'm scared I'll just get burned out again or that I'm not cut out for it. And now

I'm stuck in this job, and I . . . *I'm sick of it.* I can't do it, but I don't know what to do."

"Lena . . ."

I swallowed, the saliva growing thick in my throat. I never cried, but now it wouldn't stop. It was more than just the party and the anger. I was tired in a way that I'd been ignoring ever since my plane landed. Every frustration, every ounce of nostalgia, every mistake, every hope. All of it had gathered in a corner I could ignore and had told myself didn't matter. Now it bubbled up, and I couldn't get it to stop.

"Is it so bad that I miss when the biggest stress of my day was learning how to read a manuscript or having to remember what old family used poison? I know it isn't practical, and you guys don't get it, but I miss just sitting in pubs where my beer came with stories of kings and historically overthrown tyrants and not the fucking *guilt* of knowing that each pint might mean I couldn't afford money for the train. And these . . . these fucking people, think they can get away with it. With how they treat us and—"

I couldn't go on.

Rumi sat, quiet for a moment, and then kindly reached forward. "I mean . . . for what it's worth, it doesn't seem like you've strayed that far from the shitty kings. So . . . at least you've got that going for you?"

A small laugh at his poor attempt at a joke slipped through my sniffle.

"It's just a shame you can't poison them anymore, eh?" Rumi asked. "Although with the way you talk, it sounds like they're doing a decent job of that themselves."

"Don't even joke. Please, Ru, not today."

"Fine," said Rumi with a sigh. "But c'mon. You clearly need some sleep."

"I can't," I objected, finally feeling my cheeks a little less wet as he took the coffee from my hand and urged me up from the chair.

He walked me to my room. With each step on the aging carpet, a new and terrible thought blossomed. An idea so cruel that I was helpless to resist it, one that pulled at every bit of rage in my sinews, begging to become real.

Poison.

Poison, Rumi had suggested, and it hung in my mind, refusing to disappear.

7

IN A.D. 79 PLINY THE ELDER DIED, leaving behind a thirty-seven-book catalog of the natural world and among it a list of over seven thousand poisons. Almost five hundred years earlier, the famous philosopher Socrates felt his legs go numb and sat helpless as the hemlock spread upward through his body until it at last stilled his heart and lungs.

More than six thousand years separate us from the origin of poisons and the notion that as humans we have other methods of murder than how sharp we make our arrows or swords. From the baffling hebenon of *Hamlet* to the catatonic belladonna sleep of Juliet and the grasp of monkshood or cyanide on Romeo, I had come to know too well the toxic lore of the botanicals that lay in my aunt's garden. Beneath the warmth of the sun and her guiding hand, I had received an education on the subject of poisoning beyond my wildest dreams and as a result had unintentionally developed a predisposition to the thought of such an act and how shockingly easy it would be if ever a reason found me.

The modern age did not want to believe in poisons. The fear of poison had been replaced by that of guns and nuclear attack and disease. In each of these was a monster more bold and less archaic, and so the poetry of poison faded in favor of its brothers, but the deed itself never left. In the New York of the Roaring Twenties, poison killed more people than did car accidents, shootings, and stabbings combined. Even today someone will die because of a poison. Every minute, every hour—we just refuse to think of it as such.

As a society we have learned to strip nature down to white powders and chemical compounds, smaller and smaller until we forget their origin. As a med student, I knew precisely the usage of atropine on the system, but it was Aunt Clare who showed me the leaves and the plump, dark berries that too many hikers accidentally consume in the height of German summers.

The fear of my own knowledge, once sparked, was immeasurable. Too easily did a catalog of plants filter into my imagination alongside numbers that together spelled out ratios. The sort that could divide a cure from a casualty. I had been there, in her lab, as the juice of *Atropa belladonna* was harvested into vials to mimic the recipe once used by wide-eyed Venetian women. I was there for the reconstruction of propagandist Roman tales and to have a glimpse into the brews behind the Borgia family crimes.

Rumi knew nothing of what he'd done, the impact of his words that afternoon, but it was too late. The temptation was there, and every thought of the party—and of Mrs. Gainsborough or of my father in her place—coalesced into a single realization that Martin Verdeau was to blame. That Martin Verdeau needed to suffer and fall and be humiliated just as he had done to others like them.

And I knew precisely how to do it.

It wouldn't be murder, but it would be close. It would be just as satisfying.

For each helpful herb that grew in Aunt Clare's garden, there was another that carried with it a reputation of woe, and she had tended to them all with motherly affection.

"Plants aren't good or evil, Lena," Aunt Clare used to say. "We decide that for them."

I knew that my decision would not be a good one in her eyes—but with each passing second I cared less. My anger had grown until it was the only thing that mattered, and I could see it all so clearly.

To mess with Martin Verdeau would be easy, and the idea, once planted, flourished. It wasn't something I was proud of, but the potential of revenge occupied my daydreams from that weekend onward in a way I couldn't shake.

Too quickly I found myself considering which poisons would blend with his coke-rattled brain, which would be easiest to slip into wine. I played out on paper which would be the hardest to detect, the easiest to procure, and the quickest to act. The cruelest to his ego.

Hurt. I wanted to see Martin Verdeau hurt. I wanted to see him stumble and fall surrounded by his colleagues in the same way Mrs. Gainsborough had, that my father likely had, and poison would be my way to make that happen.

There were hundreds that would fit my needs, and I imagined each of them so carefully that by the time Monday had arrived, my embarrassment following the party had vanished and my heels felt sharper as I walked into the town house.

I had e-mailed Aunt Clare with an odd but specific list, framed by a nostalgia for our work and a little humor that she was happy to indulge in. After that it was just a matter of taking a grand from my bank account for equipment like beakers and a small portable burner I could sneak away into my closet. Then I had only to wait.

Perhaps I was too quick to judge, my muscles too taut with an eagerness for revenge. At the time it didn't bother me. This was what hatred and humiliation could do. At its best, hatred was not a blinding rage with popping veins and curled fists. Rather its strength lay in its power to persevere. To seethe and simmer and bubble, seeping into everything it touched like a brilliant contagion. Transfixing anything once good into something unrecognizable.

AS I TOOK THE TRAIN to the brownstone again, my stomach twisted with a coldness. I'm ashamed to say that at this time any concern I'd managed to develop for Jonathan Verdeau fell to nothing. I saw him only as his father's heir and, on occasion, just as guilty. As cruel as it was, he could have tripped the whole way down the stairs and my muscles would not even have twitched with a thought to move and help. After the course of the party, it was too easy for me to recall his cutting tone and the leers of Dylan and the others. Still, my job was to tend to him, via Prosenko, and I knew that. I just didn't have to care.

True to form, the state in which I found Jonathan that first Monday I returned to work was not a well one. He had been dragged back to Boston with grease in his hair and a drowsy manner that meant he'd slept through my arrival after lunch. The moment he was awake, the doors began to slam on the second floor. As my hands sorted paperwork and claims from the party, Martin stormed past and out the door, leaving the entire house to shudder in his wake, the small crystals of the foyer chandelier jingling.

"Fuck it," Jonathan said, his voice echoing down the stairs.

"Which office do you think he's going to?" said Audrey beside him, dully. "You might have angered him all the way to Beijing with that one."

"You're welcome to take your leave, too."

"Hm, but how will I hear your moping from all the way in China?"

Every word Jonathan spoke that week was tired or crazed with bitterness, to the point where Audrey appeared even less often than before, which was just as well given my mood. I failed to see Martin again until the following Friday. That left Jonathan alone in the town house to wander in the same phantasmic stupor, avoiding Prosenko and myself at all costs.

In corners he would cough, hard enough to leave him trembling, and then I'd catch him sprawled on a chair on the wooden balcony with a sickly sweat on his lips. As horrible as it was, with every new weakness I saw in him, I saw an opportunity. Jonathan was not my focus, but still, watching him I couldn't help it. The image of a new plant would burn behind my eyes, and I'd imagine too easily the effect of it on his system. The red flush of cyanide to his face or the blue as it built around his lips and dropped him in seconds. I'd imagine methanol slipped into a drink and the five-day descent into blindness, the shock on his face as his body truly and genuinely failed him. Each scenario crueler, more deadly than the last. It didn't matter that I wasn't planning to *kill* Martin. Or that Jonathan wasn't a part of this. My mind wouldn't stop.

As a businessman Martin often left early in the morning, long before I arrived for my shift, and returned only once I was home, if he returned at all. When I did see him, it was like watching a lecherous villain out of Elizabethan theater. Martin Verdeau worked and drank, never permitting himself to be seen without a glass of some amber liquid in his hand. His favorite argument was the slam of a door or a phone, and I learned how his time was split between countless cities and offices and phone calls and, very seldom, his children. Audrey never spoke to him, and Jonathan only invited shouts and screams the same as everyone else.

As time passed, I began to wonder if I would ever return to Arrow's Edge and if all my waiting was going to be for nothing. By the third weekend at home, I began to grow paranoid that the parties happened without me and that somehow, George or Prosenko had caught a whiff of the plot. Perhaps they found an e-mail receipt from an order for herbs, and even though it was innocent on paper, somehow they'd detected my motives. I foolishly worried that my thoughts were audible or that Prosenko was psychic and that at any moment I could be discovered, that the family in turn would grow distant from me. However, it was by some miracle that the opposite occurred.

In the October of my employment, Prosenko at long last asked. It was a Wednesday, and not the night of a party. Jonathan had made a point to drive all the way to the Berkshires at 4:00 A.M., stealing the car before it could be taken to the airport for a flight to Los Angeles by his father, and Prosenko had been unable to convince him to return. The more the doctor tried, the more Jonathan pulled away, and so it was just after 8:00 A.M. when I got the call from a very tired Prosenko and was told to please pack a bag of clothes and place a call to George.

By 10:00 I was in the passenger seat of a convertible with the Verdeau family butler silent and stoic behind the wheel, traveling for the most uncomfortable two and a half hours of my life. There was no music. No conversation. There was nothing but the buzz of the air conditioner and the white noise of the tires on the road. After the party George had done his best never to be in the same room as me, and it was an effort I respected with the utmost sincerity.

The only benefit was that by the time we pulled up to the Arrow's Edge gate, which had so strongly provided me with nightmares and hatred over the last month, it actually felt like a relief. A twisting and uncomfortable one, which made my mouth go dry and my hands twitch, but a relief nonetheless. By the time I saw Prosenko, his face weary from the chore of my apparent charge, he still managed to hold some degree of positivity. However, the state that I found Jonathan in that morning still sticks out vividly—as it was the day he regained some semblance of humanity in my mind.

After Prosenko met me on the steps, he led me back into the estate with a familiarity that suggested he'd been there too many times before. He paid no attention to the details of the sunlit manor house that now captured every bit of my interest, nor the fact that Arrow's Edge was truly immense. He was on a mission to return to work, but still I walked with an increasing and unshakable curiosity.

Without a mass of people and the chaos of a party to steal my attention, Arrow's Edge eagerly revealed its strange enchantment. Compared to the breezy opulence of the gallery and the clear, framed glass of its windows, the remainder of the home was closed off. The dark rooms from the party remained hidden in the same shadows of statues, only now the space seemed to stretch wider and longer—and altogether lonelier than I knew a room was capable of feeling.

We did not go into the gallery when Prosenko led me onward. Instead I was ushered through gilded rooms with gaudy and oppressive details typical of the homes of Victorian oil barons. Here minimalism was a sin, and every bit of wood was carved to form curious beasts and plump breasts and fruits dripping off vines. Ivy leaves adorned mahogany doorways, and every chair or couch came with claws and velvet cushions. Even the walls refused to give onlookers a breath of reprieve, and as we paced across warm parquet floors, the images of portraits, seascapes, and bucolic villages danced through chandelier-filtered light. Still, although the rooms were overflowing with art, each seemed to wail with a profound sorrow of abandonment and a craving for the din of life.

Much like the town house, Arrow's Edge opened with a magnificent staircase at its center. Only here the marble of the foyer stretched into a series of curved steps, covered in a dark stripe of red, which Prosenko hastily led me up.

"The second floor is the same layout more or less as in the town house—Martin's room at the end, Audrey's on the left, and Jonathan's on the right closest to the stairs," he said. "But everyone remains in the western wing. George has found you a room on the third floor in the old servants' quarters." The term felt dusty and cramped, and already I was not looking forward to it, nor had I known I would be expected to stay for that long.

"What's in the eastern wing?" I asked, realizing that Prosenko had likely avoided bringing it up on purpose.

"Repairs," he said gravely. "And remnants of their mother's."

"Their mother's?" I repeated, again finding myself wondering about the absent Verdeau matriarch. The portrait of a blond woman in the brownstone's study coming curiously back to mind.

"Yes," Prosenko confirmed, "and untouched for twenty years. It's an old house, Miss Gereghty, as I'm sure you noticed. Some areas just aren't safe."

"And the servants' quarters?"

"We renovated five years ago," he assured me. We came upon the floor and turned to see many small doors and narrow halls. "George will be staying in the room next to you. Daniella is across the hall."

"Where is Sascha?"

"End of the hall and on the right. Now, here's your key if you should need it. There's a bathroom across from Sascha. Everything else should be accounted for—bedlinens, towels. I'll leave you to change."

"Oh."

"A problem?"

"No, I just— Where's your room?"

Prosenko made a face. "Just find me in the office when you're ready. I should be getting back."

The room wasn't as bad as the name would have implied. Instead it was like a small hotel room complete with an antique armoire, a twin-size bed, and a rug. It wasn't fancy at all, but given the age of the house, it could have felt considerably more haunted. On the back side of the armoire door was a long mirror, and I used it to wrangle my dark mess of humidity-worsened curls into an even messier but more practical nest atop my head. Then I changed into some cleaner jeans and a basic black Henley. It wasn't much, but it was enough, and after splashing some water on my face I hurried back down to find Prosenko.

My footsteps echoed loudly in the space, and the house seemed to amplify every noise with a pettiness. As I approached a large suite near the main staircase, the sound alerted Prosenko to my arrival, and he turned in a leather chair.

"Excellent, you found it."

"I think I'm slowly learning my way around."

"I suggest you do so faster. That'll make today easier."

I gave him an inquisitive look.

Prosenko sighed and rolled back to his desk to grab a clipboard. "Jonathan's disappeared again, and if I leave to find him, it'll put me behind in submitting this order for Martin. I've already called the supplier, but their cutoff for shipping is in twenty minutes."

"So that's it? You just want me to find him?"

"Find him and get his ass over here. He's been giving us all the chase since this morning, and I've rather had enough."

"Oh, sure. Where does he—"

Prosenko had already returned his attention to the computer monitor and was scrolling past pharmaceutical supplies at a record pace. He motioned absently for me to go, and upon realizing that there was no more information to glean from him, I did just that.

I wandered the estate for a half hour, taking in its charm and tracing my steps from the party to where I thought the Verdeau son might be hiding, no doubt already drunk with wine stains on his shirt. The library, however, was empty, and no room that had once held the party showed any signs of life.

It was not until I was thoroughly lost amid the portraits and hidden hallways that I caught the familiar scent of tannins and found Jonathan at last—stubborn, upset, and precisely as I'd imagined he would be, framed by the couches of an old music room complete with a grand piano. He sat, lounging back with an old book in his hand, long lashes, and a pensive set to his lips that my approaching footsteps unfortunately interrupted.

He paused and glared up at me.

"It's Lena, right? Like Helena."

"That's right."

"Hmph," he said, his attention drifting back to his book, turning another page. "Not exactly a face worthy of a thousand ships."

"Excuse me?"

"Maybe a paddleboat."

"What's wrong with you?"

"You should know by now, shouldn't you?"

It took everything in me not to smack him. The image of my fingers on his cheek flashed quickly, but I doubted that someone like Jonathan Verdeau had ever been slapped in his life.

His lips curved into a short, bemused grin. "I assume you're here to fetch me for Doc, yeah?" he said. "Well, if you want me to go, you're gonna have to gimme an oxy. I've got a brutal headache. Can't possibly walk."

Beside him on the floor was the glint of a green bottle, its cork rolled a few feet away near another antique chair.

"Ask Prosenko when you see him."

"Now, where's the fun in that?" Jonathan reached for the bottle, raising it to his lips. He swallowed once, then twice, and released it from his mouth. "You're his *assistant*. He should at least trust you with a little bit of pain meds. Unless of course you're really that terrible at your job."

"You know, water helps hangovers more than wine."

He turned back to me, lips a dark shade. Eyes darker still. "Who says it's a hangover?"

I looked to him and then to the bottle with a raise of my eyebrow.

"Fine," he said. "Then who says I want the help?"

"You *just* asked for a narcotic."

Jonathan considered it and shrugged. "Fair," he said. "But if you're not going to help me, then why don't you just go on and run back to Doc and tell him why I won't come?"

I started to think I preferred him unconscious on the steps. The scathing, manipulative tone was one I had heard only in patchy insults echoing from the hallways of the town house after his sister had wandered in, and I didn't care much for being the brunt of it now.

"Why did you come all the way out here?" I asked.

He frowned and eyed me over the leather binding. Then he raised the book with a small wave of his hand.

"Yeah," I said. "I know, I'm distracting you. I get it."

"The book," he said.

"You . . . wanted to come back for the book?"

"Well, I wasn't going to find it at the city library at three A.M., now, was I?"

"You dragged us all out here for a book."

"No," he said. "I came, you just followed. And now you're wasting my time with redundant revelations."

"Don't you have business in Boston?"

"Don't you need to be a bitch somewhere else?"

I watched as thin fingers twitched in anticipation of another page turn. How his eyes hurried over lines of print and thick lashes blinked. With ease Jonathan had abandoned the conversation and relegated me to the status of a ghost. As I lingered, my resentment and rage grew, the same as anytime I'd been around him after the party. Only this time, for a moment, it dulled at the realization that his reading was not as flippant as it seemed. His eyes hurried over the lines, but in a cautious way, with an odd, obsessive love behind them.

I realized then that whatever it was he held in those hands truly had consumed his thoughts so powerfully the night before that he drove almost three hours just to get it. Although such an act was childish and selfish in the same absurd manner I'd grown to associate with Jonathan Verdeau, for a moment the chaos of his existence quieted into something almost tender.

From behind me the sound of footsteps signaled George's approach, and I watched as Jonathan's face soured all the more, were it somehow possible. Any hint of that tenderness flickered and promptly faded.

"You have a call," said George dully. Jonathan looked back to his book and ignored the family butler even as George motioned forward with the phone. Finally George said, "It's your father."

Jonathan cursed and got up from the couch. Then, slamming his book shut, he brushed past me as he ripped the phone from George's hand on his way out, not seeming to mind his headache too badly after all.

"What?" he shouted into the microphone, his voice echoing with each step. "I told you I don't care! I'm not going! I don't know why you keep promising them I'll show up when I've told you a thousand times that I don't want anything to do with it. . . ." His words trailed off as Jonathan turned the corner, disappearing into the belly of the house and out of sight while his battle continued away from my curious ears.

As I returned to Prosenko, my mind was busy with an attempt to piece together what had just unfolded. The whiplash of Jonathan's wit and strange affection. What kind of esteemed heir to a man like Martin would drive across the state in the middle of the night to read an old book? What alcoholic twenty-something would insult me with Homeric references? He was nothing like his sister, I thought. Not in mannerisms or speech. If I didn't know any better, they would have seemed entirely unrelated.

I found Prosenko busying himself with restocking equipment in the same room as earlier. Only then, as I approached, did he reveal that it was his office there at the estate. I could have realized it sooner, had I only looked deeper into it to see a doctor's chair, file cabinets, and a workstation cluttered with papers.

"It's the main one," he said, shoving a packet of gauze into its place on one of the metal shelving units. "Or it used to be, before they all started preferring that old brownstone."

Looking around the space, I saw it was clear that Prosenko's words were truer than they sounded, and the intricate setup of the parlor room during the party all those weeks ago was but a cheap caricature of what now stood before me. It was decked out in medical equipment, everything from plastic-lined walls to portable X-ray machines and shelves upon shelves that made Prosenko's office look entirely the part of a pharmacy back room. It also made the office in the town house resemble a closet.

"Martin had it built years ago," explained Prosenko, "for Jonathan. The nearest hospital is miles away, and the care is atrocious. Downright pitiful."

"Does he really need all this?" I asked, staring at a shelf stocked with nothing but 800-milligram ibuprofen. Bottles of it.

Prosenko paused to look back. "You've met him. You tell me."

Whether or not Jonathan Verdcau actually needed a full doctor's office in his palatial childhood home didn't much matter to me, especially at the time, but the level of medication was enough for anyone to question whether part of the problem was a family proclivity toward hypochondria. Then again, the circles under his eyes told a different story. In the aftermath of our conversation, there were more questions I wanted to ask Prosenko, but my mind's wanderings regarding Jonathan's state were put on hold as shouts echoed up from one of the home's expansive halls.

Prosenko sighed. "Another conference call," he said, and promptly returned to his task of sorting small boxes—this time needles by their gauges. "You told him to come by, right?"

"Not exactly. . . . We were interrupted."

"Damn. Well, he'll be by soon enough." He paused, raising an ear to the air. "I give it three more minutes."

"How can you tell?"

"It's Martin on the phone, right? These calls never run long. Neither can stand it. You'll learn to detect these things soon enough. Doesn't change the fact that whether he likes it or not, that boy has a job to do."

I peered out into the hall, half attempting to listen in and half bewildered by Prosenko's implications.

"He really works with Martin? Jonathan, I mean. In his state?"

"He helps, and it's a state made better by you and me, Lena. Don't forget why you were hired."

"I'm not, I just—"

"Jonathan stands to inherit Avelux."

There was a newly acquired gravity to his voice in the moment. Something unspoken but unmissable to my ear. A severity.

"What about Audrey?" I asked. "With his health—"

Prosenko merely laughed, short and insulting. "Martin knows who his heir is, and it won't be someone who prefers Chanel stock over his own."

Oh, but cabernet is fine, I thought cruelly.

I tried to understand it but couldn't. In all our conversations, however brief, Audrey seemed every bit the ideal heir from my outsider's perspective. She had a background in law, and I recalled Martin's flippant dismissal of her that first day of my interview. Summa cum laude. Yet at home there were no laurels. No reward for her efforts. Nothing but the shops on Newbury and yes, some Chanel, but who could blame her?

Was it wrong for me to feel so infuriated on Audrey Verdeau's behalf? Possibly. I hardly knew her, but a part of me was enraged that Jonathan could act in the way he did, storming down those halls and running off at all hours of the night, and still be able to sleep soundly with the thought of a crown in his future.

Something was missing from the equation. A hidden piece that I wasn't yet privy to. As the thought passed, my eyes located a stray fleck of glitter on the hallway floor, no doubt overlooked by the maids and cleaning crews.

Was it the parties? Did Jonathan simply play Martin's game better than Audrey? I didn't want to believe that any more than I wanted to believe that someone who tried as hard as Audrey Verdeau could have been so easily shoved to the side. There had to be something else I was missing, some small detail that could offer rationale to the twisted logic Prosenko now offered, that boiled Audrey down to something useless while the family disgrace stood proud.

In a flash every bit of hatred returned. A fitful wave lapping over my mind and my imagination. At once I recalled the plan. I just had to make it back home to Roslindale.

8

ARSENIC, LEAD, AND BELOVED BELLADONNA. These three ingredients formed the Aqua Tofana of the seventeenth century and secretly fouled the husbands of angry and abused women. Over six hundred of them, vindicated. The poison was colorless and flavorless, perfect for a subtle death, and had been the first thing that came to mind when my plan began almost a month prior, but I knew that whatever I constructed had to be smarter. Softer. Especially while I remained there at Arrow's Edge.

My life at this time became split into two. With physiology books sprawled out on my temporary bedroom floor, borrowed from a back shelf in Prosenko's office, I rehashed the effects of certain toxins. There was no Internet at the estate, but it didn't matter. My laptop was filled with hoarded PDFs of research articles from Italy, and I drew charts of drug interactions in Sharpie in secret, as if I were back in the heyday of my schooling. It had to be perfect, and each word I studied gave a new hit of adrenaline and the satisfaction that I was doing *something*. I hadn't felt such a passion for medicine in years.

A toxin is no different from any other drug. It's the dose that matters.

It was after another day of watching Jonathan nurse whatever had been pilfered from the estate cellar that I got the idea to arrange for the poison to be cumulative. Its effects were to be mild and undetectable alongside inebriation. Something more like an unintentional drug trip than a shock-and-drop attack. This way, I prided myself, the dose, if it *was* deadly, would be on his own idiotic hands. Martin's, I mean. If it was in the wine or the scotch, then one glass wouldn't hurt, and anyone else exposed would get by without much more than a dizzy spell and a sick stomach. But five . . . five and Martin Verdeau would fall in front of everyone, the laughingstock of his own party. Six and he might not wake up.

The more I recited the formula, the smarter it seemed, and I was damned proud of it. The new blend would work with the plants that had already been ordered, and as soon as they arrived, I could get to work. No backtracking was needed. From there it would be a matter of dilutions.

After a few days, the walls of the estate began to close in. Every morning I would report downstairs, attempting to take notes on a clipboard while numbers and chemicals occupied my thoughts. All the while Jonathan Verdeau continued his torment of keeping us there.

His mood shifted wildly from day to day, and in the evening he could be found in any one of the darkened rooms of the home, his robe blending into the velvet sofas or the lush antique curtains. He moved about the place in a daze, permitting himself to be detected only after an hour's search and a few shouts from the doctor about his daily dosage.

This was how it went, to such an extent that almost two months into my position under the Verdeau family I'd come to know little more about them than I had in the first two days. Jonathan was perhaps more of a mess than I had thought, and the brief instance with the book soon paled in comparison to the sound of his shouts and drunken stumblings. In every interaction with him, I became the victim of some new insult—half slurred and near archaic.

As for Audrey, despite my anger and contempt for her family, she remained a glowing presence that I longed to catch around every corner, but during those days at Arrow's Edge, she remained absent, favoring the intimacy of Back Bay and her Pilates classes and tapas-catered business meetings over the dusty corners and antique paintings of the estate. I imagined, too, over the bickering with her brother.

But each hour she was gone only made me miss her more, and I began to wonder if I would see her at all before the next party came. That is, until the fateful Saturday when the wheels of her Bentley crunched along the gravel as it arrived from its journey up that winding road to the estate.

"Georgie mentioned you lived in Italy," Audrey said, waltzing into the large kitchen for a fresh cup of fair-trade Guatemalan coffee. The scent of citrus and frangipani filled the room, and I was helpless if not ashamed at how quickly I was overcome with a sense of peace. It had been more than a week since we'd last crossed paths, almost two, and seeing her there before me again filled me with a hopeful chance for civil conversation. Or civility at all. "Where about?" she asked as her shoulder delicately brushed my own and she turned around to face me.

"Oh . . . um, Umbria," I told her, pausing my butter-covered fingers halfway through ripping open a fresh croissant. The reprieve had come as she caught me midbreak and mere moments after a chaotic round of laundry and errands that had taken up my morning. "Just outside of Montefalco."

Audrey sighed with a nostalgic air.

"Europe is wonderful, isn't it? Good coffee, croissants . . ." She looked down at my hands, slick and messy, and smiled. "Not all that different from here, I suppose, but it's more the air of it, don't you agree? Old bricks and flower markets. Kisses on cheeks."

I swallowed, finding my mouth going dry as she eyed me closely. In my pocket I felt my cell phone begin to ring, the call vibrating against my thigh, but I knew it was only Rumi, and I could call him back later. As the call faded, Audrey's eyes drifted from my thigh and back up to my eyes with a small smile edging her lips.

"I take it you've been?" I asked.

It was a stupid question. Of course she'd been.

"Mm-hm!" she said, finishing a sip and leaving a ring of soft rose lipstick lingering on the porcelain. "I went to my mother's old boarding school in Montreux." I tried to recall the place, and then Audrey simply smiled wider and said, "Switzerland."

"How long were you there?"

"Six years or so," she said simply, as if it had been a summer vacation and not a quarter of her life. "What were you doing in Umbria?"

I took another nervous bite of pastry before answering. "I . . . uh, worked for my aunt. She has a garden out there."

"A garden! How picturesque."

After a week of Prosenko and Jonathan, her words felt sweeter than sugar. I couldn't help but smile. "It was."

"You must miss it."

Desperately, with every millisecond I was trapped in Arrow's Edge. Especially with my evenings filled doing the research for the poison again. But I didn't need to tell Audrey Verdeau that. Seeing her again almost made me ashamed. Almost. Suddenly she pulled herself up from where her elbows rested on the marble countertop and straightened her back.

"Well, Lena, play your cards right and maybe you'll get a chance to return."

"You think?"

"I have a hunch," she said, and I watched as she twisted to look around the room. "You haven't seen my brother, have you?"

I motioned in the general direction of the music room. "He was by the piano an hour ago. Pretending to play."

She sighed and grabbed her coffee. "He always goes to her rooms. . . . Well, thank you."

"Are you staying for dinner?" I asked, perhaps too eager and with Audrey halfway out the door.

She paused. "That depends entirely on how long it takes Jonathan to agree to come home."

9

BACK IN ROSLINDALE THE GLASS BEAKERS were cool against my fingertips as I unpacked them from their cardboard boxes. A pile of shipments had been waiting on my bed for my return, and by now my mother had stopped asking what they were for. If they had an Italian return address, she didn't care, and anything else I could easily explain away as tea or clothes.

As it rested against my hand, the simple, smooth glass of the beaker took me back to the days of chem labs in college, and the sound of the glass droppers as I pulled them from their amber vials sent me back to Umbria. A shiver traveled up my spine. A feeling like I was . . . back.

It should have seemed odder, I think, to be just some girl in Boston, knees bent in dirty jeans on the floor of my childhood bedroom, pulling bulk herbs from plastic bags hidden safely behind boxes stacked high with comic books that hadn't seen the light of day in a decade. This, however, felt familiar and comforting, unlike anything else since my return home, and once the motions had begun, I clung to them eagerly. To be able to feel the crushed leaves between my fingers again, and my eyes reading the scale until it reached the perfect weight. This was my element. This was where I thrived, and even as I poured poisonous barks and leaves into a simmering pot at just past midnight, I couldn't help but smile.

The scent rose from the beakers, and I watched as the glass clouded with a noxious fume, careful not to breathe it in. With a mask on, I shielded my eyes and opened every window as discreetly as I could.

It wasn't the safest, and I could practically hear Aunt Clare lecturing me on proper protocol, but I didn't care. I was overcome by the fact it was really happening. That I had taken a daydream and in a fit of late-night orders and typical impatience managed to make it this far. It was only when my head began to spin from the fumes that I finally stopped, put everything away, and went for a walk, only to return a few hours later and get right back to it.

As off as it may seem, I wasn't all that angry during the process. Not at this time. Every thought of the party and Mrs. Gainsborough on the floor fueled me, sure, and I wanted in every fiber of my being to make Martin Verdeau suffer for what he'd done to people like her and like my parents, but . . . as I sat there watching the liquid darken, day by day, tinkering with it after my shift at the brownstone, I found myself more transfixed by the simple act of making my poison than by the underlying reason.

It was only in momentary flashes of weakness that I would see Martin's red, bloated face. His lascivious grin and how he treated everyone who made less than six figures a year, and it was these small reminders that kept me grounded to the task and mindful of every gram added to the brew.

I didn't want him to die. I didn't want to do that to Audrey, even with the knowledge of how he had mistreated her and misjudged her all the time, but I wanted to make him suffer. To knock him off his high horse and watch him slip. I wanted him and his colleagues to know what it was like to lose control. To be ridiculed and embarrassed and unable to buy their way out of things the next morning.

Cautiously I adjusted and readjusted my formula, using gloved hands to cut leaves, roots, and berries by the milligram. Hours of planning strained to come into being through the mere minutes I could slip in after everyone in my house had gone to bed, but I had no choice. Time, at that point, was far from in my favor.

The following Wednesday, Martin returned from abroad, and by Thursday word had begun to circulate that the next party neared. The announcement hung on his lips with excitement. There was something under his tired, aging demeanor that each one of his employees came to know during our time in his employment. A mania and a craving for release that ran through him like something akin to an addiction.

Something had happened on that trip, but to this day I can only guess.

Martin Verdeau's return marked a new chaos in the Back Bay household. He replaced half the art on the town house's walls in a fury and canceled almost every meal with a shout to Daniella and then another shout to wonder where the food was less than an hour later.

His displeasure at Jonathan was even worse.

After Jonathan's refusal to fly with him, Martin had tried to remotely loop him into calls, which Jonathan only further refused, aside from one. That day of Martin's return, the town house was filled with the two men's pacing and a continued argument with neither soul willing to surrender.

"When will you stop humiliating me?!" I heard Martin shout, the depth of his anger causing Sascha and me to stop in our tracks as they passed. "What you did at that meeting was inexcusable! You can act like that at parties, but in the boardroom I expect you to have a different attitude!"

"How many times do I have to tell you I don't want anything to do with the stupid company!"

Martin's face turned furious, his arms shaking as he raised a pointing finger. "No, you *will* step up like the man you are! You don't know what I've done for you, boy! You don't know how long—"

"I don't care!" Jonathan shouted back, a humorless laugh in his voice. "The only thing I've ever asked of you is to leave me alone! Like I'm trying to do now, but you never seem to get the message, do you?"

"Because that's not an option! Stop this right now, Jonathan! I'm warning you!"

Their voices grew muffled as they moved farther down the hall, and soon Prosenko was brushing past us, following them in a frantic attempt to mediate the dispute.

That day in particular was a bad one.

So much so that that week, despite what I thought had been a growing bond between us, Audrey took off for New York without a word. It was a trip even George had to discover from the newspaper articles and her social-media feed. Jonathan, though a perpetual staple of the house as much as the furniture between its walls, simply did what he could to disappear from his father's eye.

Due to the costs of manufacturing the poison, I had lost around two grand, but there, in the face of Martin's anger and continued cruelty, it all seemed worthwhile. It felt like a purpose. Something every step of life had led me toward, and looking back, perhaps it had. To be close to Martin with a poison I'd concocted in my hand felt like a divine gift, or one of terrible temptation. I saw how the ways of the world had positioned themselves for me to be there, to avenge my parents, and Mrs. Gainsborough, and everyone else whose lives Martin had carelessly hurt, and I was determined to not mess it up.

In the weeks after the first party, I had waited to see if Mrs. Gainsborough would call. If she even remembered me from that night and would tell my parents what I was doing. The fear hung in the back of my mind alongside my concern for her recovery, but I never heard a word. Tom, despite the look of recognition in his eyes as I knelt down to tend to his wife, never called the house either, and they both appeared back on Facebook as if nothing had happened.

I only found out that Tom had been let go from what remained of Ellerhart when his status changed subtly one night. No announcement, no anger. Just a quiet slink away, same as my father. Another person who couldn't afford the recovery of his reputation and likely wasn't allowed the opportunity. I wondered if his wife had the orange pill bottles to match.

I told myself it was better that way. If I knew they were going to be at the party, I don't think I would have been able to go through with my plan. Knowing they were safely out of the picture made gathering the poison that morning an easy task.

That Friday afternoon, with everything ready, I put the keys into my new Honda. It wasn't actually new, but it was a purchase made out of desperation and the desire to avoid any more fights with my mother now that I would be at Arrow's Edge a lot more than I'd initially realized. The car was a basic black and a decade old, but Anna's brother worked at an auto shop and had been able to snag me a deal for an easy twenty-five hundred dollars, no questions asked. She and Rumi had been thrilled at the idea, and with a simple lie from me about savings and a last-straw fight with my mother over work, they didn't pry any further. They didn't need to know I'd planned it to be a getaway car in case things went south.

In the bag beside me, I had a small suitcase with a dress, some heels that were easy to run in, and a toiletries bag. A summary of my previous mistakes.

One lesson learned at the first party was that there was no substitute for a uniform, and the uniform that a Verdeau party required was one of sleek dresses and suits and skin. Over the course of my week at Arrow's Edge, I'd seen enough of the siblings' style, and with the walls surrounding me it became easier to remember the details of the night I'd willed myself to forget. The hemline lengths, the makeup, the hair—every detail I could don like a form of camouflage to keep me from attracting too much attention. So another hundred bucks from the bank account got a clearance dress. Black, body-hugging, and with enough stretch to be practical. As practical as a pocketless outfit could be, anyway.

It was all just a part of the plan.

Martin favored scotch above anything else, but much like his son he would drink whatever was around. Still, for me to get close enough to slip something into a drink would have been impossible. There was only one break in the party: the central champagne tower in the ballroom, with its midnight toast and the waterfall of straw-colored fizz flowing past freshly shined and brightly lit crystal.

To go after Martin alone was tricky, but the drama of the tower made it a prime target. While I knew that the champagne Martin drank was different from the one flowing for his guests—his hubris would not allow for anything less than what was fit for a king—its flaw was that it still popped with all the rest. And so my opportunity would lie in wait, unassuming and within reach just as soon as I could make it to the manor home's kitchen.

The eleventh hour of the night would signal a turn in the crowd, and at the last party it had been in that eleventh hour when people seemed to grasp more readily for any gift of pleasure or escape and so by midnight the gates of hell would have already been opened. By midnight Martin's grin would be manic and eager for applause, and that would be my chance, if I were to have one at all.

The setup for it fell into my lap.

Earlier in the week, Sascha had been complaining about the pace of popping bottles for the previous party, and while I picked at a stale muffin, I had been able to easily offer my assistance. Altogether, twenty bottles of champagne were needed for the mechanics of the tower, and so twenty-one bottles were waiting.

At 10:35 P.M., my palms were beginning to sweat. The party that night began the same as the one before, with the cars pulling in to the circle, their headlights flashing, and I watched as the guests entered through the gallery to pay their respects and down the first shot of whatever liquor was handed to them. Pacing the rooms, a purse filled with condoms and a bottle of Narcan at my side, I scanned the faces and all the couches and chairs for a sight of where Jonathan could have been lounging about, trying to see if he would be there for the toast or not, and that was when Audrey caught my eye, a vision in spaghetti-strapped, golden glitter.

"You look nice!" she complimented loudly over the music, reaching forward to take my hand in a shockingly friendly motion.

I didn't know what to say. Instead I followed Audrey's gaze as she looked out across the ballroom at the growing tower of glasses, twirling her fingers together with mine.

"It's stupid, right?" she asked, forcing me to lean in closer, straining to hear.

"Yeah," I said, trying not to let my fingers fidget as she held on. "Seems kind of a waste."

"Oh, I know!" She rolled her eyes, gave my hand a squeeze, and let go. "They always pick the worst person to pour it, too."

I raised an eyebrow and shouted over the booming bass of the music, "Who's pouring it tonight?"

Audrey met my eyes and then smiled.

"I've got to go, Lena, love," she said, leaning in to brush our shoulders once more in parting. "See you at midnight."

Her petite form disappeared into the crowd again as I watched, confused and still distracted by the memory of her fingers in between mine.

Trying to refocus, I took a breath and headed deeper into the house, shifting past the same group of drunk and high forty-somethings as if I were invisible. I moved through them for what must have been an hour, until at last I came upon Jonathan, laughing and standing atop one of the antique sofas in the music room. At first glance I could see he was play-wrestling in some very close way with Elliot Hayworthe, his hands shoved into Elliot's copper-colored hair as their bodies trembled in laughter and teasing shouts, while Dylan sat on the other side of the small room, obscured by the rolling hips of two women.

I didn't linger. Instead I looked at my watch and realized I had just short of eight minutes to spare, so I hurried back into the kitchen, where Sascha, Daniella, and some of the party staff had already begun preparing the bottles. It was there, amid the bustle of frantic bodies, where I felt my heart rise into my throat, the nerves at last taking hold.

"What can I do to help?" I offered.

Sascha looked to me with relief in her eyes. "Lena! Thank God! George just went back to grab the Clicquot for Martin, but I've still got to finish preparing the hors d'oeuvres. Can you just— Ugh!" She yanked another cork out, the fizz coating her hand in sticky alcoholic foam. "Take over for me? Just put them on the counter there when you're done!"

The Veuve Clicquot was Martin's favorite. Not the standard you could find at any liquor store but a limited three-liter release with an ostrich-leather label that he kept in the cellar under lock and key. He bought a case of the stuff for every party, purely for himself and those among his inner circle. Exorbitantly expensive and leagues above your standard Dom, it was highly pretentious, and that night it was to be the instrument of my revenge.

As agreed, I busied myself opening bottles, keeping my eye on the door for George's sullen face or his aging hands holding that familiar yellow label. One by one the bottles for the average class were popped. A mix of Dom and cleverly disguised six-buck Brut, each fizzing and bursting forth into a sticky blend on my fingers.

Like a good helper, I moved to pick up the next bottle and offer my assistance, all the while waiting for my chance and praying it would come. The kitchen around me was crowded, and time was short. The music was blaring, rattling the walls just a few rooms over, and the hour of the toast was dangerously near.

At last it arrived. George hurried over with the bottle in hand just as Daniella shouted from across the room with another request, causing him to do a double take. Seeing my only chance, I leaped into action and reached out.

"I've got it!"

And then, like that, the Clicquot was in my hands.

The foil wrapping was twenty-four-karat gold, and I tore at it with such enthusiasm that I was still finding flecks under my nails a month later.

As I yanked the cork, I recited the formula again in my head. I would need no fewer than thirty drops to make a difference. If I wanted it to kill him, I'd need over a hundred. Knowing his drinking rate and that of the men around him, however, a bottle with thirty would be enough to embarrass him.

No one noticed.

The vial was tucked under the tight sleeve of my dress, a little plastic dropper hidden by a cheap gold bracelet to trick the eye. Small and easy to conceal and control, it worked marvelously. With each drop that fell, a new kind of adrenaline struck my veins.

After the weeks of waiting and planning, the souring juice that had sat hidden in the shadows of my childhood closet was now lying in wait to touch Martin Verdeau's lips. All I had to do was wait a little bit more along with it.

"How are we doing on time?"

A single voice penetrated the clamor of the kitchen, and I turned to find none other than Audrey. From behind me George hurried over.

"Everything is ready. We just need to bring the bottles out."

The color in my face drained as he reached in front of me to grab hold of a single green glass bottle. The ordinary stuff. "Here's yours for the pour. I'll follow you out."

She smiled at him and then looked to the bottle in my hand. "No.

You know, Georgie, I think tonight we'll share the best with the crowd. Give them a taste."

Her manicured hand took the Clicquot from me then, fingers wrapping around the neck, where I knew three drops of the poison had slipped out and lingered along the rim. Her thumb fell over the opening. "Thank you, Lena," she said with a wink, and hurried off as quickly as she'd arrived.

I faltered.

The world around me instantly came crashing down.

"What . . . ?" The word came from my throat more out of confusion than anything else, but Sascha came up to grab her share of the bottles to deliver, the movements of the night still continuing like a well-oiled machine.

"Didn't you hear?" she told me. "Audrey's doing the toast tonight! I guess she secured some kind of deal when Jonathan skipped out on a conference call last week. Kind of huge. He never trusts her with that stuff. Anyway, thanks for your help, Lena! We've got this now. I'm sure Prosenko's looking for you!"

Panicked, I froze until at last I let myself be ushered out behind Sascha's fiery hair and short-legged scurry. Hesitantly, fearfully, I moved through the clouds of perfume to the ballroom.

10

THE SCENE WAS MORE ABSURD THAN I HAD IMAGINED.

Martin sat at the back, watching as a large rolling staircase moved up to the glistening tower amid cheers and celebrations. I had missed the event last time, catching only the aftermath as I guided Mrs. Gainsborough into the parlor. Now, as the spotlights shone and the crowd parted, I watched with unshakable focus as Audrey addressed the crowd, her voice kind and melodic. She delivered a series of words I failed to hear over the pounding of my own heart, then raised the bottle high, took a long sip, and began to pour.

I watched as poison fell in sheets among the glasses and as George, and Sascha, and Daniella, and others each came up with a bottle in hand and began to pour on the lower levels.

Never had I watched a clock so closely, nor had I been filled with such a clear sense of paranoia. I had spent weeks planning the mixture and its effects on Martin from a single bottle, but I had in no way planned on widespread dosage. Certainly not with such a degree of variance. The image of Audrey taking such a large gulp at the beginning, her lips precisely where I knew the stray drops to have fallen mere minutes prior, kept repeating and repeating until my soul felt torn with revenge and guilt and something else I dared not place.

Fifteen minutes later the house began to fall.

The waiters were the first to notice, shouting requests to dim the chandeliers as the darker rooms filled with more and more people and individuals began gulping liquor like horses. But the delusions were what signaled it to me. That despite everything my poison had worked. With a far greater potency than I'd intended.

I watched as men in sharkskin suits stumbled through the space, their pupils wide as they ran from some horrifying yet imaginary act. Their fearful shouts and their faces, so painfully red and full of guilt, were the only cue I needed.

From that moment on, my fun was over.

I went into action.

Within a half hour, the already busy ambulatory clinic of the parlor room was filled to the max, and Prosenko stood bewildered. He had readied a shot of atropine before I stopped him and suggested we try physostigmine instead, judging from the excessive thirst but puffy cheeks that spoke of obvious water retention. Prosenko said he didn't keep a lot of it in stock, and I told him it was on a recent order sheet. There should be enough. So I ran to his clinic room, the real one, and we agreed to take the most severe patients there.

It wasn't pretty, and it kept me busy, but I still waited for the entire night. To see Martin falling or even Jonathan stumbling in with some plastered and delirious grin on his face like a satyr of great myth. It felt like a promise, biding its time as my hands busied themselves with the others. The accidentals.

Instead at close to 1:00 A.M., as I was running from the parlor to find Prosenko in his office, I crashed into a thin body draped in glittering silk and golden rings.

Audrey's face was flushed pink, the brown flecks in her hazel eyes blown wide, like a ravished angel teetering on high heels, and I shouted for her, catching her just before she could trip over her own feet.

She giggled and looked to me with a little "Oops!" and then frowned, focusing on my arms. She patted them with clammy hands, slick from sweat instead of their usual imported lotion.

"So strong," Audrey said, and gave my forearm a squeeze.

"Come on," I told her as my heartbeat rose into my throat. "You need help."

She slapped me away. "I'm fine," she said, although it was so painfully apparent that she was not, and I was left to wonder how many times she'd been in similar situations and not realized it. If she were so pre-exposed to the drugs of her familial pastimes that she couldn't even recognize when she'd been poisoned. At the same time, she felt like the friends in undergrad who had called me from the dusty confines of some frat cellar, scared and shaken to their core as their bodies betrayed them.

I clung to her as another dizzy spell overtook her, watching as she whined and looked at me.

"I'm so thirsty. . . . Can you get me some—"

"No," I told her sharply, and flung her arm over my shoulder. "I'm getting you help."

But the motion only seemed to endear Audrey further. I tried to stumble her away from the crowd, the fabric of her dress pressed close to my chest, and as she hung around me, I realized we had never been so close. After months of my employment and watching her drift in and out of the estates, never once had we actually touched like this. Not a hug nor a handshake. Despite how much I dreamed of them.

Her feet stopped moving, and before I could realize what she was doing, Audrey had twisted around and was looking me in the eye, so close I could see her mascara running from the sweat of the evening. And despite it she was beautiful. God, she was beautiful.

She pulled herself up, and before I could think anything else, I was tasting her lip gloss. It was not a small kiss. It was short, but Audrey had initiated it eagerly, leaving me in a daze. At once I knew how soft her lips were and what it meant to taste champagne on someone else's mouth. It was a flash of sensations that left me stunned and stupefied as I held her there in the mess of that house, with ignorant jeers sounding all around us. Then, as she pulled away and licked at her lips, the thought crept in as to what was on them.

Would the poison also reach me? Did enough of a drop linger on her tongue?

Every inch of my body felt warm. A mixture of fear and a fire beneath my skin that I wanted to feel the flash of again, and then hated myself for, because as I stared at her, left with the stickiness of her lip gloss smeared across my mouth, I knew that she had done it only because of the Saint's Fog. The poison that I'd made to hurt her father. It didn't matter that this was something I hesitantly, naïvely dreamed of in the months of my employment. It felt stolen and, worse, because of the drug she likely wouldn't even remember it.

IT WAS SOMETIME AROUND 4:00 A.M. when the music died down and most people had run off to secluded rooms or nearby hotels, that I at last left the infirmary again. My head still swirled with the memory of her, and there was a growing unease in the pit of my stomach as I tended to the patients in Prosenko's care. I tried not to think about it, though. I forced myself not to.

She had been fine, guided by Sascha up the stairs and left to sleep in her room. Whether she remembered what had happened, I wouldn't know. The fact was, I had poisoned her, and I felt sick for it. I hadn't meant to hurt her. I hadn't meant to hurt anyone other than Martin, but especially not her.

When I saw Jonathan again, he was laughing, ecstatic, with a glass of champagne in hand and more alive than I knew he was capable of. Clearly Dylan and the others were enjoying it. Jonathan's face held a color that was less sickly than before, and I realized with an unwelcome sense of relief then that the poison must have missed him. Either that or he'd received such a small dose that by the end it just aided in one of his trips.

My relief turned to resentment, and I hated myself even more for it.

I hated that I'd followed a plan precisely one month in the making, only to see Audrey and some bystanders suffer the effects of a toxin hand-crafted to make Martin and his circle suffer. Martin who, as it stood, appeared fine.

For hours he had sat on that pretentious throne of his, motioning for men to walk up and pay respects with an offering of some golden pen or glass bottle, or for a woman to sit on his lap and give a little dance. When I wasn't trapped in the parlor curing a chaos of my own making, I watched him eyeing his kingdom with the face of a man who was lost in rapture. His movements held none of the telltale signs of my concoction. I had meticulously studied historical accounts of similar poisons and dispersion rates. I had memorized the interrogations of Madame Tofana and the dinner accounts of Cesare Borgia. I knew what I was looking for. I had seen it in an unfortunate (but not entirely undeserving) dozen others, and I had seen it in Audrey. Flushed faces, wide eyes, and a delirium building as the heart beat faster and faster, mouths going dry with thirst just before the sickness took hold. The five bathrooms of the open part of the manor all had lines out the door, and Prosenko was quickly running out of bio-hazard bags, to the point that even George took it upon himself to go to the storage room and fetch a few boxes to help.

But here, even with the knowledge that I'd failed, something sinister had settled into me. A sort of power, or a godly and energizing force that could only come with creation and only be fueled by a secret.

I had done this. The fruits of my labors, ripe and dangling more boldly than the mahogany grape leaves of the corbels. No more were tales of the Renaissance a daydream or a joke. Arrow's Edge had made them into a truth. A reality that, as I watched Martin's hands clasp onto some blonde thirty years his junior, could clearly be improved.

The more I listened that night, the more I realized that no one had noticed anything was wrong. There were no shocks nor gasps in the crowd, for the reasons I had naïvely striven to instigate. The party, despite Prosenko's and my increased workload, was a success. Another terrible notch in the Verdeau family's belt and another slap on the back for their reputation.

And this time I had helped.

11

THE CHILL OF AUTUMN SWEPT in overnight, and as I walked the long road down to my car that October morning, my breath caught and twisted up to deadened leaves. I was lucky to be leaving with such ease, and I knew it.

Martin hadn't stopped me, nor had Prosenko realized that anything was off, despite what I felt were a thousand neon signs pointing to me as the guilty party. Not a word was spoken, and that night the house slept easy and hushed.

When the party had at last lulled and drivers could be hired for the commute of some sicker patients back to their hotels or homes, Prosenko and I were running on the fumes of a few 2:00 A.M. espresso shots. I kept waiting for the shoe to drop. For him to stop folding white sheets or curling IV cords around his hand and turn to me and say, *What the fuck did you do?*

Instead he said, "Long night, wasn't it?"

And I agreed.

But paranoia doesn't care about getting caught. It cares about the potential for it, and so every second that went on with invisible red ink coating my hands was a second I struggled to let my shoulders loosen.

I got maybe three hours of sleep. Twenty minutes here, an hour there. My sheets, when I returned to the servant's room, became a knotted mess wrapped around my ankles from all the twisting and turning I did, and with every movement the aging bed frame gave a loud and horrible creak that I was certain would alert someone in the house to my distress. One I couldn't easily explain. So I would lie there, frozen with nerves as sweat gathered on my temples, waiting for what felt like the inevitable as the scenes from the party replayed in vivid color, but no one came. The house remained silent.

Dawn arrived with a pink sky and blinding light. Birds chirped and lawn mowers roared while I pried my eyes open and changed into a flannel shirt and jeans, moving to the bathroom with hushed footsteps to brush my teeth.

The previous party had not required me to stay, and so I thought it was best I didn't that morning either. I couldn't stay another night or hang around for Audrey to find me after the kiss. I wouldn't survive it. I didn't know what to say. What I *could* say, if she remembered what she'd done. Downstairs I watched as hired help swept up the glitter and broken glass and came in with new rugs still rolled up and wrapped in plastic to replace the ones that now resembled maroon-and-gold watercolor paintings. Arrow's Edge seemed to sigh, its walls breathing out with a tired satisfaction in the morning light.

As the sobriety of the day lingered on the horizon, my guilt told me to run. A car was waiting for me, and a suitcase of clothes had been prepacked in case I couldn't go home. I planned for it to go worse than it did. After all, there was no way to test the poison beforehand, and I wasn't about to put it on a cracker for the neighborhood rats. That just seemed cruel.

I drove straight to Slick Rick's. Like any other time when I didn't want to go home or was scared and had nowhere else to turn. I climbed into one of the booths with my cell phone in hand, anticipating some dreadful call or a news alert to flash across the screen with my face and the headline WOMAN ON THE LOOSE. HALF OF WALL STREET POISONED.

But my phone had been silent on the drive, and an hour into the booth and with my fingers greasy from picking over a basket of French fries, it remained unsettlingly so. I wanted to call my friends. I wanted their chatter to distract me from the terrors that kept playing in my mind, and I had prayed that perhaps Rumi or Anna would be there when my car pulled into the parking lot, but the booths were empty, and I couldn't bring myself to call them and risk bringing them into this. They would know immediately I had done something. Especially Rumi.

An hour passed, and then another, and then, slowly, I began to realize that true to form for all of the Arrow's Edge parties, it seemed like the world was unaware that the previous night had even happened. Any mistake, any injury, any fault that occurred within the home was left with no more power than a dream. Sealed shut in the manor's old framing. Although I was sure at least five men and women were now suffering and shaky in their beds somewhere because of me, their stomachs sick and heads spinning with hallucinations, the world heard not a peep. Social media was silent. Not even Brodie's Instagram had its usual photos.

More and more my world divided. As the distance between myself and that terrible house grew, a breath of ease at last began to seep in. The party now felt far enough away that with an empty basket of fries in front of me and the familiar smell of grease that had comforted me since eighth grade, I was left wondering: Had I really done that?

Had I watched as men swallowed a poison that had sat on the floor of my closet for weeks? That I'd tended to personally each day as the roots steeped into a quiet tincture? Had I really treated them and saved them from the brink of death?

Lives. I'd held lives in the palm of my hand and played with them. Yet still this voice within me cried out, loud and ashamed of failure. There in that worn blue plastic booth, that smile of Martin's haunted me.

THAT WEEKEND I GOT LITTLE SLEEP. Since I owned my own car and with my paychecks I'd taken to helping with groceries and the utility bills, my mother had no more reason to complain, so she mostly left me to my own devices. For the rest of that Saturday, I remained cooped up in my room, constantly checking the news and fearing every new text to my phone from Rumi or Anna. I was ignoring them again, and I knew it, but I couldn't help it. Even with a growing sense of clarity and the silence of the news, I still couldn't convince myself that connecting with them wouldn't bring them into this. In my closet, a few steps away from my hunched form on the bed, sat the plastic bags of chopped-up roots, carefully dried and labeled in Sharpie. I thought how obvious they were. How foolish I'd been. Couldn't I have had the foresight to predict a police investigation? How obvious was it that there, beneath my sweaters and coats, were bags filled with poisons labeled so clearly a kindergartner could read them? It was stupid. I was stupid.

Again and again the scene played out. The bottle in my hands. Audrey's thumb over the lip. I knew what had happened. Still, I couldn't process how exactly it had gone so wrong. How I had lacked the foresight to imagine any other end than with the poison in Martin's glass.

But he hadn't been affected. Instead my poison seemed to have claimed everyone else, including Audrey, and no matter how hard I tried to wrestle the fault away from myself and relegate it to chance and a lack of luck alone, I knew that any error that night was my own.

I could recall Audrey's lips on mine so clearly but couldn't bring myself to enjoy the memory. I couldn't believe that the kiss had been real or that someone like her would have honestly meant to do that if she were sober. As much as I secretly hoped for Audrey to see me in that light, I didn't want my poison to be the cause.

It sickened me.

The plants on my windowsill sat bright green and eager for water, but those wide leaves of the Saint's Fog were just another reminder of my failures, never producing anything of its claim in lore, and perhaps through some delirium it seemed to mock me as it sat there half hidden by shadows and gathering a thin layer of dust.

I had clipped a few of the leaves. A bit of the root, too, and added them to the poison on the off chance it still might have been redeemed as an entheogen—a divine hallucinogen, as the original monks who grew it claimed. Yet even in that, it seemed to fail me. There was no way the images that haunted the victims last night were remotely holy. Their fear had been all too clear.

There is no greater agony than waiting for a punishment, but if there is to be one, then it may just be waiting for confirmation you've gotten away without one. My wait that weekend was dreadful. My palms were so perpetually sweaty with nerves I became a dehydration risk, and food lost all appeal. Time and again I came up with excuses, one after another. A reason not to eat. A reason not to watch TV with my father. A lie here, a lie there. I couldn't stop. Then, by Sunday, my phone was ringing again with Prosenko's number, and by Monday I found myself once again on those steps in Back Bay, just as nervous, just as out of place as that first day.

Showing up for work, I half expected one of two things. Either another bonus was waiting, just as after the first party. Or, what I thought seemed much more likely, I would be fired. An arrest was also in the mix, though I tried desperately not to think of that option.

When Martin called me into his office not ten minutes after my arrival, before the tea George had made could even be steeped, I thought for sure that was it. I'd been found out. Everything else had been a ploy to keep me comfortable. The pause, the silence over the weekend. My suspicions had been correct and there was no other option than this—there never had been. I was a fool for even imagining that another scenario could take place. The evidence was so clear. It was right in front of them.

The thoughts and the fear swirled on and on in my brain, swallowing up any small shred of hope that remained in a matter of seconds, until I was drowning in it.

Still, I opened the door.

"What a party," began Martin from his desk, slowly, with a voice far deeper than I recalled its ever being before. "Eh?"

Nerves forced me to swallow. His office was claustrophobic. Four walls of floor-to-ceiling wood, lined in bookshelves filled with leather-bound texts and what were clearly display gifts from colleagues. It reeked of power and wealth that morning in a way that felt far stronger than when I'd first sat in that chair and signed my contract that bore a letter-head I wish I'd paid more attention to before the ink hit the paper.

The pen still sat on his desk.

"I stayed busy."

Martin laughed and then nodded. "Yes, I heard. You left before any of us were up, but then Prosenko told me you weren't on the schedule, so I thought I'd just wait and give you the weekend. Please, sit."

He motioned, but I stood, frozen, as sweat began to gather on my palms. "I'm all right."

"I insist."

Hesitantly I looked to the chair, and then in one, two, three steps I crossed the dark red of the Turkish rug and sat down. We were close enough that I could smell the coffee on his breath and the aged cigarette smoke that clung to his clothes. I hadn't known he smoked, but sitting two feet across from him, there was no denying it.

There was also no denying his ill health.

"All right, Lena, let's cut to the chase. There was something . . . different about that party. Folks knew it. I could see it on their faces clear as day, and you and I both know something new appeared at the party. Something that got everyone all worked up." I swallowed, my fingers gripping at the fabric of my jeans just out of view. "My phones have been ringing off the hook. See that flashing red light?" I watched as he pointed to the phone on his desk. "That's the people waiting for answers. Waiting," he said with a lowered voice, "while I talk to you."

My world imploded. Here I was, so clearly guilty and in the office of a man rich enough to ruin my life, have me arrested, and force me into abject slavery or a thousand other terrible things. He knew it, I thought. He knew I'd gone after him. This was my Italian-leather electric chair. I fought to calm my nerves enough to speak. To ignore the sweat pooling at my temples.

"I'm . . . I'm sorry, sir, I—"

"Sorry?" he boomed. "You misunderstand, Miss Gereghty, I don't want *sorries*. I don't want apologies."

"Sir?"

"I want *more*."

What?

"What?"

Martin grinned. "I don't know where it came from, this new drug, but it got everyone thrilled. Had me more blissed out than in the heydays before '87. And I'm counting the quaaludes."

I didn't understand. My heart rate refused to slow down as I sat there stunned while Martin went on.

"I interviewed each of the staff. Daniella, Sascha, George, and every hired hand who set foot inside that party. But even with all my questions, no one seemed to know a thing. I phoned my colleagues thinking surely one of those assholes would claim it for their own, but I've been calling and calling, and, Lena . . . no one, not a single person, owned up to bringing it in. Which is a shocker, since usually whoever brings the good stuff can't shut up about it. Hah!"

My lips remained tightly sealed. I was terrified to the bone of what was going to happen next.

"Lena, there's no hiding it. It all comes back to you. I know you helped with the champagne. I know the shit hit after the toast—and you? You're the wild card here. My dark horse."

He stared at me. As if he knew every step I'd taken. Every detail of my being. All my nightmares. As if the truth were already out.

"So my question is, Miss Gereghty . . ."

Fuck. Fuck. Fuck.

"How much do I owe you?"

What?

He waited.

"Um . . . what?"

"I'm not sure where you got it, but I'm guessing you got it from somewhere, right?"

I stayed quiet, and then, slowly, he nodded in understanding.

"Okay, protecting the source. I got it!" His hands slapped the wood of his desk. "Well, you still did us a favor. You help my parties, I'd like to help you. My colleagues and I, we appreciate what you've done, so I want to pay you back. For services rendered. I called you here to ask one thing: How much?"

"I . . ."

"Three thousand seem fair?"

Deep inside, a part of me registered that number the moment it left his lips. Another part hastily switched from disbelief to anger. Enough to know he was lowballing me for what he thought he was buying and force a number out to demand for myself as much wealth as he could afford.

"Five."

Martin leaned back in his chair. Thinking.

"Four," he said. "And a thousand down for the next order."

Again my brain had to readjust to what was happening. Was I really sitting there being offered five thousand dollars? For attempting to poison my employer and his friends?

Fuck the world, I thought. *Fuck dreams. Fuck fairness. I didn't do this to be a drug dealer.*

But I needed the money. He had stolen it from my family anyway.

"You really want more?" I asked.

Martin frowned. "You can get it, can't you?"

"Depends. How much do you want? For the next party?"

"Double it. Whatever you did last time, double it."

I paused again to think. He didn't know how close his guests were to the emergency room. He didn't know what doubling it would do to them. Either that or he didn't care.

"If that's doable," he said.

"By when?"

"A month from now. That gives you plenty of time."

I considered it. At this rate I wasn't sure my heart would survive another four weeks in his employment. I wanted him to suffer, and looking at him then, just two feet of polished wood and paperwork between us, I still wanted him to suffer. Hell, knowing what he was planning now, I wanted him to suffer more. He wasn't just buying this for his friends. He was buying it to drug anyone who came to his party. People who didn't want it. People like his daughter.

Then again, I couldn't say no to the money.

"Five for last night," I told him, feeling my veins run cold. "And I'll double it for eight. Still with a thousand down."

Martin looked at me, and then he grinned. I watched as he pulled out a checkbook and wrote the sum of eighteen thousand dollars to my name. He handed over the check, and I sat there, unable to believe what had just transpired.

"I added your bonus, too, since you didn't grab it Saturday."

"Thanks."

"You did good work, Gereghty," said Martin. "What do you call it, by the way?"

"Call it?"

"The drug. What's its name?"

"It doesn't have one."

He raised an eyebrow.

"I mean, there's a lot," I said. "Nothing official."

"Then what do *you* call it?"

My eyes locked down on the bit of paper in my hand. The potential. The sum of a bit of a failed experiment and some dusty leaves. The anger. The largest failure I knew.

"Saint's Fog," I told him.

The name earned a nod, and like that I signed myself over to a devil's deal.

My father always said that when a man offers his hand, look at the wrist. In middle school, back in the days when a wrist showed nothing but angry red cuts and shame, I mistook it to mean something merciful about compassion and the unknown struggles of others. As Martin extended his hand to shake mine that day, I found myself face-to-face with a glimmering two-grand Armani watch, and I realized too late the truth of my now-unemployed father's words. In Martin's world, compassion, like respect, depended entirely on the sum in your bank account. Apparently mine was now filled enough to earn some.

It was the longest conversation I'd ever had with him and by far the nicest, and although it ended with a small fortune to my name, every word out of his mouth only confirmed his own perceived infallibility. An immortality given through his white face, his dick, and his financial status, and the same could be said for each of his associates. I'd never thought poisoned men would come back begging for more, but I shouldn't have been surprised. They'd poisoned themselves for decades. A trip was a trip, and whatever didn't kill them made them invincible. They lived in their own heaven, their own arcadia, where nothing, not even death, could touch them. Nothing except for me.

12

THE DAY AFTER THAT MEETING, Martin left for another business trip—Utah, I think it was. I willed myself to see sweat on his forehead or signs of lingering symptoms as he departed, but none appeared.

Not everyone got away clean after the party, though. Jonathan had apparently spent that previous Saturday in bed, with Prosenko having tended to his retching all the way back to Boston. Come Tuesday, Martin's son could not be bothered to take the car out to the airport to bid his father farewell. Instead Audrey had to go, her ill and quickened heartbeat safely hidden from view for the purpose of familial duty and last-minute business discussions, despite not having been invited on the trip herself. She still put on a deep blue cotton dress and heels and her finest coat and was there to wave good-bye with all the flair of that scene from *Casablanca* and none of the signs of acute anticholinergic syndrome.

After Martin's departure Jonathan only seemed to get worse. Instinct and a sick desire tried to tell me it was the poison taking a delayed toll on him, making him refuse the trip that morning and not delight in the usual torment of his sister. Even Prosenko noted a sharp decline in Jonathan that day, and a dulled and dreary temper.

Where before his malaise had come across as laziness caused by little more than a hangover, after the party Jonathan retreated into himself and barely said a word to anyone. All that came from his throat that morning was a soft muttering as he flipped through the pages of another old book and the occasional curse as a dizzying pain overtook him. This continued until the afternoon, when the alarm in Prosenko's office beeped in a reminder of his dose, and the doctor was nowhere to be found. Just the same tray that was used every day for the task on his desk, with its glass of water and the plastic cup with the small black pills already inside.

After waiting for what seemed like a reasonable amount of time, I decided to take the tray and administer the pills to Jonathan myself. When I found the study empty and the lounge and all the bathrooms unoccupied, I headed to his room upstairs. I found him there in the dark, in bed with his back to the door. The wrapping from one of Elliot's packages the week before was left on the floor.

"If you're going to yell at me this time," he said dryly, "don't. I'm at a good part."

"I'm not here to yell," I said, and watched as Jonathan stiffened at the sound of my voice, then turned his head just enough to see me standing in the doorframe.

"Well, you can't make me take them either."

"I don't care if you take them or not."

"Hm," he said, and turned back. "Great. Then you can leave."

Everything about him signaled that the conversation was over, and despite our daily encounters my ability to coax a conversation out of him had not improved. Then, just before I could surrender and go find Prosenko, I saw a curious motion that I couldn't ignore. A fiddling of fingers as Jonathan's hand rested atop the covers. A flicking of nails against skin, almost absently.

"Did it fall asleep?" I asked, unable to help myself. "Your hand."

The motions stopped. "No."

Jonathan closed the book and sat up properly, turning to face me. The room was dark, but the sun filtered in through a pair of curtains in small streaks, and the light from the hall behind further illuminated his uncovered frame. Part of me wondered why he didn't have pajamas on. The other part wondered how the hell he was alive. Especially after the party.

Before me was a man near emaciated and pale. His collarbones left dark shadows, and his face looked progressively unwell. I wondered if peripheral neuropathy were a symptom I had yet to calculate for the poison.

"S'just numb again," Jonathan said, and the motions of his hand resumed.

"Again?"

"It happens sometimes. It'll pass."

"Here," I said, the guilt rising regardless. "Do you mind if I check your stats?"

It wasn't my job, but I knew enough of Prosenko's usual procedure to be comfortable going through the motions. As I took hold of Jonathan's hand, his skin was noticeably clammy and his breathing was shallow. Still, he was handsome in a way. I couldn't ignore that. His eyes were dark and sunken, but it only made his lashes seem longer, and his lips, though paler than they should have been, were still an arresting shade of crimson. Even without the purple tint of wine.

Gently, I pinched the tip of his thumb. "How's that?"

He shrugged. I pressed the remaining four fingers to little response. No sharp hiss of pain and nothing to denote a reflex either.

"What other problems have you been having?"

Jonathan seemed to pause as I moved to take his pulse. It was slow, quickening for a moment to a normal pace although it remained noticeably weak and thin, which explained why he passed out so easily. It just didn't explain the numbness.

Sitting before me, he seemed far from the victim of a hangover and rather more like a boy with leukemia. His skin in the light was an eerie gray, and for once, so close, I realized the dark and solemn air about him. A scent that was sweet like rancid fruit or figs. It lingered on his breath, passing through chapped lips and clinging to his hair like a cheap cologne.

Something was definitely wrong. The question was how much my mixture was the cause.

Curious, I let my hands linger too long, and my eyes focused on the trembling of his pale mouth as he took in weak breaths one after another.

Down the hall a door slammed, and Prosenko's loud and booming voice echoed just beyond the room.

"Gereghty! Do you have the pills? Has he taken them?"

Jonathan looked at me, eyes wide, and I froze with the tray resting on his bedside table. Prosenko's footsteps rang out as he walked closer and closer, and before I could open my mouth to say something, Jonathan grabbed the cup and downed the pills. He winced, eyes squinting as he swallowed, but in a moment the meds were gone.

"Yeah!" he shouted. "And they taste like shit as always!"

Weakly, he shoved the tray back at me, shuddering with the acrid taste, and then waved his hand for me to leave.

I had just enough time to turn around to see Prosenko, who eyed the tray.

"Just took them," I told him. "When I couldn't find you, I . . . well, I didn't want him to be late, so I went ahead and brought them up."

Curious, Prosenko leaned over to peer in the doorway and watched as Jonathan frowned and rolled back onto his side.

He eyed the boy's face and, seeming satisfied at something—perhaps

Jonathan's displeasure—turned back to me. "Well, good. Thank you, Gereghty, but I'll remind you that you are not to—"

"I got his stats, too. I'll go record them."

After a quick and confused thank-you from Prosenko, I shut the door behind me, leaving Jonathan once more in the doctor's care as I hurried down the stairs to his office. I had only just turned the corner, my pulse rising, when a wisp of blue caught my eye, heading into the study. After the notes were recorded, I found that Audrey was still there, curled up, the fabric of her dress pooling between the arms of the antique chair.

She lifted one hand off her coffee cup to cover up an oncoming yawn.

"You're back," I said, in a voice probably more surprised than was warranted.

"Oh! Lena. Hi."

"How was the airport?"

She smiled softly. Politely. "Fine, thank you for asking."

There was a beat, and I followed her gaze as it fell on the small pile of books. As well as the empty bottles and bags of chips.

"Are these from today?" she asked.

"I don't think so. He hasn't left his bed all afternoon."

Her eyes turned back to me, a hair wider. "He's still in bed?"

I nodded.

"Has Prosenko seen him? Has he taken his pills?"

"Just now. I only came down here to make note of his stats."

"Oh," she said, and looked away again.

Even in the dim light, I could tell that Audrey's brother was not the only one who was unwell. Her face was puffy, and her eyeliner, which usually looked so sharp, was shaky and uneven. If I didn't know better, I would have said she'd just been crying.

"How are you feeling?" I asked, finally willing myself to step closer. "After the party, I mean."

"Oh, me?" She smiled. "I'm fine, Lena, love. Better than the others. That was a rough one. I barely remember anything."

Something in me winced. Another part was grateful. I still didn't know what I would say to her if she remembered.

"Has Prosenko checked on you at all?"

She only laughed. "No, why would he?"

"Well . . . you're clearly sick."

Audrey smiled, a gentle sadness overcoming her face. "No. He's always busy with the boys. Besides, Jonathan really doesn't seem to be doing well lately." Again she looked at the empty bottles. "His anger this morning was . . . different."

I motioned for her to stand. "Come with me to the office. I want to check your stats."

Something in her brightened, and she stood. "Mine?"

"Of course. You're a part of the family, too, aren't you?"

"Depends on who you ask."

I SAT HER DOWN IN PROSENKO'S CHAIR and stretched out her arm for the blood pressure cuff, keeping my hands as gentle as I could while searching for her radial pulse.

"Is it common?" I asked her after a moment. "His anger, I mean."

Audrey nodded with years of experience. "Jonathan hates the city. I think there's too much to do that he just . . . can't. Not anymore."

"Is that why he goes back to Arrow's Edge?"

"Among other reasons," she said. "I think he likes it because it reminds him of our mother. The town house was purchased after she was gone."

Listening, I released the cuff and took measure of her systolic pressure. "I'm surprised he hasn't tried to go back yet. Now that Mart—Mr. Verdeau is going to be gone for a few days."

Again Audrey smiled. "Maybe we should let him. What do you say, can you spare a weekend?"

"Me?"

"Well, of course. If Jonathan goes, Prosenko has to follow. Haven't you realized that by now?"

"I don't know," I said, slipping the cuff off and putting the stethoscope away. I had only just returned and had been sleeping in my own bed for a few days. Still, something in Audrey pleaded, and as I imagined Jonathan curled up in bed and deathly pale just above us, I found myself weak, and folded to her suggestion without protest.

We left for the manor house within the hour, but this time Audrey came along—luckily, with enough spare clothes in her suitcase so that I didn't need to worry about my own lack of preparedness. As odd as it seems, I was glad of it, really. The quickness of our return. For no sooner had the car pulled up to the imposing estate than the veil lifted from across Jonathan's face.

This, I realized, was his home. Unlike Audrey, who reflected the clean lines of the town house so well, Jonathan belonged to Arrow's Edge, to every dusty corner and to every page of the books within. It was during this trip that I at last began to wonder whether the parties were simply a small part of his affection for the home, an excuse to feel alive within its framing.

The longer I spent with Jonathan, the more perplexing his condition seemed. The numbness of his hands haunted my daydreams with their small twitches of a pianist's fingers. With each passing glimpse I caught of him, another strange and unexpected symptom appeared. A slurring of words once dismissed as a symptom of drunkenness soon gave way to greater suspicion.

It was my first time back in the home after Saint's Fog's release, something that should have mattered more to me on my drive up than it did. But as soon as I crossed the threshold again, the tinge of paranoia returned. In the short time we were away, the house had been cleaned, its rugs removed and floorboards waxed, but echoes of that night remained in my memory. The towering glasses and the sickening scent of champagne. The note of bitter herbs on their breath. The bile.

I realized I should have said no to Audrey's request, but I was weak to her more than anyone else. Especially now. The fear of coming back to the scene of my crime paled in comparison to the thought of disappointing her after what I'd done.

After checking in with Prosenko, I met her in the kitchen. She was fiddling with a cup of cold coffee, her eyes distant.

"How are you feeling?" I asked, stepping into the room.

She turned to me. "Fine, thanks to you."

The kitchen seemed larger than it had the weekend before. Without the extra staff and the rush of bottles and ovens hot with food, the space was cold and barren. I followed Audrey's gaze to a shelf in the back of the room.

"Do you know what those are?" she asked suddenly, realizing I was staring at the same beakers as she was. From the looks of it, they were antiques, the glass warped and burned at the bases. In the back were the remnants of distillation equipment. The kind people with quirky hobbies would pilfer from consignment stores just to look edgy. Or just the kind of stuff I tripped over all the time at Aunt Clare's.

I told her as much.

"They're Mother's," said Audrey, still staring at them. "She collected them. I thought he got rid of it all years ago."

I looked back to them with a new curiosity. "Your mom?"

Audrey nodded, and her hands tightened around the rim of her mug.

"When we were children, they were displayed all around the house. I used to make up stories about them with Jonathan. We would pretend our mother was a witch, away in her cottage brewing up medicines to save him." She looked down, smiling softly. "It's silly."

"What happened to her?"

Audrey looked to me, furrowing her brow. "No one told you?"

I shook my head. "Prosenko said not to bring it up."

"He would. . . . No, it's all right. She left us, that's all." Audrey paused. "Martin, rather."

News that their mother was still alive was arguably more shocking to me than any alternative.

"Left you? You mean, she didn't . . ."

"Die? No. She has a business back in Zurich that keeps her very busy. Which is just as well. I don't think she's set foot in the States since she left, to be honest. I really don't think she ever will. Not as long as he's here."

There was something odd about her tone. The reemergence of a disappointed young girl, but I didn't say a word.

"Do you know how to use it?" Audrey asked me suddenly. "That old equipment?"

"We had stuff like it in Umbria, but this is old. The glassware may be fine, but the tubes and valves are probably worn."

"Mm . . ." A sadness overtook her face.

"Why?"

"Nothing, it's just . . . looking at them now, I can't help but imagine using them to brew up something for Jonathan for real. A cure for melancholy. Or maybe to figure out what's in those stupid pills of his."

Her words caught me. "The pills? You mean his medicine? You don't know?"

"No, why would I?"

"I don't know, but . . . Prosenko's been your doctor forever, right? I thought surely you—"

"Prosenko only came around after the divorce began," she clarified sharply. "Him and his treatments." Her tone had become something darker. Something I dared not ask about. She turned to me again, deep, doll-like eyes meeting my own. "You don't know, do you? What's in them?"

"No. I never thought to ask, and he—"

"Doesn't tell you anything?" She rolled her eyes, and turned back away. "Yeah, I know how that goes."

For a while we both stood there in the emptiness of the kitchen. The chill from the large windows spread through the air.

"What's wrong with him?" I asked her at last.

"With Jonathan?" she said, attention snapping back. "A lot . . . nothing. I don't even know at this point."

I raised an eyebrow at her.

"He gets these . . . attacks," she went on. "He's always sick, but sometimes he passes out or forgets things. Sometimes he can't stand to walk or move and parts of him will go numb. That's why we have a doctor around all the time." She gave a soft, bitter laugh. "What, you thought it was just because he drank too much? I'm sure that's what my father believes."

I had nothing to say. She continued without needing an answer. She knew it already.

"Our mother left a few years after he was born. Martin became paranoid about Jonathan's health, but we were really young, so I don't remember much. Just that one day Prosenko was there and Jonathan was taking all this medicine. He was always sick as a child, same as now. Fine one day, bad the next. . . . I was shipped off to boarding school before long."

"Switzerland," I said, and she nodded.

"From the sounds of it, he was doing a bit better until he left for college. Then . . . well. You see him now."

I tried to imagine it. The Verdeau siblings, younger. A bright-eyed Jonathan shaking and scared on the steps where I'd first found him months earlier. The idea of sending Audrey off in the midst of it seemed cruel, and I struggled to wrap my head around it. As I pondered the family dynamics of two decades prior, she looked to me, eyes glassy with a sorrowful desperation.

"You really don't know what's in the pills?" she asked again.

I shook my head.

"Then . . . can I ask something of you?"

Anything, I wanted to tell her. *Anything if you keep looking at me like that.*

"Will you help me find out?"

13

WHILE THE POISON CONTINUED BREWING IN MY CLOSET, biding its time until the next party and paycheck, my mind found a new
obsession. Albeit a healthier one than the image of Martin Verdeau col-
lapsing on that throne of his in a sickly mess, face red enough to match
the velvet cushion.

Audrey's curiosity had quickly become contagious, and after agreeing
to help I soon found myself on a mission to get ahold of those pills and
find answers for not only her, which would have been enough, but myself
as well. I had never questioned what I was giving Jonathan, but once I
realized this error, no part of me could be satisfied until I knew.

The only problem was the fact that Prosenko watched me like a hawk
at every turn, and aside from the afternoon I found Jonathan in his bed,
I was never entrusted to give him his pills. The timing of his dose during
that week even changed, occurring earlier and earlier in the day, until it
happened that by the time I walked downstairs for brunch, Jonathan was
either already sick from the aftereffects or nowhere to be seen.

I knew where Prosenko kept them. Sort of. I knew the little cabinet he would open with a key to fetch the pills with a pair of physician's gloves, but there was no way into the cabinet. Besides, if I took them from the source, then he would most certainly know. The man knew his inventory with obsessive detail, and something as apparently prized as those pills were without question at the top of his mind.

In the days after the fateful conversation in the kitchen, I tried to be patient. I went through the motions as expected and monitored Jonathan with an even closer eye. Time after time Prosenko would have me grab multivitamins or fetch an ibuprofen when Jonathan complained, but never was I allowed close to the container with the small black pills.

It only made my suspicion grow.

Audrey had given me a mustard seed, but in the following days we remained trapped at Arrow's Edge, that small inkling of an idea grew and grew into something relentlessly larger.

Then, at last, it happened. As November arrived and another unplanned week at the estate began, I headed to the office only to find Prosenko missing, and, same as before, the tray was out.

I eyed the little cups. One of water, one of pills, and I waited.

Fifteen minutes passed, and there wasn't so much as a shuffle. The scent of Prosenko's herbaceous cologne was gone, and time was quickly getting away from me. The decent-employee part of my brain told me to take the tray and give the sick boy his medicine. The deviant part of me said to steal the pills and please his sister.

At thirty minutes past the doctor's usual time, I took up the tray at last, balancing the water, and wandered the halls of Arrow's Edge looking for Jonathan. Cautiously, I searched the usual hiding places only to come up short, and I began to wonder if Prosenko had taken him somewhere without my knowledge. A new attack, a hospital visit of some sort that had made him abandon the tray like that.

Finally I opted to find my way back to the kitchen for coffee through a back corridor of the servants' quarters. The hallways were walled off and small, used in the past so people such as me and Sascha didn't have to be seen or heard. Now they were just creepy shortcuts that Sascha liked to use to avoid running into George when he had an undesirable task for her to do. I thought I knew these passages well enough, but the more I walked, the more I realized that I was wrong.

Somehow I had taken a wrong turn, and as I opened the door to what should have been the back hallway to the kitchen, I found myself instead in the eastern wing.

The chill of the air hit me almost immediately as I entered the un-heated, uninsulated space. It was a time capsule of dilapidation. Not the sort with sunken floors or water damage, but eerie with disuse. Forgotten.

A few more steps and something else made me catch my breath.

"Lena!" Audrey gasped as we nearly crashed into each other. "What are you doing here?"

"How are *you* here?" I asked. "I've been looking all over for people. Everyone is gone. I thought Prosenko took Jonathan somewhere, and I was starting to think I'd been abandoned for a return to Boston."

Audrey frowned. "Oh, Lena, no! I mean, I did take the car and drive back last night for a meeting, but I think I saw Sascha heading into town with Daniella for groceries."

That all made sense. Still, I looked to Audrey, confused by our sur-roundings. "What are you doing here?" I said, motioning with my elbow to the darkened hallway around us.

"Oh, I was just"—she glanced at the tray—"looking for Jonathan. He wasn't in the usual spots, so I thought I'd wander back here and see if I could spot him. Clearly we had the same idea."

She eyed me closer, then my hand with the tray, and grabbed my arm to pull me toward her. "Lena, are those . . . ?" Nervously I moved the tray a bit away from her. An absent, work-minded motion. "Have you been able to . . . ?"

"Prosenko hasn't given me a chance."

"Then this is it! He won't miss them! It's perfect!"

"He'll still know, Audrey. I can't!"

"Lena," she said severely. "Please."

"I don't know."

She thought for a moment. Both our minds were focused on the same intention, but neither was willing to commit, not to mention the fact that we were coming at it from two very different perspectives. Her decades-long curiosity and my vulnerable and increasingly at-risk employment.

Something to my left creaked, heavy and metallic like iron, and I watched as Audrey's eyes brightened at the sound.

"What?"

"You haven't been here before, right?" she asked me.

"No, Prosenko said it was closed off for repairs."

"Follow me," she said with a mischievous air, grabbing my wrist again to pull me along with her.

After a few feet of running while trying to balance a tray of now-spilled water, I saw the eastern wing open to reveal the entrance to what appeared to be a large Victorian greenhouse.

Even with orange flecks of rust marring the white-painted iron details, it was stunning.

"What is this place?" I asked as we approached.

"It was our mother's favorite. I'm surprised Prosenko never mentioned it. We used to find him in here all the time as children."

As we entered, I was hit by the familiar scent of soil and musk. The slow decay of plant matter, the lingering moisture from years upon years of watering, and the unmistakable density of life. It was November, but inside, the air was sticky with warmth, and the shocking green of foliage framed Audrey as she stepped farther within.

"Prosenko?" I asked, trying hard to imagine the doctor loitering about in a place like this. It was beautiful and lush, the opposite of his pristine office space. After the shock wore off, my eyes at last began to take in the finer details, including the varietals that lingered along the glass wall.

It was a little more than a half circle, the greenhouse, and structured in such a way that it took over the corner of the eastern wing, allowing the rounded glass panels to look out upon the lawn. In the sunlight I could barely see it through the warped glass, the old and stately lawn with stone urns and steps that stretched down into smaller, manicured gardens and fruit trees. In the cooler temperatures, the lawn beyond the greenhouse had lost its brilliance. Inside, however, everything was still bright and standing proud.

"You said you worked in a garden, right?" Audrey asked, turning on the edge of her heel to face me. Realizing how close our bodies had become, she took a step back. "Do you know any of these plants?"

Her hand motioned to the row of green beside her. A series of large shrubs and overgrown plantings. There were no plaques.

"Let me see," I told her, stepping closer to the plants. I set the tray cautiously down beside me. "Well, this one is just an azalea," I said, kneeling. "It's been trimmed back, and the flowers are mostly dead, but it's just a flowering bush. Pretty common. Our neighbor had one when I was a kid."

She looked disappointed.

"B-but the blue that's here means the soil is acidic," I said, hoping to be of some better entertainment. "They change color based on the pH. Some people will even add rusty nails and coffee to the soil if they don't want the flowers to be pink."

Audrey smiled. "Interesting, but personally I think they'd be better pink. Is there a way to change it back?"

I shrugged. "You can make the soil more alkaline?"

She pondered for a moment and fondly felt one of the leaves. "Hmm. What else?" she asked, then looked around and pointed to another cluster, this time of ferns. "What about those?"

A smile formed on my face. "I don't know. The bigger one might be cinnamon fern. Or a royal fern, but I really don't—"

She didn't listen. Her golden hair moved about her face as her eyes darted to find more things to ask about. She didn't care that I'd been trained in Italian plants and medicinal herbs, not the average fare of a conservatory meant to be beautiful.

We wandered the garden, eyeing the various plants on display. Audrey would point and ask me a question, and I would rifle through my mental catalog from Aunt Clare and take my best guess. There was lily of the valley, delicate and small, and some Queen Anne's lace in the far corner. Most of the greenhouse consisted of common plants on display, overgrown and lush despite the approaching winter. It wasn't until we followed the path to its end that a small white patio set came into view— and with it Jonathan.

Audrey stopped, and as the sound of her clicking heels ceased, he looked up.

"Was wondering how long it'd take you," he said, returning his attention to his book. It was a different one from the one I'd seen him clinging to the day before. This one was old and bound in leather, its edges worn away to reveal the binding.

"Have you been hiding here this whole time?" Audrey asked sharply.

"Here? Yes. Hiding? No." The ease of the past few minutes gave way to a near-palpable tension. Jonathan looked to me. "You know a lot about plants."

Nervous, I swallowed. "A bit."

He closed his book. "That sure sounded like more than a bit. Wouldn't you say, Audrey dear?"

Were she a bird, her feathers would have ruffled. "Yes, she's quite smart."

The compliment would have been nicer had it not come as the product of sibling rivalry.

"Where was it you worked, again?" Jonathan asked, but instead Audrey answered before I had the chance.

"Italy. Umbria."

Jonathan smiled soft and wicked. "Ah, right," he drawled out. "Now, how's that go, again? . . . '*Sotto la cura di Santa Chiara*,' no?"

His pronunciation was off. Slurred. It didn't change the fact I'd heard worse from fourth-year students in college. The fact that he spoke some Italian at all was shocking. Then again, I knew the sorts of Romantic books he read.

"If you met my aunt, you wouldn't think her work very saintly," I quipped in an attempt to not seem surprised.

"Mm," said Jonathan, reaching for a bottle of wine on the table beside him. "Good company, then."

Audrey frowned, watching as he poured a glass of pinot grigio. "You're so annoying."

The bottle hit the table, heavy but substantially lighter than before.

"Don't you have a hair appointment to get to or something?" Jonathan said, turning cold once more.

"Business, actually," said Audrey, straightening her back as she dealt a death glare to her brother. "Someone has to answer Martin's calls today."

"Too bad it's such a disappointment when *you* do it."

"You know what," said Audrey, turning her attention back to me. "Give him the pills. I don't care. Let him suffer on a stomach full of acid." She looked at him again. "Maybe his *face* will turn blue."

Sharply, Audrey took her leave, abandoning me in the greenhouse with Jonathan Verdeau a mere two feet away, a prince to be waited on.

In that setting, with his dark hair, heavy brows, and sickly pallor, Jonathan looked the part of his bygone heroes. Someone trapped in time and in an apparent state of madness and perpetual melancholy.

"So," he said loudly once the metal of the door had slammed shut and

Audrey was safely gone. I watched as he took a sip from his glass, and every bit of him relaxed and returned to a more jovial, mischievous state. "Do you need something?"

"It's time for your meds," I told him, walking over and at last putting down the small metal tray.

The mask of humor fell from Jonathan's face almost instantly.

Slowly, and with a groan, he sat up straighter, slamming his book shut from where it had been held open absently with his free hand. It allowed me to read the spine. As much of it as I could see anyway.

"*Edward II*? Another Marlowe?"

"What do you care what I read?"

"I don't," I said quickly.

Jonathan merely hummed and then waved his newly empty hand. "Just . . . get it over with. Check my pulse. Be disappointed or whatever it is you do."

Lacking my usual equipment, I had nothing to take his stats with but my hands. The only things I'd managed to bring with me were the tray with the little cup of pills, a now-spilled cup of water, and paper to record the time.

I stepped closer and motioned for his wrist. Miraculously, he gave it to me.

"It's a terrible play," he said. "Marlowe only writes terrible things."

I tried to count the beats but could focus only on the feeling of his sinew under my fingertips. How easily my fingers wrapped around the bones of his wrist. "Then why read it?"

"Terrible things are always the most honest," he said. "Shakespeare, he took what Marlowe wrote and made it sweet. Did you know that? He didn't just copy it all. He . . . he *dulled* it."

"I wouldn't call Shakespeare's work sweet," I told him, at last letting go. "Or a copy."

"They're *nice*. Marlowe's work always shows people at their worst."

"Anyone ever tell you you're a bit of a pessimist?"

Jonathan paused and stared at me as I scribbled down notes. "Hey, what's my pulse today?"

"Terrible," I told him. "But you've clearly been drinking this morning, so I can't be surprised."

He went quiet again. Long enough for me to test his circulation with a press to the fingertips. I watched as the purple flesh beneath his nails paled into something white, and then pink, then red.

"Why's it bother you?"

"What?"

"My drinking," he said. "I know Audrey hates it, but you're new. No one else here cares."

"You're really asking me this?"

"Yeah. It's not your problem."

"Because I'm hired to help you," I told him. "And I feel like one of these days I'm going to walk into a room and find you dead."

It was too much, and I knew it. The words flew out of my mouth too fast to catch them, but Jonathan sat there, examination done, his wineglass forgotten.

"It won't be the booze that does that."

He eyed me for a moment, a too-long one, and then his gaze slowly dropped from my lips to my chin, then lingered just above my chest.

"You're Catholic," Jonathan said, focusing on the small golden crucifix hanging around my neck. A gift from my aunt that I never took off but often forgot I had on.

"So?"

"You're young."

I turned away from him to busy myself. Pretending to take more notes. "I'm Italian, remember?"

"Yeah, but your name's Irish."

"And my grandma's Brazilian. What's it matter?"

"How Catholic are you?"

"What's that supposed to mean?"

The book caught his attention once more. A flicker of a motion. "Do you buy into it? Confession and all that. Sinning and such. This is Sunday, and you're here."

I frowned. I hadn't realized it was Sunday, but he was right. "I'm working."

"Still a sin, though."

"I guess."

Jonathan thought for a moment, eyeing the crucifix again. "They say . . . the reward of sin is death. Do you say that?"

It was a strange question, but a quote I nonetheless knew, even if the topic broke a standard code of conduct for employer-employee relations. Despite that, I realized this was the longest conversation I'd ever had with Jonathan Verdeau. I also realized that with all the talking, and Audrey gone, his wineglass remained untouched. His eyes, too, were a bit more alert.

"I think if we say we have no sin, we deceive ourselves and there is no truth in us."

It took only a moment, a millisecond as the words left my mouth, and something in Jonathan brightened. "Then how about this—" he started.

"*Che sera, sera?*"

His expression was more joyous than a child's at Christmas. A startling switch had occurred. Progress, I thought. A breakthrough.

"That," he said, "is *Faustus*. So you *do* know Marlowe."

A small, pleased smile threatened my lips. "This last semester in Italy, my aunt had a few Ph.D. students visiting. They were mildly obsessed. Strange group."

"But you haven't read Marlowe yourself?"

"Oh, I had to in high school. When we studied Shakespeare."

"But not for fun."

"Why would anyone read Marlowe for fun?"

"Because he's brilliant!"

His sudden excitement was enough to make me laugh. I had never seen such a smile on his face. Not a true one. Not a happy one. In the space of the garden's greenery, it was beautiful. Striking.

"Is Marlowe all you read?"

"Of course not," said Jonathan, affronted.

"Then who else?" I asked him as I recorded another note about his complexion and then reached to pick up the little cup. A motion more out of habit than anything else. A follow-through of steps. He'd been watching me, though, my hands as they moved, and when our eyes met again, Jonathan stopped and the air about him fell.

"Something wrong?" I asked.

His face paled, more than usual, and I watched as he swallowed thickly and saliva gathered on his lips. He was going to be sick.

Hastily, I moved the papers and tray of pills out from under him, just before Jonathan grabbed a cloth napkin from his table and covered his mouth. I watched as he bent over, away from me, and imagined the cloth stained a rancid green blend of bile and pinot grigio.

His eyes focused on the cup in my hand.

"Please . . ." he practically begged. "Not today."

I looked around for water but found nothing except the wine.

"What happened?" I asked, abandoning the cup back onto the tray. "Have you been nauseous this whole time?"

Jonathan coughed into the napkin. I waited as he coughed and retched, his entire body trembling with some horrible sickness that had yet to be given a name. I stood there silent as he crumpled the fabric into his fist and threw it to the ground.

"I always am," he said, voice thick. "Among other things."

"Nauseous?" I asked. "Then why do you keep drink—"

"Don't start," said Jonathan weakly. "Some pains are better than others."

My eyes fell onto the pills, and at last I broke my resolve. "Okay," I told him, a scheme forming. "Not today."

"What?" he asked.

I watched his bewilderment as I shifted my position and took the two small black pills in my fist and walked over to the plants a few feet away.

"Wait, what are you doing?" he asked, eyeing me as I knelt down and shoved my hands into the dirt.

"Not today."

14

WHEN I BURIED THE PILLS, I did so with a plan to go and get them back, but on the following morning, as I snuck my way through the dusty, darkened halls of the eastern wing and dug my hands into the moistened soil beneath a dying sprig of foxglove, they came upon nothing. The pea-size pills had disintegrated, disappearing into the roots and earth, relegated to fertilizer and therefore useless to Audrey and myself.

It was disappointing, but there were more pressing matters.

That week Martin returned from his trip and immediately announced another party. We knew it was coming, but the timing came a week earlier than anticipated, catching the whole staff off guard. We were all expected to remain at Arrow's Edge until after it had occurred, which would have ruined any attempts to poison Martin had it not been for his own new involvement in the matter.

He permitted me to drive back to Roslindale for a night, with the expectation that I would also take care of some of George's errands on my return. So I hastily returned to my closet that afternoon for a much-needed reprieve from the Berkshires and an odd and unwelcome return to what should have felt more like home.

After my two weeks away, the household felt just as foreign as it had that first night I returned from Italy. I had barely spoken to Rumi and Anna in weeks, not since the last party, and I had ignored their texts for one too many days without meaning to. I couldn't help that a text would come just as Prosenko shouted my name or as I was exhausted from the day, too tired to talk. Half of me debated calling them for dinner. The other half knew I had a lot of work to do and that they likely would not have picked up if I bothered. My heart couldn't take the risk of knowing.

Over three-fourths of the batch from the Saint's Fog brew remained. It was more than enough for another party. A mason jar that now, thanks to an absurd demand, was worth thousands of dollars. The idea was still laughable to me.

I tried to will myself to prepare it, slipping on the protective gloves and fetching the same small dropper from less than a month prior, but the fire was gone. My anger, whatever bit that had been left to fester since that first party, had lessened in my distractions. In its place had arisen a new and unwelcome sort of sympathy for Jonathan Verdeau. A guilt from ever thinking that all his ills and woes were attributed to hedonism rather than a sickness that I saw the symptoms of but in those flashes of anger was once willing to ignore. Something like a self-hatred that had even Audrey worried, despite his cruelty to her a few days before. Or any day for that matter.

Then there was Audrey herself.

Too easily could I recall holding her hair away from her sweaty brow as she shook, trembling in my arms. How she smiled at me that night, her cheeks warm and pink.

I put the jar back into the closet and sat on the floor of my room with legs splayed, taking in the scent of dried roots and bitter herbs. I looked back at the Saint's Fog. The original.

The dust that had once covered the leaves had given way to a kind of mold. A gray, fluffy sort of film that clung to the tops of the leaves. I had waited for the plant to die, thinking surely it was doomed from its stay at customs, but it had not.

I looked back to the little jar and the dropper in my hand and cursed myself.

Despite my intentions, despite the anger, I hated what I'd done and hated worse that Martin had paid me and would pay me again. The money was nice, but I just kept thinking of Audrey. Of Jonathan, in bed, sick for a week while Martin got off scot-free. I thought of everyone else I had poisoned. The people who were just invited, and out of place, and had finished their night shaking and scared—and I thought of my parents. Of what would have happened if they'd been there and been unlucky enough to take a glass from the top.

Tipping the dropper over, I drained out half the poison and replaced it with water from the tap.

With a trunk full of champagne and a purse full of (weakened) Saint's Fog, and yet another dress and heels and spare clothes just in case, I drove back to Arrow's Edge in record time. The party was set for Friday as usual, and so with my return that Wednesday afternoon I still had to prepare.

Audrey, meanwhile, had other things on her mind.

Now that her curiosity was out, her insistence about the pills never faltered, and the moment she caught sight of me again, I had the unfortunate experience of having to explain what had happened in the greenhouse that morning I went to retrieve them. Still she did not let up.

"Fine. I'm going to Boston until the party," she told me, voice curt. "Keep trying."

"Why the hurry?" I asked with an armful of champagne halfway up the main steps.

"There isn't one."

Yet everything about her said otherwise, and so after unloading the car and doing my part of the setup, I returned to do my job with Prosenko distracted and useless for it. Frustrated, Prosenko banished me from the office and assigned a series of chores that had so little to do with the medical aspect of my job that despite all reasoning a creeping paranoia began to build. Did he know? Had Jonathan said something? Had Jonathan seemed too sick? Too happy? That night I barely slept. I needed to, with the party drawing near, but I couldn't, and the next day wasn't much better.

Protests echoed from outside Jonathan's room on the second floor, its mahogany doors failing to mute Prosenko's familiar voice and the crash of a metal tray onto the floor.

The door slammed heavily behind Prosenko.

"Don't just stand there," he said, storming past me and down the stairs. "Grab his pulse when he stops acting like a child and bring the tray back to my office!"

For too long I stared at the carving on Jonathan's door. The shape of the paneling, the diamonds and leaves that made up its border. Even something so beautiful couldn't hide a rough scene like that. Or any of the others I'd been witness to the past few weeks. I could feel him wrestling in the shadows. A fit of discomfort and agony as Jonathan waited for the nausea to hit him.

I waited for it, too.

At least five minutes passed with nothing to signal it was safe.

"Gereghty!" Prosenko shouted from downstairs, and hastily I opened the door.

In the darkness Jonathan sat, spine bare against the pillows as he held his face in his knees. Same as the last time I'd entered his room, there was no light to be found anywhere, except for where it peeked in through his curtains and the hallway behind me.

I saw the metal tray, upside down and in the corner.

"Bastard," Jonathan mumbled weakly.

"Are you . . . okay?"

He turned to me, eyes sharp and bloodshot. "What the fuck do you think?"

"Did you—"

"Take them? Yeah."

I forced myself to remember the smile from the garden. The sympathy as it battled against the old, rising resentment.

"I told him I didn't want to!" he shouted, then shoved his face back into his knees, knuckles white as he gripped the fabric, making fists. "The party's tomorrow, and—"

The party. Of course, that was still on his mind.

"Is it really so much better without them?"

A long moment passed where I stood silent in the darkness of that room. Surrounded by the smell of sweat and rancid breath. Then, "It was."

Were it not for the fact that Audrey seemed convinced the pills were nothing good for her brother, I would not have entertained the idea at all. You don't mess with medications. You don't mess with the dose. You don't even skip a dose. It can be the very difference between life and death. A heart attack or a functioning brain. Without knowing what was in the pills, I couldn't know what I'd denied Jonathan before. Still, the fact that I had done so and he was still here, begging me again in his own way, told me maybe it wasn't so serious.

"If you skipped them in the morning . . . do you think you'd be okay until the evening?"

I hated suggesting it. My tongue felt cursed by the words as they fell, but I would be lying if I said I didn't see another benefit.

His eyes widened.

"Yes," Jonathan said, hopeful, then, "How?"

I picked up the tray from the floor. "If you convince Prosenko to let me give them to you. Instead of him."

"Really?"

I nodded. "He'll listen to you."

"Tch." He pressed his face back into his knees, but I persisted.

"Otherwise you fight again tomorrow."

Jonathan eyed me suspiciously. "Why would you help?"

"How did you feel after the greenhouse?" I asked him, and the look in his eyes showed he understood. "Drink some water," I said, stepping out the door with tray in hand.

The door creaked.

"Wait!" he called. "What about my pulse?"

"Same as always," I told him. "Shit."

He gave a small laugh. The barest hint of a smile, and the rare beauty of it was enough to convince me this was worth it.

It would have to be.

THE MORNING OF THE PARTY CAME, and with it another series of shouts behind closed wooden doors. I was midway through my morning coffee with Sascha when Prosenko wandered in with a wearier look on his face than normal. He was quick to cut to the chase.

"The tray is waiting on my desk," he said. "Jonathan has . . . apparently taken a shine to you. . . . The task is yours today, and for however long it takes this fit of his to pass. Just make sure he takes them."

Sascha looked to me, her eyebrows arched in curiosity just above the rim of her mug.

It took every ounce of me not to smile.

With the little cup of pills in hand, I walked to the library, where

Jonathan chose to linger that day, slumped in a velvet chair and reading a copy of *Faustus*. He grinned as he shouted his usual string of protests for good measure and was grinning still as he saw me crumple the paper cup and shove it behind one of the many books on the library shelves for later.

"Hey, do you know what they are?" I asked softly after a moment.

"What are?"

My eyes motioned to the newly hidden cup.

His lips curved up. "All I know is that they're custom. Herbs and stuff the big man formulated himself."

"Does he make them? Prosenko, I mean." A thought turned over in my head, but at the time I couldn't grasp it. Just enough to ask the question.

Jonathan simply shrugged. "I think a company we own makes them."

"Oh."

"So you're telling me you're a doctor and you don't know?"

"I'm not a doctor."

"Mm." Something in him looked clearer, and I noticed that for once his glass contained not wine but rather water.

"How do you feel?"

"Terrible as always, but with the distinct impression I'll be feeling better thanks to you."

Jonathan eyed me closely then, his hazel eyes narrowing with an expression that made my skin warm uncomfortably and sent a shiver down to my feet. I didn't dare think about what it meant.

"I shouldn't be doing this for you, you know. Like I said, I'm not a doctor. It's dangerous."

"Mm, maybe you're not a doctor *officially*, but official things are boring." As if to make his point, Jonathan stretched his arms up and gave a yawn, large and dramatic. Despite his jokes he did seem better. Alert . . . more human. Though I didn't know whether to attribute it to the water or the lack of pills.

"Boring is safe," I told him.

"It's unfulfilling. Hardly sustainable," he said, letting me watch, *knowing* that I was watching, as his spine settled back into the cushion. "What nourishes me destroys me."

"That," I told him, at last averting my gaze, "is because you choose to nourish yourself with wine and narcotics."

"Grapes are fruit," he said with a wave of his hand. "Liquid, but fruit nonetheless."

"With that logic opium is a bouquet in disguise."

Jonathan smiled devilishly. "Isn't it, though?"

"You're hopeless. And you read too much Marlowe."

"Well, he was hopeless, too. Like a brother from another mother."

"God, do people still say that?"

"Dylan insists the phrase merely went into hiding and is coming back for revenge."

"He better be wrong."

"Oh, Gereghty, Dylan's wrong about a lot of things, but for better or worse the man understands society in ways my father only wishes I were capable of."

"Audrey seems to get by just fine."

"That," he said poignantly, "is because Audrey is a wolf who looks better in wool than most sheep."

Even given his jovial attitude at the possibility of a day without nausea, his distaste for Audrey lingered, and it surprised me. If only he knew, I thought. If only he knew how much she cared. He wouldn't be saying those things.

"What's the deal between you two?" I asked him.

Jonathan rolled his eyes "Where to begin?"

"Some days you like her and some days you don't."

"Oh, I like Audrey just fine, Gereghty. I just don't trust her, is all."

"Why not?"

A frown appeared on his face as Jonathan took a moment to think of his reply.

"Well, you've met her."

I nodded. I had more than just met her.

"Then you know."

"That's hardly an answer."

"She's just wicked!"

"Wicked!" I said, fighting back a small, absurd laugh. "She's your sister, and she brings George frappés on her way back from Newbury!"

"And she's devilish about it! George only likes drip. Black. Darker than his nights back in 'Nam."

"Jonathan . . . really?"

"You'll see, Gereghty," he told me. "She's a witch. Always has been. It's in her nature, the way she's always going behind my back to do stuff at Avelux. How she's got folks wrapped around her finger. I know they all prefer her."

"Jonathan, come on. That's not fair. You don't even try to answer the calls. I've seen you."

"That's not the point!"

"Then what is?" I asked him.

He went quiet. A shadow of genuine emotion coming over him. Sullen and rare. "I just . . . don't get why it has to be like this. Why she doesn't understand that the company isn't that great."

"What do you mean?"

He ignored the question. "If I answer the calls, she's mad. If I don't, she's still mad. I can't win with her . . . and I just . . ."

"What? You just what, Jonathan?"

He shook his head. "Nothing."

I could tell that something was on the tip of his tongue, but I didn't know what I could say to draw it out of him.

"Well, Prosenko's going to be expecting something," I reminded him, coming back to myself and focusing on the pills again "And drink that water and a few more glasses of it before the party. Do your kidneys some kindness."

"Noted, Doc."

With that, I memorized the book I'd hidden the pills behind with one last glance to the shelves and then left with a reminder for Jonathan to run to the bathroom in five minutes.

He made a show of it.

15

I DIDN'T SEE AUDREY AGAIN until the party. As she'd said, she remained in Boston until the lights dimmed and the bash had already begun. It didn't matter in the long run. As much as I wanted to hand the pills off to her, the party took priority. Arrow's Edge demanded it.

It wasn't until the final round of checks during setup that I snuck back to the library and retrieved the pills, placing them in a small plastic bag and tucking them hastily into my dress. With my zeal for making Martin suffer temporarily replaced by both his patronage and the knowledge that the worst of the poisons within the Saint's Fog had been reduced to near nothing, the party, when it arrived, seemed mechanical. That night the music blared, same as before, with crowds filtering in from their rented limos and Rolls-Royces in the same obnoxious display of wealth that had once made my blood boil. I watched as the fabric of the women's dresses glittered and how necklines plunged deeper between breasts than I thought dresses were capable of without falling open. Everywhere I looked, something glistened, and in its shadow something more sinister put a smile on eager mouths. It reminded me why I'd done what I did—and also just how far I'd come.

By that third party, I had learned the faces of the most prominent attendees. In the gallery I passed Albert Reicher, an old friend of Martin's who Sascha told me had also worked in manufacturing and production in a very hands-off way. He had an investment portfolio worth billions and a house in Malibu he stayed at with his fourth wife and her sister. In tow behind him was Bill Acton, a silver-haired forty-something and short seller who had been the bane of Albert's business until he caused the competition to fold, turning a tidy profit of $5.2 million in the process. Judging from their faces, another scheme was in the works. Bill winked at me, and I took my leave to move into a side hall.

There were faces I only knew existed because of the hoarded cutouts Anna once taped to her walls back in high school. Former models turned trophy wives with Botox to battle their aging faces and others with fillers to look a few years younger. Even with close to three months under Martin's employment, I didn't understand the constant emphasis on upkeep and image, when all they seemed to do with it was drink, and snort, and dance until it didn't matter. There had to be more, I thought, more people who didn't buy into the rampant debauchery and delight that so powerfully reeked of desperation for approval.

An hour into the party, my old disgust had bubbled up, only this time it was softened with a strange and unwelcome sense of pity.

I found Jonathan. Accidentally. His thin fingers, shockingly pale in contrast to the darkness of the music room. His face was obscured by a head of cascading blond hair and another girl, vying for attention and failing. It wasn't an uncommon sight, Jonathan surrounded by strangers in adoration of him. At the first party, I had wondered if it was because of his notoriety—the fame of his father and his own reputation as an heir without a care. But that night as I looked on, and looked away, I wondered instead whether he had drunk enough wine to mask the bitter memory of those pills. What his tongue was like, now a day free from the constant taste of bile, and if those girls could taste the same saccharine scent of rancid disease that I met daily in the hidden rooms of this very house.

Did they know how weak he was? Probably not, and because they didn't, an ache arose in my stomach the more I watched. I didn't trust them to handle him gently enough. I didn't trust *him* to handle himself kindly.

Hidden in the shadows, I stuck to my role, eyeing instead the crowds as they filtered in and out through the portal of the music room. I watched as Elliot waited, quiet in the corner with his hand twirling a glass of scotch, keeping distant from the women. Instead his eyes remained drawn to every flicker of emotion on Jonathan's face. Every smirk. Every frown. Nothing seemed to pass without Elliot's knowledge, and so of course as I stood there, he noticed me, and his eyes turned soft in a way that, had I known any better, I would have called pity.

Beside him Dylan drained the last of a vodka bottle and used it to smack the ass of an unsuspecting woman passing by just as Brodie took a picture, and together they burst into a fit of laughter. A familiar hatred seethed at the sight, and I remembered the eyedropper under my sleeve.

Back in the kitchen and with twenty minutes until the eleventh hour, I was met by George. Behind him the champagne bottles stood in a row, same as before, lined up and forgotten amid the frantic shuffle for more small bites of finger food.

"Miss Gereghty! What are you doing back here?" George asked sharply.

"I . . ."

He raised an eyebrow. "Does Mr. Verdeau need something?"

An idea flashed. "Yeah, yeah, he says he needs more scotch. Or whiskey? I'm not sure. He held the bottle up."

George looked perturbed. "What was the label like?"

"Um, silver? It had a crest. Maybe some deer?"

I waited quietly as George racked his brain for stock similar to whatever I'd made up. "Ah, I think I know the one. It's in the cellar. I'll go fetch it," he said, and started out the door. "Thank you."

I nodded.

Suddenly the room was empty and the little dropper was out, cap off, with my fingers squeezing for the first of many drops as my hand moved from bottle to bottle with increasing skill. Because of the dilution, I didn't worry so much about the exact amount. Any series of drops would suffice, but I aimed for three. So the liquid flowed, into one bottle, then two, then ten, until, as the music blared and the walls trembled, the last of the bottles received their dose.

I had only just managed to tuck the dropper back under my sleeve when Prosenko rushed by the door with a patient and Sascha and Daniella ran in with sweat on their brows and red in their cheeks.

"Lena!" Sascha shouted. "Are you able to help again tonight?"

She arranged a tray of lobster rolls while Daniella shuffled behind her with a hot pan, fresh from the oven.

I ducked out of Daniella's way.

"The bottles are all opened," Sascha continued. "Maybe you can go ahead and bring one to Martin? I heard he wanted his own bottle from this batch along with the Clicquot."

I stopped. "Why?"

She shrugged. "Dunno."

With an increased rhythm pounding in my heart, I agreed and grabbed the neck of one of the opened bottles. I then made my way out the side entrance and into the crowd of the party.

There had to be a reason, I thought, that Martin would have asked for his own bottle. Did he expect something to go wrong? Was the request nothing but a ploy to catch me red-handed?

As I wove through the myriad of people, choking on the unholy blend of designer and drugstore perfume, I tried to think as Martin would. Whether there was some ulterior motive I couldn't see, something beyond a madman's request to drug his entire party without their consent. In every hand I passed, there was some glass filled to the brim with liquid, and unconsciously the image flashed. That of the drops, oil-slicked and hovering silently in the champagne without their knowledge.

It hit me just before the busy hallway opened into Martin's realm. The request wasn't one that arose of suspicion but rather selfishness. He wanted his own supply of the drug that he'd paid for his subjects to receive.

And I had lowered the dose.

Hastily I turned my back to the crowd to slip a few more drops into the bottle, just as a couple shoved me as they laughed, running in seconds before the show began. In the brush I nearly dropped everything, struggling to maintain my delicate, nervous hold through sweaty fingers. I managed to save it, but in my desperation the squeeze of my fingers pressed too hard, rendering double or triple the intended dosage of everyone else. Possibly even more.

I wondered if it was too much. If it would be the dose that did him in at last. A fateful mistake to take me back to how this all started. If this could be the dose to have him flat on the floor through some holy intervention. I had no way to know.

The flow of the crowd ushered me into the ballroom, and almost immediately Martin caught my eye. He looked at me, aging eyes focused on my form from across the room while his mouth continued its discussions with a balding man in a pinstripe suit. I watched as he smiled and motioned with his hand.

The heels of my shoes had only just landed among the inner circle of men when the music died and the flashing lights ceased. There, holding the opened bottle, I stood frozen beside Martin Verdeau and his ilk, helpless and undeniably at the center of it all. I could feel my heartbeat in my throat. A nervous, panicked pounding so loud it drowned out everything else.

The speeches for the tower's toast began a few yards away, and Martin reached for the bottle. I handed it over, earning a wink in return.

A spotlight glared, cast on Martin as he stood and raised the bottle high into the air with a grin and a shout to signal the start of it all. He raised it with a motion toward the star for that night, Bill Acton, and concluded the toast with his wrinkle-lined lips clasped firmly around the bottle's rim.

My face felt hot from the light, and I wanted desperately to run away. To hide before the chaos began and anyone could look and say, *There she is, that* bitch.

She handed it off to him. She's to blame.

The champagne poured, and my legs began to tremble, but as my eyes wandered, the only gazes I received were from those around me. Around Martin.

I tried to study their faces to see a semblance of suspicion. Instead I saw nothing but a leer at my dress and lasciviously curved lips at the light shining on any bit of exposed skin. Martin eagerly poured the bottle's contents out into his glass and swallowed it down, and then one by one the other men offered up their own. Being without a glass, and nowhere near a friend, I assumed it would pass over me. I prayed it would, thinking of the dose. Then it stopped, and upon realizing that my hands were empty, suddenly the men were shifting wildly and offering me their own.

"Aww, c'mon, boys," Martin boomed with a slurred and alcohol-graveled voice. "Give'r a break. Be kind! She's working tonight."

A man, the same one I'd seen in the striped suit before, leaned in close. "That's all right, so are we," he said with a wink.

I tried to shift away.

"Todd," Martin warned, "show some mercy, will ya? She is after all the reason your ass didn't end up in the emergency room at Hillcrest."

The man looked at me, close enough so that I could see the red in his eyes as they widened. "Well, damn. You mean this bit of yours saved me from missing that deal in Qatar?" His hand landed heavy on my shoulder before giving a loud, self-amused "Hah!"

All around me the other men laughed, shaking one another's shoulders as they fell easily back into their old conversation. A clamoring of voices, excitedly and sloppily overpowering one another. Grateful to have their eyes off me, I stepped away to take my leave.

Just before I could turn my back, Martin's eye caught my own, and again I watched as a grin grew across his face. Slow and menacing. Or rather not menacing but . . . a motion that made my skin feel dirty.

And I realized it at last. Something that had evaded me in all the seconds prior. When my body shook with fear and unease, even as I stood there being welcomed in by this disgusting group of men.

I was no longer a fly on the wall, no longer a peasant in a foreign king's court.

No. I had been adopted. Absorbed into their circle and their games at some point over the past few hours. Days. Weeks. I was just the last to know.

It made my stomach turn.

It also straightened my back.

Armed with this revelation, I wandered through the pulsating rooms with confidence shrouding me like armor. All around were people with coupe glasses in their hands, and these I knew were sticky with the diluted drops of Saint's Fog. I passed through the gallery and beyond the library, with every room the same, every manicured hand holding a cocktail of my own making. At the sight a dark part of me delighted in it, that same part from the previous party when I first saw the crowd begin to fall. It wasn't nice, and the emotion felt like an ill-fitting suit, but still, as I paced the darkened halls, I resigned myself to it over any guilt that might have lingered. I had become the arcane magician in the court of a king. Then Jonathan Verdeau stumbled past me in the crowd, face pale, and too easily my eyes found a coupe glass in his hand, and all that power slipped away.

Like an anchor tethered, my emotions sank. Plummeted into a dark space just as quickly as they'd risen from it. I could practically feel Audrey in my arms again, her warm skin against me, so clearly ill. Now I feared the same for Jonathan. Despite everything, his health hadn't been good leading up to the party. Even worse, I'd neglected to give him his medication, and for all the good it might have done to allow him a night away from the nausea and pain, I didn't know for sure the effect it would have. I lingered there, pausing in my journey back to Prosenko, and waited, watching.

Much like his father, Jonathan never strayed far from his inner circle when a party was afoot. Wherever I found him, that whelk of a human being Dylan Westerly was never far behind, and so I watched as Jonathan, egged on by Dylan, raised the rim of the glass to his pallid lips and swallowed.

I yearned to reach out and rip the glass away. To see it shatter on the floor into a thousand pieces. Instead, before my hands could move beyond an impulsive twitch, Dylan grasped the glass and downed the remainder of the liquid in one fell swoop.

His long and skinny face was sweaty and red. Eyes bloodshot and breath stronger with the scent of alcohol than an overturned shelf at the bar. If anyone deserved the Saint's Fog, it was him. I'd seen enough at the previous parties to know that he supplied half the drugs there. If he wasn't around Jonathan, he was handing over baggies of powder and stuffing hundred-dollar bills into his pocket or slipping pills one after the other and chasing them down like a teenager at a rave. So as he drank his fill of the poisoned champagne, that wave of guilt that had arisen within me at the sight of Jonathan sharply faded.

I was not naïve. I knew I had a growing concern for the siblings that I didn't want to admit. One that crept in on the nights when I lay alone in my bed and wondered if Jonathan was finally getting some rest, or if Audrey was sneaking into the kitchen for a late-night cup of coffee. I knew it because of how easily and how often I could picture Jonathan's eyes poring over another set of antique text, lost in thought, his mouth relaxed, or Audrey's lips on the edge of the cup, her fingers clasped around the porcelain as steam rose to kiss her cheek.

But another part of me could not deny that I liked this new power that came with the Saint's Fog. The power of knowing something they didn't. Of being able to curse or cure people like Dylan or Brodie if I wanted to. Sure enough, as I waited there a few minutes longer, Dylan and others began to show the signs of having one too many glasses stolen from the prized bottle at Martin's side. Their smiles turned to panic, and their skin turned a sickly green as they reached for phantasmal horrors.

It had begun.

Elliot looked to me, the closest one to sober in the room, with worried brows.

"Do you know what's wrong?" he asked.

Yes, but I didn't say so. Instead I took up my role and reached for Brodie's arm as Elliot swung Dylan's around his shoulder in an effort to help. Almost instantly Dylan pulled back, flinging his hand in a weak punch at Elliot as he shouted an F-slur I'd heard too many times in high school and that Anna, Rumi, and I knew too well. A word that made me wince, then well up with rage as I watched Dylan stumble away. Elliot's eyes mirrored my own, but before I could say something, he ran off into the shadows.

Alone in the crowd, I did my job and dragged Brodie as best I could toward Prosenko's clinic and only just made it before my own muscles tired from the effort of keeping him upright.

"Dylan's back in the music room!" I shouted to Prosenko as Brodie collapsed into one of the chairs. "Can you get him?"

Prosenko eyed me and then Brodie's pathetic form as he began to shake. He sighed, a quick "For fuck's sake" beneath his breath, before rushing out with a barf bag in hand and years of experience.

"Give him the standard treatment and put him in the back with the others. It's the same crap as last time."

I did so, easing into the job while surveying the room. All around me I saw the familiar symptoms of the Saint's Fog. The ruddy faces and sweat-soaked oxford shirts, the blown-out pupils and dazed, panicked expressions. Unlike at the previous party, the faces held within the room that night belonged not to unsuspecting victims and unfortunate women on the arms of billionaires but rather to the top tier. To those in Martin's circle.

I saw economic advisers and portfolio managers, and there, in the corner of the room, I saw the familiar silver hair of Bill Acton. The dilution had actually worked, despite everything, and the effect of the Saint's Fog blended seamlessly with the generic effects of alcohol abuse. Again a sense of pride flooded me. This time I did not try to shake it.

Prosenko barged into the room with Dylan, waving his arms wildly. A bit of sick dribbled down from Dylan's lips.

"It's that bitch!" he cried, flailing while Prosenko pinned him into the closest empty chair. "She did something," he slurred. "Put something in the . . . in the booze."

The world froze, and despite the claustrophobic air of bodies pressed tightly in the clinic room, it felt cold.

"Now, now, Mr. Westerly, you and I know that's not the case," said Prosenko, reaching for a rag to wipe the spit from Dylan's mouth. Then, slowly, he looked to me, gray eyes focused on no one else.

There was no doubt that he knew. Earlier, when he'd passed the kitchen with a patient, he'd seen me, probably with the dropper in hand, just before I'd finished, and said nothing. He had been treating everyone all night with the knowledge that they'd been poisoned, and still he said nothing.

When he finished, Prosenko stood up and calmly walked toward me. My heart began to pound. "The boy's in bad shape," he said. "But he'll pull through. Lord only knows he's taken worse shit than what he got tonight." I waited as Prosenko pulled a clean handkerchief from his pocket and wiped the sick from his shoulder.

"Sir—"

"There's no need, Gereghty," Prosenko said before I could give myself away any further. "It's just senseless babble. He won't recall a thing come the morning."

"But in the kitchen . . ."

"We all do what we're told. Whatever that is. Now, go check on the drips we have going in the corner. I'll make sure these two get what they need."

Upon hearing his words, I was once again filled with the same rush I'd felt standing there at Martin's side. Despite all my weeks as an outsider in their realm, envious and oblivious to how they mocked their own power, here at last I had received it myself.

That night in Arrow's Edge, I had become invincible, too.

16

RETURNING HOME TO ROSLINDALE AFTER that third party was harder than any time before. The mocking tone from my younger brother, Tony, as he watched me hang up the black dress from my suitcase made me debate putting drops into his cereal the next morning. Even worse was the look from my mother, as there was no doubt that after our previous conversation she suspected precisely the kinds of parties I now returned from. The ones the Gainsboroughs no longer attended and the ones that, as the weeks went on and I saw my father's state, told me the pills he took were not for an injury that still lingered months after his mysterious fall but were an addiction that he now couldn't seem to shake.

I knew she wanted to ask. I imagined the few mothering instincts that had been around for most of my childhood and recently lay dormant inside her begged to make sure I was okay. But she was never good at expressing herself, and so her lips remained sealed and it was, never discussed. Same as with my high-school girlfriends, my college boyfriends. Same as everything else.

That Saturday as my shift ended, Prosenko informed me that Martin had another long business trip planned and would be leaving later that evening for New York, only this time with Jonathan and himself in tow. As a result he was giving me the week off. Initially the convenience was worrying, but when the local news reported a large tech summit, I realized it was the truth.

By Tuesday I'd been welcomed back into the fold of the Gereghty clan and their daily, lower-middle-class monotony. Forgotten were the buttery layers of Daniella's croissants and the scent of fair-trade, single-origin coffee. Instead at home I was met with the stench of bacon grease and the odor of body spray emanating from the family bathroom upstairs, a scent from my childhood that I had willfully forgotten.

With Rumi and Anna still being distant and the knowledge that a text from me might not be the most welcome thing, it wasn't long before I reached out to the only person left who had always been there to talk to. No matter how small the problem or how terrifying. If there was anyone in the world I could rely on for comfort, I knew it was my aunt, and so I pulled up her latest e-mail.

In our last exchange, she'd announced that a new company had been funding her latest schemes and that an exciting new contract was in the works. Something about a research grant by a place called Kinlex Labs. After that I began reading her articles again and quickly realized that so much had been published in my absence. Old colleagues whose dissertations I'd pored over and line-edited in exchange for a pint at the pub had gone on to graduate. There were articles attributed to Clare Ricchetti in languages I couldn't begin to identify, and at this knowledge a source of pride swelled within me.

I missed her terribly, like swords piercing the muscle of my heart.

Beside my computer sat the small bag of black pills, two little spheres the source of more anxiety than they were likely worth. Aunt Clare would have known what to do with them, I thought. In all the days I'd had them, no ideas had come, despite how much I willed them.

By Wednesday I had begun to think that there was nothing I could do until I was back with the Verdeaus and could ask Audrey herself what she preferred. It was then, as I sat alone that afternoon, with my brother at classes, my father at the hardware store, and my mother running errands, that a knock came at the front door, and moments later I found myself answering it wide-eyed, face-to-face with Audrey herself.

Inviting Audrey Verdeau into my childhood home felt like something out of a dream—or a nightmare—and given the task I could only assume she had arrived with in mind, it felt more likely to be the latter. Soon her perfume overwhelmed me, masking any scent of bacon or the mildew of aging carpet, and I willed myself to drown in it. I had missed it at the party. I had been away for only a few days, and yet already I had missed *her*.

"It smells just like you!" she said, delighted as we rushed up the stairs and opened my bedroom door. With all the vigor of a magpie, she was drawn to the shelves of plants that filled any free space between my books. Her manicured fingers fiddled with the leaves. "Like herbs, I mean. You always smell like them. It's all over your clothes."

Embarrassed, I resisted the urge to sniff at the fabric to check, but when she looked at me, she giggled and said, "Don't worry. It's charming."

"I . . . I . . . uh, I thought you were in New York," I told her, trying not to blush, but the statement only earned a frown.

"Oh, I went. Without an invite, of course, but a few days and I'm done. I had my share of brunches."

"You mean you weren't at the summit?"

"I try not to spend all my time where I'm unwanted if I can help it." She looked to my door, a brief spot of hesitancy crossing her face.

"It's fine," I assured her. "You're more than welcome here. My home is yours."

Audrey beamed. "Oh, good! In that case, Lena, love, let's get to work."

"Work? With what?"

"The pills, of course."

Audrey quickly made herself at home, taking my words to a whole new level. Every item in my room was hers for examination, and as she roamed, she asked me what I knew about the pills and if there was a way we could perhaps distill them. As she eyed some of the brewing equipment in the corner, holdovers from the first batch of Saint's Fog, I hastily had to tell her no.

"Jonathan says a company you own makes them," I explained, trying to refocus her attention away from the most obvious evidence of my crimes.

"Well, he's wrong," she said. "Prosenko's the one that makes them. I saw him once with a little press. Back before I was sent to Montreux."

"Why would he tell Jonathan something different?"

"I don't know. But if he's lying about them, then that's even more reason to not trust them. Don't you think?"

It did seem suspicious, I gave her that.

"Can I . . . ask what you're so worried about? Why all the curiosity with the pills?"

Audrey plopped herself onto my bed in a graceful thump. "You've seen him after he takes them. It's absurd. He's so ill. Medicine shouldn't do that. After all these years and constant care, he only seems to be getting worse, and the only thing I can think to explain it are those pills. . . . I'm just tired of not knowing."

"Some medicines have side effects, Audrey."

Something in her face changed, and she looked to me. "No, not like this. Don't you get it, Lena? That's why I need your help. I'm worried they're not medicine at all."

"What else would they be?"

"Poison."

I watched, running over the word in my mind as Audrey stood from my bed and paced to the wooden desk, placing her fingers over the grain before at last landing on the small plastic bag. She picked up the pills.

I raised an eyebrow.

"I know it must seem absurd, but I can't keep waiting like this, Lena. By the end of the day, I want to know what's in them. What that man is doing to my brother."

"Audrey," I tried again with growing nerves. "It's just not that easy to pick something like that apart. You need a hypothesis, a few guesses, and then tools. Papers and dyes and . . ."

Her fingers fiddled with the seal of the bag and popped it open. For a long moment, she said nothing, instead giving the small pills the entirety of her focus. Her delicate fingers reached in and slowly pulled one out to examine in the light. "You said you would help me."

"I'm *trying*. I got the pills, didn't I? I tried to find you to talk about it before the party, but I haven't seen you since, and—"

She sighed and looked to me. "I've seen the studies from Umbria. The ones you worked on with your aunt. She's listed you in over twenty papers as a lab assistant. You're not naïve, so don't play like you are. If anyone knows poisons, it's you, Lena."

"But we're not even sure it *is* poison! That, that idea, it's absurd, Audrey. I mean, listen to yourself! He's your brother's doctor."

"That's why we need to figure it out!" Her usually composed voice was edged with a rare desperation. She walked over to me holding the pill still clasped between her fingertips. "I need your help with this, Lena. It's you. No one else. Just you and me. Just today. Do it for me. *Please*. I've been waiting so long. This is my only chance."

The air around me choked with the scent of frangipani. Heavenly and soft. "I just don't know how to help."

Audrey raised the pill up. "Poisons have symptoms, right?" she said.

A dark idea blossomed between us. A flash of something that she clearly recognized. A stupid, impulsive idea that had me panicked in an instant and reaching forward to stop her.

"Audrey. Don't," I pleaded.

As if it were a film reel playing in her pupils, I saw the scene. The pill I'd seen placed on Jonathan's tongue day after day, watching him tremble with disgust despite having a lifetime of experience to numb him to it, placed between her lips. Audrey Verdeau, pale and shaking on my bedroom floor. Collapsed into my arms and pupils wide in horror—again—only this time with none of Prosenko's tools to cure her.

"You can't."

"It's just a pill."

"Audrey—"

"He takes them every day."

"I know, but—"

"Do you trust me?"

I eyed the pill in her hand, then shakily said, "No."

"Good."

"Wha—"

Audrey placed the pill into her mouth and swallowed swiftly, without a second thought. I watched as it disappeared behind her pink lips. Then I heard the plastic bag crinkle open again.

"Audrey! Why would you—"

"I'm really sorry about this, Lena, love."

Suddenly, as my mouth hung open in confusion at what she could have meant by that, her hand shoved the final dose between my teeth and clamped my jaw shut like a dog's. I felt the pill slide down my esophagus in reflex, and my hands turned clammy as the panic began to set in.

I wanted to gag. As soon as I realized what had happened, I wanted to reach my fingers down and fetch the cursed little pill, but Audrey, somehow sensing it, perhaps knowing it from her own shared emotions, took my hands and held them as if in a vise.

"We want to know what's in them, and we don't have the time or the equipment to reverse-engineer it, right?"

I nodded, feeling spit flood my mouth.

"One pill won't kill us if it's medicine," she said. Then, "Right?"

I swallowed and cursed the motion.

"Right?" she said firmly, and jerked my hand until I nodded.

"R-right." I swallowed again. "Right. Probably."

Audrey searched my eyes with her own. Hazel eyes, with the same flecks of brown and black as Jonathan's. It was the first time I could remember seeing her scared.

It terrified me.

"Even if they're poison?" she asked.

I nodded. "If you're right and he's been taking them for years . . . it should be fine."

"What's that mean?"

"It probably won't be lethal."

Her hands loosened their grip. "Why would it be lethal?"

My mouth felt dry, the soft tissue burning with the taste of something noxious and bitterly acidic. Even after swallowing, the flavor lingered everywhere, tingling my mouth and causing my throat to close from fear. I coughed and then gagged, and tried and tried to source enough spit to swallow again, as if it might clear the torture overwhelming my tongue.

The symptoms came on quick, though I'm not sure if their impatient arrival could be considered an act of mercy. When a girl like Audrey Verdeau, daughter of the sun and summer and as gilded as the walls of her palatial home, comes over, it's easy to want everything to go well. I wanted my room clean and for the air downstairs to smell less like a morning fry-up, and I certainly wanted not to be doubling over with a wave of nausea and an impending sense of doom, but there I was.

Within minutes my stomach was cramping.

The thought of bacon made it flip.

"Paper," I said sharply, reaching out my hand. "If we're gonna make this worth it, I need . . . I need paper. Hurry, hurry—" I swallowed down the sting of bile, and immediately I understood Jonathan's response to the pills. The expression on his face that day in the greenhouse.

I watched Audrey, her condition playing out my own very near future as she stood up and braced herself promptly on my desk. "Where? Where do you . . ." She paused, closed her eyes, and shook it off. "Where do you keep it?"

"Printer!"

"Well, where's that?"

My hand flew in the direction of the bedside table holding the small printer. My world spun and my body ached, and I thought surely, surely we had really fucked up. Surely this was not something I would make it back from.

I think most people know what it's like to be poisoned. Ten shots of tequila and some questionable 3:00 A.M. tacos aren't that far off from a low-level poisoning, and on a scale of one to ten that scenario is probably a three.

I opened my eyes to grab a stack of paper, and my situation quickly moved to a five.

"I'm gonna be sick," I said, and scrambled up just in time to rush to the bathroom across the hall, leaving Audrey in my confused wake.

The door slammed and not thirty seconds later was pulled open as Audrey rushed in and slammed it again.

Once my world stopped spinning and the worst felt over, I tried to make a record. Sketch out our forms in shaking lines as on a medical sheet or an autopsy report. Mine looked more like skewed gingerbread men than like anything with a medical or anatomical origin, but it served our purpose well enough. I wrote down the times, or as close as I could. From the moment we first swallowed and everything after. Each sharp pain in my side and each flush of the toilet and new symptom received a time stamp. My hands were sweaty, and my thoughts weren't clear, and my lips felt increasingly numb, but at some point the fear had dissolved. At some point between the heavy breathing and the pounding in my chest, I had lost all trace of it.

Maybe it was seeing Audrey's own.

The truth is, after that first party with the Saint's Fog, it was too much to see her like that again. I didn't even blame Audrey for shoving her fingers into my mouth and forcing me to swallow. I merely regretted that I hadn't stopped her from doing the same.

"WHY ARE WE DOING THIS?" I asked later as Audrey stared vacantly out my window with her knees pulled to her chest. It had been an hour since the start of the symptoms and a few minutes since they passed. We were dizzy, and our bodies ached, and we should probably have gone to the hospital after a brief wave of mild hallucinations and flashing colors, but we didn't. Instead I fetched us some water from the tap and some saltine crackers, and we sat there, silent on my bedroom floor. "Taking the pills, I mean. It's stupid."

"I told you," she said, her voice weak and tired. "I need to know."

"*Why?*" I asked. "Why the urgency? Why today? Why . . . why take them for him? After the way he treats you, I don't get it."

Audrey looked down. Her hair fell in a series of small, delicate strands. Just enough to shield her face. "We were close when we were younger," she told me. "Did you know that?"

I had assumed.

"We don't seem like it now, but . . . we're not even two years apart. Jonathan, he . . . he wasn't always so sick. We would play together all the time, running through the rooms, through the gardens back at Arrow's Edge. If you think the house is big now, just imagine how it must seem to a toddler."

I watched, waiting as Audrey got lost in a memory. How her face softened. It didn't last, though. Soon the small smile on her lips disappeared and her eyes widened. She swallowed and blinked away the wave of what must have been nausea.

"Whoo . . . I, uh. Sorry. I think I just tasted gin," she said, amazed. "I haven't had gin since Monika's birthday party six months ago."

"You should drink water," I suggested, already reaching for my cup. The world spun slightly, but Audrey shook her head.

"No, no. I'm fine. I think the worst is over. . . . Anyway, Jonathan. Right," she began again, refocusing. "I guess back when we were kids, he always followed me everywhere. When you're little, you don't really understand the whole heir-versus-heiress thing, even if your parents wished you did. But, Lena, we were thick as thieves, and when our mother left, we just became closer. I can't remember spending a minute without him there, you know. Even in school he was always in my class. My father convinced them Jonathan could skip a grade, so we were always together. At least until the private tutoring started. I must have been eight or nine." She swallowed. "It was after the divorce was finalized that it all went downhill. I remember I was so angry one day that Jonathan wasn't in my class anymore that the minute I got home, I ran out to find him and stole him away from his lesson in the study. I don't even remember what it was. I just yanked him out of the chair and chased him through the hall and through whatever rooms we came across. Laughing. We were hysterical. It was so *good*, and then . . ." She paused. Memories flashing again behind her eyes. "And then Martin burst in and scared us. Jonathan fell off the couch and into a side table.

"He was fine. I think. There was blood, but . . . After that . . . well, that's when Prosenko moved in with us and our worlds separated. We spent less and less time together, and Jonathan spent more and more time with the doctors and the tutors and the special meetings. Eventually they sent me off to boarding school. First a place in Connecticut, then to Switzerland. . . . I missed his birthday that year. Martin, I think, must have planned it. Because I was still on the plane halfway over Amsterdam when he was probably blowing out the candles."

"Audrey . . . that's horrible."

She shrugged. "We were kids. Jonathan was upset, but I was . . . I was so *mad* . . . and then after that we just grew apart. We saw each other grow up, but it was through little postcards and Christmas visits and brief family phone calls with the company lawyers. Disputes over business ownerships we were too young to understand, that sort of thing. One summer he was going to fly out to visit me, but at the last minute he had some sort of attack and Martin canceled the trip."

"When did you move back to Boston?" I asked.

"Just before law school," she said. "After Jonathan turned twenty-one, I made the decision. He had dropped out of undergrad, drunk all the time, had a car accident—it's still all over the Internet. It made every tabloid. He was a mess, worse than now, and I guess I thought maybe Martin would realize I could help." She laughed bitterly. "I was wrong.

"He was like a ghost," said Audrey, continuing after neither of us said a word. "He'd become so ill and would only talk to me if I drank with him, and of course that only made Martin angrier, so . . ." She shrugged.

"That's who you became."

"In short."

"I saw those photos, too. On the Internet."

She smiled bitterly. "It wasn't my best. . . . Jonathan's not a bad guy, though, Lena," said Audrey. "Not really. Not like the others around him."

"He's a complete asshole to you."

"It comes with the territory," she said. "You should know. I can be an asshole, too."

"What? No, I—"

Audrey laughed, soft, her throat sounding raw. "It's okay. . . . I mean, I did poison you, after all."

Yeah, I thought, feeling a new, growing weight in my chest. *You're not the only one.*

17

WE HAD BEEN POISONED. THERE WAS NO QUESTION. I knew too well the symptoms of a substance not agreeing with your biology. The problem was that didn't mean *Jonathan* was being poisoned. Despite Audrey's concern, all it told me was that her brother was on some kind of medication that we had no business taking for a joyride.

I tried to tell her that as she lay there, huddled for warmth beneath my childhood blankets, but Audrey didn't want to listen. Instead she continued on, with a cold sweat on her brow and determined as ever, as she made me chart each new symptom and the time it occurred.

All I could do was tend to her and try not to be too obvious with my affections as I brushed the hair from her face. I went back and forth with myself that night, but in the end I just couldn't be mad at her. What Audrey had done was stupid and reckless, but . . . I would have done the same. If I were that worried or finally saw my chance at getting answers. Isn't that what I was doing with the Saint's Fog? Taking my own reckless chance to punish Martin for what he'd done to my father and Mrs. Gainsborough and others like them?

———————

IT TOOK US DAYS TO FULLY RECOVER, but we had the time. With Prosenko gone and most of his office at the town house open, Audrey wasted no time in paying for a taxi to Back Bay. As nice as it was to wake up to her curled against me in the morning, I could hide her from my parents' inattentive eyes for only so long. We needed to be somewhere safer, with enough of a medical-supply stash to get us through the after-shock. Luckily, George stayed away from us with our excuse of the flu, and Daniella happily made a giant pot of soup, with the scent of simmering chicken left to filter through the entire town house.

My balance was fucked up for days. Minor ataxia made it so I'd reach for something—a glass of water, the door handle—and miss entirely. I watched, too, as Audrey stumbled on her heels and how as soon as we arrived at the town house, she switched into a pair of flats. The confusion was the worst of it, though. It was lucky that almost everyone was gone, as more and more it seemed I'd confuse words. I was barely able to think of a full sentence at times, much less say it out loud in any manner that made sense. I assumed Audrey suffered this, too, as we began to talk less and less.

I guzzled water to flush the pill from my system. When there was no sign of kidney pain and the symptoms faded with no lingering issues or signs of encroaching blindness, I was at last able to relax, assuming we were in the clear.

But God, I was scared. Whatever was in those pills seemed worse than the Saint's Fog, medication or no.

The thought of Jonathan taking something as rough as that daily, and with twice the dose, haunted me worse than on any occasion prior. The shock of it all was equally apparent on Audrey's face. How long, I wondered, had she watched him suffer? Watched his health decline? How powerful, too, was whatever illness plagued him, if it called for such a potent dose?

We didn't have much time to debate it. The end of the week signaled Martin's return and with it my own back home and another order for Saint's Fog. Only this time, I was warned, it wasn't for just any party. It was for New Year's Eve. His biggest bash of the year, and the shock of his order size had me scrambling despite the twenty-thousand-dollar check.

With Audrey distracted again and my own assignment clearly given, I spent my days working on fulfilling the order for Martin, watching as Black Friday sales soon gave way to lights and wreaths and Christmas-tree lots, with children running around and every café in Boston filled with the same holiday playlist that had been going since I was in high school.

I was so busy that when the moment came that Audrey pulled me aside to ask about what progress I'd made, I shamefully had nothing to show for it. No more than I had as we'd lain sprawled on the floor of my bedroom.

"Tell me there's an update," she pleaded. "Anything. Anything at all."

"Maybe. I . . . I don't know. I was thinking it could be something like mercury with the ataxia issues, but that wouldn't make sense, and even still, there's like twenty potential options. I've been comparing notes, but our symptoms were a mess, and I'm . . . I'm sorry, but nothing is lining up yet."

"Lena, *please*! Don't make me regret swallowing that shit more than I already do."

"It was your idea!"

"Yes, and if we hadn't, then we'd still be at square one!"

Something was off in her tone. A new concern that made me stop. "Are you okay?"

"I'm fine. Just . . ." She sighed. "Just business. Please, hurry up."

"Why? What's wrong?"

My question fell into empty air. She was already walking away, a wisp of camel-and-cream satin.

"Audrey?" I called after, now worried as well. "What's wrong?"

"What are you yammering about now, Gereghty?"

Jonathan rounded the corner just then, still in his robe and boxers and looking like a rent boy for the Reaper himself.

Shit.

"Nothing," I said, and took a breath. "Do you need something?"

His eyes looked to where Audrey had disappeared and then slowly moved back to me. "Yeah, Doc is gone. Said I needed to . . ." He sighed and waved his hand in a circle. "Said I needed something."

"Did you take your pills?" I asked suspiciously. "From Prosenko?"

"An hour ago," he said, and then laughed, weakly but with a wink. "Maybe. Must've given me memory loss. Can't remember a thing now."

I rolled my eyes and walked over to guide him to the chair before he had a chance to collapse. Something didn't feel right, but I couldn't tell what. At least he was talking.

"Did you drink last night?"

"What do you think, Gereghty?"

"I think you need to tell me."

"Pff. Boring. I want you to guess."

I noticed then that his eyes, strangely, were not bloodshot. That after reaching to take his pulse, I observed it was thin but not out of range. Not slow. For once his breath smelled more like toothpaste than stale cocktails or bile. For Jonathan Verdeau, he seemed . . . healthy. Shockingly healthy.

"Prosenko didn't give me any notes," I told him. "Nothing more for you to take today."

"Tch, then fuck if I know."

"Jonathan," I started. "Did you . . . did you really take your pills?"

After a second he rolled his head to look at me. "I accepted them."

There was no need to say anything else. Although I hadn't expected it, our scheme from the week prior had clearly been continued. Even in my absence.

"You won't say anything to him, yeah?"

"No," I told him.

"Good."

While I was happy to see him feeling so well, a part of me worried that surely there would be some sort of long-term side effects if he kept this up, even knowing what had happened with Audrey and me.

That December, despite everything, I had anticipated another one of Martin's surprise parties. A holiday bash of some sort to precede the larger one planned at New Year's, especially since he'd been at the town house more often in that closed-off meeting room of his, stepping out only for a snack or to request more jam for his croissants. However, his presence merely drove Jonathan to seclude himself in the Berkshires once again, and so, same as before, we followed.

Snow had yet to come to the city beyond a few flurries, but back at Arrow's Edge every barren tree was laden with white, and the rooftop of the estate stood draped in it. Picturesque and far less imposing than in the height of summer.

Mid-December came and passed, and the Advent season showed no signs of being welcome at either of the familial homes. No tinsel was hung or holly displayed. Ribbon remained missing, as did any plans for a tree.

Instead, a day after being asked by my father if my own family would be lucky enough to get me for Christmas that year, I received a letter at my home address. A custom, gold-embossed envelope bearing an ornate *V* and sprigs of Yuletide botanicals.

I wondered if it was a Christmas bonus. Not that I necessarily needed one—by this point I had made a substantial dent in my student loans and still had cash on hand—but the courtesy would not have been beyond the range of Martin's standard actions. Yet when I opened it, it was not a check but an invitation and, to my surprise, a plane ticket.

Helena Gereghty,

Martin wished to type this up, but I thought it too impersonal, so I intervened. Handwritten letters are nicer, don't you agree, Lena, love?

We are leaving for France after the solstice, the 22nd of December. You are encouraged to join. Prosenko says required, but that's neither here nor there.

It's been a busy few weeks, but we have the long-standing tradition of visiting the "home country" for Christmas. I hope your family will understand. If it helps, there's grand shopping in Strasbourg, so perhaps the promise of souvenirs shall warm their hearts. Then again, you were away for the last few Christmases anyway, right?

The ticket in your hand is just for proof—don't worry about losing it. George will be in touch about the logistics.

I'm overjoyed you'll be joining us this year.

You must have played those cards right after all.

Warmly yours,
Audrey Verdeau

Warmly yours.

I reread the line over and over again and fought not to smile.

Strasbourg. The name conjured up a variety of thoughts. Warmed wine, snow on cobblestone streets. The strange but enchanting intersection of French and German charm. Almost immediately my imagination was plagued by an onslaught of fantasies that now seem childish but nonetheless gripped me as my fingers held the paper. Snow-topped timber-framed houses.

Europe, I thought with a warmth to my heart. *I'm actually going back.*

The discussion that followed at dinner that evening, with the Gereghty clan all seated in the living room, plates balanced on our knees and a Patriots game on the television, was not a good one. Tony informed us he was bringing his new girlfriend to Christmas Eve dinner, an idea my mother promptly attempted to get him to reconsider. My father turned the volume up as she began to list the details of the meal, and finally she turned to me and said, "Lena, that means I need you up at six to get the roast marinating."

To which I said, "Actually, about that . . ."

My father muted the television. "It's Christmas!" he shouted, and so the flurry of protests began. I remember being silent, staring as the bodies crashed into one another on the television screen. The absence of sound where I knew there were cheers, and music, and announcers giving the score. It felt like forever, the plate of baked chicken and macaroni growing cold on my thighs as my mother's voice rose above everything. Shrill, panicked, and above all furious.

"Well?"

I blinked.

"So will you call them or not?" she asked. A redness had risen in her cheeks.

I stared down at my plate. "I'm sorry," I said. Then added, in a soft tone of resignation learned from childhood, "I'll be sure to get you souvenirs."

Neither of my parents wanted gifts. I knew that then as much as I know it now. In all their protests, there was only the same kind of argument. *Where will you be to help? Who will go get groceries? What about Mass? Don't you want to meet Tony's girlfriend? Don't you care about this family?*

Audrey was right. I had missed Christmases back in Roslindale when

I was in Italy, but that was different from missing my *family*. And with the stress of this year, it didn't matter how much I loved them or what I was willing to do to help my father. I needed a break, and I was being offered one. It felt foolish to say no.

There was a week between the letter and the proposed departure, and so it was spent in preparation for New Year's Eve. Tending to the contents of my closet and securing them from prying eyes. I still bought presents and even wrapped them nicely to put under the tree before leaving, but they were tokens.

When all the work was done, I turned to the only other people I cared about, ones I had regrettably forgotten over the chaos of fall and whom I begged to meet up with again before I risked losing them entirely.

Thankfully, they agreed.

"I can't believe they bought you a ticket," said Anna as I shoved a french fry into my mouth. It was late, and the roads were iced over with melting snow, but even at night Slick Rick's was open, and so we came.

"Are you excited?" Rumi asked. "You'll be trapped there with them."

I shrugged. "I'm trapped here with them anyway."

"They've held you hostage," said Rumi, sounding frustrated. "For months. I was starting to think they'd even stolen your phone."

"And that's just in the Berkshires," said Anna. "That's a hell of a lot different from France."

"I'm sure it'll be fine. Things have been going better," I tried to explain. "Busy, but better."

Rumi gave me a look of disbelief through his curly dark hair. "They have?"

"Well, better than before."

"Are you sure about that?"

"What do you mean?"

Anna looked nervously at me from across the table. "Well . . . you've been AWOL."

"I know, I . . . I'm sorry. Things just got busy, and—"

"We haven't heard from you in weeks," she continued. "It's like you're back in Italy."

"Yeah, only then you sent us postcards and DM'd us, but it's been radio silence lately, Lena. What the hell?"

I didn't know what to say. A part of me felt guilty and knew that I had let too much time pass, but another part of me just felt angry. I thought of the presents, wrapped and waiting in bags under the booth to give to them. Hopeful peace offerings that I'd bought with the money from the Saint's Fog that I thought maybe I could finally tell them about. But the look on their faces now told me they weren't in the mood to understand. At some point something had broken between us, and I had realized it, just not soon enough.

They came that night not to catch up as I'd hoped but to accuse.

Without revealing anything I couldn't take back, I tried to explain to them what my time with the Verdeau family had been like. The parties, and Prosenko, and the pills. Except every word came at the cost of their patience, until finally I was too tired and too frustrated to keep going. They didn't want to listen.

I pulled the bags out from under the table and set them heavily on top.

"Here," I said to them as I stood up from the booth and grabbed my things. "Merry Christmas."

18

THE SNOW IN STRASBOURG WAS BITTER. The air around my face stirred crisp and painful from the moment of our arrival until at last we settled into our hotel. By the time I was carrying in my suitcase and stomping my slush-covered heels onto the marble tile of the foyer, the warmth was a welcome reprieve.

It had been a long journey. The family and Prosenko had first-class seats for the flight. To be honest, I almost expected Martin to have owned a private jet to fly us there, but that level of luxury was beyond even him. Instead, as he sipped his scotch alongside his children, I sat uncomfortably next to George, relegated to business class.

The flight was long and filled with stuffy silence, and an odd blend of excitement and the dread of unknowing. It seemed I had only just come home from Italy, and while every fiber of my being yearned to return to Europe, never could I have imagined that the opportunity would present itself less than six months after my arrival Stateside. There I was, flying back, listening to the murmur of French and German and the barest hint of Italian echoing from the rear of the plane. It was comforting. The seats in business class were also more comfortable than the coach I'd experienced during all my flights before.

I missed Aunt Clare.

Just before leaving I'd checked my e-mail to find a message from her with a flurry of updates about the garden. The new contractor had procured a large grant for them, allowing her to move forward on some plans to acquire yet another plot of land. This time farther north, she said, near the French border, and with more sandstone in the soil composition. She'd be able to test new Gallic varietals and get more students to help her now that I was gone. The funded project was for theriacs, she said. The same composites of poisons meant as miracle cures that she had introduced me to during my first year there. It was just the sort of thing she loved. Things that were fake, that she could try to make real. Bad things she could make good.

As I stood in Strasbourg, much closer to her but still so far, the mere idea of it was maddening. It was with her where my future had first begun to feel bright again after so many dark months. When her comforting presence filled me with encouragement and helped me to realize again that somewhere deep inside me, beyond the burned-out husks of prior passions, there still existed a love for medicine. She pulled it out of me day by day until it felt like there was potential bubbling over everything.

Now it all felt bittersweet, knowing what I was doing at the parties, with the warmth of Montefalco so far away.

After a car drove George and me to the city and our hotel, Prosenko met us alone in the lobby, already looking aggravated.

"Martin's left for a meeting," he said. "Come on, I've got your room keys."

Tan, polished marble flooring stretched underfoot, reaching all the way to the elevator, which slowly took the three of us up, not stopping until it had landed at the very top. The hotel wasn't tall. It was an older building, layered with brick and stucco and altogether no more than six or seven stories, a far cry from the sleek high-rises of New York or Shang-hai that Martin frequented. Still, it felt very Verdeau, antique and uncom-fortable with a modern coating.

The upper floor had a series of suites at the farthest end and windows overlooking the picturesque rooftops of the city center. Prosenko mo-tioned down the hall.

"Martin and the children are down this way." He fished out a series of room keys and handed George one and myself another. "Your rooms will be here, by the elevator. Oh, and George," he said, turning toward the older man, "follow me for a moment. I have a question about the ar-rangements you made for Jonathan's setup here. . . ."

Prosenko trailed off, forcing my own exit from the conversation as the two men abandoned me to the hallway and disappeared toward the cen-tral suite. I looked at the paper sleeve of my room card, which read 604, and as it happened, so did the door just a step away.

Inside I tossed my bag onto the floor and fell down onto the mattress face-first, playing the part of a drowned body waiting to be fished from the Charles. Silent, mouth agape, unmoving, arms spread.

I had only just begun to drift asleep when Prosenko knocked on my door to tell me that Jonathan had run off before George could so much as set up the suite. Between that and Martin running between appoint-ments and business calls on this so-called family vacation, I was officially deemed free for the rest of the evening. Sightsee or whatever, he told me. Shop. Sleep. It didn't matter to him.

I bade Prosenko a quick thank-you and debated each of his sugges-tions with my jet-lagged brain until at last I resigned myself to the more responsible and boring task of unpacking my suitcase.

I hadn't thought to pack much. A few sweaters for the cold, some pants, and one formal dress because of an embarrassing belief that I'd be invited along to whatever fancy events the Verdeaus might have had planned for the holidays. Truth be told, from the minute I'd opened that letter from Audrey, I hadn't a clue about what the trip would entail. Even less did I understand what it meant for me.

For months I had lived under the shadow of the Verdeau family. First fearful and then falling into line as I surrendered myself to the role of Prosenko's assistant. It was bizarre to imagine then the nerves that once enveloped me as I stood on those sun-covered steps in Back Bay. Summer had become a distant dream.

The desperation of a job hunt felt foreign, and the parties that had come so close to forcing my hand into resignation now held little power over me and only added funds that I had never dreamed of to my bank account. Where revenge had once been my sole purpose for remaining with them, now, after spending time with Audrey over break and my hours with her brother, there was something else that had begun to stir below the surface.

I thought of Audrey's fingers. How delicate she looked holding the pill, how forceful as she shoved it into my mouth and watched me swallow. Even there in France, the thought made saliva build beneath my tongue with an impending sense of nausea. I still couldn't summon an ounce of hatred, though. Instead all I recalled of that day was her body, shaking and scared on my floor, and above everything the scent of her perfume where it still lingered on my pillow.

The reality was, despite my belief about the nature of the pills, Audrey deserved answers. She deserved to know what her brother was taking, especially now that we understood the depths of its potency.

It had been weeks since our fateful night and since Jonathan had been rejecting the pills, and I was certain that soon Prosenko would catch on. We weren't geniuses, the three of us, and even worse was the fact that while Audrey and I could handle taking one of Jonathan's pills, this was her brother's life we were playing with, and time felt like it was running short. If he did need his pills, I was putting him in danger by letting him skip them. If they were poison as Audrey believed . . . well.

Prosenko would surely notice an improvement in Jonathan's health and be looking for someone to blame.

In the hotel room, I picked up a journal from my suitcase. It was basic fake leather, and it held every bit of the evidence of my crimes. The printer paper bearing shaky figures from that night with Audrey was folded up into the cover, and on page after page I'd recorded my theories from all the nights that I was kept up by the mystery.

I wanted so much for swallowing the pills to have yielded more results after the punishment it inflicted on our innocent bodies, but it did not. Our symptoms were too much of a mess. Nausea, dizziness, dysmetria, blurred vision, hallucinations, red faces, sweaty palms—the list went on, and unfortunately, as I'd told Audrey before, it was still too vague to make heads or tails of.

Beside me on the nightstand, I saw a phone, and before I knew it, I was dialing Aunt Clare's number. I listened to it ring and ring, my legs bouncing nervously as I sat on the edge of the bed, until the sound of her voice came through on the other end and my heart stopped. At her simple, melodic "Hello?" I became so overjoyed that it took a moment to compose myself—before I could force my throat to say, "Hey, it's Lena."

Even just the sound of her voice made that dim hotel room seem flooded with light.

She asked what I'd been up to. How I was. I must have told her something about how much I missed Italy, because she wasted no time in giving me an update, repeating all the details she'd mentioned in e-mails, only this time with more notable emotion behind them than I could read through text.

She was so excited about all the sudden interest in her work following the contract with that new lab, and how the plot of land in the north was shaping up in record time. With any luck, she said, they could plant it by spring. It was only afterward, when the conversation turned to the plants she'd mailed me, that I was reminded of a question I'd almost forgotten to ask. One that had been pushed to the back of my brain with my focus on the pills.

"Hey, Aunt Clare. . . . Do you remember the Saint's Fog?"

"Yes, of course!" she said. "How is it responding to the climate there?"

"Well, that's the thing. It started to get this film on it. Like a sort of dust on top of the leaves. I was wondering if you might know something about it."

Aunt Clare laughed. "How long was it abandoned in customs?"

"No, I mean since being in Boston. I thought for a bit it had died, but it's still growing."

"The plant?"

"The dust. Well, the plant, too."

"Hmm . . . it may be a blight of some sort. You said it's still alive?"

"Yeah."

"I don't think anything like that has happened to the ones here, but I'll have James take a look when he gets back from town."

"James is still there?"

Quickly she explained to me how one of her oldest and yet least-published assistants was supposed to return to Penn around August but had submitted a new proposal and gotten piggybacked onto some secondary research grant that extended his visa. In reality we both knew that James was a graduate student terrified of actually graduating. He was brilliant but horrifically stupid when it came to planning his life. In hindsight I had been a little hard on him one too many times at the pub.

"But how are you, *gattina*? All is well over there? How is that job of yours treating you? All right, I hope."

"It's . . . yeah, it's all right."

I didn't want to tell her the truth. What could I have said? *It pays great, but even better after I tried to kill them with the plants you sent.*

There were so many things I wanted to say to her. I wanted to sit on the bench overlooking the garden, with the sunset lighting the hills, and feel her gentle fingers combing through my hair. Every inch of my soul yearned for her advice, and my tongue begged me to request it, but I could not. To tell Aunt Clare what I'd done would plant a seed so dark into her mind that I feared it would dull her shine forever. That it would dull me to her.

"I miss you," I said after a moment, in a voice small and weak.

"Oh . . . oh, Lena, I miss you, too. Is everything all right?"

I swallowed back a wave of sorrow. Ignored the sting of tears at my eyes. "I'm fine."

"Hey . . . do you remember that day you first arrived?" she began, voice warm and tender. "And I scooped you up from the airport?"

A tiny smile formed on my lips. "Yeah."

"You were so scared. You hadn't slept the entire flight, and I could have sworn you would pass out right there in my truck."

"I wanted to."

"But you didn't, and I don't know what's bothering you now, *gattina*, but I know something is. It's in your voice. And I know you'll beat it. All those worries you had when you arrived, about school and your future, were swallowing you up, do you remember? You didn't speak to anyone when you first got here. You hated James and Delphine and the others—and do you know what solved it?"

By this point I had not stopped smiling. "You made us all have dinner together."

"Yes! With lots of wine and fresh bread and—"

"We used herbs from the garden and put them in everything. In the pasta, in the bread . . ."

"Mm-hmm . . . we did, and you said nothing for the first hour of the meal. Not until everyone had tasted what you'd cooked. You just sat there and watched."

"I was nervous. I had to make sure they liked it—"

"You were waiting to see if they liked *you*. But liking your food is not the same as liking *you*, Lena. I told you that then, and I will tell you that now. You worked so hard at everything. Hours and hours in the gardens or in the lab with me. You barely slept. Everyone else saw that, except for you. You get so mad if someone doesn't like what you make or if you do something wrong, but that is not you. Whatever is hurting you right now, whatever problem you are having . . . take a breath for me. You're so scared of doing wrong, but you never will. Not to me, okay? You're so good, *gattina*. I love you so much."

Tears streamed down my face.

I missed her, more than I had realized, but her words stung deep. I *wasn't* good. I hated lying to her after everything she'd done for me, but I couldn't bear to tell Aunt Clare the truth. Everything she believed about me was a lie. If she had known what I was doing with the Saint's Fog . . . if she knew that I was hurting Martin . . . or what I'd done to Audrey . . . the risk I was taking with Jonathan . . .

I had already lost so much.

I couldn't bear the thought of losing her, too.

Aunt Clare had always been the pinnacle for me, an ideal of childhood admiration built through birthday cards and brief visits every few years, a hero that no woman or man on earth could come close to. In my time in Italy, she had become something of a mother to me, too, someone who coddled me on dark nights when the future had me trembling with frustrated tears and a fear of the unknown. She held me so often, cradling my body, her curls tickling my face.

I missed her so much it ached, and I yearned to break away and abandon my post for one more holiday with her. To run far from the Verdeaus and the parties and return to her side where I belonged and forget everything I'd done and planned to do, but I could not.

I could just resolve to be better.

If not for me, then for her.

19

It was early the next morning when George knocked on my door in a rhythmic pattern and ushered me into the suite where Audrey and Jonathan sat eating their catered breakfast. Since I had skipped dinner due to the pains of jet lag, my stomach grumbled easily at the first sight of coffee and pastries. As the light filtered in through their window, it softened the scene into something idyllic. For a moment I wondered if I had awoken at all, if such a peaceful scene of pastoral wallpaper and gauze curtains was something my imagination had conjured while I remained sprawled out, drool dripping from my lips on the cotton sheets.

Thankfully, that wasn't the case.

"There you are!" said Audrey, her voice as warm as ever. "Lena, come, you must join us for breakfast!"

Prosenko, I discovered, had already gone with Martin for a meeting across town that Jonathan was meant to attend as well, but he insisted on having a chance to finish his meal. Considering his son's track record of eating at all, Martin allowed him to stay.

"How was your night, Gereghty?" Jonathan asked as I pulled up a chair.

The table was not large, so I ended up between them both, uncomfortably close, and near enough to notice how Jonathan's eyes were foolishly bright and how there was color in his cheeks—a gentle rouge and olive hue usually lost to his sickly pallor. There was no scent of alcohol around him, nothing to overshadow the smell of the fresh coffee or the shampoo still detectable in his hair from a morning shower.

"It was all right," I said.

Audrey smiled politely and handed over the basket of assorted pastries. "Is it nice to be back? Georgie said he heard you on the phone last night. Did you call your aunt? Is she close enough to visit?"

"Don't be stupid." Jonathan sighed.

"It's not stupid. When I was in Montreux, I could easily train to Lyons. It only took a few hours, although it was faster with a car."

"She said she was in *Umbria*, not Milan."

Audrey frowned just as I grabbed a pain au chocolat. "It's okay," I said, trying to swallow the sorrow as I remembered the call. "We're both too busy to visit anyway, but it was nice to talk. And no, I've never been here. I'm looking forward to getting a chance to explore a bit later. Prosenko hasn't given me my schedule for the day, though, so I don't know how much time I'll have."

"Well, Doc is gone for who knows how long," said Jonathan. "If he didn't drag you to the shareholders' meeting this morning, then I guess you're meant to be stuck with us."

His voice was like a child playing hooky from school.

"You should come with me!" said Audrey. "I'm going out shopping after breakfast. Oh, you have to join, Lena, it'll be so much fun."

Audrey's enthusiasm was startling. An earnest tone I immediately craved to hear again.

"It'll be nice," she then added, "to finally have a chance to talk."

Midway through my croissant, still somehow not as good as Daniella's, there was a call for Jonathan, and a car parked out front to take him to a newly planned meeting Martin had arranged. How he had managed to arrange meetings at the last minute on Christmas Eve I still do not know. Either way, the disappointment on Jonathan's face was all too clear.

Audrey and I watched as George hovered over Jonathan, helping him into his black pea coat and trying to encourage him to carry a proper suit jacket to change into in the car, but Jonathan refused. Instead he left little more dressed than he'd been at breakfast, his skinny legs shoved into a pair of dark chinos and a thick, plum-colored sweater across his chest. I tried to offer him the last of my croissant, hoping the convenience would be enough to convince him, but it was ignored. He had only managed half a piece of toast and two cups of coffee. A Byronic diet if I'd ever seen one.

With Jonathan gone, there was no reason to stay. Audrey finished her cup of coffee and delicately wiped at her lips. "Well, are you ready?"

After grabbing my coat and bag, I met her outside the elevator. She had changed into something more comfortable. Or what appeared to be more comfortable and was actually remarkably chic. Jeans, slim-fitting and high-waisted with a cream-colored cashmere sweater, not unlike her brother's in design, French-tucked into the front, and a pair of heeled boots. Her coat and bag were matching Chanel.

"Come on, Lena!" she said as the wind whipped her golden hair around her face. Stepping onto the streets of Strasbourg, we were met with a new dusting of snow and the bustle of people as we began our trek to one of the main shopping destinations in the city, the Galeries Lafayette, a large indoor mall with Christmas decorations hung about and a tree at the entrance. In all the hurry and travel of the past few days, it had been easy to forget the season, but there it was, painfully picturesque and doing its best to encourage a regret or a yearning for my family in the depths of my chest.

I imagined that my parents and brother were again being reminded of my absence, and I'd resolved to pick something up for them as an apology of sorts. I would have bet money that at that moment Aunt Clare was teaching the new batch of assistants to make the delicate pinwheel shape of the cartellate or, even worse, forcing James's clumsy hand at it. I could imagine the scent of honey filling the space of the house we had shared, how it mixed with the aroma of warmed wine, almonds, and spices. The sound of the olive oil popping on the stove as another nest of dough is tossed in. My mouth watered.

Cool wind slammed into my face as Audrey opened the door back onto the street, and still there was no one. No Martin, no George, and no Prosenko. It was the morning of Christmas Eve, and instead of being with my family I was with *her*, alone again, and I couldn't believe it.

Audrey turned back to smile at me. "Let's find a café, shall we?"

In her small blond body, Audrey Verdeau held a preternatural ability to find caffeine no matter her surroundings. As if guided by some ghostly force, she led us through the crowds and down the main streets of the city center until at last we landed upon a suitable shop, where the scent of coffee, sweet and aromatic, greeted us the moment she opened the door.

With our hands each holding a warm cup and elbows linked, we continued on. For hours I followed her as she darted around people, her eyes scanning windows and taking in the scenes with a pleasured sigh. I knew she had spent time in Europe, but it was here where I saw that we shared the same affinity. The urge to let our eyes linger upon an antiquated street or a seventeenth-century house more than the average tourist. Only where I longed for the stucco and warm tones of Umbria and all its summer charm, hers was a nostalgia linked to the Alps, snow and timber-framed houses and the lush greenery of Central Europe.

Still, I waited for her to bring up the subject of the pills. She had hinted as much over breakfast, and so with every step into a quiet corner of a shop or a turn down a side alley I held a breath in anticipation. Only she never did. That morning her mood and her smiles were easy. A spirit of genuine relaxation had come upon her that told me this town and this region were as much a home to her as Boston—if not more. I did not dare to break that peace. We continued walking, my hands willfully holding the growing multitude of shopping bags for her as we paced the historic district, and I did my best to tell myself that this wasn't a date.

Strasbourg was a stunning town. It was smaller than many would imagine, a far cry from the polish of Paris, and intimate in the holiday season. True to my imagination back in Boston, the buildings held a unique, Germanic charm—a result of proximity to the Black Forest region and likewise to its German history. I never found out if it was really this town that Martin believed his ancestors called home or if it was just a one-off vacation that had resulted in favoritism. Looking at Martin Verdeau, however, ruddy-faced and stout, it made a bit of sense. In the countenance of every passerby and shopkeeper, I attempted to find some sort of familial link or feature.

We walked in the direction of one of the Christkindelsmärik—the light-filled Christmas markets for which Strasbourg, I was told, was famous.

"Can I ask you something?"

Audrey turned to me and made a face as if to say, *Of course, go ahead.*

"Do you celebrate Christmas?"

She smiled. "It doesn't seem like we do, does it? Are you asking because we don't have a tree?"

I smiled as well, fighting a laugh. "Kind of, but more because it's Christmas Eve and your father—"

"Ah," she said, cutting me off. "Yes, well. That's Martin Verdeau." Her voice turned grumbling and low, in a comedic mimicry of her father as she quoted him: "The Chinese markets don't stop today, so why should I?" She shrugged. "It's just his way."

"And you?" I asked.

"What about me?"

"Do you celebrate?"

Slowly she looked down. "No, but I like to think I celebrate how it makes the world. Everything is more beautiful this time of year. Cozier, you know? Like I can breathe."

Before I could reply, I followed her gaze as it lingered over my shoulder, and then, as her eyes widened, she shouted, her voice carrying across the cobbles on the square. "Jonathan!"

"What are you doing here!" she called out as we rushed over to him, kicking the snow beneath our feet. "Why are you out here alone? Where's Prosenko?"

He froze. "Shit."

Audrey frowned as we arrived, closing the distance. "What happened to the meeting?" she asked, catching her breath.

Jonathan looked away and shrugged. "Finished early."

"No, there's no way. I saw his schedule. That meeting goes until three."

"Yeah, well, I decided I was done with it."

"Are you feeling okay?" I asked him, interrupting the scuffle before it could get any worse and break the pleasant mood of the morning. I scanned his face for any symptoms.

Aside from a bit of red to his nose from the cold, he seemed fine. His eyes, however, continued to dart around, reading the signs of every shop. I then noticed the piece of paper in his hand.

"Are you looking for something?" I nodded to the paper.

Audrey also stopped and eyed it.

Jonathan held his fist around it tighter, crinkling it. "It's nothing, forget it."

"Jonathan," Audrey urged.

After a moment of silence, he sighed. "Yeah, uh, have you seen an antique store near here? With books in the window? It's closing early today."

I thought back to the streets we had wandered and then nodded, motioning. "Yeah, actually, a few blocks down and to the right—"

In a dash he was off, leaving Audrey and me to follow hastily.

For someone as sick as he was, Jonathan ran quickly, his long legs carrying him far more efficiently than Audrey's heels on the cobblestones would allow her. By the time we found him, he was already transfixed on a cart of books just outside an antiquarian bookstore, silent as his fingers brushed the aged spines so ardently it was as if the world around him had ceased to exist. He rummaged and rummaged before disappearing inside the store for a long moment, to where the rarer texts no doubt lay in wait.

We remained silent, patient until at last he appeared again at the threshold of the door, an open book with faded red binding in hand, his eyes scanning it with the greatest of attention.

"'We decay,'" he said softly, standing just inside, where the warmth of the shop could still reach his face and beneath the shopkeeper's watchful eye. "'Like corpses in a charnel; fear and grief / Convulse us and consume us day by day . . .'"

His nails, bitten down to the quick, beds blue from the cold, lay in stunning contrast to the yellowed parchment. Tenderly, so tenderly, I watched as Jonathan stroked the book's binding in admiration, reading the text aloud.

"What is that?" I asked him.

"It's from 'Adonais,'" he said, distant. "By Shelley. . . . It's about Keats. An elegy."

Audrey looked to him and then reached for the book with an unreadable expression.

"You need to stop with this," she said sharply.

Jonathan gripped the book, his hand tight as a vise, letting his voice grow equal parts sharp and deep. "Let it go, Audrey."

She promptly did. "You promised you'd give it up."

Once it was safe again, her brother held the book as one might hold a baby sparrow. Impossibly delicate. Adoring. For a flash of an instant, Audrey's face was furious, and then her anger faded.

"Jonathan . . ." she pleaded.

"I'm buying it."

"You know what Martin thinks about this death shit. He—"

"I'm buying it, Audrey. It's a first edition. Elliot said if I ever found anything, he could have it repaired for me and—"

"You're not *listening* to me."

"And you're ignoring me the same as always!" he shouted. "Just let me have this!"

Something in Jonathan had changed. Something tender and ferociously melancholy that left Audrey and me standing there on the street corner watching our breath cloud the cold winter air as his pea coat disappeared deeper inside the small shop so he could pay.

Beside me Audrey shuddered. She seemed completely at a loss.

"What's that about?" I asked.

She shook her head. "Nothing, it's just . . ." Her gloved fingers tightened around her arms. "Just some old obsessions coming back. That's all."

"What do you mean?"

She stared at the cobblestones. "Has he ever mentioned them to you? His idols? . . . Marlowe? Shelley? Keats?"

The answer was clear on my face. I had found Jonathan too many times in that old library at Arrow's Edge or in the music room lost in the pages of another antique book, as often as I'd caught him with liquor on his tongue.

"You know why he likes them, don't you?" she asked me.

"They're sad?"

"No," said Audrey, her voice a tired hush. "They died young."

I had briefly turned back to the opened door, watching as the older man at the counter handed Jonathan a package wrapped in brown paper.

"I hope we get to the bottom of this soon, Lena. I really do. I'm not sure how much longer I can stand to wait. I need to know the poison or the medicine or . . . or what they're treating him for. I just need to know."

"And we will," I assured her. "He's been doing better at least, since we stopped the pills."

"You think?"

I nodded. "He's more alert."

"Hmph. Maybe that's why we're fighting more."

"A small price to pay?"

"Hardly one at all."

"Ready?" Jonathan asked, stepping back into the cold with a smile, the package tucked under his coat. Audrey remained silent, so I nodded and did my best to smile, too.

"Lead the way."

"The market should be just a few more streets up. The shopkeeper told me you can get gifts for your parents there, Lena. If you still want to."

I was surprised he'd thought to ask at all.

We walked the winding streets, but the day's joy yielded to a darker cloud as my mind wandered back to my first genuine conversation with Jonathan, to his exhausted body framed by the lush plants in the greenhouse and his eyes glued to the old copy of *Edward II*.

In all my time with the Verdeau family and in my months of tending to Jonathan daily, I had never seen him smile as softly as he did there in the streets of Strasbourg. How much lighter the burden about his shoulders seemed.

There were few occasions where that somber air he clung to faded, and the only ones I could recall were in the early hours of the parties when Elliot sat beside him, hands waving in the air as he told Jonathan the details of a newly found sketch by Joseph Severn or a poem by A. E. Housman. Never had I thought his predilection for history had a more macabre cause, but now that I knew, it all added up.

Beside me Audrey stayed quiet.

With every passing street, her distaste for the book seemed to grow, occupying every bit of her mind until the lights of the Christmas market appeared.

We were greeted by wooden stalls, all laid out in rows with painted signs and everything you could imagine for sale. There were pastries, and roasting meats, and little carved houses, and ornaments alongside stuffed animals and mulled wine. It looked entirely like something out of a fairy tale, and despite everything I was utterly charmed. A cacophony of scents surrounded us, each delicious and tantalizing.

Jonathan was in good spirits and clung to the new book with a loving grip all the way through our tour of the stalls. In the December cold, his face was an eerie shade of pale, but his nose and cheeks were bright with blood. Blood, I thought, and life.

Audrey led the way through the many rows of stalls, stopping only for the most charming or glittering of objects. We found rows upon rows of ornaments, some a crystalline white and others rustic and made of carved wood, more to my taste. There were painted dolls and figurines and little churches that mimicked the grand cathedral only a few streets away. After a while of looking and no decisions made, the cold at last seeped too far into our bones to ignore, and the smell of mulled wine was irresistible.

We shared a cup, the three of us. A small sampling of the local Alsatian white, warm with spices and steam rising to greet our eager eyes. Audrey took the first sip, holding the cup like a goblet at Communion before passing it to me.

Of all the occasions in my life I've had mulled wine, both before and after the Verdeaus, that simple paper cup remains my unequivocal favorite. No wine could ever surpass it. When it was my turn to hand it to Jonathan, I let the warmth linger in my throat, willing time to stop. Then, to my surprise, he took a single sip and passed it off to his sister once more.

Both of us were shocked. Shocked and grateful.

Without the fog of alcohol to mask him, the real Jonathan had begun to surface, and an energy floated about him that I quickly came to admire. He was something akin to a six-foot-tall and lanky child with dark, messy hair and wide hazel eyes, a child full of wonder and none of the pessimism that plagued him back in Boston. Yet I noticed that in his growing curiosity and excitement, he stumbled over himself. It was an act I had previously attributed to his near-constant inebriation, but there in the light of Strasbourg there was nothing to hinder him but his own ailing body.

We had just finished our first round of the market when he began to slow. Audrey and I would walk, only to realize he had stopped three stalls behind. With every glance he feigned interest in something nearby, but the reality was clear to see. It had been weeks since he'd left the house for this long. Walked more than the length of Arrow's Edge or from his room to the kitchen.

Still, Jonathan knew the city. Like his sister, he knew French, and German well enough, too, which I had never known or expected, and aside from forgetting words, he was happy. Genuinely so, and I yearned for it to last forever. The image of the three of us, arms laden with Audrey's discoveries, the bustle of the surrounding crowds, the scent of hot wine and bread. If heaven were to exist, I think I caught a glimpse of it that afternoon.

Unfortunately, our return to the hotel was far less peaceful. Almost as soon as we set foot inside, the ice dripping from the soles of our shoes, Martin appeared. A dark shadow passing across our joy to yank Jonathan into a side room like a delinquent puppy.

The shouts began almost immediately, echoing through the walls so that the foreign luxury of our hotel instantly mirrored the halls of the town house. Audrey gripped her bags tightly and hurried off to her room.

I lingered. I lingered long enough to catch a glimpse of Martin, his face bearing all the fury of Mars, repeating the same words I'd heard months before. *How dare you embarrass me? You don't know what I've done for you.* To this day it is the image of Martin that remains at the forefront of my mind. The hatred. The rage at his prodigal heir. It felt inhuman.

20

JONATHAN SHOUTED, HIS VOICE PIERCING the late hour with a manic and desperate joy as it echoed through the door. A heavy hand slapped at the wood in rapid beats, echoing for my attention. "Leeena! Lena, Lena, Lena, wake up!"

I threw the comforter back and ran to the door, only to open it and find Jonathan still in his clothes from earlier. His hair was a mess and his face frightful.

I glanced at the clock on my bedside table. "It's . . . it's after midnight."

He grinned. "Yeah, I know."

"Go back to bed."

"Can't. Was never in it to begin with."

"Then you should try and get acquainted with it!"

"Mm, now, why would I do that when I have you?"

I faltered and started to close the door. "Go to sleep."

"I'm going out."

"That's a terrible idea. It's freezing."

He lifted a hand to reveal a half-empty bottle of wine. Surely not his first of the evening. "That's what this is for."

It was the first time I'd seen Jonathan since returning to the hotel, when Martin whisked him away, and something told me Jonathan had been drinking steadily since. It was such a stark contrast to the man I had come to know on our walk that afternoon. The calm face. The gentle smile as his fingers so cautiously flipped the pages of antique books.

"I'm going out," he repeated, slurring his words.

"You'll get sick."

"Well, you're my doctor. You're supposed to take care of me, right?"

"No, that's Prosenko. Go drink with him."

Jonathan frowned, letting the bottle droop slightly in his grip.

"But he's a bore, and you," he emphasized, leaning closer, "you, Helena Margaret Gereghty, are a mystery."

I was surprised Jonathan somehow came to know my full name, but not surprised enough to indulge him. Not until he refused to let me shut the door and made me watch as he easily drank another quarter of the bottle. It stained his lips a darker hue and sloshed onto the crisp white of his shirt.

Despite my better judgment, the memory of Jonathan hours earlier was enough to convince me to reach for my coat and scarf and follow him out the door into the chill air of the city.

I followed Jonathan down the winding streets as he searched for a bar worth staying in that also was not closing. We went from door to door, peering into the window display of every restaurant and bar in hopes of seeing someone behind the counter or a single light still on.

For me now the night remains something snowcapped and strangely cozy. A night of small spaces and wooden stools in pubs. The sanctuaries he managed to find were almost tacky, Anglophilic interpretations of Black Forest charm. Imports that had a tourist menu and little else. They were also the only places willing to serve us on Christmas Eve, when the rest of the city was shut up tight.

"Lena . . ." said Jonathan at some point past 1:00 A.M. "Lena."

"What?" I asked, exhausted but clutching onto my Märzenbier. He had made me choose something. The foam still met the top of the glass. I hadn't taken a sip. Jonathan stared down at the countertop and his own empty glass. "He took it."

My brows furrowed. This seemed to come out of nowhere. "What?"

"Martin," he said, and swallowed. "The book from the . . ." He paused, then motioned. "Well, you know. Shelley."

My heart sank. "Why did he take it?"

Jonathan shrugged. "He doesn't like them. . . . They're not dumb, right?" he asked, almost nervous. "You like them, too. You get it. The Romantics. They're not dumb."

"No, Jonathan. They're not."

The chair creaked below him as his body shifted, unsteady. Despite my protests Jonathan had chugged two glasses of mulled wine in the short time we'd been there and ordered a third. Which is not to mention the half-pint of beer from the place before, which he got bored of and stumbled out of, leaving me to run back and pay.

"Do you have a favorite?" I tried asking him. "Poem of theirs."

His eyes stared at the grain of the wooden counter, his body easing back and forth on the stool as if he wavered between realities. "Yeah."

"Tell me some of it?"

For a moment I thought he was going to ignore me entirely, leaving the inch of vulnerability he'd given to fade away and hide back behind the warmth of his alcohol. Then he spoke. Softly, face unreadable. The same poem he had purchased earlier that day.

"'With me / Died Adonais; till the Future dares / Forget the Past, his fate and fame shall be / An echo and a light unto eternity!'"

I was surprised he had any of it memorized. But he did. Even despite his drunken stupor, the words that began the poem flowed from Jonathan's lips with such a sorrow that my very heart ached for their story's hero. He said only the first few stanzas, but I was sure that if I'd asked, he would have recited the entirety of it.

"I'm sorry," I said, meaning it more than should have even been possible.

He turned to me, eyes glazed over and empty with sorrow. I thought he would say something, from the way his mouth hung open, but nothing came. Instead he waved his hand with a flick of his bony wrist and mumbled for the check.

No sooner had our feet hit the snowy pavement than Jonathan stumbled forward into the street, his body framed only by the dim light posts and the strings of red and green overhead. Then he screamed. A loud, hysteric, and guttural "Fuuuuck!"

He screamed again.

His voice bounced between the buildings, and I'm certain that a few curtains opened and windows cracked to see the commotion of whoever dared to disturb the Christmas tranquility, but there on the street all I saw was Jonathan, incredibly drunk, incredibly broken and overwhelmed with grief I could not begin to understand. Everything in my heart ached for him. Helpless and hurting as he shattered further and further in front of me.

"Fuck you!" he screamed to the sky. "Fuck you, you fucking asshole of a man! Fuck your business meetings! Fuck your cars and your CEOs! Fuck Germany and Zurich and your trade plans and fucking Utah! Fuck!"

His body was shaking by the time I reached him, and as my hands grasped his shoulders, his entire body flinched, throwing me back. His arms wrapped around each other, cradling himself as he choked down rage and the rise of stale wine.

"Piece of shit . . ." he mumbled, and gasped for breath.

I had started to reach for him again when his body lurched.

"Why'd you . . . why'd you have to burn it?"

"Jonathan."

The cold had stung his lungs, leaving his breath hard and raspy. Cautiously I put my hand on his shoulder, and this time he let me pull him up onto his feet.

"Hey," I told him, placing my other hand on his cheek, stained with tears. "Hey, look at me."

He refused.

"It's just a book, it—"

Again he lurched away. Violent with grief. "No, s'not! For fuck's sake, why can none of you people see that?"

He was heaving, and as I reached out, Jonathan stumbled on the packed ice of the curb, crashing into a nearby tree on the sidewalk.

"I'm sorry," I urged louder, in an attempt to get closer to his level. "I know that. I shouldn't have said that."

For a moment he sobbed, a choked, silent sound impossible to mistake for anything other than a deep-felt hatred at letting himself cry. I watched as his hands formed fists, grappling with themselves, and as he weakly punched at the flesh of his thigh. Over and over again, thin fingers balled up in Italian leather.

I waited for what felt like hours, the snow gently falling around us and the streets so painfully quiet that you could hear it settle. A crackle of ice onto the frozen world and the whisper of the wind as it passed through the alleyways and into our hair. No cars, no voices or laughter. Nothing but that same white snow. A silent night.

"I didn't want to go," he mumbled, so soft I nearly missed it. "To the meetings. I told him that."

"The ones today?"

He nodded. Still Jonathan refused to face me.

"They kept saying I agreed to stuff, but I hadn't. But they had my signatures, and so I guess I had, but *fuck*, the way he looked at me . . ."

Every word that came from his throat was strained and so very, very tired.

He barked a bitter, stunted laugh. A grin of rage across his lips as he looked up at the sky. "I don't know what I expected. The minute he saw it in my hand. Barely through the door and he took it." Finally Jonathan looked to me, dead in the eye. "He ripped it from my hand."

"Jonathan—"

"I punched him," he said. "Right in the cheek." Weakly he motioned a punch into his hand. "Couldn't even hit his fucking eye . . . but that was it. He took the book and . . ." Again he acted it out with his hand. "Poof. Into the fireplace."

"I'm sorry," I told him, at a loss for anything else.

"You didn't do nothin', Gereghty," he said, finally calming down, and with the calm a visible numbness settled over him. The next thing I knew, I was watching him stand up, pants soaked dark from the melting ice. I was mildly surprised he had enough body heat to melt it at all. Despite the darkness I could see the bluish tint edging his lips through the stain from the wine. I watched as he stumbled, still drunk, down the road and farther into the night, and then I chased after him, calling his name once more until he stopped.

"Where are you going?"

"To find another place," he slurred.

"Jonathan, there *isn't* another place. It's Christmas, everything is closed."

He paused and looked up. Then pivoted on his heel to look around at the street and the decorations hanging from the corners of buildings, the lights reflecting in all the windows.

"It's . . . Christmas."

"*Yes.*"

He looked to me again, only this time with gentle surprise. "You didn't go to Mass."

"What?" I asked sharply. "Jonathan, no, I . . . I don't go to Mass."

"But why?" he said, words laced with concern. "You have a reason to go. You wear a crucifix. You . . . you're *Italian*."

I could not believe that the conversation had turned into this. The snow continued to fall around us, the cold gripping me harder with each second we remained outside. I almost yearned for the pub again.

"That doesn't mean I go to Mass."

"But you should! You should be with family and sitting in those wooden pews and singing hymns and stuff. Looking at the plastic babies. Welcoming the real one."

"Well, I . . . I was working."

Jonathan blinked, his lashes heavy and flecked with snow. He stared, growing quiet until at last I looked at him with the same genuine attention.

"But *why*?" he asked, leaning dangerously close.

"Because," I started, "I was asked to. Because you're here."

"Me?"

Against my better judgment, I let my voice soften. "Yeah."

Standing there, I was surrounded by the smell of cologne and wine, with so little distance between us that I could feel the falsified, alcoholic warmth radiating from his cheeks. His lips hovered so close to mine that if he slipped, there was nowhere else for me to turn. So close I could practically feel him blink. That if he stumbled, if a hard enough wind brushed against his back, we would—

My heart skipped, and my head grew angry that it had. Then, at the last moment, as if something sobering had crossed his mind, Jonathan straightened his spine and pressed his lips instead into the curls of my hair, letting them linger. So long that I dared not breathe and felt my lungs ache with impatience.

"You're right," he said after a moment. "It's late. . . . I'm tired."

I stood there, awkwardly silent. Hesitant to move.

"Good night, Helena," Jonathan said somberly, and then, as easily as he had leaned down and twice as quickly, he turned and left me to watch as he stumbled along the snow-covered street toward the hotel.

I had not realized it, but in all our going in circles we'd managed to return to the same small street where we'd started, with the golden light of the lobby calling to us at the end.

I went to bed exhausted and tipsy, and when morning came, the peace of the snow and the tenderness of the previous night were forever gone.

21

IN THE MORNING I AWOKE with great alarm to the sound of banging on my door once more. By the time I opened it, my brain had yet to catch up, and so I still expected to see Jonathan, snow-covered or perhaps grinning madly once again, as if mere seconds had passed since our parting. Instead I saw George, tall, wrinkled, and even more somber than usual. A great worry in his eyes.

"Jonathan has taken ill. A flight has been arranged."

The words processed.

"Ill?" I asked. "But he was fi—"

"I'm sorry to say that your services are not needed today, Miss Gereghty," he told me shortly. "His doctor is tending to him to ease the pain. You are simply to pack your things so we can leave."

"What?"

I refused. It was foolish of me, but my heart rate was increasing, and so I rushed out the door, past George and toward the room where I knew Jonathan had been sleeping. Outside I saw Audrey, draped in her cream silk robe with mascara streaked down her cheeks. The fact that it could be seen from so far away meant Audrey didn't even care that she was in such a state, and it told me all I needed to know.

As I approached the door, she moved, startled, and tried to prevent me from going in, but I was taller than her when she was without her usual heels, and so, peering past her tousled blond hair, I saw Jonathan on the hotel bed. Pale, his back bent, writhing as if his body were confined to an invisible torture device. There are no other words to describe it. He was in agony, and the sight of him made tears gather at my eyes.

His name caught in my throat. "Jonathan!?"

Audrey shoved me back as I shouted. "Stop it!" she said, and wiped at her face. The fear in her eyes was gone, for a moment.

I listened as Jonathan groaned, and I saw as Martin's eyes turned sharply to me before Prosenko slammed the door shut.

"What happened?" I asked, a growing panic in my voice. "I should be in there! Why didn't anyone wake me up? What's going on?"

I can count on the fingers of one hand the number of times I'd seen her angelic face angry. The way she looked at me then was one. To this day, it stands out with a crystal clarity.

"Audrey?" I asked again, trying to calm myself but failing. "What's going on?"

"I don't know. I just went to get him for breakfast and heard him scre—" She stopped, choking on her words. "Screaming. Through the door."

I watched as Audrey took a breath and calmed herself, swallowed every bit of anger and loss of control, then stared at me with the venom of it all condensed.

"What?"

"When did you two get home last night?" she snapped. "Three? Four?"

I didn't know.

"Audrey . . ." I started, my voice softer. "No, it . . . it wasn't that late."

"Do you think I'm an idiot? His room is right next to mine. I heard his door shut! I saw you two from the window when you—"

Again the sounds from his room traveled down the hall. The slam of a body into a bed. An agonized moan. It was too much for either of us.

"He hasn't been taking his medicine, Lena. Because of us he hasn't been taking it, and—" Audrey's shaking hand quickly covered her mouth. "Oh, God . . ."

I didn't want to hear the echoing screams any more than she did. My own body ached with sorrow at imagining whatever was going on behind those doors. Still, I didn't understand the sharpness of her eyes moments before. The kind of look that made you feel guilty in an instant, and I did. I knew that nothing had happened between Jonathan and me, but in Audrey's eyes something had, and for that my conscience burned with guilt regardless.

"What happened?" I asked, looking again to the shut door just ahead. "Has Prosenko been in there the whole time?"

Suddenly she shoved me, her hands shaking and weak. Instantly they recoiled, wrapping around herself in regret.

"Of course! He's the doctor."

I stopped, and with another brief glance to the door, pulled Audrey closer. When I spoke again, my voice was a harsh and cautious whisper, filled with a sense of betrayal.

"How can you still say that? After everything?" Audrey yanked away from me, but I persisted. "You were the one who didn't trust him! That's why you made us take those pills! And you were right, Audrey, you saw what they did! How can you trust him now?"

"I think you should go."

"Why? I didn't do anything!"

"Enough!"

In a moment my hand was empty, and I was left watching as her golden form rushed back to the door where her family was and slipped inside.

It didn't take long for George to meet me again and guide me back to my room to pack up my things. With tears rolling down my face, I folded each shirt haphazardly into my suitcase, and I listened as another wretched cry came from too far away for me to help. With each sound the image of his face haunted me. Jonathan's smile outside the bookshop. The way he walked along the cobblestone streets. Every ounce of happiness from the day before became a device of cruel punishment, because somewhere between when my head had hit that pillow and the dawn of today, Jonathan had taken a turn for the worse. Only I didn't want to believe it was the lack of pills. That it was my fault. I had seen his improvement from the days of not taking them, and then for Jonathan to be in such a pained state after Prosenko got his hands on him again . . . I couldn't fight the feeling that Audrey's suspicions had been correct. Maybe it was willful denial. After talking with Aunt Clare and promising to do better, maybe I just didn't want to believe I could have hurt him, but still . . .

I was back on the plane in a flash, with only George and Audrey as company. A dazed drive from the city to the airport where no words dared to be spoken. Banished from the situation and ordered back to Boston, Audrey sat in the front seat during the drive from the hotel, her jaw clamped tight and her fingers holding firm to her cell phone. I was forbidden to speak.

They didn't tell me what had happened to Jonathan. Instead I was left to imagine the scene over and over again as the distance between us only grew. Jonathan, now helpless and alone, in a foreign hospital with no one to tend to him but his father and the person I increasingly trusted less with the task.

When we landed in Boston, another car took us straight back to the town house. I presumed, initially, that it was to continue and drop me off at home as well, but I was wrong. Perhaps that was the original intention, but something shifted. A block away from the town house, a small crowd began to appear. A cluster of curious eyes and eager hands on cameras. The car slowed at their sight, but Audrey urged our driver forward.

"I asked to be dropped off at my house. Not my neighbors'. Make them move."

He did, and, almost rehearsed, the small crowd of seven or eight parted, scattering like rats. I'd seen them on occasion, one or two circling the building after Audrey had returned home from shopping, but nothing like this.

George motioned for me to wait, then slowly got out on his aging bones and opened the door for Audrey. He helped her with the luggage, and no sooner did her foot hit the pavement than hell itself broke loose.

Within seconds a group of men with cameras and flashing lights accosted her, shouting. "Audrey!" "Audrey!" they boomed. "How was France?" "Is Jonathan okay?" "Audrey!" "Audrey, over here!" Endlessly it went on, a scene I had viewed only as an outsider, but the lights that day were different. Now they were crueler and more invasive in their hunger. I watched Audrey, the way she shielded her face, a cold airport coffee in her hand and her Birkin dangling from her wrist. The way misery was laced in her mascara. She stood there, alone with all the indelicate rage of a wick on its last thread.

Without thinking I rushed out of the car.

Two men from the crowd came after me.

My body was soon thrown back, held by the force of the men before I could reach the immaculate steps. Audrey paused, startled, with her hand on the door and turned to me. George tried to usher her inside.

"Audrey!" they shouted again, screeching like seagulls. "Why are you alone?!"

"Audrey!"

"Audrey!"

"Is he dead?"

Something flashed bright into my eye, and I stumbled, falling into a man who smelled like too many cigarettes and too much sweat.

"Stop!" yelled Audrey then. The pitch rising above everything else. "Stop this! Leave her alone! Don't photograph her!"

More flashes of light. Blinding. Harsh.

Finally I felt a hand grab my wrist and saw George, tired and sympathetic, as he pulled me through and slammed the door shut behind me.

A disorienting silence greeted us.

No sooner had I realized that my suitcases remained abandoned in the vehicle than Audrey grabbed hold of my wrist once more and dragged me down the hall and into a dark room. The study.

"Never answer their questions," she said, avoiding my eyes. Everything else in the room was a focus for her. The spines of books. The corners of tables and the details of the Oriental rug below. "They only ask terrible ones. To get your attention. They're vultures who shouldn't even be here. I don't even—" She shook her head, shaking something off in a huff. "The hotel must have leaked it."

My eyebrows furrowed. I couldn't help it. "Are they always like that?"

Still she avoided me. A frown forming on pink lips. "No. Not since his last— Not for a few years."

I followed Audrey's gaze to an abandoned wineglass. The once-red liquid now a ring of residue, dried out from the day of departure.

"I know you don't want to tell me, and I don't know why. . . . I don't know, maybe I do know why, but . . . please . . . Is he . . . is he okay?" I asked, desperate for an answer.

When Audrey spoke again, her voice was quiet. "He's stable," she said. "I got a text from Martin on the drive over."

"What happened?" I asked, to no response again. "Audrey, *please*. Talk to me."

"I don't know!" Her fingers curled in on themselves, forming a fist until her knuckles went white, releasing and closing again nervously as she went over the details in her mind. "We were all getting ready for break-fast," she explained. "I had knocked on his door to wake him up, passed Prosenko on his way for his usual checks. He . . . he asked me if I knew when Jonathan got in last night, and I mentioned I saw him with you, but . . . Then I went back, put on my makeup, and just . . . There was this awful sound. It was terrible. I've never heard him screaming like that. Never."

Something in her words didn't add up.

"Why did you talk to Prosenko?"

Audrey frowned deeper, her eyes becoming daggers. "Don't start with me, Lena."

"Why not?!" By this point my patience was exhausted. Worn out by the ill-placed blame. By too many hours spent wondering if Jonathan was okay. If he was even alive. If I had done something the night before and what any of this meant. The silence of the plane had swallowed me up, and I couldn't even cry anymore. I had wanted to for hours, off and on, I was so scared for him, but now . . . now I was just mad. "Then what have we been doing all this time?" I said, my voice cracking. "Think *back*, Audrey. Put the pieces together. I'm not going to defend Prosenko when all the evidence tells us otherwise!"

"What evidence?!" she shouted. "Lena, you haven't been able to tell me anything! All this proves is that he went off his medication, you went out drinking with him, and it put him in the hospital!"

"That's bullshit and you know it! He was doing well! He was *smiling*! He was fine last night!"

"He was plastered! I saw him! And you—" She was furious again. Undeniably so. "You're his doctor, too. You should have been helping him. Let me tell you, Lena, my brother kisses dozens of men and women who don't mean a damn thing to him. No one does. No one ever has. You're not special."

"I was helping him!" I screamed, finally matching her tone. "I was the *only* one helping him! I didn't make him drink, Audrey, that was Martin when he threw the book Jonathan had bought into the fireplace and destroyed it right in front of him!"

The tension in her shoulders froze, her eyes going wide. The air around us went quiet.

"He what?"

Finally I had a chance to catch my breath. A chance to realize that my hands were shaking as adrenaline raced through me. "He was upset, Audrey. I . . . I only went with him to make sure he didn't hurt himself. Nothing happened between us. He was distraught."

"Martin burned it?"

"*Yes*, the Shelley book. 'Adonais.' The one from the store."

She looked away again. Eyes wandering back to the wineglass as everything in her seemed to break. "Lena, I . . . I'm sorry, I don't know what to do."

"I tried telling you. Something happened this morning. Jonathan was . . . he was fine when we got back to the hotel. Drunk but fine. I *promise*."

Glassy, dark eyes looked to me then. Tired. Worried. There was another question she wanted to ask but didn't. "You really think he did something?" she asked. "Prosenko?"

"After you passed him in the hall? Yeah. I do."

"But why? Why *then*?"

I dared to inch closer, taking a seat on the chair in front of her. "I don't know, but it must have something to do with the pills. I've been trying to think of what could be in them. What Prosenko has been using with him. Why I haven't been able to get an answer. Why our symptoms matched with dozens and dozens of poisons and medicines and not just one."

She arched an eyebrow, ever so cautiously, "And . . . ? What? Could you think of anything?"

I couldn't, and that was the problem. After reading Aunt Clare's e-mails, I had tried to remember all our studies. I thought of every poison I knew, and every mixture, and still I couldn't think of one that could cause so many symptoms. But I couldn't think of any sort of herb or plant or drug that would have been used for a medication either. Not one that would have been strong enough to cause such harm to us from one small dose.

"Lena?"

It was like a mixture of everything.

A compound of every plant, and poison, and—

That was it.

"A theriac."

Audrey looked to me, barely hearing the word as it escaped my mouth. "What?"

I swallowed, wondering, could that really be it? Could it be so simple? I thought back to Aunt Clare's e-mail again. The garden. The plants she described and everything she was working on. I'd only briefly known what they were, but . . . it was possible. I hadn't thought of it until now, but it was possible.

"A theriac," I repeated. "It's like a blend of poisons. All of them. Or maybe not all but a lot."

"*What?* That's absurd."

"No, no, it's not," I insisted as more of the pieces seemed to come together. My weeks studying them with Aunt Clare. "Not really. Have you heard of Mithridates?"

"Is that a company?"

"A Persian king. He was so terrified of someone killing him to seize his power that he had his doctors give him poisons. Every poisonous thing on earth, but in very small doses. Very, very small. He thought it would build up immunity."

"That's crazy."

"It is, but . . . according to lore, it worked. It's like a vaccine. People have been using the method of these theriacs for centuries. They're not common, but . . . I think . . . This may sound crazy, but is it possible that's what Prosenko was hired for? That that's what he's been doing to Jonathan all this time?"

"I . . . I don't know, Lena. It seems like a bit of a stretch. . . ."

The more I thought about it, the more it made sense. I had known it only as a story from the history books and the late nights spent in Montefalco over campfires as we traded tales. The tactic of a paranoid and tragic king, so desperate to evade death that he poisoned himself with everything possible to make himself immune. It was strange, but it fit with everything I knew about Martin Verdeau, the risks he was willing to take. The knowledge of it gnawed at me and clawed at my consciousness with the fierce and terrible wonder that only truth can give.

The image of a young Jonathan falling, and Prosenko being ushered in to save the supposed sole heir to Avelux. Martin's obsession. The fury at Jonathan's morbid hobby. Every minuscule fact I had learned over the days of my employment added up to this single and terrifying conclusion of the things Martin would do to save his only son. His reputation.

Beside me sat Audrey, thoughts flying behind her eyes. "What did they use them for? These . . . theriacs."

"Everything. Every ailment, every sickness. From trying to cure cancer to stopping blood—"

"What?" She turned sharply. "To stop bleeding? Like a coagulant?"

I nodded. "A lot of things. Why?"

Audrey's eyes transformed into something suspicious and wild. "Jonathan got sick after that fall. That first one I told you about. You don't think— He just told us the pills would stop the bleeding. Then Prosenko, he came back with more. There were always more issues after that. Bleeding, bruising, a cough, a sick stomach, too tired . . . until Jonathan was taking something daily. Until he couldn't leave the house. That was when the drinking started. . . . I think he just always felt so bad."

"But *why?*" I asked her, trying to get her to realize what I already had. "Why would your father let Prosenko do something like that?"

"Because," she said with a newfound certainty, "Jonathan was all he had to inherit Avelux. I was never going to be an option."

That evening we didn't leave the study for hours. Even as George knocked on the door to inquire about dinner and the paparazzi grew bored and left, we remained. Two souls, finding ourselves alone in a world with the burden of an unwanted truth.

Without my asking, Audrey began to explain to me how she'd fought with Martin for years. How she had to pitch him three times to be allowed into the same meetings as her brother. To have a say in her future, same as she felt she'd earned. Only when the day finally came and the conference-room door opened, there was no one there. The meeting had been canceled. For the last twenty-five years, every step Audrey Verdeau took to impress her father and prove herself worthy of her family name seemed only to curse her. Every award she received that should have been a mark of success was an award stolen, in Martin's eyes, from Jonathan.

Jonathan's health always took a turn for the worse when Audrey's life began to get better, an odd pattern of fate that I learned she had come to blame herself for. Meanwhile, with every failure on his part, Jonathan secluded himself away more. Every ache in his body was a reason to be unworthy, and the more he tried to run, the more Martin pushed and the worse Jonathan tried to become.

Alcohol was the only thing that dulled the pain of his body. The pain of Martin. This was what Audrey suspected, and from everything I knew about the man, I saw no reason to believe otherwise.

I didn't know it then, but six brief days were all that separated us from our return to Arrow's Edge. The next party lingered, uncanceled despite our not knowing Jonathan's condition, and so it became a dark phantom over every thought and passing hour.

Armed with the knowledge of how far Martin's cruelty went beyond his parties, I was no longer satisfied with simply humiliating him in front of his colleagues.

No.

He needed to fall, and he needed to never recover.

22

THAT NEW YEAR'S EVE, WITH THE AIR CRISP and the old rooms of the estate filled with lights and sounds ten times greater than at that first party, I saw Jonathan again for the first time since Strasbourg, barely free from the hospital and already dressed in a half-buttoned oxford shirt. His hazel eyes were rimmed in purple, his cheekbones sharp as Martin circled him. As that devil of a man handed him a glass of amber liquid, my blood ran cold.

Did I plan for Martin to die that night?

With every fiber of my soul's construction.

Did it happen how I wanted?

No.

Not at all.

And that's what I regret.

It felt like slipping into an old skin, easy and comfortable. A rageful state I wore so readily in the aftermath of that initial descent into their world. Before the failure, before Martin's demand for the Fog. But if the sight of Mrs. Gainsborough the night of the first party had been a spark, the thought of the siblings now, with everything Martin and his world had done to them, was a bonfire.

The amount of Saint's Fog that Martin had requested was absurd. To make the cut took brewing a new batch as well as diluting the entirety of what lingered in the old jars in my closet. And I *had* diluted it. Despite everything in my body urging me beyond the edge of war's thin moral line, I diluted it to near nothing. All except for one vial. A little dropper, hidden underhand, with the gray-dusted leaves of the drug's namesake shoved in among the liquid for luck.

The afternoon before the party, apparently now unbothered to hide his intended mass druggings from the staff, Martin asked George to relay to me that the doctored drinks were to be available only in the ballroom. A large table, like many of the others scattered about Arrow's Edge, with glasses and glasses in tidy rows, each with a measured dose. Then, same as all the parties before, a glimmering pyramid of glass. The champagne tower.

After Strasbourg I expected it all to be canceled and my ticket to the event stripped from my hand. That somehow Prosenko, or perhaps even Martin himself, would blame me for Jonathan's attack in the same way that Audrey had. But upon their return a mere two days after our own, Prosenko had called me at home, personally giving me the schedule and telling me when to arrive, a courtesy I couldn't help but find odd.

He was pleased, he told me, that Jonathan's condition had improved, and the party would now take on a celebratory tone. He seemed chipper, overjoyed, and the idea of his smile settled like venom in my gut. The feeling remained as I arrived during setup and he handed me a bag with a few of Jonathan's pills.

"Enjoy the night, but don't forget you're still working. I want you to find him," he'd said to me, "and when you do, be sure he takes them this time."

I pocketed them and went on my way.

When I next saw Martin, he beamed with a wicked grin, unkind like an old god as I administered the first few drops into the glasses. This night my role had been lifted from the shadows. No longer was my hand hidden in the corners of the kitchen; it was there under the spotlights and before his velvet throne as Martin watched me. Every motion. Every ordered drop. I imagined grabbing one of those glasses and throwing it straight into his face. The shards puncturing his eyes.

Despite everything, I told myself it was fine.

The New Year's party was bigger, flashier, the music louder, filled with glitter, confetti, and all the trappings of the high life. A vaudevillian affair, more extravagant than anything before. Even the staff who had been under the Verdeau spell far longer than I were alarmed at the vulgarity and magnitude.

At the back of one of the rooms, I saw Sascha, running around in a fury, her red hair a beacon of friendly civility and innocence among the wavering crowd. In another I saw George, stoic as always and with a rigid spine. It was, I think, the first night I'd seen the soldier in him. The patience and resilience.

I was numb. The human body, I believe, if it possesses a soul, can only contain so much anger before it surrenders. In the span of those few hours, I watched Audrey sloshing martinis. Pouring them down, one after another, and avoiding me at every pass. She hated being there as much as I did, and at last I saw before me the same Audrey Verdeau that the websites and newspapers had once loved. A tight dress, white and sparkling, and her lips full, cheeks flushed from the alcohol.

The crisp, pragmatic Audrey that I knew was gone, replaced by a changeling of a girl who only knew how to cope, and I couldn't blame her. She had spent her life coping. This was just a mask she knew how to wear, and the knowledge of what Martin and Prosenko had been doing with her brother had been the final straw.

There was a story I'd learned as a child, about how Apollo and

Dionysus shared the same city, Delphi. Apollo inspired order and precision as much as light. He got it for most of the year, but the mortals, he realized, couldn't bear to be so precise all the time. Eventually the madness had to come out. Eventually Dionysus got his turn.

Before long, midnight neared. I watched as Martin, already wild and lost, glanced to the glasses and beckoned to George to top them off more. "Champagne to the rim!" he said, and Prosenko himself ran off to fetch a bottle with an eagerness I'd never seen before.

With anticipation in their eyes, a hundred people all turned, every bit of their focus on Martin, their king. He stood from that throne of his as Prosenko handed him an obscenely large champagne bottle. A Methuselah.

Martin poured, messily drowning the table in golden liquid as it fizzed and sloshed its way onto the floor. It was a spectacle only someone so debauched could have managed and not been ridiculed for. Soon the servants and hired hands stepped forward to file the glasses onto trays, handing them off and leaving me to watch, silent in the background, as each one was passed around to the eager onlookers. To people who innocently thought that all they held in their hand was simple champagne.

The music stopped. The countdown began.

5 . . .

They shouted.

4 . . .

The lights flashed.

3 . . .

Audrey looked to me in the crowd.

2 . . .

Martin smiled.

1 . . .

They swallowed.

As the liquid poured down their throats and crashed into their stomachs, it was only moments before they seemed to be catapulted up into an enormous high in spite of the dilution I had prepared. A slow warmth spreading from their core to the fingertips, tickling their skin straight through to the bone, and the heat would continue to spread. Up, up into the head and settling behind the eyes to give a brightness to everything they saw. So great it was painful, but it didn't matter. The joy that night flooded them like a prayer answered straight from God, and then they would linger there in heaven. A pride swelling within and a belief that everything was right and good and beautiful enough to make you cry.

Then something would happen. Something to snap them back. A touch. A sound. A memory. It always came, and I stood there in the crowd waiting for it.

Only that night, for some reason, it was far worse than any of the times before. More than Dylan's wandering eyes and shouts and more than the red-cheeked flush of drunks and their imagined monsters. That night an encounter, any encounter, appeared to have them dropping, plummeting from the highest point to the very pits of hell itself, where an agony of hatred waited. Whatever embarrassment or shameful thought that passed through their minds seemed to take root and grow into something tangled and dark and torturous, until the guilt threatened to swallow them up.

I watched as men caught sight of lipstick left by their mistresses and tried to rub it off their face. They scratched and clawed at the growing smudge until their skin was stained with tears and blood, and still they scratched more.

There was nothing but bared teeth and animalistic drives to rid themselves of . . . everything, it seemed. In front of me, a woman ran by, stopping only to rip the jewels from her golden necklace, the metal so forcibly removed that it dug a sleek line of red into the skin of her neck.

When I turned away, the view wasn't any better. Everywhere I looked in the shadowed rooms, I saw designer clothing being shredded as if bugs clung to the fibers and the disgusted owners' hands couldn't destroy the garments fast enough.

Beside me faces fixated on the mercury-glass mirrors as fillers and implants were frantically pinched and pulled out from beneath the skin. The very sight of it forced me to find another room. But there was no safe place. No room in that party with more sanity than the last. Running through the darkened halls, I passed men in nothing but socks and underwear, the soles of their feet growing dark with the splatter of blood.

I had never seen so much blood.

Not in person.

Glass was everywhere within minutes, and not a single person managed to avoid a shard in the heel or a cut from a broken stem. I saw women brandish the shattered pieces like swords and lunge, puncturing things with a messy fury and gargled screams.

Terror did not come close to it.

This was not Saint's Fog. It was not the poison I knew, even if the air was thick with the scent of it, a rotten sort of sweetness that once filled the foot of my closet and now stood powerful and unmistakable. Figs, anise, and mud.

The hallways of Arrow's Edge were a mess of panicked bodies, and by the time I at last found her, after searching every blond and terrified face, Audrey was sick like all the others.

She was drifting in one of the hallways, pupils blown wide and spinning. Finally I reached out and caught her.

"Audrey!"

Upon seeing my face, she drew close, until her eyelashes brushed the skin of my cheek. Her breath was warm and ghosted over my lips, just before she leaned in to kiss me again.

"Audrey!" I said sharply, panicked, and as she refocused, her smile fell. Plummeting into something ashamed and sorrowful in an instant. She shook her head and lurched away.

"Sorry, sorry . . . sorry, sorry, sorry," she repeated. The words mumbled from her mouth.

"What's wrong?" I asked her, my hand firmly on her forearm. I needed her attention. My body shook with the need to solve this before fear overtook me entirely.

For a brief moment, she seemed to come back. A clarity passing over her eyes as she looked down to my fingers.

Suddenly she ripped them away.

"No, no, no," she repeated as the same familiar panic of the crowd around us overwhelmed her face. She began to scratch. Hurried and furious, with a building mania precisely where my fingers had been.

"No, no, no, no!" she screamed. "No!"

"Audrey!" I shouted, and grabbed her hands, fighting with all my strength to stop her before she could sink her manicure in any deeper.

"Why did you do this, why did you do it?!"

"What's happening? What's going on?" I asked her, still doing my best to force her to focus on me. If only we could make eye contact again. "Think, Audrey! You've been poisoned. We've done this before. Tell me what's going on!"

My words fell on deaf ears. The more I pushed her for answers, the further she drifted from me, her eyes staring off into the distance. When she looked to me again, her mascara was running down her face and blood was trailing down her wrist from the few wounds she had managed before I'd grabbed her.

"Fuck!" I screamed, unable to fight it any longer as the helplessness completely overran me. It slithered its way into every nerve and filled every bit of my bones, making its home deep in my very marrow. All I could see was red. Red streaks, violent and wet against the once-pristine fabric of her dress.

I felt sick. My hands would not stop shaking.

"Lena!"

I heard a voice shout, and I turned back to see Sascha, terror-stricken on the other side of the room. The usual half apron over her hips was stained too many colors to count.

She hurried through a break in the wandering bodies, at last coming over to me. When I saw her and her beautiful, clear, comprehending eyes, I pulled her close. "Thank God."

"Lena, what's—" She'd been sobbing. I could feel her chest pressed against mine with every heavy breath. "I don't know what's going on. Miss— Oh! Oh, Miss Audrey!"

"Stay with her!" I told Sascha. "Try to get her somewhere quiet. The kitchen, I . . . I don't know."

"Where are you going?"

"To get something that'll help!"

By now pockets of the house had been abandoned. Broken furniture lay strewn about the marble floors as I hurried through the space, little more than splintered chair legs and velvet cushions to mark the passing of the manic crowd.

It was in this desperate search for something to help Audrey that it sank in just how much of a genuine horror show the house had become. Screams echoed off the gilded walls, bouncing about the space as I ran, a crunch of glass beneath my feet with every step. But I couldn't stop. I had to keep focused.

If Audrey were to have a chance, I needed the physostigmine in Prosenko's office.

There was no safe way to give a shot, not with the mania going rampant, but I didn't care. I would hold her down, help her, even if I couldn't help anyone else. I only needed to help *her*.

Her, and Sascha, and Jonath—

Jonathan.

There in the darkness of one of the side corridors, I remembered him at last.

My body stumbled in the dusty silence, conflicted and trying to decide what to do. If the Saint's Fog had affected Audrey so much, I was terrified to think what it had done to someone like him. If blood covered him now the same as his sister. If one of the hundreds of screams had been his.

A few rooms over, a chandelier came crashing down, and the sound of its shattering glass snapped me out of my thoughts, urging my feet onward. Prosenko's office was just around the corner.

I could find Jonathan once I had the shot.

Dodging another group, I made it at last to the small office and slipped behind the door, half expecting to find Prosenko and instead finding myself alone in an almost shocking stillness.

Compared to everything else, the lingering scent of his cologne felt impossibly fresh. As if the ghost of him were there with me, watching. Around my feet sat boxes of last-minute arrivals for the party, their packaging seals not yet cut open, and no time for me to do so. I stepped over them toward the desk, my eyes scanning for the familiar white-and-blue label of a physostigmine box that had already been opened.

The desk was covered in Prosenko's usual notes and mess of pre-party paperwork, along with hastily opened boxes of drugs, and then at last I saw it. A stack of the thin boxes, some ripped open already but a few unharmed.

I grabbed one, knowing it would have at least five doses, and ran back toward the ballroom to find Jonathan.

Only a few minutes had passed, maybe three, maybe five, but in the time it took me to cross the length of Arrow's Edge, the entire building had transformed into something I could no longer recognize. Especially the ballroom.

Especially, to my surprise, its king.

It was the first time I really stopped. Everything around me seeming to freeze as Martin Verdeau, center stage as always, stared back at me from his velvet throne with empty eyes. Foam bubbled out of his mouth, and his clothing stuck to his skin, soaked with sick and torn to shreds. Not from himself, I think, but from the claws of others. Blood oozed into the fabric from a cut on his hand, and all I could do was stand there.

I wanted to take it in more. To allow myself a moment to realize that this man I'd so deeply hated for so many months was no longer breathing. That his eyes were empty and his mouth would not smile again. I had envisioned it for so many nights, and it didn't seem real now that it was actually there in front of me. But a glimpse was all I got, as from behind I heard the rush of footsteps and spun around just as a man hurried toward me, heavy and panicked. I jolted back, my foot landing on fallen glass, hissing at the pain of a shard burying itself into my skin through the cheap sole of my shoes. Still I managed to avoid him as he continued on, screaming into the air and past, I realized, what was the side entrance to the music room.

Immediately I ran toward it.

The tang of freshly spilled liquor greeted me as I arrived, that and the sight of Dylan, crazed and fighting Brodie over a piece of some poor girl's clothing. In the corner I saw Elliot, shoulders trembling, face streaked in blood as if someone had run their fingernails from his forehead and over his eye to his jaw.

He saw me, I think, but suddenly Brodie was pulling me back by the fabric of my dress.

The next thing I knew, I was being yanked again, away from Brodie and the music room and back into the ballroom.

"Gereghty!"

Jonathan was drunk, that much was obvious, but even teetering on his feet, he seemed oddly calm. He pulled me aside into a corner, where together we hid, bodies close and hot.

I reached out to grab him with the hand not holding the shot, feeling the texture of his shirt beneath my palm, desperate for a sign that he was really there. He wasn't on the floor or screaming in a hotel bed. There was no blood. He was okay, I kept telling myself. He was okay.

"Thank God!" I shouted, a choked sort of sound, but he put his hand over my mouth.

"Shh," he said, and then raised a glass of liquid closer.

I felt the cool glass touch my lips and tried to spit it out.

"Easy, easy. It's just scotch," he said. "Scout's honor. M'fine."

Still, I shook my head and refused.

"You're okay. How's—" I watched as he took a sip. "Stop it! Don't drink that!"

He grinned, the entirety of his thin body shaking with a gigglish laugh as he downed the rest of the glass's contents, the hospital band from Strasbourg still wrapped around his wrist.

This close to him, I realized his pupils were blown out almost entirely to the edge of the iris, where none of the warm hazel remained. His cheeks were red through their usual pallor, and I reached forward, trying to press my trembling fingers to them.

"Jonathan, you're sick."

He laughed again and leaned his back to the wall, body shaking, and coughed.

"I'm always sick, Gereghty."

"No, you're— Shit." In one of the rooms, another roar of screams echoed, and it was then, when I looked out the gallery windows, that I saw flashing red and blue.

Police.

I grabbed his wrist and tried to pull him along, back toward where Sascha had taken Audrey, back toward what felt like safety, where I could give him part of the physostigmine shot I still held in my left hand. But something in him changed, and he forced me away, causing my arm to fly back. With the motion the shot fell from my hand, skittering across the floor along with, to my horror, the small bottle of Saint's Fog I had hidden under my sleeve.

Jonathan froze and eyed the bottle.

Before I had the chance to follow, he lunged forward and grabbed it. All while what must have been a dozen ambulances coming up the drive filled my ears in a chaotic, disorienting song.

"What is this?" he asked, his voice barely audible as he looked to me.

"It's . . . Martin wanted it. He told me to—"

Jonathan's eyes widened, and he looked to the bottle again. Then he unscrewed the small cap.

"Stop!" I screamed, and tried to knock it from his hand, but he turned, refusing to let me get closer. "Please!" I begged him. "Stop, don't take it!"

The bottle was raised, hovering over his tongue, when the police entered the room next to us. At the sound of their boots, Jonathan paused in alarm, giving me the chance to grab it from him.

He looked to the police, then back to me, where I held the small bottle upside down, the dropper end of it overhead.

"Take it," he told me, with a newly sober voice. "Take it, Lena."

I didn't understand why, or what he wanted from me, but then the police edged closer, and in a motion I nearly missed, Jonathan had turned to block me from their sight, shielding me with his body while the bottle still lingered in my hand.

My eyes caught sight of the drop just about to dangle down from the bottle's tip, and in an instant I lowered it to just above my tongue and squeezed.

"You there! What are you—"

The room around me spun, as if the tiles below my feet had switched places with the ceiling in a single leap. When I looked back to where I thought the police had been, there was no one. Not even Jonathan. I had no idea whether seconds had passed or minutes, but at some point I blinked and the room itself seemed to disappear, or maybe I had moved to somewhere else.

I don't know.

But a part of me did know what was coursing its way through my system, and the sting of it had me nauseous, feeling the heat spread itself from my mouth and down my throat, my arms, my legs—everywhere.

In that moment what felt like decades of sadness, and guilt, and disgust that had been pooling between my ribs were now setting me on fire to get out. A frantic, hateful energy that caused my muscles to twitch, fueled by a violent need to act. To rid myself of the shame.

Blue, and red, and golden, filling the space between each blink with memories blending into the walls of Arrow's Edge. By the time I had remembered Audrey and looked down to the floor for the dropped shot of physostigmine, my hands had morphed, seemingly covered in something grotesque and glistening and sharp as my vision blacked out.

Then something hit my head, and I fell.

23

MY HANDS STUNG.

That is what I first remember upon waking. The tips of my fingers stinging as if pricked by a thousand jagged needles.

A headache pounded its way in my skull, but my hands hurt, and so I forced myself to look down and found them bandaged.

Too many seconds passed before my brain could register the reality. The scent of liquor was gone, and the colors and screams of Arrow's Edge were nowhere to be found. They had been replaced by the stale smell of a county hospital and the unfortunate beeping of a heart monitor just out of sight.

There was no way of knowing how long I'd lain in that hospital room before I awoke. Minutes? Hours? Every bit of time seemed to stretch on endlessly as I remained there, taped up and attached to drips whose labels my eyes were too blurry to read, staring at the cheap yellow wallpaper and a pink vase of fake flowers. The art on the wall was the same as in a two-star motel room. Then I saw it, the large printed calendar date on the wall reading JAN. 2.

I had missed New Year's Day entirely.

Despite my blurry, medicated state, the events of Arrow's Edge clung to me so much that it still felt as if I was there. Any half seconds of peace I received would be short-lived. Then my heart would pound and I'd be flung back into that corner with Jonathan, anticipating the screams of others.

It's impossible to forget something like that night. Once you've survived horrors such as that, they live with you, haunting every crevice of your mind and taking hold. Even now I could be sitting dreaming of the bees over the lavender in Umbria and the image of blood will flash before my eyes from deep within my brain. An unforgiving presence of something real and quick and slippery. Their faces, the champagne, and the bile mixing with the foam at their lips. I've heard them called intrusive thoughts. Aunt Clare once called them devil dreams, and I must admit I find that term to be more accurate.

After I'd lain there for what felt like half an afternoon, a nurse at last came in, old and round-faced with frizzy bleached-blond hair done up in a half-fallen bun. When she saw that I was awake, she opened her mouth to say something, then closed it and pointed to the TV remote.

"On?" she asked, apparently failing to find any other words. I nodded, and a local channel came on. Loud and with a string of commercials. Too loud for my ears to handle. The nurse tried to change it, seeing me wince, but I stopped her, mumbling to turn it back. "Please," I said, and I didn't need to say anything else.

She soon handed me a plastic tray bearing food and a candy-apple-red Jell-O cup, followed by a sympathetic, "Try to eat." But I couldn't. Every bit of my being was still anxiously awaiting the end of an evening that was by then long over. I needed to know what had happened. If Audrey was alive. Or Jonathan.

I thought, too, in a sort of wordless fear, that there was no way the story hadn't gotten out. It would have been stupid to assume otherwise. I knew who was at that party, and I had seen enough to understand the impact in some small semblance of a way.

Then, at long last, the television finished its break.

CONTINUING STORY

BOSTON BILLIONAIRE
BROUGHT DOWN IN BERKSHIRES

It flashed in a bright red banner.

Martin's face appeared in a photographic rectangle beside the anchorwoman's head. Regal in a blue pinstripe suit, complete with a smile. Not the lecherous one. Not the one he gave me so many times when he knew what was coming or when he stared at the ass of a redheaded twenty-something secretary trying to save her job. The one on the screen that day was kind, and warm, and ten years younger. Nothing less than a grotesque PR stunt.

"Yesterday, just after 12:45 A.M., officials were alerted to a large party outside Lenox, Massachusetts, in Berkshire County," she said with the usual telecaster cadence. "The party, hosted by Avelux CEO Martin Verdeau of Boston, was a New Year's celebration attended by his circle of friends and employees at his familial estate. Information is currently slow to come, but the victims who managed to escape and have been released from care are now reporting that a drug may be to blame for up to thirty deaths. We have more on the story now with News Channel 7's own Richard Gonzalez. Richard."

The banner below her changed.

DOZENS DEAD IN LARGE
BERKSHIRE PARTY OVERDOSE

The scene flashed to a familiar street a mere seven blocks from the hospital.

"Hi, Stacey, thanks. Yes, residents of the surrounding area here just outside Lenox have begun to come forward with information that a new drug may be to blame for the tragic and bewildering catastrophe that occurred here almost two nights ago. Now, we are still waiting for confirmation, but friends and family members of victims are reporting that they believe drinks handed out for the New Year's toast were laced with a new kind of street drug, unbeknownst to the guests." The reporter paused and looked down at a series of cards in his hand, then continued, "It says here that victims describe it as 'a nightmare. We were surrounded by friends out of their minds. Angry and shouting, running through the rooms and using anything around them as weapons to attack others as well as *themselves*'—quote." Richard shook his head. "Many victims are still in recovery from that night, but we will be staying here in Lenox to keep you updated on anything new that comes forward. Stacey."

"Thank you, Richard. Absolutely tragic. As always, please stay tuned to News Channel 7 for the latest in local reporting. Now on to our sports update. The Patriots—"

There had been nothing useful. No answer to my most urgent of questions. I grabbed my phone and began to Google for anything else I could find, checking news sites and gossip pages. I saw talk of cults and mass suicides. Satanic connections with Wall Street, which, I should add, was already taking a hit.

But there was no mention of my name, no mention of Audrey or Jonathan. With every part of me, I prayed that the lack of their names in the reports meant something good, but I also knew too well that the gravitas of Martin's name could overshadow anyone.

A sudden wave of nausea slammed into me at the sight of the Jell-O, and I flung myself back onto the pillows in a violent dizzy spell. Even with my eyes squeezed tight, I still saw their faces. My stomach ached with a terrible tightening pain as small black, vinelike tendrils danced at the edge of my vision.

Fuck, I thought. *Fuck.*

The fear traveled through me, building adrenaline, instantly convincing me that I was going blind. Same as that night with Audrey in my room. The more I worried, the longer the tendrils stretched, snaking their way everywhere I looked. I shut my eyes tight again and tried to breathe. To pray a healthy round of shitty Catholic, "Please God."

Lord have mercy. I didn't mean to fuck up this bad.

Mary Mother of God, don't let me die.

WHEN I AWOKE AGAIN, A TALL FIGURE lingered, peeling back the hospital curtain, but it wasn't the doctor. Not unless he was dressed in a pair of pajama pants and a pea coat. Initially I thought it was a dream. Some cruel phantom of my imagination to taunt me, but instead he looked at me with the same set of familiar hazel eyes.

"Hey, Gereghty," said Jonathan. "You okay?"

The door to my room opened, followed by the shift of the curtain and another familiar and welcome voice.

"There you are. I—" Audrey froze, looked to me, then around the room, then back to me. "Oh. Lena . . . good morning." She shifted awkwardly on the balls of her feet. There were bandages all along her forearms, thick and padded with gauze. The same place, I noticed, that her Birkin bag would normally hang.

She turned back to her brother. "The car is here. We should go."

But Jonathan ignored her. Instead he just stared at me like he was trying to find the words to something. It was the first time he looked genuinely better than I felt.

"What happened?" I asked them both. No *Hey*, no *Hello*. I should have asked something better. Been more relieved or shown a sign of how overjoyed I was to see them both alive and upright, but I didn't. My brain didn't work fast enough, and besides, everything about them told me they were not entirely okay. Audrey's face was pale, her nails stripped of their usual manicure and filed down to nothing. For once her pristine clothing didn't look at home on her. For once she more closely resembled Jonathan.

"Don't talk to them," said Jonathan with something off in his voice. "If the police come. Don't talk to them, Gereghty, okay? It'll be fine."

The words didn't make sense to me, but already Audrey was motioning to get him to leave.

"And try to rest up," she said, almost as an afterthought. "We'll be in touch just— He's right. Don't say anything yet. We'll take care of it."

I sat up, pulling against the IV cord, but it was too late. Almost as soon as they had appeared, the siblings were gone, and it wasn't long before a terrible pain ravaged my body, excruciating in my abdomen, until I had no choice but to double over as another wave of sickness hit me.

THERE WAS NO TIME TO PROCESS what they meant. I faded in and out of that yellow hospital room, either due to meds or some kind of concussion I wasn't aware of, balancing between pain and sleep, thinking that their visit had in fact been little more than a drug-induced dream.

As the news played, apparently left on despite my lack of consciousness, there was still nothing of Prosenko, nor George or Sascha or Daniella. Just Martin and the big shots in his circle. With every new story, there were sobbing wives, clients, and escorts all vying for their shot at a television interview. The smaller people, the poorer people, as always, were forgotten and ignored.

The Berkshires residents, filmed standing in front of their homes, acted appalled. "We had no idea," they said. "Been here all my life. This sort of thing doesn't happen here." But of course they knew. Small towns talk. If you worked at the sheriff's office or the gas station, you knew. They were just embarrassed it got out. Same as everyone else.

Their perfect world had been shattered.

Later, after my pain medication had started to wear off, I surveyed the room again. There, on the other side of the inner window, I saw a nurse through a crack in the blinds, this one middle-aged and frowning, with pinched brows and blue eye shadow. She was chatting with someone, a plastic bag of fabric in her hand. Clothing, it looked like, and I tried to crane my neck enough so I could see who exactly she was talking to.

Then I saw the navy blue uniforms and the flash of a badge, and my heart lurched with panic.

Helpless, I watched as the nurse paused and dug her hand into the fabric, then finally pulled out a small clear plastic baggie with two black pills inside. The police took it.

24

THERE IS NOTHING GOOD ABOUT finding strange men next to your bed.

Worse if they have a buzz cut and a badge.

When I next awoke, an hour (three?) later, a stern-faced police officer was in front of me, eager for me to confirm that I was an employee of Martin's. His words came in an unsympathetic clip, and if he had explained why it was important, I missed it. Luckily, before I could remember Audrey's and Jonathan's words and let answers slip with a half-conscious nod, a nurse took pity on me and wouldn't allow them to continue the interview.

Still, as she adjusted the medication in my drip, I could only stare ahead at the badge as it caught the fluorescent light, barely paying attention to the officer's speech about wanting to talk to me at the station when I was feeling better.

He glanced down at the bandages around my fingers.

The pain in them pulsed.

I tried to keep calm and tell myself it was fine—that yes, okay, they'd found pills in my pocket, but surely I'd be able to prove they were just Jonathan's pills. That it was a part of my job.

Except that Jonathan's pills were made of poison.

But, I thought. But the pills weren't in the champagne. The pills weren't what had made everyone act like that. I'd felt it myself, a little too much admittedly, and without the dropper there would be no way to tie the Saint's Fog to me—not unless they searched my room.

I had to get home.

I WAS IN HILLCREST HOSPITAL in the Berkshires. The worst of the cases were sent to Boston, transferred out as soon as they arrived. Some others were sent up to New Hampshire or Connecticut, depending on their family's preference. I, however, had arrived late and in apparently terrible but stable condition and so was lucky enough to stay.

And now I needed to leave.

My parents had to have seen the news, if only because my father insisted on keeping up with football every evening before dinner and would likely have seen a clip or something of the events. They had to have known where I was. Why I didn't come home. They knew I worked in the Berkshires, they knew about the parties.

I didn't want to think about why the phone never rang with a call from them. Why I'd been stuck there for days and not once had my mother bothered to drive up and see me. I couldn't let my mind go there, because if it did, there would be no stopping it.

I couldn't stand to know how deep her uncaring went. Her shame.

Or how much I might have put my father at risk.

Instead it was just after checkout when my phone rang showing an unlisted number. The OxyContin that lingered in my system had put me in such a daze that I answered it without question.

I'm grateful I did.

"Lena," Audrey said brusquely. "Have you spoken with anyone yet? I'm sending a car for you. Just . . . don't talk anymore to the police. I'll handle it."

"Audrey? What's going—"

"There's a gas station about three blocks from the hospital. The owner's a family friend. Go inside and wait. It'll be there at a quarter past seven. Try not to be late, okay?"

I waited.

"I'll call again when everything settles. Just give it time," she said, and then paused. "I'm sorry. I— Take care of yourself. I'm glad you're all right, I just . . . I'm sorry."

THE BELL ABOVE THE GAS station's door chimed as it opened, and with a quick glance around for safety, I walked inside to wait under the fluorescent lights. It was 6:53 P.M.

No one said anything. The balding man behind the counter never removed his eyes from the television screen, and he was the only other soul in the place. Just the radio and the vibrating hum of the ice machine tucked away in the corner.

When the car arrived, no questions were asked. It pulled up, and soon I traded the fluorescent lights for the back seat of a sleek black car, driven by a man who didn't say a word. After I reached for the handle of the rear door and missed, he opened it for me, shut it again, and drove. When I asked if he knew where he was taking me, he merely nodded, and after that I didn't ask anything else.

I arrived home with the hospital band still on my wrist and my fingers bandaged and bloody as I hesitantly opened the door. My parents didn't know what to say. I don't know what I expected.

At first I think they were just happy to see me alive. My mother with her arms outstretched and my father standing with a stern jaw and a grumbling "Glad yer home," but it didn't last beyond those first few minutes. Soon I was being ushered up the stairs and to my bed, and by the next morning when I awoke again, the house was empty, with a note taped to my door saying, *"Went to run errands. There's soup in the fridge if you need it."*

And just like that, things did their best to return to normal. Time passed with an agonizing pace as I waited for what seemed like the inevitable. A knock on the door from the police when they realized I had no plans to show up at the station. Angry partygoers, paparazzi, and others waiting for answers. But it was silent. Painfully so. I could only guess that Audrey was the reason.

After she'd sent me the car, I expected to hear something more from her, but a call never came. Nor a text, or an e-mail, or anything to tell me what the siblings were doing or if they were even okay.

After a week of silence, I finally tried to call Audrey again with a re-dial, but I received nothing more than the error tone and a robotic, "We're sorry. The number you are trying to reach is no longer in service."

I had been abandoned. By everyone, it seemed, and so I did what anyone in my situation would do. I watched TV.

That's how the story came together.

When asked, the prosecutors and the courts didn't know what to make of the event. Murder? Suicide? No one could agree on what exactly had happened to Martin Verdeau and the others at his party, and so the process of pressing charges was messy, and despite filling the news and being on the lips of every Bostonian and New Englander, the investigation ended quietly behind closed doors and in wood-paneled rooms.

One thing that did come out of it was that Saint's Fog was deemed not a poison but a drug, and one with a terrible and now very public reputation.

In total forty-three people died that New Year's Eve, the overdose accusations quickly spawning news segments and social-media campaigns about the drug habits of the elite. It happened so fast, touching every family among New England's 1-percenters, that it became a race to see who could survive the fallout.

In that sense I suppose I got what I wanted after all. A party they could never recover from. A reminder that their wealth could hide only so much. Now I didn't feel like the only one angry at the things people such as Martin Verdeau could get away with. Now the world felt my rage, too. I was just too tired to care.

Still, when after a month Prosenko remained missing, all those who needed an answer found themselves presented with one. A face they could finally blame. My stomach twisted, given how close it had been to being me. Had Jonathan not insisted I take the Saint's Fog, had the cops not seen it hovering over my tongue . . . I saw now what he meant. What he was trying to do.

After all, this was a game he'd played so many times before, and in the chaos he'd been the only one with the clarity to see a way out.

In the end the investigation had come down to three things: Martin's parties, the drugs at the parties, and Prosenko's pills. The pills the police happened to find in my pocket that day they visited the hospital.

I watched every news clip I could, waiting for them to come forward with the truth about the medication. The only thing that would save me. But the days passed, and there was nothing. A familiar anger rose up each morning as the segments played with no new word, but by the end of them, all I seemed to hear was Audrey's voice.

I'm sorry. It'll be okay. I'm sorry.

So I tried to trust her.

Meanwhile, bit by bit, I watched as the dominoes fell in a cascade of small consequences.

My brother's girlfriend was caught trying to sell cell-phone pics of me to the paparazzi, and she gave a bad interview to a local newspaper with stories about drug addiction in the family and the pill bottles around the house. As a result Tony dumped her.

With my father, unfortunately, it wasn't much better. When it came out that I had worked for the Verdeaus and, additionally, worked their parties, Benny down at the hardware store let him go. He couldn't stand the loss in business, he said. He hoped my father understood. My father took triple his usual dose of meds and was useless for days. He hid in the bedroom, refusing to talk, refusing to do anything.

I couldn't blame him.

As for my mother, she didn't know what to say. So she just did what she always did when she couldn't rightfully be mad at me for something. She stopped talking. Despite the news and our nightly dinners, I received little more than a few glances from the corner of her eye.

Then, on television one morning, almost a month later, my attention was pulled from browsing jobs on my phone by the familiar sound of heels and a woman's voice breaking through the clicks of cameras flashing. A voice I'd missed far more than I thought.

25

"WE WANT TO THANK YOU ALL FOR BEING HERE TODAY," Audrey began, the sound of her voice more welcome than I cared to admit. "Your kindness has meant a great deal to our family and the others who lost loved ones that night. . . . I called you here in hopes that I could clarify a few things."

From my position on the couch, I watched Audrey speak, following every small motion of her eyes. Her straight back and firm, beautiful face. Her perfect makeup. The only thing that gave her nerves away was the twitching of her fingers. Small, fidgeting motions as she held on to the speech cards in her hand.

"The truth is, there has been a lot of blame going around and a lot of questions being asked of people who, to be frank, know nothing."

Was she talking about me? Was this it?

"My father was a drug addict. He was a businessman who achieved a great deal of success and, like those who found it, celebrated well.

Because of his continued success, he never learned how to stop. The fact we must face is that the lifestyle men like Martin Verdeau found themselves living is not one any of us should be proud of. Not least of all because it went beyond himself and has so clearly destroyed the lives of others. There is no reconciliation to be made or sum large enough to mend the hearts of those who lost their loved ones to my father's party on New Year's Eve. I say this knowing well that my brother and I both played a part in it and"—she paused, glancing back to Jonathan—"and suffered, too. As survivors of that night, we owe it to everyone to tell the truth and end this before it can destroy the life of anyone else. Simply put, enough is enough.

"The drug used that night is known as Saint's Fog and was sourced for Martin by our family doctor, Denis Prosenko, who as you may have heard is now missing. Nine months ago, at a party in June, I first caught my father with it, wandering the house. It was not until the following party, just before July Fourth, that he began to share it with a small group of others. For those who do not know, the drug itself is a liquid compound. Not a pill."

Her voice emphasized the final word, and all I could do was sit there.

It was a lie.

The timeline she gave put the Saint's Fog months before I was hired. At first I couldn't understand, and then it clicked.

She was covering for me.

"I am telling you this because for too many months my brother and I have known the reality and stayed quiet. We have attempted to hold up the honor of a man who does not deserve it. Denis Prosenko tended to my family for years, and we have known him since we were children, but his influence has never been a positive one. He has done immeasurable harm to each of us and those in our employ. My only wish now is that he come forward and confess his crimes."

Immediately the gaggle of reporters transformed into a rush of voices and flashing lights.

"Miss Verdeau! But what about the pills? Why were they—"

"All charges related to the individual possessing those have been dropped," she cut in, her voice sharp.

"But the toxicology reports on them proved they were—"

"The pills were Prosenko's own invention," Audrey insisted, and as soon as her words began, I wished the camera would turn to show Jonathan. "They were the same pills he'd been giving my brother for over a decade. He had tasked a new hire with helping him tend to Jonathan, and this is why she had them in her possession. She was doing her job. The pills have nothing to do with her.

"A few months ago, I opened an investigation into Prosenko and the formulation of the pills in question. As you all now seem to know, it was discovered they were a composite of poisons. He was approached with this just before a family vacation to Strasbourg, where reports now show that he administered a small dose of strychnine to my brother early on the morning of Christmas Day. We believe this was an attempt to secure his job as well as place blame on his assistant. There is now reason to believe that Prosenko mixed the poisonous pills with the first round of beverages served at the party in the main ballroom. It is likely that this, in combination with the Saint's Fog, is what resulted in the deaths."

The reporters paused.

Then, "I'm sorry, did you say he *poisoned* your brother?"

Her fingers gripped the notecards tighter. "If you have any further questions, or information about the pills from that night, we have provided a number you may call. It will direct you to the laboratory that has conducted a full investigation into the matter, and the women and men there will be able to answer your questions in full. Thank you."

I'm not sure how long I sat there after the press conference ended.

Long enough for the jingles of commercials to echo in the silence of the house. For the coffee in my cup to grow cold. Still, I couldn't believe it.

I was . . . free.

I had gotten away with it.

It just didn't feel that way.

26

THE CHILL OF JANUARY SOON carried into February, which became March, and then April, and at last the snow that covered Boston melted into mud. Back at Slick Rick's, the plastic of my old booth welcomed me sooner than my friends.

I couldn't blame them really. I had turned into someone they didn't know a mere month after gaining new employment, and they might as well have ended things with the way I acted toward them just before Strasbourg. Poor Rumi especially. After that day he dragged my ass to my room and instilled in me that terrible idea, I had barely said more than a few words to him. To my regret, I had traded him, and everyone, for a few plants, a couple of mason jars, and richer company.

After all was said and done and I'd been granted my release from the informal house arrest my parents had me on after the press conference, I took to going back to Slick Rick's alone, almost daily. Being at the family house for months without reprieve was almost enough to make me yearn for the prison sentence I once thought I was destined for.

I had passed the time searching for another job. My eyes scanning over every want ad and job posting remotely in my field day in and day out, but nothing had come through. Despite the damage control of the press conference, my name seemed to become public knowledge after it was aired. At least for anyone curious enough to look up my role. I had hoped that I could just wait it out and eventually something would come up, but thus far it hadn't. Trial or not, guilty verdict or not, Audrey's words helped only so much. The police left me alone, and angry families with homes in the Hamptons eventually got on with their lives, hiding from the scandal as best they could, but not my neighbors, and certainly not potential employers.

The final check from New Year's had never arrived, and I did not expect it to. Four months into unemployment, and paying off the last of my loans, I was running low on the small savings I'd built up from my crimes.

Besides, with every new advertisement for a job, I struggled with the feeling of wanting it to be more. A hysterical fact considering that in all my time working for the family I'd yearned for something simpler.

The reality was that those two worlds I lived in were far apart. The coffee shops at home all had the same coffee, which lacked the rich scent of toasted hazelnuts, toffee, and blueberry that signified Audrey's favorite. The walls were all painted white and had cracks and water stains on the acoustic ceilings. Every building smelled like the same flat scent of mass production. I was the only one who would open doors and expect to find antique furniture and large, framed oil paintings.

I knew that none of it belonged in Roslindale either. That if the shops started importing the expensive coffee I missed, and the signs and streets and tiles were all replaced with something new that Audrey or Jonathan would like, then it wouldn't be home anymore. It wouldn't be the same place I'd grown up in or that my friends and family could afford to live in. Everything that made it mine would be lost, and in that it was just another reminder that my world and the Verdeaus' couldn't exist together. Not without destroying each other.

Still, I knew what I wanted, and I hated myself for it.

I hated that I couldn't let my phone out of my sight for more than a second, because even after months of silence I hoped they might call. Despite everything, I still waited for them.

Every day before I checked the job boards, I checked the news for word of the siblings or of Avelux. Two months prior, in February, after the funerals and the dust had settled, I'd seen that Audrey had flown to Switzerland, but the news never reported if she'd returned. There was never a word about Jonathan.

As far as Avelux was concerned, the stock slowly rose again. A result of wise connections and too many rich men invested in the company to let it dip too low for too long. Scandal or not. I kept the articles on my laptop, saved alongside tweets and Instagram photos from accounts I had no business stalking.

The bell on the door chimed overhead as I walked in at last to Slick Rick's. From behind the wooden counter, Theo, the owner's middle-aged son, gave a noncommittal wave as I walked past and toward the booth just on the other side of the door where I dropped my bag.

Then, as every day for the last eight weeks, I ordered a basket of onion rings and a dollar iced tea and got to work.

For an hour I sat there with my onion rings growing cold, their grease leaving fingerprint stains on the paper of my notebook. My eyes must have passed fifty postings, for everything from an attendant needed for the reptile room at an exotic pet shop to a graveyard-shift baker at the local Mexican *panadería*, and while each would have been preferable to the continuous gaze of disappointment from my family, I still couldn't bring myself to apply.

It was close to noon when the door behind me chimed, and I popped my head up in time to see a familiar mess of thin, mousy, green-and-blond hair and a black hoodie entering. Anna stood at the counter, ordering something to go, and I watched her, waiting until she made the mistake of looking back.

I offered an onion ring.

She ended up eating there.

By the next week, Rumi finally started answering my texts again, and it wasn't long before he came, too, squishing himself into the booth, and it began to feel like maybe, just maybe, things would be okay again.

THE FOLLOWING WEEK WHEN THE DOOR CHIMED, the table was full and loud with life. Anna was smiling as she dipped a fry into the communal ketchup, laughing as Rumi continued arguing with her over whether his boyfriend, Alex, would make as good a drag queen as he thought. It was the kind of debate we'd occupied ourselves with throughout school and which, despite everything, I had not realized precisely how much I'd missed.

The hours spent filled with laughter and grease in those blue plastic booths were bright and joyous enough to remind me of a time before the Verdeaus had ever entered into my life, and I longed for it to continue, just like that, just like before, as I forced the memory of it all to fade.

And it could have continued to fade had there not come a ring at the door one chilly afternoon. Where from above the top of the booth I saw him, that head of dark messy waves, and instantly my heart sank.

27

"FOUR MONTHS. IT'S BEEN FOUR MONTHS."

We were outside, feet on the broken-up gravel pavement of Slick Rick's minuscule parking lot. In front of me, Jonathan looked on the edge of life, trembling and barely able to stand. As if his father's negative influence had only strengthened in his absence. I watched as his thumb flicked against the numbness of his finger again, saw how the clothes that hung on him looked like they hadn't been washed in days, and I hated that still, after four sobering months without him, he was beautiful.

Before he had even seen me in the booth, I was standing up and ushering him out the door. He stumbled with every step.

I was starting to be okay, I thought. *How can you come in here looking like that?*

In front of me, Jonathan shrank into himself. His gangly arms in an oxford shirt stained with various wine blotches of purple and amber and red. He was little more than a spine left to poke through the thin fabric, and when the spring wind blew, his body shuddered.

"Do you know where it is?" he asked me as soon as we had stopped. "That stuff from the party. The . . . the Saint stuff."

I must have given him an awful look, because instantly his eyes turned down, then back up at me.

"I mean, is there any left?" he slurred. "You gotta have some left, right?"

"That's why you're here?"

He avoided my eyes again.

"Jonathan!"

With a wince he reached up to cover his ears. "Stop it, shit hurts."

I punched him. It was an impulsive motion, meant to be softer than it was, but every muscle in my body was tense with adrenaline and relief and something else so strong and unnameable that the mere sight of him again made me want to put my fist through a wall. "How can you ask me that?"

Instinctively he reached up to rub at his arm, frowning. "Forget it. I shouldn't have come."

Jonathan tried to turn on his heel back toward the black Bentley he'd brought into Roslindale. Absurdly shiny for the area, it stuck out like a sore thumb, and I hated him vehemently for it, but I was also damned glad to see it. *Yes*, I thought, a glimmer of gold against the concrete. No rust. Just wax smooth enough to reflect my own face from five feet away.

I pulled him back. "Why *did* you come out here?"

Please give me another answer. Please tell me something else. You have my check. You're sorry. You have a job. Audrey lost my number.

"I told you."

Fury hit me, lightning-fast. "No. No, no, no. *No*. Of all things you finally come back and it's for *that*?"

"You don't understand," he mumbled.

"Then tell me! Why?"

Jonathan stepped back, and I saw the white of his shirt reflected in the black paint just behind him, a crisp streak along the car. "Stop it."

I stepped forward. "Why would you want something like that?"

He didn't reply.

"Just tell me!"

Nothing.

"For God's sake, how could you come here and *ask* me for that? It killed people! Jonathan. JONATHAN!"

"BECAUSE I NEED IT!" His scream stopped me in my tracks. It tore through his throat, squeaking before his vocal cords could give it any kind of depth. It was weak, and tired, and childish, and still the words rang out, angry and frustrated, and then softer as I stood there in silence. "I just . . . I just need it, okay?"

I didn't understand. The scars on the tips of my fingers began to sting.

"You *know* what it did."

Jonathan avoided me, turning back to face the car. "You heard Audrey. That wasn't the Fog."

"Still . . . you don't . . . you don't need something like that. You don't need it any more than those pills—"

"Fuck *off*, would you?" The sharpness of his voice shot straight through the air. "You don't know shit, Gereghty, all right? You think you can just disappear and . . . and get to hide away while I'm shipped off somewhere to go through withdrawal in that fucking boring room while they bury that bastard—" He stopped and turned back, holding curled fingers at his sides.

"Jonathan—"

"Leave it. I shouldn't have come."

I closed the gap between us just as he pulled at the keys from his pocket and fumbled with them, the metal jingling and then scratching the paint, as he had to lean against the door to find the right one. Nothing in his body seemed to work. Even worse than when he was on the pills.

"Hang on," I said, and reached for the keys. They were all too easy to grab. "You're not driving. I won't let you."

He frowned and tried to protest, but from that close I could smell it.

Drifting over to me from his lips. The cabernet on his breath. The usual notes of tobacco, dried fruit, and a rancid stomach. The scent itself was so strong he must have been drinking since the morning. How he managed to drive at all, I had no clue.

"What happened to you?" I asked him. "Audrey said you'd call."

"Tch, yeah, she's been saying a lot of shit lately, hasn't she?"

I thought back to the press conference, to his form just out of view, and felt like I was seeing it now. "Where is she?"

He shrugged, and standing there looking at his newly hollowed, relapsed, and weak self, I realized the severity of the situation.

Prosenko was gone. I was gone, and George, and everyone else who had ever tended to Jonathan and forced him to eat and drink water. Everyone his father had placed in his way to shield him from his own destruction. Somehow in the months of our separation, while I'd been complaining about a lack of polish and missing a world that never served me, Jonathan had been haunted not only by the fallout from his father's doings but the abandonment of everyone who'd ever cared for him. Including, from the sounds of it, even his sister.

God, I hoped she was okay.

He didn't move, just continued to use the door as a crutch. I looked around at the parking lot, where Rumi had stepped out from the restaurant and now hovered, glaring at Jonathan.

"Rumi—"

"Why don't you just go back home?!" he shouted across the parking lot. "Leave her alone! You people have already done enough!"

"Shit," I cursed, the word a quiet hiss through my teeth.

In front of me, Jonathan had looked up, his dark-rimmed eyes searching until he found Rumi, and now seemed to bounce back and forth between us. I felt him as he tried to pull away again, a hesitant, guilty sort of motion that I couldn't exactly blame him for. Still, he was here again, and something in me didn't want to let him go.

I could see Anna's critical gaze peering from behind the window, her shoulders scrunched up inside her hoodie, and prayed that she would understand. That Rumi would. Maybe not now, but someday.

"Lena!" Rumi called out again, this time in warning. The tone twisted my stomach into guilty knots, and even as time seemed to slow, I couldn't bring myself to turn around. To turn my back to Jonathan as my friends were begging me to do.

Instead I avoided meeting Rumi's eyes and stepped closer to Jonathan. "Get in the car."

"Wha—"

"I'm driving you home. Get in the car."

Before he could protest again, I opened the door to the back seat and urged him inside. With his frailty and wobbling state, it was easier than expected.

"Lena, what the *hell*?!" Rumi yelled.

I shut the door and ran back to Slick Rick's, brushing past Rumi as fast as I could, giving a quick apology as I shoved my way to the booth. "Who is that?" Anna asked. "No one." "It's him, isn't it?" "I've got to go." "Jesus, Lena, don't—" "I'm sorry." And just like that, the onion rings forgotten, I grabbed my bag, left a twenty on top of the table, and didn't look behind me as the door shut.

I DIDN'T KNOW WHERE I WAS DRIVING. The car was so expensive that my hands were nervous to even hold the wheel, and so I just turned vaguely in the direction of my house and went around the block in a large circle while Jonathan sulked beside me. He had climbed into the passenger seat before my return and was curled up like a sour, angry old cat by the time the engine started.

He hadn't moved much when he finally decided to speak again.

"It helped, you know."

I glanced over, my fingers tight around the leather wheel. "What?"

"That's why I wanted it."

"The Saint's Fog? No, it's . . . it's a drug."

"Everything's a drug," he told me. "Still helped. More than those fucking pills."

Jonathan looked away and out the window, leaving me to glance between him and the road, trying to study his face. It wasn't how I expected him to find out about the theriac game being played. I thought perhaps Audrey would sit him down or the doctors in the hospital would explain it to him after a standard blood draw, but . . . there on TV, with all the world to gasp as he stood, forgotten in the background . . . it was far from ideal.

It was also clearly something he was struggling with and I reckoned was part of the explanation for his present state.

"You look like shit."

A short, breathy laugh escaped his lips.

"And you're clearly drinking again."

"Never really stopped."

I tried to focus on the road. I didn't know where I was. I just kept turning onto streets and turning again.

"You can't have the Saint's Fog. It was a poison. Even I know that." *I know that more than anyone.*

"But it didn't *do* anything."

"That's not true. I watched you. You were clearly affected at the party."

Jonathan looked down. "No. It just made me . . . it made me feel *good.* Better. Like nothing *hurt* anymore."

His answer didn't make sense. I had seen his pupils blown wide and felt the heat radiating from his skin the same as Audrey. I had seen the glass he held in his hand that night, one clearly from Martin's lot.

The lot that also would have held Prosenko's poison.

"But at the hospital. You were there. You were hurt."

"Yeah, I woke up there. But it was just a mild concussion. That and this." Jonathan shifted in his seat and then rolled up his shirt to show a large pink scar, right between his ribs. "And before you ask, I don't know who did it."

I turned the car toward the signs for the highway.

"I'm glad you're okay."

"Don't say that, Gereghty," said Jonathan. "That's the worst thing you could say."

JUST AS I HAD TAKEN the turn to get onto I-95, the phone in my bag began to ring, muffled and insistent, and finally Jonathan reached back to hand it to me.

"Hello . . . ?"

"Lena," said Audrey. "Have you seen Jonathan?"

"It's been four months."

"I know. Have you seen him?"

"Why didn't you call me before? Are you okay? What's going on?"

"Have you seen him?"

"You said you—"

"I know, I know, I'm sorry. I can't explain it right now. Mother's been here."

I had forgotten that the former Mrs. Verdeau was even still alive, and when I did at last recall our conversation, I remembered that Audrey had made it clear that their mother would never set foot back in the U.S.

"He's with you, isn't he?"

I didn't answer.

"Can you please bring him back to the house? It's a long drive, I know, but—"

"I'm in Roz. It's not that far."

"No. Not the town house. We're in Newport. At the summer house."

"Newport? . . . *Rhode Island?*" I paused and turned to him. "You drove here from *Rhode Island?*"

Jonathan shrugged, shrinking his body further into the corner of the door.

"Please, Lena," said Audrey. "Bring him back. I'll compensate you for your time."

I didn't want the money, and Audrey knew that. Even after all the time that had passed, she knew it was impossible for me to say no to her. As I hung up the phone and tossed it into the cup holder, Jonathan shifted again, agitated when I exited to go south.

"You can't take me back," he said. "It's insufferable there."

"You disappeared on her, and I'm sure your mom is—"

"She doesn't care," he said. "She only came back for the company."

"Jonathan . . . I can't just keep driving in circles. I need to take you somewhere."

"Why?" he asked me. "Why do I need to be anywhere? No one *wants* me anywhere."

My fingers gripped the leather of the wheel tighter. "That's not true. What about the town house?"

"Abandoned."

"What?"

He looked over at me. "Do you believe what she said?"

"About what?"

"Prosenko," said Jonathan. "And my pills."

I didn't know how to answer. In my silence Jonathan continued.

"I don't understand it. They keep saying there's these toxicology reports and investigations, and Audrey mentioned this story about kings, but I— It couldn't have been him. My father would never have done something like that. He wouldn't have let that happen. He was shitty, but he hired Prosenko to *help* me. I was . . . I was sick before he worked for us.

That's what my father always said. I just don't understand it. I keep trying, but I don't."

"But, Jonathan, you stopped taking the pills, and it made you feel
better."

"I know! It's just that it's been months, Lena, and I still . . ." He
shifted his body awkwardly, clenching his hand into a fist and then letting
it go. "Something is still wrong."

I glanced down at his hand again, recognizing the same signs of
numbness from before. Remembering what he'd said when he arrived.

"So that's why you wanted the Saint's Fog."

"I know you made it. . . . I'm not mad, but my father talked about it
too much, and I mean, I saw you with it at the party."

My stomach plummeted. "But I thought . . . If you knew that I was
the one making it, then why did Audrey say—"

"Audrey says a lot of things now," he told me. "We wanted to clear
your name, and she figured that was the best way to do it. Didn't mean it
was all lies."

"Then it was really the pills? That's what killed everyone? Not the
Saint's Fog?"

Jonathan looked away, toward the window at the passing cars and the
growing gray clouds. "I don't know. That's the other thing I don't
understand."

"What?"

"It was just a few pills, Lena. Just a few that they found, and yet they're
saying it killed . . . everyone. It killed so many people, but . . . I *took* them.
I took them every day. That *couldn't* have been the same ones."

I didn't say a word. I just drove forward on the highway as a million
thoughts fought for my attention. On one hand, I had believed Audrey the
first time. I had known enough about Prosenko and my own diluted blend
that night to convince myself of my innocence. On the other hand, the
thought of something else had kept me awake. A worry that the Saint's

Fog really had done it. That it had twisted into something else, despite my intentions.

The symptoms had not been that far off. The hallucinations and the guilt and the blackouts—it had been different when Audrey and I took Jonathan's pills that night. Audrey hadn't been terrified and scratching her arm as she lay there on my bed recovering from our experiment. That part was the Saint's Fog, and I knew it.

But if that were true, then . . . maybe we were both guilty, Prosenko and I.

Though why he had attacked everyone, I still didn't know.

"There!" Jonathan shouted suddenly, pointing to the exit for the Mass Pike. "Take that exit."

I turned on the blinker. "Why?"

He kept his eyes forward, watching as the car curved around the exit and westward onto the Pike, toward the Berkshires.

"Because I need answers," he said. "And you're going to help me find them."

28

THE LAWN WAS OVERGROWN, THE LIGHT of spring giving the
grounds new life as I drove up the winding gravel road. The air was silent
in the way that it never should have been, not at a place like Arrow's
Edge, the sort of lonely absence of sound that shouted of abandonment
and hungrily welcomed us in.

As I stepped out of the Bentley, the misty air of spring rain met my
face, and we came upon the front entrance unlocked, the door ajar and
covered in obnoxious yellow sun-bleached police tape. Jonathan ripped it
off, rushing inside with the heat of the engine still warm.

"How could they leave it like this?" It was the first thing he'd said in
an hour. "We need— I should call the groundskeeper. George . . . he—"
Jonathan looked around, stepping on broken glass before I could reach
forward and stop him.

"Be careful."

"How could they leave it like this?"

He had not been back since New Year's. Before growing quiet on the
drive, Jonathan had told me as much. That with the investigation they

weren't allowed and then with the funerals and the risk of vandals and the company's flailing PR, it wasn't "advised." That Audrey had forbidden it and that their mother had made a point to move them farther from the scene to lessen the sting.

It was the longest Jonathan had ever spent away from the house not counting college, and even then I doubt he went longer than a month without a party.

The dim, golden light of late afternoon pushed through the curtains as he explored deeper inside. First through the gallery, then the ballroom and the myriad of hallways that stretched outward from it. Each of them with dark red stains that upon my seeing them again burrowed themselves into my memory forever. In all that time, nothing had changed. There was no staff to clean up and unroll new carpeting. No vacuums to suck up the glitter. So it was here, in the shadows of its missing light, where the reality of it sank in for me at last. There would be no more parties. Arrow's Edge had nothing left.

"We should go," I said, increasingly nervous. But Jonathan pushed on.

In the music room, he stopped to stare at the corner behind the sofa. For too long he stared and then lurched forward and retrieved a painting that had fallen from its spot on the wall. The very one I had seen Elliot cowering beside that night, face scratched up and eyes wide with fear. In a flash it came back to me, so strongly that my heart still ached with a need to help him.

"It's not broken," he said softly, running his thumb over the golden carved details of the frame. "I thought for sure it . . ." Jonathan trailed off and gripped it tightly, taking it with him.

I followed as he wandered the empty hallways again, the disarray not seeming to deter him. Jonathan walked with an ease, dodging the fallen side tables and the glass and the broken furniture. All the while I remained in continued disbelief at the damage. In the space of the party, the chaos had its place and the disorder of the shouts and the crash of chandeliers and furniture fit. Now it was alone there, dust-covered and cold and half molded from a winter of mistreatment.

Arrow's Edge had fallen, and it was not happy about that.

"You don't remember, do you?" Jonathan asked me as we neared the library, staring down at a series of shards and broken glassware. It was the first thing he had said in a while. "After you took it."

"I remember . . . some. But after I blacked out—"

"You ripped the glass from my hand. Shattered everything you could. Even if it was already broken, you picked it up. Nothing was broken enough. You'd break it and then pick it up, and break it and then pick it up, and sweep it all aside like you were trying to hide the pieces. The police tried to stop you but you . . ." He laughed oddly. "Your hands were all red, and you just looked at them. Finally an officer hit you on the head. Knocked you out."

It added up. My hands twitched at the reminder.

"How do you remember?" I asked him, trying not to think of the pink scar between his ribs.

"S'like I said. I felt fine."

"You didn't black out?"

Jonathan shook his head, and I watched as he opened the door to the library and wandered over to the shelves.

"But in the hospital . . ."

"I got knocked out, Gereghty. Being slammed into a marble floor will do that." He paused. "Shit, at least I think that's what happened."

"But you remember drinking the Saint's Fog? How? Didn't it affect you?"

He shrugged and knelt to look at the books, setting the frame he'd been carrying onto the chair beside him.

He didn't say anything more.

———

WE EXPLORED UNTIL NIGHTFALL, THE LIGHT fading from golden shadows to a stormy black with no stars to see. Never once did the nervousness leave me. With every step in that forsaken estate, I could feel their ghosts following. Waiting in an eternal party, bubbling unseen just below the surface, and as the darkness grew, it was too easy to anticipate their hands reaching out for me. Running from around a corner. It was so quiet. Every creak echoed throughout the space, foretelling a scream or a crash.

The smell followed as well: a scent of stale alcohol and fermented sugar. Liters of spilled champagne left to evaporate, now nothing more than a trail of sticky spots to catch our shoes. Then there was the mold. The decay. The scent of their blood abandoned in the space. Left to transform from something fresh and metallic to a darker scent, faded but still there. It will always be there, I think.

My hands grew sweaty, and I wanted to ask Jonathan again to leave. Say that this was a bad idea and there was nothing left here for us. Any answers about Prosenko's motives or the pills were sure to be gone by this point, but Jonathan insisted, increasingly sober with each minute that passed.

By the time we circled back to the grand staircase, Jonathan's steps had quickened, and my eyes turned to the door that was Prosenko's old office.

The lock had been pried open, likely by the police during their search, and the antique mahogany had splintered and now stood jagged as Jonathan reached forward and entered without hesitation.

My own feet remained still at the threshold.

Despite having been in that office more times than I could count, on that day I felt unreasonably unwelcome. Jonathan wandered in, running his hands along the cluttered desk and the edge of the metal shelves where medications sat, filed and organized for use. It was still partially stocked from the party, each shelf of items in disarray after the initial raid by the police and likely having suffered months of pillaging since. From the rows of ibuprofen to the Narcan, few boxes remained undamaged or unopened. Some had been marked with evidence tags, but aside from the mess everything was exactly where I remembered.

Hastily Jonathan began to grab at some of the bottles, fumbling to open them and look inside. After the third or fourth frantic search and handful of pills tossed onto the floor, I stepped into the office at last.

"They've got to be here," he said as he poured out a series of white pills I couldn't recognize in the dim light. He shoved them back into the bottle, spilling more than managed to make it back inside, and threw it onto the shelf. "I know they do."

"Jonathan . . ."

He paused and turned to look at me, hands clasped around a large jar. "I need to know if the ones from that night were the same ones he was giving me. Where did he keep them? You should know, right?"

A beat passed between us. A moment for him to realize how heavy his breathing had become and how tightly his fingers clasped the bottle.

"I took them my whole life. My whole *life*, Lena. You heard her. If he poisoned the party, if he's really the one who killed my father and everyone else, then why did he do it? Why?"

I waited, unsure of how to answer.

"*Why?*" he asked again.

My eyes drifted to the metal file cabinet below Prosenko's desk. It was an instinctive motion but one that did not go unnoticed. Jonathan abandoned our conversation to rush over to it, jostling the cabinet as he fought with the lock. He shook the handle again and again, harder with each attempt, until at last he hit it with his hands and cursed into the air.

"Jonathan," I started, nervousness bubbling over my tongue. But he ignored me. Or maybe my voice was too soft. Instead he ran a frustrated hand through his hair and then rummaged through the desk.

"There's got to be a key around here somewhere," he muttered.

I swallowed. "There won't be. He always kept it on him. I've never seen him let go of it, but, Jonathan, listen—"

In the small office space that had stolen too many hours from me, I watched as Jonathan Verdeau fought against himself with a desperation for answers to questions he didn't know how to ask. In that moment he was just a boy with a failing body, fatherless and abandoned and left without a reason for it.

Jonathan paced to the back of the office, where the shadows grew darker and the ceiling lowered due to the staircase above, making him crouch.

Unsure and too weak-willed to speak, I distracted myself by looking around the room: past the doctor's chair and the heart monitors, the row of rolling IV drips and the folded partitions used at every party. Some were still strewn about and knocked over in the old parlor, but here two remained, half unfurled and against a wall.

"He's been gone for months, Jonathan, and this place has had police crawling through who knows how many times. What if . . . what if there's nothing here?"

Ahead of me he continued searching, picking up every bottle he could find and reading the label of standard drugs and drips, each effort fruitless.

I looked around the room again, and that's when I saw it. Just above the partition, behind Jonathan's head. The corner of something. He turned toward it and rolled the partition away, leaving me to watch as his shadow disappeared behind it and then disappeared altogether.

29

THE ROOM WAS SMALL AND SIMPLE, like a refurbished butler's pantry or a linen closet, but still large enough to fit us both. In it a workbench lined the wall to our right, with shelves above and below it. A pharmacist's station, frozen in the moment of its last act. Glass bowls sat on the wooden tabletop, with papers and pens scattered about and small metal spoons in a neat little row. At the center was a scale, with folding papers on top, still holding the residue of a finely ground dark powder that had been measured out.

Even in the darkness, it matched my setup back in Roslindale almost entirely, down to the mortar and pestle. Only this room, unlike my closet, had a hundred amber jars, some small, some large, but easily stretching back into the cramped shadows of the room. At the edge of the workstation, I saw a framed photo and, squinting, made out the image of what seemed to be a younger Prosenko, lankier, with dark wavy hair, beside a smiling blond woman in a lab coat. Next to that sat a book that had been left open and Prosenko's notepad, the dust around it smeared with recent movement.

As Jonathan stepped inside, I pulled out my phone to use as a make-shift light. Slowly the beam illuminated the details into something clearer, and as I focused it on the book, I found Prosenko's handwriting and a series of abbreviations and numbers.

In an instant Jonathan's hands slammed onto the desk, shoving the spoons off and leaving them to clatter and clink their way to the floor as well as whatever was on the papers to fly into the air. I raised my arm to cover my nose, shielding it from the potential for inhalation.

I tried to read the masking-tape-covered labels and their formulas written in messy cursive, but even my months under Prosenko had not gifted me a better ability to decipher them. On the floor around us there were more jars, only these were imported and in the standard pharmaceutical plastic containers. A sterile white, with Chinese characters I didn't know how to read. A few feet away, Jonathan stood in a cramped alcove, staring at it all and growing more upset by the second.

"That's them, isn't it?" Jonathan asked.

Quickly he darted back to the shelf and began to pull one of the nearer, larger bottles out, unscrewing the black lid. I watched, helpless, as he poured a few of the little round pellets into his hand and how at the sight his face grew paler.

In the limited space, it didn't take long to reach him. As I did, I looked down at the small, almost black orbs in Jonathan's hand. The smell coming from the jar was noxious. A scent beyond rancid, so much so that it smelled sweet, and metallic, and undeniably familiar.

Jonathan looked ill and shut the lid as tight as his fingers would allow.

Again he cursed under his breath.

Then, louder, "These are them. This is what he gave me as a kid. They're the same."

"But . . . hold on a second. That doesn't mean they're what was used at the party."

"You saw them!" he shouted, turning back to me. "He gave you pills, the police report said as much! Tell me these aren't them! That these aren't what he put in our drinks."

I opened my mouth to say something but lacked the words. It still didn't make sense to me that the theriac Prosenko had used on Jonathan would be what he'd used at the party.

Sure, the pills I took were toxic, but the motive didn't make sense, nor the tool, and the more we ventured into Arrow's Edge, the less I understood. Something would have had to make him do it. Just like something made him use the strychnine in Strasbourg.

I turned back to the book and tried to read through the numbers, thumbing through the pages in an attempt to find one from the same date as the party, hoping for some new kind of clarity. Instead my fingers stopped, landing on a page that held a date from five years before. The year Audrey had said Jonathan's health got bad again.

I wondered. . . .

I flipped until I found a date from earlier this year, but there was nothing beyond it. Nothing anywhere close to the date of the New Year's party, or even my employment. As if whatever he'd been working on had stopped its development a year ago.

Still, what was written there was clear.

"Formulas," I said, my eyes scanning the series of twenty to thirty initials, with milligrams written out beside them. "These are the original formulas. For your pills, I think. Here," I told him, moving the light to see his face and guide him over.

"Does it say what's in them?"

"No, he . . . he didn't write the names of what he used. He wrote in code."

"Give me that," said Jonathan, and before I could stop him, he had stolen the book from me and moved it into his arms to flip through urgently.

I tried to refocus the light but caught the edge of a larger amber bottle instead. As Jonathan continued to tear through the pages, distraction got the better of me and I moved closer to examine the bottle.

Covered in a layer of dust stood a row of jars larger than my head, with crude paper labels taped to their sides. As I pulled one off the shelf and unscrewed the lid, everything in me stopped.

They were flowers. Dried, but still strong-smelling and still a darkened purple with a shape that I knew well.

Too well.

Because a bag of them sat at the bottom of my closet.

"Monkshood."

The name flowed softly over my lips, and upon hearing it Jonathan stilled and returned his attention to where I stood with the little light.

I turned the jar over in my hands and read the name and then, at the bottom of the label in parentheses, the initials (ACTn).

Aconitum napellus.

"Check the book," I called over to him, newly horrified as I added up the symptoms in my head and read to him the abbreviation.

It didn't take him long to find it.

I screwed the lid back on and hastily returned the jar to its spot before moving the light along the row with the intention to read out more. As I did, I saw through the tinted glass a series of crushed leaves and chopped-up stalks and knew now that here in this hidden room were the ingredients Jonathan had been seeking.

The ingredients to the theriacs.

There was no denying it. This was Prosenko, caught red-handed.

In the darkness I stepped to the side, trying to discover more, and then, as my foot creaked on the aging floorboards, I saw a dangling string and followed it up.

Dozens upon dozens of plants hovered overhead. Shielded by the rafters and out of view. Each wrapped and bound into bushels, left to hang and dry in the dark, still air.

There were hundreds of them. Poisonous shoots and leaves and stems that I knew from Aunt Clare's and had failed to retrieve for my own blend thanks to regulations and red tape. There were so many in that small room, none of them reduced to powders or tinctures, which would have been easier for someone like Prosenko to acquire.

I moved the light farther along, following the lines and the plants until it hit something else, and the next thing I knew, Jonathan had bolted and disappeared yet again down some dark corridor whose entrance I'd missed.

"Where are you going?" I shouted, but he didn't answer. Jonathan had abandoned me to the space, and so I followed.

He moved quickly, tripping but determined, through the strange door and through the cramped back passageway. It likely dated from when the house had first been built and was similar to the servants' corridor I had discovered so many months earlier.

Helpless to the bones of Arrow's Edge, Jonathan continued on, moving through the shadows and past the cobwebs without care. As if somehow he knew exactly where it was heading. Then, as we came to the end of the passageway, Jonathan took a sharp left and we nearly stumbled. A series of buckets and shears sat tucked away just before the door, surrounded by the smell of dirt. And at this I at last realized our destination.

30

THE STORM OUTSIDE HAD GROWN, the thunderous rain becoming all too apparent the moment the door opened and we could hear it echo on the expansive glass roof of the greenhouse. In a flash Jonathan blew past the bushes and the palms at the entry and beyond the small time-worn placards that dedicated the space. Past the springtime blooms and the small Victorian patio set at the center, and then I watched as he disappeared behind a large azalea, to a corner I had somehow failed to notice in all my visits prior.

There he stopped and stared, his breathing heavy and wheezing. Surrounded in winter-wrapped greenery as I caught up.

"*Aconitum,*" he said suddenly, ripping the plastic off. "*Napellus.*"

I looked at the small, withered plant that drew his gaze. The tiny, shriveled brown stalks. Flowerless, they were dried and broken, but it was clear that before being abandoned a few had been trimmed with something sharp. On the ground was a single faded flower, the purple-blue tint now dark and dead like that of its brothers in the jar.

Jonathan stared and then pointed to another small series of

uncovered plants. "*Atropa belladonna*," he said, as if it were a game he had played with himself as a child. Then pointed to another across the way. "And there, datura." I followed his motion. "Digitalis . . . delphinium," he continued, and pointed to every small bush and half-dead branch in that forgotten corner of the greenhouse. He said their Latin names, but my mind translated them with a sickening ease. Nightshade, angel's trumpet, larkspur. All, I realized, matching the abbreviations I had read in Prosenko's journal. The precise compounds of his pills.

At each glance from the jar in his hand to another plant, Jonathan's eyes twisted further into something chaotic and pained. I watched as he shattered, the pieces coming into place so clearly that they could not be denied anymore.

This had been a refuge for Jonathan. This greenhouse with its peeling white paint and Victorian glass. It had been where I found him months earlier, where he first smiled, surrounded by the verdant hues of foreign palms and flowers. I realized, too, that this place had been more than some hideaway for him. It was a significant part of his attachment to Arrow's Edge.

It was this garden that had offered him a reprieve from his father for over two decades. A small but lingering connection to an absent mother. The only gift, really, he had ever received from her.

One that now, it seemed, he had used as a teacher. To memorize every plant that grew here, as if they were friends to help him pass the time.

It should never have been where he found the source of all his suffering.

"Did you know?" I asked him, my voice hushed.

"Know what? That the plants were poisonous? Yes."

"Then—"

"But I didn't know *this*." His fingers squeezed the jar. The edge of his voice, just beginning to crack. "I never thought— *Fuck!* It was always just a bunch of exciting plants, and I was a kid who just thought here was my mother, not here, not with me but *still* somehow taming all these things. Look at how *powerful* she is . . . that she could grow these things. . . ." He swallowed back the urge to cry, but he was quickly losing the war. "I thought something in this greenhouse was going to be my *cure*. That my mother and Prosenko were working on something to help me. I . . . I used to think something in here would be my savior."

He stopped.

"My *savior*, Lena."

"Jonathan—"

"But no! This is where he got it all from! What he used to hurt me, and . . . and not just me. But my dad, and Audrey and everyone . . . to kill all those people! Audrey was right. He never tried to help me at all. He took her garden and he abused it! He . . . he *made* me sick," Jonathan said slowly, with a voice strained through teeth and spit and fury. "When she first said that, I didn't think . . . I thought she just—"

As Jonathan broke in front of me, teetering on the edge of an emotional collapse, everything grew slow. I thought back to Prosenko. To the pills. To the timeline and the fifteen years that separated the birth of that journal and the pills Audrey and I had taken.

The ones in my pocket that night of the party.

"We really could have died. . . ." The words were spoken just over my breath. Horrified. Astounded. Disbelieving, as Jonathan knelt to the ground and began to rip at the deadened stalks with his bare hands.

Audrey and I could have died.

Beside me Jonathan screamed, his hands growing torn and blistered, and I pulled him up from the dirt and braced him against the winding metal staircase.

"Stop it," I told him desperately, examining his hands. "Even if they're dormant, some of those leaves can burn you. They—"

I stopped, feeling his body sob, and then I stood there watching help-lessly as Jonathan reached up to his eyes, rubbing back the growing tears with sap-covered fingers as he sank to the floor. While a part of me winced at the disregard, the other part of me abandoned all plans to tend to his wounds, and instead I knelt and pulled him close to me. Rocking him as the realization slammed into his boney, weakened body. That everything he loved was now gone and there was no refuge left. Not even in his memories.

Outside, thunder boomed, the rain falling heavy. Yet even in the darkness my senses were overwhelmed. Attacked by the scent of an army of plants, rich and green, protruding from the soil with roots as old as Jonathan himself. A petrichor of poison that made the man before me tremble in an ever-growing disgust that I could never begin to truly, genu-inely empathize with.

A flash of lightning made his hand into something phantasmic. Something so pale in contrast to my own that it seemed alarming, un-natural, as it reached up to my neck.

The kiss itself was not that startling. I had seen Jonathan panicked before. I had seen that switch go off in his head that made him reach out for the nearest pair of lips as if they were more efficient than a prayer. I had seen him enough times covered in five shades of lipstick. None of them had mattered any more than the couple of jeers they got from his friends at a party.

And then of course there was Strasbourg. His face in the snow.

His tongue was bitter with herbs. Sweet with wine.

It wasn't pleasant.

And it wasn't romantic.

Jonathan tasted like death as much as he looked like it. A mouth of soured berries and honey, and yet in the chill of that forgotten place his lips were alive, and warm, and they were gentle. There was no smirk that pulled at the edge of his mouth as it normally did just before the paparazzi bulb could flash or someone handed him a drink at a party.

In the large expanse of the manor house, it was only us. He knew that, and I knew that, and I knew in the pit of my stomach that the Jonathan before me was not the corpse of the one that society expected. This was the tired, truthful, world-weary form of a boy who spent over twenty years grasping for the sun in every empty cavern of society he could. In glasses. In pills. In books. Anything away from the life his father planned for him and from the obligations he knew he could never meet even if he wanted to.

Our lips touched for less than four seconds.

I hadn't moved.

Jonathan looked at me, eyes glistening in the pale light. Searching desperately in my own for some answer that I wanted to give but didn't know how. Even with the taste of him still on my tongue, all I could think about was his sister. How it was still her I wished I held in my arms. About the anger in her eyes that morning in Strasbourg.

I couldn't do this to her.

I don't think even Jonathan wanted to.

He didn't need a lover. He didn't need a kiss or whatever he thought he was seeking in that moment.

He just needed someone to care.

Miraculously, I did not cry, although I should have. Holding him in my arms, I wanted to absorb every bit of his suffering. Every bit that had once been and every bit that I myself created. I wanted to suck it out of Jonathan like a merciful monster of lore so that his tears dried and his lungs didn't wheeze. So that he could smell like the rain and old books and not like cologne and sweat and bitterness. I kissed his hair as he had done mine that night, and in return he kissed the warm skin of my neck so tenderly and cautious of harm that it seemed chaste.

"I'm sorry," I said quickly. My eyes fighting against the water building within them. "I'm sorry for everything."

"Why?" he asked, pulling away from where he had burrowed himself in the crook of my shoulder. "You didn't poison me, Lena. You're not the one who hurt them."

31

WE SAT THERE ON THE DAMPENED GROUND until my legs went numb, and still I held Jonathan close. But soon the chill of the air raised the hairs on our arms and became too much, and so he stirred awake and mumbled that maybe, finally, it was time to go.

The wooden floorboards shifted below our weight, creaking as we walked into the abandoned passageway back toward the main wing of the house. Beside me Jonathan's steps were a soft, tired shuffle.

Even with the knowledge of the garden and the extent of Prosenko's decades-long plans, I didn't understand why he would have poisoned the guests on New Year's or why he had taken it so far. All our visit had proved was that the conclusion I'd reached with Audrey that night in the library was correct. I just underestimated the depth of Prosenko's involvement, and now, knowing that it was her garden, I wondered about Jonathan's mother, too.

I tried to not let my mind wander to what Jonathan would do when I took him home. Or rather not to his home but to the house in Rhode Island, where Audrey no doubt had spent the day anxious and waiting for his return.

I wanted to call her. To hear her voice again. To go back in time to when we were together and warm and safe on my bed, her perfume seeping into my pillow as we schemed a way to save her brother. Only those days felt long ago.

I didn't know what I would say to her now.

Ahead in the darkness, the corridor split into two paths, and Jonathan and I paused to try to recall the turns we had taken in our urgency. Then, out of the corner of my eye, a thin flash of light appeared, and I heard the floor to our left creak with footsteps.

"Did you see that?" Jonathan asked, just as alarmed as I was and fully awake again.

"Stay here," I told him, keeping my eyes focused on the shadows, but as before he ventured on, ignoring the risks and leaving me to follow.

It was as we neared the end of the corridor that we saw the open door to the apothecary room, and I heard the quick creak of the door being forced closed, shutting us in.

"Shit!" Jonathan said, and already I was running past him, my fingers clinging to the thin edge of the old wooden door to try to pry it open, but from the other side I could hear the crash of amber bottles as shelves were tipped over.

Whoever it was was doing everything they could to keep us out of the office.

Jonathan's body met mine, pressing me to the door as he worked to force it open. His hands slammed into the wooden panels until I choked on an inhale of dust. With his thin legs, he gave a hard heel kick to the door, and more bottles crashed and rolled along the floor on the other side, but it was enough. He reached his hand in through the small gap he had managed to create and forced the door open, slipping inside.

The inside of the apothecary was destroyed, the previously organized shelves now a mess of scattered pills and shards of glass. Jonathan stepped uneasily over the top of them, crunching the pieces beneath his shoes as I scrambled to keep up.

"Slow down!" I urged him. "You don't know who—"

"I don't care! They shouldn't be here!"

There was no time to look as we moved on, but with a passing glance I noticed the workstation in disarray, the scales toppled but the desktop emptier than I recalled. In Prosenko's office another crash echoed, and together Jonathan and I picked up speed, my heart pounding as I tried not to think of what lay up ahead.

When we reached the office, I nearly fell, my face slamming into the back of Jonathan's shirt as he stood there, paused for a moment to discern where, or whom, he might have seen.

Then, without another word, he was stepping over the tipped boxes and leaping past the doctor's chair and out the door, into the stark, cold silence of the house.

I stared at the open front door, where the chill of the night air seeped in and met our cheeks.

"Forget it," I tried. "We should just go!"

"No!" Jonathan insisted again, determined. I didn't care who was in the house. It could have been a vagrant, a partygoer, the police, anyone. None of the options my brain thought of were good.

"This is stupid! We need to get you home. Audrey is probably worried. It's late."

But my words fell on empty ears. At the sudden loud, echoing creak of a door, Jonathan was off again.

I looked back to the door, my fingers making anxious fists, but I couldn't leave him. Alone I listened to the hurried sounds of Jonathan's footsteps, tracing them back through the house, beyond the gallery and the bloodstained furniture. Past the smell of rot.

When I came to the library, I caught sight of his leg just before it disappeared into the music room, and I hastily followed, worried that we were running headfirst toward some kind of robber or group of squatters.

What I didn't expect to see was Prosenko.

32

THERE HAD BEEN NOTHING OF HIM after the party. A manhunt across state lines had come up empty. For months he had remained a ghost, to the point that everyone, including myself, thought he must have been dead. But there he was, in the aging, abandoned space of the room, no longer in his white lab coat or the blazers he had once worn as his uniform. Instead he was in stained chinos, his usually styled salt-and-pepper beard now overgrown, and the previously gelled curls an un-bound, undyed mess of gray atop his head.

It was a shadow of the Denis Prosenko I had known from the parties and somehow the truest version of the snake I had come to know under-neath. All the polish that once surrounded him gone. All the rigidity and formality abandoned.

Beside me Jonathan was frozen, his fingers forming anxious, angry fists as his breathing picked up.

"You."

"Jonathan, I—"

"Why are you here?!" he shouted, taking a step forward toward the old man. As he did, Prosenko took a step backward, and I saw in one hand the metal glint of a gun.

In his other I saw the journal from the workstation, as well as a picture frame.

"I can explain."

"No, you had your chance to explain!" Jonathan yelled, the anger flooding him. "For months you had your chance! Over twenty years! You could've—"

"I couldn't!" Prosenko argued, a strange sort of sadness seeping through his tone. "I wanted to, but . . . God, you're alive. You're alive. It worked after all."

In the small room, Prosenko stepped forward toward Jonathan, but the motion was rebuked as Jonathan lurched back, shouting, "No thanks to you!"

"No! It's *all* thanks to me!"

Jonathan seethed, and standing there before me the two tall men seemed to occupy the entirety of the room, the air between them tense. Once again I felt invisible. As much of an onlooker as I had been in the first weeks of my employment. But looking at them then, I noticed for the first time a sympathy in Prosenko's eyes. Something that whispered to my instincts that his hesitancy to raise the gun at Jonathan now was not fear but something else.

Something almost loving.

"He never cared for you," Prosenko began. "Not like me! That man only cared about himself. About Avelux. And your mother, she . . ." His fingers clutched the picture frame tighter.

"What about her? What does she have to do with this?"

I looked to Prosenko, waiting for an answer, hopeful if not naïvely so. Instead I watched his face grow hard again, any weakness fading as he straightened his back and tightened his grip on the gun. Spit gathered in my mouth, and I swallowed nervously, turning to Jonathan before I heard a click and looked back to Prosenko to see a gun pointed straight at my head. "You shouldn't have come back," he said.

Jonathan quickly grabbed me and motioned for us both to step away toward the piano bench. All I could do was stare down the barrel. As if I could blink and it would disappear. Yet I blinked, and I blinked, and Prosenko remained there, arm steady and unbothered by the blood and stench of decay that surrounded him.

"I didn't mean to hurt you," he told Jonathan, still without dropping the gun. "We were trying to *save* you. That's all I was ever trying to do."

Jonathan didn't answer, not for a while. Instead he looked at his old doctor in disbelief, from the grime on his shirt to the crazed look in his eyes and the dark, tired circles underneath. When he spoke, it was a curt and simple, "Bullshit."

"*No.* No, no," Prosenko continued. "I had everything under control! But then she . . ."

My muscles tensed as Prosenko kept the gun pointed at me. "It was all meant to end in Strasbourg. I had a plan, but then your father . . ."

Prosenko glared at me. "It should have been you taking the fall. After that shit you pulled with the bars that night. It was perfect. I had been waiting for you to slip up. But that morning I tried to tell him, and he just . . . he couldn't let it go. He couldn't let the Saint's Fog go. He didn't want to blame it. Blame *you.*"

"What?" I couldn't believe it. If what Prosenko was implying . . .

"You were stupid with the drug. I knew what it was, but that idiot got addicted anyway. He ruined everything." Prosenko looked to Jonathan, his voice yet again growing sympathetic. "Your health had been declining for months. I couldn't . . . I didn't want to let you go, but she made me."

"So all of this . . . You hurt everyone—just to blame me?" I said. "For what? Why would you do that?!"

"Because he messed up," Jonathan said, his voice soft again. "And Martin Verdeau never takes the blame for anything."

"Shut up!" Prosenko shouted, moving the barrel toward Jonathan. His finger trembled against the trigger.

"I know how he works," Jonathan continued. "I know him. I was failing . . . a sick, pathetic disgrace. He told me as much when I got back to the hotel that night. So let me get this straight. You wanted me dead. Is that it? He had had enough, and you needed a way out, so you figured you'd just cut your losses and have her take the fall?"

The room grew silent. Quiet enough that I could hear Prosenko's breathing as he stared at his old charge.

"Your little experiment with my health wasn't working, and my father wasn't happy." The words came cold, and I looked to Jonathan, frighteningly sober as he took a step forward. "Hell, I was dying anyway, right?"

"No." The word slipped through Prosenko's throat in a nervous warning. "Jonathan, stop. You don't understand, he didn't know, he didn't—"

"Everyone wants me gone," Jonathan continued, now dangerously close to where Prosenko aimed the gun. "So here, now's your chance. You can finish what you started. What the party failed to do. Just like he would've wanted."

I didn't know what to do. The look on his face mirrored the one I had seen in the greenhouse. The one staring out the window on the drive over. The one Audrey had likely seen every time Jonathan read Marlowe or Keats or Shelley. Something hollow and hurt.

"I'm sorry."

The next thing I knew, the gun had gone off with a crack. Disorientingly loud. I saw Jonathan stumble, kneeling, and then too slowly I realized that my right arm felt hot. Impossibly hot, and with an increasingly painful sting.

"Shit!"

Prosenko dropped the gun, leaving it to clatter on the marble floor. He looked once more at Jonathan, and then with shaking hands held tight on to the journal and picture frame, he scrambled to leave.

My arm hurt ferociously. A dull ache that resonated through my body with each pulse, and the sleeve of my shirt became wet as a small trail of blood began to drip its way down to my elbow.

Prosenko ran. Tripping over the furniture and running along the hall and toward the front entrance as fast as he could, toward his escape. In the quiet of the house, we could hear the roar of his car's engine as it started, listening as it slowly faded when Prosenko turned down the drive.

My arm pulsed again, and I reached up to try to stanch the blood flow.

"That looks bad," said Jonathan's voice from somewhere close.

I pulled my hand away and, seeing red but not as much as I expected, swallowed and put my hand back with increased pressure.

"I'm fine. I don't think it's deep. Are you—"

"I'm fine," he said, and from somewhere I had missed pulled out a scrap of fabric. A long, torn piece of white cotton. "Hang on."

I watched him, his face mere inches from mine as his nimble fingers delicately worked at the cloth, looping it around my arm and tying it tight. Almost instantly it darkened with a small, bright red line of blood. His eyes looked up to meet my own.

"What were you doing?" I finally asked. "Why did you tell him to shoot?"

Jonathan looked down. "I . . ."

With my eyes I begged him for an answer, different from the one I already knew.

He couldn't give it to me.

33

WHEN I AWOKE, THE SUN was shining in through cream-colored curtains, warm on my face. Around me was a large bedroom, full of robin's-egg blues and botanical prints. Nothing lush or green, but classical. Simple and reminiscent of a sun-bleached cottage. As I moved to brush the hair from my face, I winced, rudely reminded of the wound in my arm. Looking down, I realized at some point my shirt had been changed and, with it, my arm had been bandaged properly.

As I sat up, a woman stepped into the room. Her hair a pale blond and in a messy but chic knot atop her head. Everything else about her was proper, from her nude heels to her crisp white dress and blazer. When she spoke, her voice was firm but kind.

"Oh, good, you're awake. You surprised us last night."

I tried to think back but only vaguely recalled the car driving up sometime before dawn. The seashell gravel crunching underneath the wheels of the Bentley and the hurry of someone from the front door. I had presumed it was Audrey—a wisp of beige and blond in the morning twilight—and I wanted it to be, but looking at this woman, I realized it must have been her.

"Come, come," she said, and motioned for me to get up and follow. In her hand was a small first-aid kit. "Let's take a look at those bandages. I've got some lunch waiting outside near the garden."

"I'm sorry, have we met?"

She paused and smiled at me, yet it was somehow cold. "In some ways. My name is Olivia," she said. "Olivia Linzinger."

I raised an eyebrow.

"I'm their mother."

I followed her outside through a set of white French doors and was instantly greeted by the smell of the ocean being carried over from a gentle breeze. Up ahead sat a white patio set in the shade of a large umbrella, its table covered in pitchers of cucumber water and lemonade. A small tower of pastries sat at the center.

My stomach growled at the sight.

"Please sit," she told me, motioning with her hand.

I did so and waited as she smoothed her dress and sat down on the chair beside me. Then she placed the first-aid kit on the table and undid the clasp.

"It's good to meet you, Helena," she said, gently taking hold of my arm to pull it closer. I sat there, letting her get to work in a mild state of bewilderment. Audrey and Jonathan's mother was not at all how I had imagined her. She was tall and imposing, with the bold carved features that Jonathan bore but almost nothing else of him. Yet her voice and her coloring made it like seeing Audrey in twenty years' time. In this there was no mistaking who she was. Who had been in that photo, smiling with her arm around Prosenko. The portrait in the town house. Still, I wrestled with the fact that she was there in front of me and not an imagined ghost of Arrow's Edge.

The medical tape clung to my skin, making me wince as Olivia pulled it off and left it on a napkin. Then she picked up a second pair of tweezers, and I realized that at some point, without my knowing it, the wound had been stitched up. Across my upper arm was a line of red and a series of blackish blue lines neatly in a row along it.

"You're lucky, you know," she said. "The bullet only grazed you. Eight millimeters or so at the worst." I fought not to wince again as she picked at the lingering residue of the gauze and then reached for an alcohol swab. "It looks like a lot of blood, but if you try not to use it, the wound should heal in a few weeks."

"Are you a doctor?" I asked her then. "Audrey never mentioned what you did."

She smiled again, this time a hair wider and more genuine. "No, but I work in pharmaceuticals. This is just a skill I've learned over time. A holdover, I suppose, from some of Martin's wilder days."

"Pharmaceuticals?"

"A drug company. Just a small one that's been trying to expand recently. You may have heard of it. Kinlex?"

She was right, I had heard the name before, but from where I couldn't remember. Yet suddenly the plants and the garden made more sense. Prosenko's words the night before made more sense. Jonathan's ill-placed trust in her garden, all of it came together. That and something else.

"I—"

"I advise you to be smart, Miss Gereghty," Olivia said sharply. "I can see that you are."

"I'm sorry?"

She grabbed the alcohol swab and wiped at the wound, the alcohol searing into my skin and causing me to flinch. She merely pressed harder and held it there.

"You had a long night. I didn't see the point in sitting you down to talk then, but I hope you're rested enough now."

"Talk? About what?"

Olivia discarded the swab, which had become entirely pink with blood, and then grabbed the tape and a fresh piece of gauze and secured it all safely before speaking again.

When she was finished, she reached for a glass of what looked like sparkling water but smelled strongly of gin.

"We fired your father."

I did a double take. A recoiling of my mind.

"Well, Martin, I suppose. I wasn't consulted in the decision, but that's what started all this, right?" she said, clutching the gin fizz in her hand. Everything about her was poised. Immaculate in the sunlight. Golden, even with the medical waste beside her. "The parties. The Saint's Fog."

I remained silent.

Olivia sighed and took a sip from her glass. "You're poor, I can't fault you for that. All they seem to teach you in school is that we steal from you and fire your fathers. I can understand how you connected the two. You weren't taught anything different."

"What?" Something in my voice turned cold.

"He did fire him. Yes. But do you know why?"

The image of the parties flashed through my brain as I pictured my father trying to keep up with the rampant alcoholism and the debauched attitudes of men and their mistresses, so much that he couldn't shake the addiction after. How his side table remained full of orange pill bottles now, almost a year after the fact.

I hated that my father ever set foot in Arrow's Edge.

"Yes," I finally said.

"Hmph! You sound so certain."

"Martin bought out the company and left him with nothing. He worked there for a decade, and your execs couldn't even spare him a severance package."

Olivia raised an eyebrow. "Is that what he told you?" I could feel her watching me through the lens of her shades as the air shifted around us.

My father had told us this a dozen times over dinner. My mother bitterly mumbling the fact while she threw a slice of cold lasagna onto a plate. I had heard this unfairness countless times ever since the Verdeaus came into our lives, and never once did I have a reason to doubt.

"Oh, you poor dear," said Olivia without any sincerity. "We gave your father the same option we give everyone we let go. Well, at his level anyway."

Again I said nothing.

"When Avelux absorbs a company, we obtain its stock. You know about stocks, you're smart, I shouldn't need to explain them. So, like everyone else at your father's level and experience, he was presented two options upon dismissal. We could give him shares in our companies, equivalent to what he would have gained working at Ellerhart for another ten years. I believe it was just shy of a million. That's about the standard. Or he could have two years' salary to do with as he wished."

What else could I do but stare?

A *million*? Even two years of my father's wages would be $150,000. Over $100K after taxes. But we saw none of that.

"Your father, as it so happens, took the two years' worth. It's a shame, but most do. And then he went to the casino and the penny stocks and he did what, unfortunately, most men like your father do. He gambled it away, and when that didn't work . . . well, pain is pain, I suppose."

"He would never."

"Your father is poor, Lena, and your father thinks like a poor man thinks. He met a man at a flashy party who contacted him after he took the deal. Then, as this man has probably told so many others, he told your father that he could make two million, or three million, or five by Friday."

"Stop."

"And your father believed him, because this is what separates us. This is where the divide grows and where mistakes happen, Lena, and this is what will always keep us separate. Because the poor want money quickly. A poor person could be handed five dollars, and if they want to make it grow, then they think the best way is the one that happens the fastest. The rich don't think like that. The rich are patient."

I felt an embarrassing wetness grow against my eyelashes, and anger had risen and settled and risen in stages of shock that left me a confused mess and longing for a chic pair of sunglasses and a glass of gin in my own hand.

"Why do you think I'm telling you this?"

"I don't know."

"You're patient, Lena," she said. "It's because you're patient."

"Why did Martin hire me? If you all knew this," I asked, now thinking back to Prosenko and his words, fighting against the sick feeling in my stomach.

Olivia shifted and took a sip from her glass. "It's a simple matter of math. Paying you for tending to Jonathan and those parties never came close to the sum of stocks your father would have gone away with, so I didn't have a problem with it. Though, really, the choice belonged to Denis in the end."

"Prosenko."

"Mm," she hummed. "More of an idiot than I initially thought him to be, I'm afraid. But it was nice while it lasted."

"You . . . you *knew*? You knew what he was doing? What Martin was?"

"Shh," Olivia hushed. "The truth is, my family was ruined before you even came to know our name. All of this was inevitable."

"What do you mean? He's your *son*."

"Do you know what it's like, running a company?" she continued, ignoring me. "It's endless work, but you become proud of it. When I first met Martin, he was ambitious. Just like me. Older. Messier. We would have done anything to keep ourselves afloat." She took another small sip from her drink. "When I married Martin, I knew that he wanted an heir for Avelux. It made sense. He had inherited it once already. This was all that mattered to him, and with my background in medicine there was an opportunity to create something that would ensure he had one. That he wouldn't have to worry. We both saw it, the potential to create something beautiful. Something that could change things. Something to help my own company, too, if it worked."

The theriac, I thought. Then she continued.

"But he was not interested, not after I had Audrey."

There was the barest shift in her tone. A swallow before she continued. All the while I sat there listening.

"He demanded a son. We fought after that, and eventually I gave him Jonathan. By this point we fought almost daily, but five years into it, before he would sign the divorce papers, there was one thing he still wanted from me. That first idea I ever shared with him. But I refused to make it. Audrey deserved the company, it was her right, and if we were going to try anything, it should have been for her. She deserved to be invincible like he wanted. Untouchable. But Martin failed to see it that way. He became terrified with the idea of our daughter taking over the company, and after Jonathan had the accident, he insisted I develop a drug to be used for Jonathan only. I refused, and eventually I had enough. I left."

"Then he hired Prosenko."

She nodded. "Right from under my nose."

"So . . . the poison . . . the theriac, that was you? It wasn't Martin?"

Again she smiled. Soft and polite. "In the beginning, yes. Despite everything. I suppose I saw it as something to help my growing company after the loss of Martin's funding. Or if it failed, in a way it would be something to help my daughter rise to her rightful place. But Denis saw the damage it was doing to the boy years ago and he refused to give up on him, bless his heart . . . refused to let Martin see what it was doing, too. He believed in it. But enough was enough. I told him last year that it was time to end it and cut our losses. That you can't control the side effects in drug trials. Not even decades-long ones. I'm sure you know that with your schooling."

I struggled with how pragmatic her tone was. How even and unemotional as she practically confessed to me that she had ordered Prosenko to kill her own son.

As if he were nothing.

"We needed a way out," she continued. "I needed the experiment to end so that Audrey would be guaranteed to take over Avelux, and Prosenko knew there was only one way for that to happen. He also knew we had to be careful about who took the fall. It was business, Helena. You just happened to be the one to arrive in the eleventh hour."

"But . . . the party. At New Year's, Prosenko—"

"Acted foolish. He panicked when Martin didn't place the blame on you. When he started to piece together what had been going on. So yes, Denis got mad and acted brash. I'd like to apologize for that. I only hope you'll be smart enough to accept my offer. Ah! Perfect, Audrey, come here, love."

Across the garden Audrey walked out from behind a large hydrangea bush. She was wearing a linen wrap dress and had a light tan briefcase in her hand. It was the first time I had seen her since the hospital, and for a moment I felt such a rush of joy at seeing her face that it pulled me away for the smallest of seconds. At the sight of me, her eyes brightened and her feet quickened their pace. Then, with the slightest motion from Olivia, every ounce of warmth and joy disappeared from Audrey's face.

"Wait," I said, turning back to Olivia. "What do you mean by that? What's going on?"

"I've got another appointment, but I think we're finished here. I believe I've made my point. My daughter will show you inside, and there you'll find a few more matters to be discussed."

Audrey looked to me, her eyes lingering a little too long before moving back to Olivia. "The press junket is setting up. They said they need to leave soon or they'll be late."

"Thank you, dear." Olivia stood up, smoothed her skirt, then grabbed hold of the medical waste and folded it in her hand before turning back to me. All it was was a look. My face reflected in the dark lenses of her sunglasses, but it was enough. I had received my warning, despite not knowing what kind.

Audrey motioned for me to follow her, and so, as always, I did. Only unlike before, her formality seemed colder in the Newport weather, more poised. She looked at me, painfully brief before going inside, and then continued walking through the living room and up the staircase.

"Sorry."

Audrey stopped and glanced back ever so slightly. "Hm?"

"That's the last thing you said to me. At the hospital."

She remained there, paused on the stairs. Her fingers gripping the banister.

"I thought about that a lot, you know. After you left. I thought about why you'd be sorry. For the party. For what happened after it. For that night in my room. But I still couldn't figure it out."

Her pink lips remained closed. Mouth tight. I saw the hint of water begin to gather in her eyes.

"But it was this, wasn't it? You knew something like this was coming."

Finally she turned and took the remaining few steps up until she landed just outside an ornate white-painted door. "Please," she said, forcing her voice to remain firm, and tried to motion me in.

I didn't move.

"How could you just leave me like that? To deal with everything. I thought you—"

"Please!" she insisted, her lip trembling just slightly. Until she heard a shuffle on the floor below and smothered it, swallowing the motion and any bit of weakness back into a forced professionalism.

Despite the lingering anger at her mother's words, my heart nearly broke.

I looked to her standing there, just a few feet above me. Her clothing pristine but her makeup failing to conceal her exhaustion and the redness around her eyes. The months of grief having taken their toll.

She kept her eyes focused on mine, silently pleading, until at last I stepped inside the small room.

When the door had shut and the lock clicked, her arms were around me, the scent of her perfume enveloping me in its confusing sweetness. Her fingers moved, threading themselves into my hair as she pressed our bodies close, hugging me, squeezing from me warmth as if she'd been starved of it. As if the winter chill of the party had remained woven into her bones ever since.

I was still angry when she kissed me. Still furious, and yet after the lonely months in Roslindale, after the previous day's return to Arrow's Edge, I couldn't help but meet her eagerly.

I thought about how nothing in the world could stop me from wanting her.

Her fingers held the fabric of my shirt tightly, gripping first where the bullet stung before apologetically moving to my waist. Her body pressed close to mine, and like I had seen with her brother before her, the months of suffering, of fallout and sorrow, all seemed to tumble from her as we stood there, hidden behind the painted doorway and away from her mother's view.

"I've wanted to do that for so long," she said, the confidence she once held in her voice all but gone. "But after the party I didn't—" She swallowed, mumbling into my chest. "I didn't know what to say. I wanted to call."

My hand moved to smooth her hair, instinctual, as if it weren't the first time it had ever done so.

I wanted to say it was okay. But I couldn't.

Behind us stood a large window overlooking the sea. White, gauzy curtains blowing in to brush against the dark wooden shelves that lined the walls. At the center was a single table, two chairs, and a folder lying open. When we pulled apart, I eyed the pen beside it.

"What's this?" I asked her.

She swallowed and wiped her tears. "Business."

Behind her on one of the shelves sat a slim television, silently playing the news, and on that small screen I saw Olivia step out onto the front porch of their estate. It was only then that I realized if I paid attention, the flash of cameras and the chatter could be heard filtering in through the window. On the TV, with a pristine photo of Audrey hovering over half the screen, the banner read that Audrey Verdeau was officially taking over her father's company. Olivia announced that due to Jonathan's failing health she and the other remaining board members felt Audrey was the best choice.

"So that's what you meant by the press."

Audrey moved to one of the chairs. "It's been eating up my life for months. . . . It wasn't—" Again she cut herself off. As if she were breaking script. "It wasn't how I wanted it. All the press conferences and the meetings . . . but she just kept saying that it had to be done. That someone had to take care of the company and it should have been mine from the beginning. But I didn't know what to do. Taking over Avelux has always been my dream, but not like this . . . not hurting you. I . . . I should have been happy, and I couldn't tell her no, and she just kept talking about how this whole thing has been hell on the other board members and how our shareholders have been pushing for a decision before the stock plummets any further."

"Right. Stock."

By this point the simple idea of a market left a sour taste in my mouth.

The folder still sat open, and finally I looked over at it. "Why am I even here, Audrey? What's this about?"

Audrey bit her lip, a small motion but enough to smear her lipstick ever so slightly.

"You're a liability," she explained apologetically. "But I'm trying to find a way to fix it."

"What?"

"After everything that's happened, despite my best efforts, your name is still connected on Wall Street to the deaths of far too many people."

"I know that. But it doesn't explain why I'm here. What's in that folder?"

Audrey stared out the window and then politely sat down, smoothing her skirt. She was trying her best to be professional, but it was clearly difficult for her. "It's taken me some time, but after vetting you I think I've come up with a solution."

"Vetting me? Wait—"

"I know I've been absent and I should have called, but I had to make sure that reaching out to you wouldn't hurt you more."

"Hurt me how?"

"Your aunt. Clare Ricchetti? Her gardens formed a contract with Kinlex shortly after you arrived back in Boston."

Kinlex, the name repeated, and finally I recalled my aunt's joyous voice on the phone. A large investment, a garden in the north.

"If the news got hold of it, they'd know enough to suspect where the Saint's Fog came from, and they would have connected it to Prosenko's pills as well."

I was stunned. "No . . . no, that can't be. Those labels, I saw where Prosenko got his stuff from last night. It was all in your mom's garden. Anything else he had was written in Chinese. No one would buy that. There's no connection."

Audrey bit her lip again. "Import laws, unfortunately. Kinlex has its subsidiaries repackaged outside Guiyang. That's likely where his boxes were from. It's also where your aunt's stuff ends up before distribution."

I was speechless.

"My mother doesn't care about it. To her it's just fallout from this mess Prosenko's made, but, Lena, look. I'm trying to give you an opportunity to save your aunt. To keep her out of this," said Audrey. "I know how much you love her."

"How?"

Finally Audrey opened the file, and I looked down to read the formal header.

Kinlex.

"This is a contract," I said.

She opened the pen. "It is. A good one."

"Right."

"You developed Saint's Fog into a recreational drug, Lena. You know the recipe."

"Wait, you know about that?"

She nodded. "For a while now."

"But that night, when you did the toast . . ."

A small flush rose to her cheeks, but she didn't indulge it. "I remember it."

"Oh."

"I also remember how that night at the party you ran to get me something to ease the symptoms. You've done it every night the Saint's Fog was out. You know an antidote."

I shook my head. "No, I don't. The stuff I used with Prosenko just treated the symptoms—"

"You know one."

"No, Audrey," I argued in disbelief, "I don't!"

"Then you will tell people that you do."

I looked at her. "What's this about?"

"Saint's Fog has hit the market," she explained wearily, as if this, too, had been a part of her months of exhaustion. "A small drug ring has popped up, and it's spread through Boston and New York. I think it was Dylan, but . . . I don't know. With Prosenko missing, it could have been him, too."

I thought of the journal in his hands. That first open page of formulas that I'd been unable to read and all the others that had been so close to my own.

It seemed possible.

"So?"

"So," she echoed. "If Kinlex is able to develop an antidote . . ."

All the pieces clicked in place. "If Kinlex gets the copyright on the antidote, it saves Avelux, too."

"It saves *people*, Lena. People that your drug—"

"Bullshit! I didn't spread my drug beyond those parties!"

She looked down, again composing herself. "I know, but other people did, and the fact is, this is your monster, and I'm trying to give you a chance to help kill it. To help *you*. Please, you've got to let me, Lena. I've been working on this for months. This is a way you can have everything."

I hated this. I wanted Audrey back so badly, but not this one. I wanted the one who smelled of sweet flowers and coffee. The one who smiled at me and linked arms with me as we shopped. Whose fingers I could still taste in my mouth. Not the calculating business side bred into her by her family. The side she used now.

"And if I don't?"

"Then you're stupid," she said bluntly. "And people die, and you shove aside all the work I've done with the press to convince people that you don't deserve to be in jail. And . . . if that's not good enough for you, then because it will save your aunt's garden. Because instead of being highlighted as a small upstart helping to rid the world of a new street drug, it becomes the Italian garden that destroyed the economy, and my family, with your name attached, and those are the only two stories. I've looked at this every way that I can, Lena. This is the only way out."

"I fucking hate you."

"No you don't," she said. "You hate my family. But so do I."

"What about Jonathan?"

She swallowed and inhaled sharply through her nose as she forced her back to straighten. Her finger moving from its resting state to gently stroke the scars on her forearm. Still pink and raised and ugly.

"This meeting is about you."

"And I'm asking about him. You've seen him, Audrey. Do you know what happened last night?"

"He refuses to sign anything," she explained. "I'm at a loss, Lena. I don't know what else I can do. He won't go to any of the meetings and refuses to speak with my mother. It's like—"

"*Your* mother," I interrupted. "You're *both* her children."

"Lena," Audrey pleaded. "If you help with the antidote, we may be able to help Jonathan, too. Like we talked about before." She reached out her hand and brushed it over my own, trying to take my fingers in hers. I had yearned for that touch months ago, but now, even after the kiss, it felt hollow. "We may still be able to reverse some of the damage Prosenko did. We know what we're dealing with now. What Martin did with the theriac. We can help him."

Martin, I thought. *What Martin did.*

So she still didn't know.

I looked to her and then eyed the paper. "Is that in there?"

"It can be," she said. "If that's what will get you to sign."

"Then I want you to write it. Add it in there."

I didn't expect her to, but Audrey took the pen and wrote in a few sentences under the final paragraph. They were numbered and in perfect cursive.

"Is that legal?"

"And binding. Summa cum laude, remember?"

I did. I stared at the contract and the addition. Then, with another glance out the window, I said, "Fine. Okay."

"Okay?"

I nodded, reaching for the pen, and then stopped as our fingers brushed again, and I looked up to her, willing myself through the anger rising inside me and trying to see a bit of her old smile or a hint of the kindness from before. Across the table she looked to me, relief falling over her face.

"Just tell me one thing, Audrey."

She waited, her large hazel eyes newly filled with an uncertainty.

"Is this what you wanted? Or your mother?"

JUST BEFORE LEAVING ME IN THAT ROOM, Audrey told me some-one would drive me home. I don't think she could escape her mother's watchful eye long enough to say good-bye. I don't know if she could trust herself.

With my arm still aching, all I could do was sit there, heavy with the realization of my situation. That somehow Olivia had known and that all this time I had been played. That my anger had been used by Prosenko and Martin, and that even now I couldn't seem to escape the Verdeau name. That I had just signed myself further into bondage.

In spite of being told to wait, I left the room and wandered the halls in search of Jonathan.

The home was not like anything I had come to associate with the Verdeau name. Gone were the ornate paintings and the shine of gold and marble. In their place I saw wood, whitewashed and painted over, with none of the rich grain to show through. All around were linens in twenty tones of beige, everything pale, everything ghostly. As a result every step deeper into the space felt stranger than the last.

By the time I reached the room at the end of the hall, there was no question as to whom it belonged. From the scent alone, I knew it instantly: the stale sweetness of evaporated wine and the sharp tang of vodka.

Through the crack in the door, I saw Jonathan in bed, hair an unwashed mess and still in his clothes from the night before, except pantsless. In front of him was another television, casting a blue light upon the sheets in the otherwise dark room, and his eyes remained glued to it, transfixed by the same sound bite I had been watching only moments earlier. The events playing out on the lawn just below him.

"Hey," I said, cracking the door open. He jumped, startled, and turned to me. It was then that I saw a glass of orange juice in his hand, the bottle of vodka on his nightstand.

"You're awake," he said.

"Can I come in?"

He motioned with a nod, and then lazily pointed to my arm. It was a brief gesture, but that told me he wasn't sober. "You got stitched up."

"Yeah."

"Now you've got a war wound like the rest of us."

I tried to laugh, however small, but couldn't manage it. I don't think he expected me to. Finally I moved closer to the bed, where I could more clearly see his face and the circles under his bloodshot eyes. It didn't look like he'd slept at all.

"Hey . . . you okay?"

For a moment he looked at me, then glanced to the screen. "They didn't tell me," he said dully, "but I can't be mad, right? They're saying how great she'll be." He paused and took a sip from his glass. "That place should've died with me, though. . . . That's what I had always hoped, y'know. That he'd croak and then I'd . . . well." He made a circle with his hand and then mimed a small explosion.

"What are you going to do?"

He shrugged. "They'll find something for me, I guess. Send me somewhere."

"Is that what you want?"

Jonathan's eyes met mine as he opened his mouth but said nothing. Then he looked over my shoulder, and as I heard the heavy sound of someone approaching, Jonathan stopped, closing his mouth and letting the conversation end. When I finally turned to see the reason, I found none other than the same man who had driven me home from the hospital.

"Are you ready, ma'am?" he asked.

"I . . ." I looked to Jonathan again, more sympathetic than my words would allow. I can't explain it, how I felt in that hallway, staring at him sprawled out and so clearly devoid of hope. The humor and wit and life all completely stripped away from him. That in all the space of his room there was not a single book in sight. Nothing to comfort him.

"Tell me you'll be okay," I said, and I waited, and waited, willing him to tell me something that I couldn't manage to ask. An excuse to take him out of there with me and away from whatever terrible plans Olivia could have devised in her coldness.

I wanted to tell him everything, but nothing came. Finally, as Jonathan turned away and back to the screen, the driver put his hand on my shoulder. "Ma'am," he said, "let's go."

34

HUMANS ARE DOOMED TO LOVE TERRIBLE THINGS.

Love, after all, is what drove me to reach out for Mrs. Gainsborough that night. What kept my hand steady as I brewed the Saint's Fog, worried for my father, and angry for my family. Leaving the house, I knew that despite everything I had loved Audrey in some way since she first appeared in the sunlit room at the town house. A crush born from a beautiful voice and a kind smile that over time had turned into something stronger, even with the multitude of mistakes and our months apart. A bond that formed between us as we found solace together in the secret of her brother's poisoning and as I held the secret of my own.

But the person that I loved in her was struggling, and I didn't know how to help, let alone help myself. Even worse, how to help her brother.

I thought of the moments back in autumn when he wandered those parties with the air of a great contagion among the socialites, champagne in his weak hand. When his lips, lonely and self-hating, were a deep and bloodstained red from the bruising kisses of strangers as much as wine.

Despite the anger that had clouded me over the course of those months, I still wanted to save him. More than that, I think, from the first moment of our meeting I wanted him to save himself. I knew that somewhere deep within her, Audrey wanted the same.

I only wished that leaving Newport that afternoon I could have been surer it was possible.

FOR TWO NIGHTS I TRIED to be content back in Roslindale. I took to wearing long-enough sleeves to cover my wound, and hiding in my room whenever possible, and being nice to my mother for reasons I didn't want to think about. I had texted Rumi and Anna to let them know that yes, I was all right, kind of, and sorry, sorry, it won't happen again. That really. It's over. I even agreed to go to brunch, and I lay there on my bed making plans with them for an hour that I willed myself to keep but dreamed of excuses not to. Because I knew that it wouldn't last. I knew the paper I had signed.

On every news channel, I saw her face. Olivia, proudly beaming down at her miserable, polished daughter. The gentle roll of the ocean, cresting behind them. The same clip over and over again from different angles in all the business recaps, and nowhere once did I see Jonathan. It was too easy to imagine him in that room, gray and white and staring at the news the same as me. Forgotten. On the sidelines. A loser in his parents' games.

Then, as the patter of another springtime storm began against my window after lunch, I got another call. This time from Olivia herself.

"Is he with you?"

"What?"

"Is he with you again?"

"Why?"

Nothing.

Then, with her voice quiet, Olivia said, "He left after lunch. After some redheaded boy dropped off a package."

I thought back to Elliot, the only redheaded boy I knew. The only other person, arguably, left to care about Jonathan, and I wondered, "What was it?"

"Some kind of book. I don't know. Look. If you see him, tell him to come back. I'm done chasing after him."

Something ugly welled up. "Ma'am, I—"

The phone clicked.

I immediately called Audrey.

Just like that I was racing to grab the keys to my Honda and driving down the turnpike as fast as I could get away with, my foot glued firmly to the pedal. There is no explaining it. The feeling that overwhelmed me then. Just that something was terribly wrong, and that feeling only grew as the skies turned gray and the rain followed me as I drove across the state. With every ounce of my soul praying, pleading beyond what my mouth could say.

When I arrived, the Bentley was already there, abandoned askew at the end of the drive, Audrey's own car not yet arrived. I yanked the keys out of the ignition and ran up the steps only to find the door ajar.

"Jonathan!" I screamed, my voice echoing into the space.

Growing up, I had always been told that Lucifer fell because of pride and that Icarus fell because of hubris. Never did I think someone like Jonathan, a frail but glowing god among men, could fall so quickly into the shadows because of his own family, and not even complain.

The truth, I realized, running back into Arrow's Edge for the very last time, was that Jonathan was a boy who believed, in every sinew and bone of his making, that he had been a worm, raised among serpents, and no one else understood that.

They were too busy trying to convince him otherwise.

I found the greenhouse empty, the antique white table overturned at its center, and dirt scattered about. Plants were everywhere, ripped out from their home with their roots exposed. I turned and ran through the side door and the dusty back hallway to the open door of Prosenko's old lab.

Glass was everywhere. Pellets still littered the floor and the shelves, fallen over from our last visit. The pills were so numerous and so thick across the floor that I squashed dozens underfoot without realizing it, and still there were fewer than I remembered.

"Jonathan!" I shouted again, louder and with panic threatening to make the task impossible. Then I ran some more, manic, through every hallway of the house.

"Jonathan, where are you? Jonathan, answer me! Please!" I screamed.

I don't know how many times I shouted his name. A dozen. A hundred. Just that I couldn't stop, and so I ran as far as I could, checking every couch and chair and corner he used to hide in, screaming until my throat felt raw. When I returned to the gallery, the rain fell thick, echoing against the old windows, and there, in the shadows on the far side of the room, I found him. Collapsed and quiet on the floor, a copy of "Adonais" beside him.

There was foam at his lips and an amber jar by his hand, without a lid.

I shouted again, something unintelligible and guttural, and ran over, stumbling to the marble floor by his side, where my hands, shaking, tried to slap him awake. Too quickly the tears flooded my eyes, and still I found it within me to hoist him up, feeling the lines of his ribs against my fingers, and I swallowed. "Jonathan, please . . . please. *Fuck*. Please don't do this. Wake up. Audrey's on her way. Come on, you idiot, *wake up*."

After a second, a decade, I moved to feel for his pulse, leaning my face so close to his own in hopes that his breath might ghost across my lips. And I waited, fighting to keep my own breath still enough and choking back sobs in the process, and then finally, in what seemed like a dream, I felt it. The barest passing of air, just enough to move a lock of my hair.

I sat him up, propping his limp body against me as I reached to pry his mouth open and shove my fingers down his throat. I pushed, and I pushed, murmuring a nonsensical prayer until his body convulsed and I felt the bile rush up to my fingers.

Jonathan doubled over, heaving, and out they poured. A mess of black pearls and liquid, dark as ink, splattered across the marble. With my body trembling, I tried to stabilize him, bending his body over and keeping his mouth open enough as he groaned, and then I tried again, and more pills followed. Fizzing and acrid with a terrible stench beyond what any layer of hell could devise.

When he coughed on his own, I finally let myself relax. As he coughed, gagged, and sputtered, I knew it must have burned his throat, but there was nothing to offer, so I sat there grateful for every breath he managed and staring down at the blackened puddle on the floor.

Given what was in those pills, there was no way he could have survived. No human should have survived five of them, and even Jonathan could not have survived fifty.

But he was awake, for now, and that was miracle enough, and I was helpless not to cry.

I tried to soothe him and rubbed circles with my hand across his back, but he shuddered and gasped, and in between the coughs and swallows of air he began to sob.

"Why . . ." he mumbled, his voice impossibly strained.

"Hey, shh . . . hey, it's okay."

"No!" he shouted, shaking away from my touch. "No, it's not! I . . . I swallowed . . . I swallowed them *all*. I . . ."

He tried to speak but in the end merely wailed, a sorrow traveling through every muscle in his body. A disappointment at waking up.

Because the reality was that here was Jonathan Verdeau. A man whose father thought the world should never be rid of him and yet who had been courting death at every corner and in every bottle he could find, and he finally thought he'd found it.

The door behind me creaked open, where the entry met the gallery, and the sound of the pouring rain echoed woefully loud as I looked over and saw Audrey, hair soaked and water running down her face. She was too far away for me to read her expression, but she saw us, and she stood there letting the rain pelt her further before rushing inside.

"God . . ." Audrey said through a shaking breath, covering her mouth. "What have you done?"

Jonathan lurched in my lap with a pained, wheezing laugh. His throat raw. "What's it . . . look like?"

She frowned the kind of frown that was overwhelmed with sadness. A quivering lip and watering eyes. Then Audrey swallowed, closed her eyes, and tried her best to smile. "You can't do anything right, can you?"

I felt his chest expand with another gasping, painful laugh.

Finally she looked to me, grateful as her face grew red and her eyes welled up with tears she quickly wiped away. She cleared her voice.

"You don't . . . really want to, do you?"

Jonathan said nothing, and still I stroked his hair. Fearing that if I stopped, he might stop moving again.

"You could have told me."

"You had a meeting."

Audrey raised her hand to her mouth, covering another sob. "I would've skipped it."

"Nah," said Jonathan weakly. "That's *my* job, remember?"

"Well, I would've missed this one. If you just told me. If you—"

"Audrey," he said, and then shook his head.

Another series of coughs and convulsions overtook him, and my arms held him firmly as Audrey stood there, helpless and yet unable to step any closer. Despite everything, his body was still ravaged by the poison, and it was a wonder to me that he was not suffering any worse or that he was still conscious at all.

After a moment she asked, "Do you really . . . do you really want to die?"

Jonathan closed his eyes and sighed.

We both knew the answer. We were likely the only two in the world who did, and despite my anger at Audrey she was there, and her tears told me that somewhere within her she cared infinitely more than she was able to show.

"Okay," she said softly, and then, louder, "Okay."

35

Death had clung to Jonathan for years, a welcomed friend that left him like a ghost in those final months, as Audrey took her rightful place among the Avelux ranks. After the overdose, though, that was it. The boy who was left on the floor amid the pills and the glass beneath the onlooking portraits had resigned himself to a fate neither Audrey nor I could dissuade him from. He couldn't keep going on. He couldn't keep smiling and showing up to meetings. He couldn't play the part like his sister, and he had never wanted to.

He had tried to find so many ways out, and none of them wanted him. In a way his father's wish still hung over him, protecting him despite it all.

As his body shivered and we held him there together on the marble floor, Jonathan recovered slowly, and then we devised one final and lasting way he could have the end he wanted.

Or at least, close to it.

With some help from the DA's office, we were able to secure a death certificate the following day. A couple of grand in the hands of a Berkshire coroner later, the papers had been signed on Jonathan's behalf. With an easy explanation of cardiac arrest and liver failure and a few other details I knew from having spent months reviewing his health reports, we exaggerated the facts and that was it. With our lips sealed and a few swirls of ink, quietly, Jonathan Verdeau ceased to exist. Away from the world. Away from his mother and everyone else, just as he had always wanted.

The popularity of the scandal and the numbed sensationalism after the New Year's party only served to make Saint's Fog even more in vogue. From the sidelines we watched as a new strain sprang up on the streets. As for Audrey, with Avelux back in partnership with Kinlex, her mother proudly proclaimed it their new mission to stamp out the drug.

We later discovered that Jonathan had secretly purchased stock in his father's company during the selloff that January as a bit of spite, arranging with a short seller to use the company's near collapse to gain money as a final fuck you to his father. It was likely the only tactic he ever gleaned from all of Martin's teachings, and it earned him a small fortune in the process. Enough to live on. The surprise only came when his will was pulled out and I suddenly received a check in the mail.

By June all the arrangements had been made. I was sent to Switzerland to work for Kinlex as my contract directed me to do, never being asked to suffer another summer away from Europe. There I was given a lab coat and 24/7 surveillance while attempting to develop an antidote to the Saint's Fog in record time, at the mercy of Olivia's shareholders.

It was slow going, even for me, with the eager but distant help of Aunt Clare. By some grace that chaotic darkness of the Verdeau family never reached her. The Fog had been traced to Prosenko, with the new evidence of it in his lab back in Arrow's Edge. She had been spared and, in turn, was naïve enough to be thrilled at my lofty new position at a company like Kinlex.

Finally, after too many midnights and mornings in the lab, an antidote came along. As with the famed magic of duck's blood in the ancient remedies, I found a secret ingredient. Something impervious to the damages. Something immune. It all fell into place, and all of America seemed to celebrate Audrey and Olivia's achievement.

At this time, in the crisp white confines of the Kinlex lab, I occupied my thoughts with ones of Aunt Clare back in Italy. Under the summer sun, with a new, strange assistant in tow. One who I knew in his spare time was discussing literature until his heart was full of the likes of Shakespeare and Keats. Laughing with her over old books and sipping cava.

I imagined the life they had and how peaceful it was, even though my only connection to him existed in the small vials they would send in insulated boxes straight to my lab. Boxes overflowing with dried herbs and absolutes, steam-distilled products and strange teas, and these thoughts kept me happy while the realities of my work kept me busy. Until the happiness faded and I found myself inevitably missing it all too much.

During that time Audrey traveled frequently, and while she had not officially moved Avelux's headquarters to Europe, she made a point to be in Zurich enough for us to have almost weekly lunch dates, an act she prioritized even over her meetings with Olivia and a deed I appreciated greater with time. Especially once we had the chance to know each other without the parties. Without the worry over her brother.

Slowly, through many kisses on the cheek and over croissants in chic cafés with her perfume wafting across to me, I realized how naïve to her parents' plans she had been and how much it had hurt her in those months where she, too, found herself alone in her mother's clutches as much as her brother.

I was just grateful to see her smile again.

Our lunches made us closer again, despite the rift that had occurred that spring. It was mended carefully, and slowly, with information exchanged between us and her hands reaching out for mine cautiously and then boldly across the table. With the summer wind blowing her hair onto her lips, she leaned in to whisper in my ear all the things I had suspected since that first party with the Saint's Fog, and after the final, when the mere touch of my hand had resulted in panicked scars across her arm. A truth she hadn't been able to admit fully, even on that day in Newport.

A truth I had been so hopeful to hear.

When she at last kissed me again, it was the most hesitant she'd ever been, and so I kissed her, and I kissed her, and I kissed her, until she realized it was okay. Whether it was what we both needed or not, it was okay.

In Switzerland my French was poor and my Italian was not popular, and I cannot deny that I was miserable. True as before, Audrey's presence made it brighter, and even if it was not enough to make my time at Kinlex feel any less like a prison sentence, she still tried, and having her there beside me made me try as well.

We continued to talk about Jonathan. At first we didn't dare, and then, without our realizing it, his name was hidden in every breath. His smile in too many passing thoughts. This is why, I think, I let it slip that night. Why, as we sat overlooking the Limmat River, with the lights reflecting in yellows and greens upon the water, I told her at last about what Olivia had done. That it was she who'd hired Prosenko, who'd planned it all. Who'd tried to cut the cord, in the end.

I told her everything.

For a moment she remained frozen, the glass of rosé still poised between her fingers. Then she looked to the river and finished it off. The next afternoon, in the empty industrial cafeteria of Kinlex, Audrey pulled out a folder, placed it on the table in front of me, and handed me a pen to regain my freedom.

I WRITE THIS NOW FIVE and a half years beyond that New Year's Day. Six years since my first step into that bright room in that timeless brownstone, with George hovering and nervous at what I might do. But now, watching the morning mist roll off the Swiss mountainsides, I think I am happy at last.

As the songbirds sing to welcome dawn, there is champagne on Audrey's breath, and already her lips are sweet with the taste as she kisses me in joyous celebration. When her eyes meet mine, they are the same determined, beautiful green and brown I first fell for, but there is a newfound clarity in them, and her smile is more stunning than I have ever seen it. Not because she is innocent but because we both know that we are not, and never will be, but it doesn't matter.

We are safe. All of us. At last, and that is why I take a sip of the champagne when she hands it to me. Because an hour's train ride away, where her mother is handed her morning coffee, she will have failed to see the small vial slipped back into her assistant's sleeve, and by the time she notices, Audrey and I will long be gone, and unreachable by the press or the flash of their cameras. Far away, across the Alps and down to the familiar fields, the news will come slow. Where we are going, no paparazzi will be able to find us. No cameras or microphones. Just the rolling of the windswept fields beyond a small, wood-framed house waiting to welcome us among the hum of honeybees.

And we celebrate, too, with an unshakable smile on our lips, because we know that there, a dark-haired man sits overlooking the rows of growing rosemary, waiting for us after all these years. Letting his tea brew stronger, a book of Keats in his hand, and, most important of all, with his pulse firm and his cologne bright, and clean, and deathless.

ACKNOWLEDGMENTS

I began to write *Tripping Arcadia* during a dark and lonely time in my life. It was a seed of self-indulgent entertainment that grew in the shadows of my mind, while lying on friends' couches, between countries, ill and uncertain of the future. Somehow, it flourished into the thing you are reading now. In that sense, this book, more than anything, has become a home for me, but it would not be here today were it not for the amazing kindness of friends and family who never let me give up, and who encouraged me to share this story with whoever was willing to listen. The greatest among these supportive stars is without question Saint, whose warmth and enthusiasm have known no bounds during this entire process, and who stayed awake with me over countless cups of tea, sharing schemes and listening to my fears with nothing but love in return. This book would not be what it is without you, and neither would I. But there are so many others to thank. My mother, Beth, who has instilled in me since I was a child a love of books, and who has been nothing but supportive in my various attempts to write something of merit over the years. My father, Alan, whose presence has inspired me more than he knows. My friends, both lost and newly found, who gave my weary head a place to rest. Even if we are ghosts to one another now, I have nothing but gratitude for the time you were in my life. But to those who are with me today, who have shared advice, opinions, jokes, tea recommendations, porch time filled with laughter, and endless movie marathons, thank you, thank you, thank you. To Emmy for taking a chance on this little book when it was hovering over the fire of self-defeat; to Stephanie for seeing the potential when even I could not and for illuminating the way for all of this to happen. To Alex for your guidance; to Elias for your wit; to Molly, Lyndall, Hannah, Sarah, Ellie, and Eliza for the countless hours of friendship, love, and much-needed critique passes and cheers. To the wonderful staff at Dutton and PRH and all the hours of work you have put into bringing this to life, I am immensely grateful. And last, to Boston for being such an inspiring home. Cheers to all the day trips and coffee consumed during drives to the Berkshires and Newport, and everything in between. I came into this process a lost little soul wandering in a labyrinthian maze, and all of you have brought me to where I am today. There are not enough thanks in the world.

ABOUT THE AUTHOR

A fan of everything spooky and indulgent, KIT MAYQUIST is a bisexual, trans masculine writer who can be found in the historic shadows of Boston, Massachusetts, hunched over his desk with a sullen Persian cat in his lap and surrounded by antiques. He has a master's in medieval history from the University of Iceland and a BA from Portland State University (and if you ask him, yes, Stumptown will always have the best coffee).